METRO

RJ NOLAN

Ylva

ISBN epub: 978-3-95533-038-5
ISBN mobi: 978-3-95533-039-2
ISBN pdf: 978-3-95533-040-8
ISBN paperback: 978-3-95533-041-5

Published by Ylva Publishing, legal entity of Ylva Verlag, e.Kfr.

Ylva Verlag, e.Kfr.
Am Kirschgarten 2
65830 Kriftel
Germany

http://www.ylva-publishing.com

First Edition: September 2011
Second Edition: March 2013

Credits
Edited by Judy Underwood
Cover Design and Formatting by Streetlight Graphics

ACKNOWLEDGMENTS

Writing may be a solitary pursuit, but without the support of some very special people this novel would not have come to fruition.

First and foremost to ETJ. Your love and support means the world to me and so do you. A special thank-you for all the extra things you do to make it possible for me to spend hours glued to my computer screen.

Once again, a huge thank-you to Pam. You are truly a beta reader extraordinaire and a great friend. It would not feel like a complete novel without your support and very able assistance.

A big thank-you goes to Jae, my critique partner. Your support and patience is greatly appreciated. You've been a great teacher. And a very good friend.

Thanks to Streetlight Graphics for creating LA Metro's cover.

Thanks go to Judy Underwood for copy editing.

And last, but certainly not least, a big thank-you to Ylva Publishing for providing a new home for my novels.

DEDICATION

In memory of Roxanne Jones, CEO of L-Book. I will always be grateful for the opportunity to work with her and L-Book in publishing my novels.

CHAPTER 1

A thick brown haze shrouded the upper reaches of LA Metropolitan Hospital. Heat shimmered off the asphalt of the parking lot. As Dr. Kimberly Donovan stepped from her car, the thick air burned her nose and the heat hit her like a wave. *Ah, August in LA. The wonder of smog alerts.* She pushed damp blond hair off her face. Despite the weather and the circumstances that had led to her being here, Kim was happy to be back in California. She was more than ready for a fresh start.

Kim made her way up to psych on the fourth floor. She smiled when she spotted the nameplate outside the door: Dr. Philip Alerman, Chairman of Psychiatry. *Seems moving to a new hospital worked out well for him. Hope it'll work for me too.*

As Kim reached for the door handle, the door swung open.

"Hey, Kim. Welcome to LA Metro. Ready to go to work?" Philip asked.

Kim smiled warmly and shook hands with Philip. "Yes. I'm looking forward to it." His curly brown hair was thinner than Kim remembered when they worked together during her psych residency, but his tall frame was still trim and he wore the same round wire rim glasses. "Thanks for getting my packet expedited with the Credentials Committee. I'm glad there wasn't any problem with the paperwork from Memorial."

Philip shook his head. "After what happened, I don't think Dr. Pruitt would have dared try to hold up your paperwork."

Kim scowled as a surge of anger at her former boss filled her. *You don't know him like I do. I wouldn't put it past him.* She sighed, pushing away the unproductive emotion. "You're right. The sooner I was gone and forgotten, the better he liked it I'm sure."

Philip reached out and squeezed Kim's shoulder. "Don't let it bother you. It's their loss. As I told you on the phone, we're short-staffed and need the help of a competent psychiatrist."

Some of her tension eased and Kim smiled. "Thanks, Philip. I appreciate the support."

"You're welcome," Philip said. He glanced at his watch. "Morning chart review should be just about finished. Let's head for the staff lounge and I'll introduce you around."

Philip led her to a set of double doors that opened into the psych ward. He stopped to enter a code into a keypad next to the door, then turned back to Kim. "The ward clerk will provide you with all the door codes, as well as issue you a pager."

Kim followed Philip down the hall, past a central nurses' station, to the staff lounge. Several people were sitting at a large round table that was covered in charts.

"Good morning." Philip strode over to the table. "I've brought us some much needed help." He turned and motioned Kim to his side. "This is Dr. Kim Donovan. She's our newest staff psychiatrist." Everyone at the table offered a wave or a smile. "Kim, let me introduce you to some of the crew."

Pointing to each person in turn, Philip made the introductions. There were two psychiatrists and three nurses. "Now that you've met everyone why don't we—" Philip's pager sounded. "Excuse me." He flipped open the pager and glanced down at the display. "I'm sorry, Kim. I need to take care of this. Why don't you hang out here for a bit and familiarize yourself with the unit. I'll be back as quickly as I can."

Kim spared a fleeting glance at Philip's retreating back before turning to face her new colleagues. She felt a moment's trepidation, then firmly pushed it away. *Time to see what things are really going to be like around here.* Kim knew from previous experience she was more likely to hear the inside scoop on the department now that the chairman of the department wasn't present.

As the door swung shut behind Phillip, Trent, one of the nurses, pulled out the chair next to him. "Have a seat, Dr. Donovan," he offered with a friendly smile.

The staff filled her in on the department procedures and the different rotations. Kim winced internally when talk eventually turned to the ER. Mention of the ER immediately turned her thoughts to her former lover, who headed the ER at Memorial. Things had not ended well between them.

"Most of the rotations aren't too bad," Dr. Roberts said. The short, stocky man with dishwater blond hair was one of the staff psychiatrists. "But watch your step when you cover the ER psych consults. The ER chief can be a real hard-ass."

Kim mentally rolled her eyes. *Great. Just what I need. I haven't even been here a day yet and I'm already hearing about the ER Chief.*

"That's not quite fair, Dr. Roberts," Trent piped up. "Okay, she does act like a hard-ass, but you have to admit she's a gorgeous hard-ass."

Trent and Dr. Roberts shared a laugh. The two female nurses at the table shared a perturbed look.

While Kim was interested in hearing about the woman she would be working with, she also curiously watched the interaction of her new colleagues.

Dr. Kapoor, a fellow psychiatrist, cleared his throat. "I'm sure, Dr. Donovan is quite capable of forming her own opinion of our ER chief." He stared pointedly at Dr. Roberts. "Maybe she would find a rundown of the responsibilities while covering the ER more helpful than a personal critique of Dr. McKenna's shortcomings."

Dr. Roberts shot Dr. Kapoor a dirty look.

The door opened to admit Philip. He walked over to stand by Kim's chair. "Sorry for the delay. Come on, I'll show you around the rest of the hospital."

Philip stopped as they once again reached the elevators. They had covered the departments that interacted with psych except of the ER. "We'll stop by the Chief of Staff's office next. I do feel I should warn you. Dr. Rodman can sometimes be arrogant and condescending, but he is a great surgeon and we just try to ignore the rest. You won't have any day-to-day interaction with him, but he does like to meet all new staff. After that we'll head to the ER."

The secretary in the outer office greeted them and directed them into the inner office. "Dr. Rodman will see you now."

Kim stepped into the office after Philip and got her first look at the Chief of Staff. Even sitting behind the desk Kim could see he was short. He had a slim build with thin, mousy brown hair that was combed over in an apparent attempt to hide a wide bald spot. When he rose from his chair and stepped out from behind the desk, he was even shorter than Kim imagined.

Philip made the introductions. Kim's eyes narrowed as Dr. Rodman's eyes traveled slowly up her body and lingered on her breasts before finally meeting her eyes.

"It's a pleasure to meet you, Dr. Donovan. Be sure and let me know if there is anything, anything at all, I can do for you." His eyes remained on her breasts as he spoke. "My door is always open for you."

Kim gave him a disgusted look. "I'm sure that won't be necessary."

"We won't take anymore of your time, Dr. Rodman. Thank you for seeing us." Philip quickly led them out of the room.

Neither spoke as they made their way back to the elevator.

Philip finally broke the uncomfortable silence. "I'm really sorry you were subjected to that, Kim."

"How does he get away with that kind of behavior in this day and age?" Kim asked.

Philip grimaced. "I'm not defending his boorish manners, but I will say he is a very gifted surgeon. Honestly, I've never seen him act that badly before, arrogant yes, but nothing like he pulled today. Then again, I'm sure having your brother on the hospital board of trustees tends to make you think you're bulletproof. And so far, that's been the case."

Kim shook her head. It wasn't the first time she had run into that type of behavior and it surely wouldn't be the last.

"Thankfully, there is no reason for you to have any further contact with him. You'll be happy to know that he stays clear of the psych floor," Philip said with a chuckle. "Anyway, enough about him, let's head for the ER. As I discussed with you when you interviewed, I would like you to act as liaison between the ER and psych. We've had some problems with staff conflicts down there."

Kim immediately thought of Dr. Roberts. *I can see why if his attitude in the norm among psych personnel.* She couldn't help wondering if he just had a problem with women in positions of power. Kim pushed aside the useless speculation. She would find out soon enough.

"If she's not busy, I'd really like to introduce you

to Dr. McKenna," Philip said. "The two of you will be working together quite a bit. She runs the ER with an iron fist. That said, she's very compassionate with her patients and a great physician. It just takes a little getting used to her very reserved demeanor. It can be a little off-putting."

Wondering just what she had gotten herself into, Kim followed Philip into the elevator.

The ER waiting room as usual was bedlam. There were a multitude of patients waiting in chairs. The admitting desk in the corner had patients lined up waiting their turn to be checked in.

Philip bypassed the admitting desk and pushed through the double doors that led into the ER proper. Medical personnel flowed in and around a large circular nurses' station. There was constant traffic up and down the hall leading to the trauma rooms. For all the chaos there was also the unmistakable sense of the underlying order of a well-run ER. Kim followed Philip as he approached the nurses' station. A woman in her late twenties, slightly overweight with short stylishly cut red hair and pretty, green eyes was manning the desk.

"Penny, is Dr. McKenna available?" Philip asked.

"Hi, Dr. Alerman. Last time I saw her she was in the staff lounge."

"Thanks, Penny. Ah, before I forget. This is Dr. Donovan. She's our new staff psychiatrist. Give her a hand if she needs anything, okay?"

"Sure, Dr. Alerman." Penny nodded at Kim and smiled. "Dr. Donovan."

"Hello, Penny," Kim said.

Philip motioned for Kim to follow him. He filled her

in on the desk clerk as they made their way down the hall. "Penny is the most experienced clerk in the ER. She's got contacts in every department in the hospital. Plus she's a miracle worker when it comes to wading through paperwork."

When they reached the door marked Staff Lounge, Philip pushed the door open and motioned Kim in ahead of him. A woman sat working at a table covered in charts. Her head was down and her black hair slightly obscured her face. Kim admired the broad shoulders and muscled biceps showing past the arms of her scrub shirt. When the woman looked up Kim couldn't help but stare. If this was Jess McKenna, Trent hadn't exaggerated. The woman was indeed absolutely gorgeous.

"Dr. Alerman, can I help you?" the woman asked.

"I came down to introduce you to the new psych liaison I spoke to you about, Dr. Kim Donovan. I know we've had some problems between our departments. With Dr. Donovan's help, I hope to improve relations with the ER." Philip turned to Kim. "Kim, this is the Chairman of the ER, Dr. Jess McKenna."

As Dr. McKenna stood, Kim allowed her gaze to briefly glide over the doctor's tall body before meeting her eyes.

"Nice to meet you, Dr. Donovan." Dr. McKenna's voice was low and husky.

Before Kim could respond, her gaze locked with the most incredible blue eyes she had ever seen. They were breathtaking. As she watched, they turned the most amazing shade of bluish silver. Hearing Philip clear his throat, Kim tore away from those striking eyes and struggled to find her voice.

"Nice to meet you, Dr. McKenna," she said, finally noticing the woman was holding her hand out.

Kim's hand was clasped in a firm handshake. She

made eye contact with Dr. McKenna again, seeing something flicker in those engaging blue eyes before they turned almost silver and expressionless.

"Well, Kim, I need to head back to psych," Philip said. "Once you're done here, come back to the floor and I'll finish up your orientation. For now, I'll leave you in Dr. McKenna's capable hands."

Kim mentally shook herself, trying to regain her composure. She had been thrown a bit off balance by her strong reaction to the ER chief. She turned her attention back to her boss. "Thanks, Philip. I'll meet you back on the psych floor."

"See you later," Philip said as he turned to walk toward the door. He stopped just before stepping out. "Take good care of her, Dr. McKenna. We don't want to scare her off right away."

Dr. McKenna nodded without comment. As the door closed behind Philip, Dr. McKenna turned to Kim. "If you'll follow me, I'll give you a basic overview of the ER layout, and familiarize you with our procedures."

Dr. McKenna walked toward the door without waiting for a response.

Kim was taken aback by the woman's demeanor. She had expected a bit of a welcome or at least some attempt to connect with a new colleague. *Philip did warn you.* Kim hurried after her.

They had only taken a few steps out of the lounge when someone called out to Dr. McKenna. Kim turned to see a young Asian woman rushing down the hall toward them.

Kim glanced at the woman's ID badge as she skidded to a halt. This must be one of Dr. McKenna's residents.

"What can I do for you, Dr. Phan?" Dr. McKenna asked.

"The patient you saw with me earlier in Bed Three is still complaining of chest pain. His EKG was normal.

I'm still waiting on his cardiac enzymes to come back from the lab. His other blood work was normal."

"He has no history of cardiac problems. Correct?" Dr. McKenna asked.

"None."

"Any sign of arrhythmia?"

"No."

"And what was his age?"

The resident quickly flipped through her notebook. "Forty-one."

"Your patient is still in pain. So what do you do next?" Dr. McKenna asked.

Dr. Phan looked down at her notes and then quickly back at Dr. McKenna. "So far, all the tests for a heart attack have come back negative." She hesitated for a moment and then continued, "I would recommend trying a liquid antacid while we wait for the cardiac enzymes to come back. If that doesn't help then possibly a nitrate patch."

"Good. Try the antacid and see if that helps. Once his enzymes come back reevaluate the situation and decide if the nitrate is warranted. Get Dr. Bates to back you up if you need more help."

"Thanks, Dr. McKenna."

Kim shook her head as she watched the young resident turn and sprint down the hall. "Let me guess, new resident?"

"Yes, she is. Sorry for the interruption."

Kim hurried after Dr. McKenna as she turned and headed down the hall without another word.

During the tour of the ER, Dr. McKenna had introduced her to some of the ER staff and shown her the whole ER from top to bottom. She explained the procedures they used before calling down psych and the protocols the hospital used for holding patients. Kim had been particularly interested when several staff members approached Dr. McKenna with questions or problems. Her responses were the same as they had been with Dr. Phan, crisp and professional. There was none of the banter and camaraderie that Kim was used to seeing among an ER staff. In a high stress environment like an emergency room it was almost a requirement.

While Kim realized that as the Chief of the ER, Dr. McKenna might feel the need to distance herself a bit from her staff, this seemed more extreme than that. She had yet to see Dr. McKenna even smile. Kim wondered if the strict emotional control extended to the woman's personal life. Despite her off-putting demeanor, Kim was unwillingly attracted to her.

Kim was pulled out of her thoughts as Dr. McKenna stopped in front of the door to the staff lounge.

"I think that about covers it," Dr. McKenna said.

Kim smiled. "Thank you for the tour. I appreciate you spending the time with me."

"Not a problem. Did you have any other questions?"

"Not that I can think of off the top of my head," Kim said.

"All right then, I need to get back to work." With that, Dr. McKenna turned and headed down the hall deeper into the ER.

Kim stared after her for several moments. When she realized what she was doing, she turned away. *Stick to business,* she chastised herself as she made her way out of the ER. *The last thing you need is to get involved with another ER Chief. Besides, you don't even know if the woman is a lesbian.*

CHAPTER 2

Jess stood next to the nurses' station as she waited for her quarry to emerge from the treatment room. When she noticed Penny watching her she randomly selected a chart from the rack.

Jess stared unseeingly at the chart. *This is not a good idea.* Although Jess had been telling herself that for days, here she was anyway. She was waiting for Chris Roberts to finish up with his patient so she could talk with him. Normally, she didn't have a lot of use for the man. He had made it clear on numerous occasions that he did not like to cover the ER. However, in this case, he could prove useful.

Inexplicably, she had not been able to get Kim Donovan out of her mind. The beautiful psychiatrist had dominated her thoughts since their brief meeting three weeks ago. Against her better judgment, she intended to try and learn more about the woman before she started her rotation in the ER next week.

Which was why she was waiting for Roberts. If anyone up in psych knew anything about Kim Donovan it would be him. Jess was sure that by now he had probably already asked Kim out. Not that she could blame him, but in this instance, she would have bet her next paycheck that it would not do him any good.

Jess was sure that Kim had checked her out when Philip introduced them, but it was more than that. She readily admitted that she had been immediately attracted to Kim. Who wouldn't be? Her curly shoulder length blond hair coupled with warm sky blue eyes were an attractive start. Add in a beautiful face and a tall, lithe body and you had a spectacular combination. Jess vividly remembered the first time their eyes had met and held. It was as if a strong current had flowed between them. It had been disconcerting to say the least. Even now, Jess wondered if she had just imagined it.

A gurney banging against a wall broke Jess out of her contemplations. She cursed under her breath when she realized Roberts had walked past her while she was lost in thought.

"Dr. Roberts," she called after him. Jess caught up with him just as he reached the elevator. The doors slid open.

"What?" he asked in an impatient tone.

"I'd like to talk to you for a minute," Jess said.

"Fine." Roberts motioned for the people in the elevator that was waiting to go ahead without him. He turned back toward Jess with a scowl.

Now that Jess was facing him this didn't seem like such a great idea. She was unexpectedly tongue-tied. That in itself was so unlike her. *I knew this was a bad idea.*

"Is there a problem?" Roberts asked. "I'm needed back on the psych floor."

Jess scrambled for something to say. She cursed herself for not thinking this out before she approached Roberts. "Do you think the record of the patient you just saw should be flagged for possible drug seeking behavior?"

"Yes. I already told your resident that."

"Okay. Good. So how is the new psychiatrist working out?" *Great segue, genius.* "Um … Dr. Donovan … Right?" *Like you don't know exactly what her name is.*

"Kim is settling in fine," Roberts said. His confusion was plainly written on his face. "Was there something else you wanted?"

"No. That's it. Thanks." Jess turned and quickly walked away. *Great, you looked like a total idiot. That's why you never do this. You're terrible at it. Stick to business. Last thing you need is to become interested in someone you work with. It worked out so well last time,* she sarcastically reminded herself.

Kim picked up an empty tray and headed for the food line in the cafeteria. She glanced up when she heard her name called. She smiled and waved when she spotted Brenda, a psychiatric nurse-practitioner she worked with on the psych floor. She made her selections, and then headed for the table where Brenda sat.

"I see you decided to descend from the ivory tower today," Brenda said.

Kim laughed as she took a seat at the table. Brenda was a feisty, middle-aged black woman. She had taken Kim under her wing.

"It does feel good to get off the floor for a little while. See how the other half lives ... so to speak," Kim said. That was one of the reasons Kim liked rotating in the ER. It could be isolating to spend an extended period on the psych ward.

"Ready to face the loony toons in the ER next week? And I don't mean the patients!" Brenda said.

Kim laughed. "I'm sure I can handle whatever they throw at me."

"I know you can," Brenda said. "Well, I need to get back to the floor. Group starts in an hour. I'll see you upstairs." She gathered her tray and with a wave headed for the exit.

Kim watched for a moment as Brenda walked away. It was hard to believe she had been at LA Metro for three weeks already. The time had just flown by. Although she was busy getting to know her fellow psych staff and settling in, she thought of the beautiful ER chief often and the brief time they had spent together on her first day. She had never reacted so strongly to anyone as she had Jess McKenna. The thought of her first rotation in the ER next week filled her with equal parts of anticipation and trepidation.

Enough of that. Kim turned her attention to the chart she had brought with her. She glanced up when a shadow covered her work.

"Hey, Kim. Mind if I join you?"

Kim smiled at Chris Roberts. "Hi, Chris. Have a seat." Despite her poor first impression of Chris when he had bad mouthed Jess McKenna, he had turned out to be a good co-worker. She had worked closely with him during her first week and found him to be very helpful and pleasant to work with. "How did the ER consult go?"

Chris scowled as he set his tray down and slid into the chair next to Kim. "Same incompetence as usual down there. They shouldn't need a psychiatrist to tell them some junkie is drug seeking. You'd think McKenna could train her residents better than that."

Kim forced her expression to remain neutral. *I bet there was more to the consult than that. What is it with him and Jess McKenna?* She still wasn't sure if his dislike was of the ER in general or Jess in particular. He had been covering the ER for the last two weeks and done nothing but complain about it.

Chris pulled the ER pager off his belt and shut it off. At Kim's raised eyebrow he said, "I'm on my lunch break."

Although irritated by Chris's behavior, Kim knew there was nothing she could do about it—yet. *No wonder there are problems between the ER and psych.*

"Well, the good news is today is your last day. I'll be taking over on Monday," Kim said.

"Ah ... that reminds me. Be on your guard when you get down there. I don't know what she's up to, but McKenna stopped me as I was leaving the ER just now and asked about you."

Concern flared for a moment, then Kim shrugged it off. It wasn't uncommon for people to be curious about new staff members. "What did she want to know?"

"That's the strange part. She asked how you were working out. I've never heard her ask about anyone new before. That's why I wanted to warn you to be careful when you're covering the ER consults."

A sinking sensation in the pit of her stomach made Kim queasy. *Don't jump to conclusions. If she found out about what happened at Memorial, so be it. You didn't do anything wrong.* She pushed away her tray no longer having any appetite. "Okay. Thanks. I should probably head back to the floor."

Chris put a gently restraining hand on Kim's arm when she started to stand. "Hang on a sec," he said.

As she resumed her seat, Kim gazed at Chris questioningly. Faint warning bells started to ring when he stared at the table, and then began to shift nervously.

"I know it's short notice on a Friday night." Chris looked up and met Kim's eyes. "Would you have dinner with me tonight?"

Kim sighed to herself. He had already tried the "let's get together as new colleagues" bit last week. *You should have told him then instead of just saying no thanks.* The one thing Kim had never been was closeted. She didn't flaunt her sexuality at work, but never hid it either. For the first time she hesitated, then immediately berated herself for doing so. *This isn't Memorial. Philip not only knows but supports you.*

"If you're busy we can make it another time," Chris

said, misunderstanding her lack of response.

Kim mentally cursed Dr. Pruitt for making her unsure of herself. *Just tell him.* "Thank you, but no." Kim held up a hand to keep Chris from interrupting. "Let me be honest with you. I'm a lesbian."

Chris's mouth dropped open, then he looked down at the table. His expression went totally blank.

Kim braced herself for his reaction.

Chris finally looked up. "Didn't see that one coming." He shook his head and his smile reappeared. He seemed to regain his equilibrium. "Are you sure?" he asked with a teasing glint in his eyes, though he sounded half serious.

Kim laughed, more relieved than she cared to admit. "Positive." She stood and picked up her tray. "I really should get back up to the floor."

"Okay. I'll see you up there later," Chris said. He grinned up at Kim. "Oh, and if you should ever change your mind about the guy thing ..."

Kim was glad Chris was taking her revelation so well. She shook her head and laughed. "I wouldn't hold my breath if I were you."

Making her way out of the cafeteria, Kim's thoughts once again turned to Jess McKenna. *Why is she asking questions about me?* Kim resolutely pushed away her worries. Regardless of what Chris thought, maybe Jess was just curious about a new colleague.

Kim pushed through the cafeteria doors. As if conjured by her thoughts, she spotted Jess about to enter from the other side. "Hello again, Dr. McKenna," she said with a friendly smile.

Jess looked momentarily startled, then her face resumed its normal placid expression. "Dr. Donovan," she said before moving to continue on her way.

"Could I speak to you for a minute?" Kim asked quickly before Jess could walk away.

Jess moved away from the swinging doors and back into the hallway outside the cafeteria. Once she was out of the way of traffic, she turned to Kim. "What can I do for you?"

"I wanted to let you know I'll begin covering the ER on Monday."

"Yes, I saw your name on the schedule," Jess said.

Knowing what Chris's attitude was like when he covered the ER, Kim felt the need to assure Jess that she did not feel the same. She met Jess's eyes. "I'm looking forward to working in the ER. I've always found it an interesting and challenging place to work."

A brief half smile flashed across Jess's face before she resumed a businesslike expression. "Your help will be a welcome addition to the ER."

Before Kim could respond, Jess's pager went off. Taking it off her belt she glanced down at the display. "I have to go." Jess didn't immediately walk away.

It seemed as if Jess wanted to say something more but her pager beeped again.

"I'll see you on Monday," Jess said. With a brief nod, she turned and headed down the hallway at a fast walk.

Kim watched Jess go as she played over in her mind the fleeting smile that had transformed Jess's face. It had softened her features for just a moment. What was quickly becoming her new mantra echoed though her mind. *Stick to business.*

CHAPTER 3

Jess stepped into the center area of the nurses' station and beckoned to Aimee Phan. The first-year resident hurried over. "As soon as Dr. Donovan gets down here—"

Penny called out a greeting to Dr. Donovan.

Jess glanced up at the clock and was pleasantly surprised. Today was Kim's first day covering the ER. *She's prompt. I'll give her that.* The page to psych had gone out less than ten minutes ago. It was not uncommon for a patient to wait an hour or more before someone from psych finally put in an appearance.

"Good Morning, Dr. McKenna, Dr. Phan. What can I do for you?" Kim asked with a friendly smile.

"Dr. Phan will fill you in on the patient," Jess said. She motioned for the resident to go ahead, and then stood by to listen while the resident gave the patient's basic history. Jess watched Kim's reactions. It had been her experience that none of the psychiatrists had any interest in working with the ER residents.

Aimee quickly finished up her presentation of the patient.

"I think the best way to start is with a full patient mental status examination," Kim said. "Have you ever done one, Dr. Phan?"

Aimee shook her head. "Just the basic questions that are part of a history and physical."

"This is quite a bit more detailed than that. Let's go see your patient and I'll walk you through the assessment procedures."

"Great." Aimee smiled broadly. "Thanks, Dr. Donovan."

Jess nodded to herself. *Better and better.* She was pleased to see that Kim had not blown the resident off and taken over the case. And best of all, she was providing a teaching experience to Aimee.

"Dr. McKenna, will you be joining us?" Kim asked.

Jess momentarily lost her train of thought when her eyes met Kim's. *Focus, McKenna.* "No. You and Dr. Phan seem to have everything under control."

Kim nodded, then turned toward the resident with a smile. "Dr. Phan, lead the way."

Jess watched as the two women walked away. Her first impression of the new psychiatrist was a very positive one.

Jess stood outside the curtained bed. She was watching Kim coach Aimee Phan through the patient exam process. Jess was impressed by Kim's handling of the resident. She allowed a rare smile to cross her face. *She's a good teacher.*

Kim gently patted the elderly patient's arm before turning her attention to Aimee. "If you need anything else just let me know."

"Thanks, Dr. Donovan," Aimee said with a smile.

Kim stepped over to the closed curtain surrounding the patient's bed and turned to slip through the opening.

Jess stepped back just before Kim plowed into her. She grimaced when she heard Kim's gasp of surprise. "Sorry about that. Didn't mean to startle you. I didn't want to interrupt," Jess said.

"That's okay. Were you waiting for me or Dr. Phan?"

"I was waiting for you. I wanted to catch you before you headed back to psych." So far, Kim had managed to surprise her. Regardless of that, Jess's previous experience with psych led her to expect problems. Most of the psychiatrists couldn't wait to get out of the ER. If you didn't catch them before they left the floor, it could be quite some time before they returned. Even if you managed to catch them, it didn't mean they were going to offer their help graciously. *She's been great so far. Give her a chance.* "I've got a patient I'd like you to talk to and evaluate. I think he could benefit from some outpatient counseling."

Kim smiled. "Sure. I'm happy to help any way I can. What have you got?"

Jess's tension eased. *Now this is more like it.* She turned and led Kim out into the hall. They headed toward one of the private exam rooms. Jess stopped outside the door.

"Patient is a fourteen-year-old male. He presented with several infected cuts on the inside of his right forearm. He claimed a cat scratched him. While there are four parallel cuts, they are too deep and symmetrical to be animal scratches. I examined his other arm and he has quite a few similarly inflamed but healing cuts on that arm as well. I think we're dealing with self-inflicted wounds. From the look of the cuts I think he might be just starting out. I didn't find any scarring that suggested previous cutting."

"Are his parents here?" Kim asked.

"His mother is in the waiting room. He refused to have her present during the exam."

"Okay. I'll tackle him first, and then his mother."

"You need any backup?" Even as she asked, Jess knew it wasn't needed. It was just an excuse. She was curious to see more of Kim in action.

Kim smiled at the offer. "Thanks, but no. He shouldn't be a problem. You've already treated the infected cuts ... Right?"

Jess was surprised by the feeling of disappointment Kim's refusal invoked. She handed over the chart in her hand. "Yes. He's good to go after you're done with him."

Kim gave a quick nod of acknowledgment and pushed open the exam room door.

Jess remained outside the door for several moments after Kim disappeared inside. She was trying to sort out the long dormant emotions coursing through her. As had previously been the case, she was aware of the strong attraction she felt toward Kim. It was now tinged with a growing respect for the psychiatrist. Jess pushed aside the unwelcome introspection. *Now is not the time or place for exploring feelings.*

Jess's attention turned firmly back to work when she spotted Karen Armstrong, one of the first-year residents coming down the hall. *Might as well get this over with.* "Dr. Armstrong," Jess called out. Jess frowned to herself when the resident visibly hesitated before making her way over. *Yeah, you know what this is about.* "I want to talk to you," she said when the resident reached her. "Let's go into the lounge."

Jess followed Karen into the staff lounge. She motioned for her to have a seat at the table. "You weren't at morning conference," Jess said. This was not the first conference the resident had missed.

"I had to take my daughter to daycare, and then drop off my husband at work. My husband's car is still in the shop."

"I'm not interested in excuses," Jess said, her tone calm but firm. "This is the fourth morning conference you've missed in two weeks. As we discussed before, attendance at morning conference is mandatory for first-year residents."

"I'm doing the best I can," Karen said, her stress apparent in her voice.

"You need to do better. You're only in the second month your residency and already falling behind."

"I can't make them repair the car any faster." Karen jerked her stethoscope from around her neck and slapped it onto the table.

Okay. Time to get serious. Jess had not wanted to turn this into a formal counseling session but Karen wasn't giving her any choice. "It's not just conferences. It's not fair to your fellow residents when you come in late or leave early. It doesn't get any easier as you go along. You need to get a handle on things now." Jess sighed to herself. Karen had a lot of potential, but she always seemed to have some problem that prevented her from fulfilling her responsibilities. "Do you want to stay in this residency program?"

Karen blanched and her hand clenched around her stethoscope. "What? Of course I do."

"Then I suggest you make some alternate arrangements so you arrive on time. I expect you to be at every conference for the rest of the month." Jess met Karen's gaze directly. "You should consider this a formal counseling session. If necessary, the next step will be to officially place you on probation. I will see you in conference tomorrow morning."

Jess knew she had been harsh, but hoped the resident would respond to the wake-up call. If she let Karen's behavior continue unabated now, it would carry throughout her residency. By the stunned look on Karen's face she had definitely made an impression on her. Without another word, Jess stood and made her way toward the door.

Kim made her way toward the staff lounge for a much needed cup of coffee. Unlike her colleagues, she had decided to remain in the ER as much as possible. It was only her first day and she already realized how bad things were between psych and the ER by the staff and residents reaction to her presence and help. The residents in particular had at first seemed shocked, then extremely grateful of her offer to work with them on the cases they presented. Philip had been right about the conflict between the two departments. If anything he had underestimated the depth of the problem. *I definitely need to talk to Philip.*

Kim pushed open the door to the lounge. She noticed Karen, one of the residents she had met earlier sitting at the table. Kim nodded to the resident and walked over and made herself a cup of coffee. Once she had her coffee, she approached the table where the resident sat.

Karen looked up, a sullen expression twisting her face. "Hey, Dr. Donovan."

"Hi," Kim said as she sat down at the table. She had been impressed with the resident earlier. Karen was bright and eager to learn. "How's it going?"

"Not so good," Karen said. Her scowl deepened.

Kim nodded sympathetically. "Want to talk about it?" Her first impulse was to try and help someone in turmoil.

Karen shook her head no.

Silence reigned for several minutes.

"It's not my fault she doesn't have a life and doesn't understand," Karen blurted out of the blue.

Confusion struck at the apparent non sequitur. "Who doesn't have a life or understand what?"

"Dr. McKenna," Karen said, her voice tinged with anger.

Oh crap! Kim did not want to get involved in anything between Jess and one of her residents. Not to mention the fact that it was also inappropriate for her to interfere. She sighed in resignation. *No help for it now.* She did not want to blow the resident off and leave. She decided her best option at this point would be to keep quiet and waited to see what if anything else Karen would say. It was a technique she had learned early in her own residency.

"Everyone says how she practically lives at the hospital. And she never talks about a girlfriend or anything from outside work. Maybe this job is her life, but I have a life outside this place. And a daughter and a husband who need me."

Kim's ears perked at the mention of a girlfriend. She was curious about Jess but this was not the way she had hoped to learn more about her. "Dr. McKenna has a lot of responsibility here. I'm sure that leads to very long hours for her."

Karen snorted. "I should've known you wouldn't understand."

Kim shook her head. "Actually I understand quite well. It's a lot of work to try and balance your professional life with your personal one, especially for a woman. A lot of people depend on you."

"I know that." Karen's shoulders slumped. "Okay, I admit I missed a few conferences, and was late a few times," she said. "But that's no reason to take my residency away."

Shock rendered Kim momentarily speechless. That seemed a bit drastic to her. Despite her best intentions not to get embroiled in this she asked, "Did Dr. McKenna actually say that? That she was going to terminate you?"

"Well ... No. Not exactly," Karen admitted reluctantly. "She did say she was going to put me on probation ... If I didn't do better." Karen banged her fist on the table. "It's not like I'm not trying. I'm not a screw-up!" Karen met Kim's eyes defiantly. That's when it seemed to dawn on Karen that she was talking out of school to someone she really didn't know. Her eyes went wide and fear chased across her face. "I really like it here. Dr. McKenna's a great teacher. I wouldn't want her to think I don't want to be here." Karen gazed at Kim with a pleading expression.

Kim laid her hand on Karen's forearm for a moment. "It can be hard adjusting to a new place and all the responsibilities of a residency."

"It is hard." Karen sighed. "But I guess I wasn't honest before. I have been screwing up. Dr. McKenna cut me some slack my first month ... and I guess I kind of took advantage of it. I got pissed when she called me on it," she admitted sheepishly. Some of the tension drained from Karen's face.

Ah. Good. Sometimes it helped to vent to someone not emotionally invested in the problem. "So it looks like you know what you have to do," Kim said.

Karen rose from her chair. She smiled down at Kim. "Thanks, Dr. Donovan. I better get back out there."

"You're welcome." Kim leaned back in her chair and sighed when the door closed behind Karen. *Not bad for your first day. Not bad at all.*

CHAPTER 4

Penny leaned over the nurses' station counter slightly to get a clear view down the hall. The ringing phone distracted her from her vigil. She answered it and dealt with the caller while keeping an eye on the door down the hall.

"Has the ortho resident shown up yet?"

Penny jumped, startled by the voice close by. She turned to face Terrell Johnson. The tall, slim black man was one of the second-year residents. "No. I haven't seen him."

Terrell sighed. "Please page him again."

Penny leaned to the side to see past Terrell. "Sure," she said distractedly. A bright smile covered her face when she spotted the person she had been waiting for walking toward the nurses' station. It quickly turned to a frown when her quarry was intercepted before she reached the desk.

Terrell turned to look over his shoulder. "What's wrong?"

"Nothing. I just needed to catch Dr. Donovan before she heads back to psych to give her a message," Penny said. What she didn't add was that the message was personal. She planned on asking her to lunch. She had been thrilled when the hot gossip about Kim reached her ears.

Terrell smiled. "Isn't she great? She's only been here a week and I've already learned more from her than from all the other psychiatrists combined."

"Hey. You guys talking about Kim Donovan?" Peter

Bates, a fellow ER resident asked, barging into the conversation. "Man, she's hot!" He looked down the hall to where Kim stood talking with another resident. "I'd like to teach her a few things ... Know what I mean?" he asked with a leer and made an obscene hand gesture.

"God, Peter. You are such a pig." Terrell's face twisted in distaste. "Grow up already."

Peter sneered. "Shove it, Terry."

Penny glowered at Peter. She knew how much Terrell hated that nickname. Terrell always treated her well. She didn't appreciate Peter giving him a hard time.

"Penny, please page ortho again," Terrell said. With one last disparaging look at Peter, he turned and walked away.

"What's got his undies in a twist?" Peter asked. He glanced down at Penny and scowled as if suddenly realizing he was talking to her.

Penny scowled right back. She was tempted to tell him that he didn't have a chance in hell with Kim. Penny snickered to herself. *I hope she tells him in front of a big crowd that she's gay.* Although Penny wasn't interested in him, it had always bothered her that the handsome blond resident had never asked her out. He had gone after most every other woman in the department. Penny was surprised when a warm, welcoming smile suddenly appeared on Peter's face.

"Hey, Dr. Donovan," Peter called out.

Penny turned to see Kim approaching with an armload of charts. Her smile was automatic at the sight of the beautiful doctor.

"How are things going?" Peter reached out and took the charts from Kim. He put them down on the counter. "I wanted to let you know if you have any questions you can come to me. I'll be glad to help you with any problems."

Penny rolled her eyes. Peter did not help anyone but

himself. The way he was talking you would think he was staff instead of a resident-in-training.

The conversation was interrupted when Aimee came trotting up. "Excuse me. Peter, I need your help with a patient."

Peter glowered at Aimee. "Can't you see I'm busy? Find someone else," he said.

Kim glanced over at Peter with a perturbed look on her face, then turned toward Aimee. "Anything I can do to help?" she asked.

Aimee smiled. "I don't think so. It's not a psych case." She peered at Peter's forbidding glare, and then turned back to Kim. "You wouldn't happen to know anything about dislocated shoulders?"

Penny could almost see Peter weighing his options. *Jerk. Now what are you going to do?* He seemed to realize his abrupt response to Aimee made him look bad in Kim's eyes.

"Come on, Aimee," Peter said with a long, suffering sigh. "I'll take care of it." He turned to Kim with an ingratiating smile. "If you'll excuse me. You know how it is with these young residents. You just can't leave them on their own for a second."

He took several steps away from the desk, then turned back to Aimee. "Well, come on. I don't have all day."

Penny watched Aimee hurry to catch up with Peter. "What a jerk," she muttered. She glanced over at Kim. She didn't look particularly thrilled with Peter's behavior either. "Just in case you didn't know, Peter isn't even a senior resident. He's a second-year." Penny felt her heart give a strong thump when Kim turned to face her and their eyes met. *God, she's hot.*

"Yes. I'm well aware of that," Kim said.

"What?" Penny asked having totally lost her train of thought.

"I know Dr. Bates is a second-year."

"Oh, yeah. Right." Penny smiled at Kim. She would be content to just look at her all day. Penny was brought back to reality when Kim began gathering up the charts on the counter. "Dr. Donovan." Penny swallowed nervously when she once again met Kim's beautiful blue eyes. "It's almost one o'clock. I was wondering ...." Penny marshaled her courage. "How about we go grab some lunch?"

Kim shook her head. "Sorry. No. I really have a lot of paperwork to do."

Disappointment washed over Penny. She tried to read Kim's expression but couldn't. Not willing to give up so easily she decided to try again. "Maybe some other time?" she asked hopefully.

"Sure. Maybe some other time." With that Kim gathered up her charts and walked away.

Penny was pleased when she realized that Kim was headed down the hall toward the staff lounge and not toward the elevators. Up until now, Kim had taken her charts back to psych to work on them. *Good. Just gives me more of a chance to be around her. Next time she'll say yes.* With that satisfying thought, Penny picked up the ringing phone and got back to work.

Jess pushed open the door to the staff lounge. Kim was seated at the table with Bates. She nodded by way of greeting on her way to the coffee pot in the corner of the room. As she made her coffee, she could hear the murmur of their quiet conversation but couldn't make out what was being said. Kim's voice rising and a clear no from her got Jess's attention. She turned toward the table. Kim had a clearly aggravated look on her face. Jess's jaw clenched. *Damn it. I warned this kid about*

his behavior.

Jess picked up her coffee and walked over to stand next to Bates's chair. "Don't you have patients to see, Dr. Bates?" she asked in a mild tone.

Bates looked up at Jess with a frown. "I'm helping Dr. Donovan while I wait for lab results to come back." He smiled over at Kim.

"I can manage just fine on my own," Kim said.

Jess glanced down at Kim. She was sure she saw Kim roll her eyes before she looked down and her hair hid her expression. That pretty much confirmed for her that Bates was making a pest of himself. And most likely hitting on Kim. *I definitely need to have another counseling session with him.* "In that case, Dr. Bates, I suggest you let Dr. Donovan get back to work. And attend to your own responsibilities," she said her tone taking on a slightly firmer edge.

"I'm waiting for my labs," Bates repeated stubbornly.

All right. That's it. "If you can't find a patient to see, I'm sure I can find one for you," Jess said, her voice cold and totally devoid of emotion.

Bates was up and out of his chair with alacrity. He headed for the door without another word.

Jess gazed down at Kim once he was gone. She shifted uncomfortably. She hated having to deal with this type of thing. *Why can't he just do his damn job!* "I'm sorry if he was bothering you."

Kim smiled up at her. "No problem. I can handle an over eager resident."

Some of Jess's tension dissipated. Kim was turning out to be a great addition to the ER. The last thing she wanted was for her to feel uncomfortable working here. "I'm sure you can, but you shouldn't have to. I'll talk to him." *If I don't wring his neck first!*

Jess gazed into Kim's vivid blue eyes and their eyes locked for a moment. Suddenly at a loss for words, she looked down and focused on the table. *Get it together, McKenna.* Quickly regaining her composure, she turned the conversation to a safe subject—work. "Working on charts?" As soon as Jess said it she realized how inane it sounded. *Brilliant, Einstein. What gave it away? The table full of charts?*

Kim nodded. "I figured since it was quiet, it was a good time to get caught up."

Jess still couldn't get over the fact that Kim was here working at all. None of the other psychiatrists worked on patient charts in the ER. Then again, Kim had already proven she was not anything like the other psychiatrists. In five short days she had turned the ER upside down. In all the years Jess had worked here, she had never heard so many positive comments about anyone from psychiatry. Although she hadn't had a chance to work with her personally since that first day, she had heard staff and residents alike repeatedly praising Kim.

Jess took a sip of her coffee to hide her struggle to find something else to say. She wanted to talk to Kim and get to know her, but at the same time resisted the urge to do so. *You don't need to know anything except that she's good at her job.*

A concerned expression suddenly took up residence on Kim's face. "It's not a problem me working in here is it?" she asked.

Jess shook her head. She realized Kim had most likely misconstrued her silence. "No. Absolutely not. I occasionally work—"

The lounge door swung open. Bates peered into the room. When he spotted Jess he ducked back out and quickly closed the door.

Jess looked down at Kim in surprise when she heard her chuckle.

"He's persistent all right," Kim said. "Don't worry.

Someone will eventually clue him in that it's a lost cause."

Before Jess could ask what that meant, the door swung open again.

Penny stepped into the doorway and looked around. "Have you seen, Dr. Bertucci?"

"No," Jess said.

"Okay," Penny said and hurried away. The door swung shut behind her.

Jess turned her attention back to Kim. "It can get—" The door to the lounge swung open one more time. Jess shook her head in exasperation.

Terrell stepped into the room. He glanced at Kim, then met Jess's eyes. Without a word he turned and left the room.

"As I was saying ..." Jess stopped and stared at the door for just a moment.

Kim laughed.

When the door didn't immediately open, Jess continued, "As you see, it can get a little busy in here. I do work in here occasionally. Most of the staff have a small cubbyhole office they share with another staff member that they use to do their paperwork if it gets too crazy in the lounge. Unfortunately, there aren't any open offices available right now."

"Oh. Well ... I guess I could go back to my office. That's where I've been doing my paperwork," Kim said. "I just thought I could be more help if I was close by and readily available."

Jess was thrilled that Kim was so willing to help. Her hard work had made a big impact on the ER. The last thing Jess wanted was for her to feel as if she did not have a place in the ER. She scrambled for a solution. "No. It's fine to work in the lounge. If it gets too hectic, you could use my office for a quiet place to work." A blast of panic hit as soon as the offer left her mouth.

What the hell are you doing! That's your only sanctuary.

"That's really nice of you, but I don't want to intrude on your privacy," Kim said.

Jess met Kim's understanding gaze. She was surprised and equally dismayed that Kim seemed able to read her so well. She quickly schooled her features. *I can do this.* Kim had gone out of her way to integrate into the ER. This was the least Jess could do in return. *And of course, if you just happen to get the chance to spend some private time with her, even better.* Jess firmly pushed the thought away. She refused to acknowledge the truth of that statement. "It's okay. Come on, I'll show you where my office is."

Kim followed Jess to a back hall of the ER that she thought only held supply closets. Stepping into the office, Kim was surprised to find it was half the size of her office in psych. It didn't even have a window.

Jess sat on the edge of her desk. She crossed her arms over her chest, looking very ill at ease.

Kim had seen the brief flash of what looked like panic that crossed Jess's face when she offered the use of her office. She wondered if this was even a good idea after seeing firsthand the distance Jess kept from her staff. Kim didn't want to make Jess uncomfortable in her own office.

"Are you sure you don't mind me using your office, Dr. McKenna?" *Yeah. See. Dr. McKenna. You don't even call her by her first name. This is a bad idea.* Kim watched Jess's reactions carefully. During the past week, Kim had noticed that after a particularly stressful trauma case, Jess would occasionally disappear for a short time. Kim was sure she retreated into her office. She was loath to intrude on what was most likely Jess's personal sanctuary from the stress of her job.

Jess dropped her arms down to her sides and stood. After a slight hesitation she seemed to come to a decision. "You're welcome to use my office while you're assigned to the ER. It's very helpful to have you nearby for consults. You've done an excellent job this week."

Kim smiled brightly. It felt good to hear Jess praise her competence. It helped alleviate any lingering worries over Jess discovering what had happened at Memorial. "Thanks."

If they were going to be sharing an office, Kim decided to see if she could do away with the formal address between them. "Now that that's settled. How about you call me, Kim?" Kim sighed in disappointment when Jess's expression closed off. *Shit. Pushed too hard.* Kim quickly tried to fix things. "Of course, I only meant in private."

Jess's expression smoothed out and her body language relaxed. "Sure. And you can call me, Jess."

"Thanks, Jess."

"You're welcome, Kim." A smile ghosted across Jess's face and just as quickly disappeared. "Okay then, I need to get back to the ER. If I don't keep a tight rein on the children, all hell breaks loose."

Kim laughed softly inordinately pleased that Jess felt comfortable enough to even make such a comment. "I'm sure they're wondering where I disappeared to as well."

"They probably figure you fell into the evil clutches of the bitch of the ER."

A bit taken aback by Jess's words, Kim frowned. Jess was firm with her residents and her demeanor could be a bit stern. And while she had seen a few contentious interactions between Jess and her residents, Peter in particular, nothing she had witnessed would make her think of Jess as a bitch.

"Oh, that's one of the nicer things the residents call me." Jess shrugged. "I'm sure you'll hear them all very soon. And you'll probably call me some of them yourself before long."

Kim easily saw through Jess's defensive bravado. It was obvious to her that underneath Jess was hurt by the name calling. "Oh, I'm not worried, Jess. I'm confident we'll work well together."

Jess smiled. "I'm glad to hear it." She glanced at her watch. "It's almost the end of shift. Shall we head back into the fray one last time?"

"Of course. Lead the way." Kim was amazed at how lighthearted one rare smile from Jess made her feel. Not to mention the fact that the more she learned about Jess, the more she intrigued her. Her first week in the ER was definitely ending on a high note.

As they made their way back into the ER proper, Kim couldn't help comparing Jess to Anna, her ex-lover. It was becoming abundantly clear to Kim that the only thing Jess shared in common with Anna was their job title. Anna had reveled in the myriad of disparaging names the residents and staff alike called her. To Anna, they were a badge of honor, as if they proved to everyone how strong she was and in charge of her world—the ER.

A resident calling her name brought her thoughts back to business. Kim glanced at Jess and smiled. "See you later," she said before walking away to answer the resident's call.

CHAPTER 5

Kim stopped outside the door to Jess's office. She looked down at the tray with two cups of coffee and a pastry that she had picked up on her way to work. Struck by the memory of all the times she had used this gesture as a segue to asking a woman out on a date, she reminded herself of the promises she had made to herself after the fiasco with Anna. *You can do this. It's just a cup of coffee between colleagues. You promised yourself things would be different this time.*

In the past, Kim had made the mistake of jumping into bed with a woman before getting to know her very well. *And lived to regret it.* That had certainly been the case with Anna. If she had known how closeted Anna was, she would never have gotten involved with her.

Conflicting emotions buffeted Kim. She had thought a lot about Jess over the weekend. That was the problem. She knew it was too soon to be thinking about becoming involved with someone. That didn't stop her attraction toward Jess. *Try being her friend and forget about it becoming anything else. That would be a real first for you.* She grimaced. That was too true. Kim couldn't remember that last time she had pursued a friendship with a woman for the sake of friendship alone and not as a prelude to sleeping with her. *You condemned Mom for jumping from lover to lover, and now you've become just like her.* That realization stung.

Kim jumped, startled out of her inner monologue by the sudden opening of Jess's office door.

Jess managed to grab the tray Kim was holding

before she dropped it. She seemed surprised to find Kim standing outside her door. She handed the tray back to her. "What can I do for you?" Jess asked. She remained standing in the doorway of her office and made no move to invite Kim inside.

"Would it be okay if we went inside?" Kim asked, gesturing toward the office. For a moment, Kim thought she was going to refuse, but then Jess stepped back and motioned her into the room.

Kim set the tray on Jess's desk. She picked up one of the cups and held it out to Jess. "I brought you coffee and a muffin. I wanted to say thanks for letting me use your office."

Jess moved over toward her desk, but made no attempt to take the cup from Kim. "You didn't need to do that."

Kim could see how uncomfortable Jess looked. "I know, but I wanted to. Cream with no sugar ... right?" Kim said as she offered the cup to Jess again.

Jess's eyes went wide, then she nodded. She reached out and somewhat reluctantly took the cup. "Um ... thanks," Jess said as she sat the cup down on her desk.

"You're very welcome." Kim smiled warmly hoping to ease some of the tension she could see on Jess's face and body language. "There's also a great chocolate muffin in the bag." She held out the bag to Jess, who took it even more reluctantly than she had the coffee. "I ended up eating mine on the way in. Anything chocolate never lasts very long around me," Kim said with a sheepish laugh.

Kim's discomfort level rose when Jess didn't respond. She was beginning to regret coming to Jess's office. The few minutes of easy interaction on Friday when Jess seemed to relax and open up a little bit had disappeared. Kim sighed. A wave of disappointment washed over her. *Okay, this friend thing may be harder than I thought. Just because you want to be friends doesn't mean Jess is going to let you. You've seen how she is with her staff.* "Well, I'm sorry to have disturbed you. I'll be in psych if anyone needs me."

"Wait ... Kim," Jess said.

Kim had almost reached the door when Jess's voice stopped her. She turned back toward Jess and raised her eyebrow in question.

Jess took the second cup of coffee from the tray and held it out to Kim. "Don't forget your coffee."

Kim had lost all interest in the coffee she had hoped to share with Jess, but took the offered cup anyway. She met Jess's gaze and was puzzled by what she thought was a bit of regret in her eyes.

"I um ..." Jess cleared her throat. "I was just getting ready to head to the resident's morning conference. The lecture today is on evaluating the emergency room schizophrenic patient. I was wondering if you'd be interested in attending?"

"Sure. I'd be glad to go." Relief washed over Kim. *Maybe I didn't screw up.* In retrospect, she realized that she should have known that her offering would make Jess ill at ease. She had never seen her share so much as a cup of coffee or have a conversation that wasn't work related with anyone. "Which one of the psychiatrists is lecturing?"

Jess glanced down and shuffled her feet. "I'm giving the lecture. I've asked Dr. Alerman several times for someone from psych to participate in a lecture series covering ER psychiatric issues." She shrugged. "No one has been willing to take it on. Dr. Alerman presented a series of lectures last year, but he said he didn't have time this year."

Anger surged through Kim. *What were you thinking Philip? The ER doesn't need a person to liaison with from psych. It needs the psych department staff to get off their collective asses and do their damn jobs.* Kim pushed aside the unproductive emotion. "If you give me a list of the topics you'd like covered, I could create a series of lectures and present them."

"I wasn't trying to foist the conferences off on you," Jess said.

"I know you're not." Kim grimaced to herself at Jess's choice of words. She would bet anything someone from psych had accused Jess of doing just that—foisting the ER conferences on psych. "I'm volunteering to give the lectures. I enjoy teaching residents. The last place I worked had a psychiatric residency. I miss presenting resident conferences since there's no psych program here. I've got quite a few lectures ready that I used with psych residents. I could tailor a number of them to apply to the needs of the ER residents."

Jess stared at Kim for a moment, clearly shocked by the offer. For the first time since she had opened her office door, Jess actually smiled. "If you're sure ..." At Kim's nod she continued, "I really appreciate you doing this." Jess glanced at her watch. "We need to get to the conference. I'll work out the schedule with you later."

"Okay. Sounds good." Kim smiled when Jess picked up the cup of coffee from her desk before heading for the door.

Jess gathered up her charts at the nurses' station. She planned on heading for her office to get some paperwork done before the rapidly approaching end of shift. The doors to the ambulance entrance of the ER banged open. Jess looked up in time to see two police officers enter. A slender, red-haired female officer was accompanied by a large, burly male officer. She was holding what appeared to be a small child wrapped in a jacket. All Jess could see was matted hair at the top and a tiny pair of sneakers sticking out of the bottom of the coat.

Jess dropped her charts back on the counter and strode over to the officers. "What've you got?"

The woman officer pulled back the jacket revealing a small, dark haired little girl. "We found her locked in a basement storage unit of an apartment building," she said. "Tenant of the building called it in. He heard what he thought was an animal crying when he went in to get his bike from his locker. When he spotted her, he immediately called 911. We're not sure how long she's been there. Guy said he didn't hear anything the last time he was in his locker, which was two weeks ago. We cut the lock and got her out of there."

Jess gazed at the little girl, but resisted the urge to reach out and take her into her arms. *Oh, little one, what happened to you?* Her hair and clothes were filthy. Jess couldn't see her face. Her little face was buried in the officer's jacket. "Have you located her parents, Officer ...?"

"Williams. We're still looking for them. According to the neighbors, no one has seen the mother for the past week. Boyfriend was around for the first couple of days after the mom left, but not for the last three days. None of the neighbors remember seeing Tara, that's the little girl's name, for the last week. But according to one of the women we spoke with that's not uncommon. Her mom doesn't take her out of the apartment very often." Williams shook her head, her anger plainly written on her face. "She's filthy, but didn't have any obvious injuries that we could see. She wasn't even crying when we found her. She did scream when one of the officers picked her up, but she hasn't made a sound since."

Jess's anger soared at the thought of the girl's

uncaring parents. *What the hell kind of sick person could do this to an innocent child?* She had seen some terrible things perpetrated on children during her time in the ER, but she never got used to it. Jess pushed her anger aside. Her focus now was Tara. "All right. It's an emergency so I can treat her without parental consent. Let's get her into an exam room."

As Jess turned she spotted Kim standing close by. She was glad that she was still in the ER so late in the day. Jess beckoned her over. "You heard the history?" At Kim's nod she continued, "I'd like you to observe while I check out her physical condition. See what you can pick up from her reactions. Afterward, you can do a full assessment if necessary."

"All right. I would recommend you keep the number of people present to a minimum. Just being exposed to a large group of strangers is stressful for a child this young. She doesn't need that in addition to whatever else she has already been through," Kim said.

"Fine. Let's go," Jess said. She motioned for Officer Williams to follow her.

Maggie, one of the admitting nurses, ran up to the group. "Dr. McKenna, there are a bunch of reporters in the waiting room asking questions. They're blocking access to the admitting desk and won't leave."

Jess scowled. *Great. Just what we need.* "How many are there?"

"I'm not sure how many people there are but two different camera crews are filming," Maggie said.

Jess glanced at the other officer's nametag. "Officer Johnson, how about rounding up the people from the media and getting them out of my waiting room? They're interfering with patient care."

The officer smiled at Jess and rubbed his hands together. "Gladly, Doc. Where do you want them?"

Jess resisted the temptation to tell him exactly

where she'd like them to go. She realized her thoughts must have shown on her face when both officers and Kim chuckled. Jess shook her head and forced her professional persona back into place. "Maggie, show Officer Johnson where Conference Room C is. If it's not empty, clear it out. Inform the rest of the staff what's happening. I don't want any reporters sneaking into the ER proper."

Jess turned her attention to Officer Johnson. "I'd appreciate it if you'd escort the press to the conference room and then make sure they stay there. You're welcome to use the room if someone from your department wants to make a statement to the press. I'll update Officer Williams on Tara's condition once I finish my exam."

"Thanks, Doc," Johnson said before turning to follow Maggie.

"Now that all that's settled, let's get this little girl checked out," Jess said. She headed toward an exam room with Kim and Officer Williams on her heels.

"Go ahead and set her down," Jess said motioning toward the gurney.

Kim moved to the head of the gurney. She wanted to be close enough to offer the little girl comfort and emotional support while Jess did her physical exam.

Tara didn't react in any way when the officer followed Jess's instructions.

Jess moved to the opposite side of the stretcher. "Officer, please wait outside while I complete my exam."

"If you can get her to talk I really need to hear anything she can tell us. I tried to connect with her on the way over here, but she wouldn't even look at me."

Jess nodded. "I understand that, but my main

concern right now is to make sure she's not injured and assess her physical and mental condition." Jess looked down at the little girl. She was huddled in the oversize jacket with her head resting on her knees. She had yet to make a sound or even move. "Once I'm finished you can come back in."

"All right. I'll go check on how Johnson is doing with the reporters," Officer Williams said. "Let me know when you're done."

"I'll have one of the nurses come get you." Jess waited until the door had closed behind the officer. She met Kim's eyes over Tara's head. "I want a detailed accounting of what I find as we go. But, I'd rather not have another person in the room. You mind taking notes?" she asked.

"No problem." Kim accepted the loose chart pages Jess offered. She watched with interest as Jess's expression softened when she leaned down to be more on Tara's level.

"Hey, Tara. I'm Dr. Jess. I'm going to take care of you ... okay?"

A slight tremor rippled through the little girl's body but no other response.

Jess tried again. "Tara, please look at me." Jess sighed. Tara gave no indication that she had even heard her request.

"Want me to try?" Kim knew Jess needed to do her exam regardless of the little girl's lack of response.

Jess shook her head. "Let me try again." Jess grasped the edge of the coat Tara had wrapped around her. "Tara ... I'm just going to take this coat off ... okay?" She waited a moment for a response. "Okay, here we go," Jess said while she carefully opened the coat. She removed it from around her shoulders and let it drop to lay on the gurney under Tara. "There we go."

Kim had witnessed how conscientious and

compassionate Jess was with patients, but this was the first time she had seen her interact with such a young child. Kim was struck by Jess's gentle, tender manner with the little girl. It showed a whole other side of her.

"That's better." Jess slowly and carefully placed her hand on Tara's T-shirt clad shoulder.

Kim tensed waiting for Tara's reaction. The little girl flinched at the first touch, but offered no other response. Kim met Jess's eyes and they shared a relieved look. "So far, so good," Kim said low-voiced.

Jess began to slowly rub her hand up and down Tara's back. "Come on, little one. Please look at me."

Ah ... that got a reaction. "Jess," Kim said softly. When Jess looked up she leaned over a bit and spoke quietly, "Use 'little one' again. She reacted to that."

Jess nodded in understanding. "Hey, little one." Jess glanced up at Kim and smiled. She had seen the reaction this time. The little girl's gaze had flickered toward her for just a second. "Come on, little one, please look at me." Jess's smile widened when Tara met her eyes and held them. "That's a good girl." She continued to gently stroke the girl's back.

Kim's tension eased. This was going better than she had hoped. While she understood the child needed to be examined she did not want to add to her trauma while doing so. She was impressed. Jess was being so calm and patient with Tara. She knew it was especially difficult dealing with injured children in the ER. *Then again some people are just lousy with kids—period.* Anna immediately came to mind. She never saw children in the ER if she could possibly avoid it. Kim's attention was brought back to business when Jess began to speak to Tara again.

"Now we need to make sure you're okay." Jess placed a hand gently on Tara's bent knees. "Can you sit up straight for me?" When she didn't get a response,

Jess lifted the hand she had resting on the little girl's knees and gently brushed her filthy, matted hair away from her face. "Come on, sweet girl—"

With an inarticulate cry, Tara launched herself at Jess.

NO! Kim lunged for Tara but missed her.

Tara slammed against Jess's chest.

Jess staggered back a step. Her arms whipped up and gripped the little girl tightly to her chest.

Kim took a shaky breath. She looked over at Jess. Tara was clinging to her for dear life. Her heart was still pounding from Tara's scream and precipitous leap from the gurney. She moved around the end of the gurney. As she got close to Jess she was assaulted by the pungent smell of urine. "You okay?"

"I'm fine," Jess said. "But I'm not so sure about Tara."

Surprise rippled through Kim at the tremor in Jess's voice. She had never seen her anything but calm, cool and collected, even after a major trauma.

"What triggered that I wonder?" Jess shifted Tara slightly in her arms. The little girl had her face buried in Jess's neck and was crying brokenly.

"She seemed to react to you using, 'sweet girl' maybe it's what her mother or someone important to her calls her. It told her you were someone safe." Kim reached out and gently stroked Tara's back. "Letting her emotions out is actually the best thing for her. I was pretty worried about her being so unresponsive."

"It's okay, little one. You're safe here." Jess moved over and leaned against the gurney. She rocked Tara in her arms for several minutes, murmuring softly to her the whole time.

Kim's heart filled with warmth at Jess's caring treatment of the little girl. Tara was filthy and stank of urine, but none of that appeared to matter to Jess as she held her tenderly in her strong, comforting embrace. When Jess looked up, Kim saw for the first time beneath the mask Jess wore at work. The open, emotion-filled look in her eyes was compelling. *Oh, Jess.* In the blink of an eye it was gone, and Kim was once more faced with the ER chief she was coming to know.

"I still need to examine her," Jess said. She looked down at the little girl. She had fallen asleep in her arms. "Poor little thing. She must have been exhausted." Jess turned to place Tara on the gurney, then appeared to change her mind. "I don't want to take a chance of waking her. How about you sit on the gurney and hold her while I do the exam?"

"Good idea. That'll work." Kim moved over and levered herself up onto the gurney.

Jess started to hand over Tara, then hesitated. "You need to get a gown. She's a mess."

Kim looked down at the pale purple shirt she was wearing, then up at what used to be a stark white lab coat that Jess had on. Tara stirred restlessly in Jess's arms. Kim didn't even think twice. She held out her arms. "It's okay. Give her to me. I'd rather not take the chance of waking her, until it's absolutely necessary."

She would have done it regardless, but the smile Jess gave her made it worth whatever happened to her clothes. Kim cuddled the little girl tenderly in her arms. She smiled back at Jess as they worked together to provide the care Tara needed.

Jess dropped her paperwork on her desk. Bypassing the desk chair, she crossed the small room and flopped down onto the sofa that took up most of the back wall of her office. Although it had not been physically demanding or even require any great skill, taking care of Tara had been taxing. Jess worked to remain emotionally detached from her patients. It was what made her good at her job. In the case of children, she always had an especially hard time, they were totally defenseless. She scrubbed her hands over her face. *You've got work to do if you ever want to get out of here tonight.*

Pushing up from the sofa, she headed for her desk only to be interrupted by a knock on the door. *Now what?* Thankfully, the last of the press had left shortly after the social worker picked up Tara. Jess had already turned over the department to the next shift. With a disgruntled grumble, she jerked open the door to her office. "What?" she asked before the door even opened fully.

"Hi," Kim said a bit tentatively.

Jess immediately regretted her sharp tone. She was glad for the chance to make up for her earlier behavior. She was remorseful for her reaction this morning when Kim brought her coffee and a muffin. At the time, her defenses had instantly gone up as her thoughts immediately turned to her ex, Myra. She had wondered what Kim's motive was behind the offering. After she'd had a chance to think about it, Jess realized how unfair she had been. *She was just being nice. Not everyone is out to get close to you, then humiliate you.* Refusing to give into the bad memories associated with Myra, Jess focused on Kim. "Come on in, Kim." She smiled warmly.

"Thanks, Jess."

Her tension dissipated when Kim smiled in return. Re-entering her office, she resisted the urge to retreat behind her desk. It was an ingrained reaction to help distance herself from people. *Let her in. You know you want to.*

Jess leaned against the edge of her desk. The silk

blouse and tailored slacks Kim had been wearing earlier had been replaced by scrubs. The dark blue scrubs set off her blond hair and made her blue eyes more vivid than usual. *God she's beautiful.* Jess sighed to herself. *And it's a lot more than skin deep.* Jess's heart had melted watching Kim's tender treatment of Tara. "I hope your clothes aren't a total loss. I know that case was a bit above and beyond the call for a psych consult."

Kim moved toward Jess, and leaned on the opposite end of her desk. "Don't worry about it. That's what they make dry cleaners for. I'm relieved you didn't find anything more serious than mild dehydration. After seeing her filthy condition, I was pretty worried about what else you might uncover."

"Me too. You were really great with her."

"Thanks, Jess. I think we did a good job with her." Kim smiled. "We make a good team."

An unaccustomed blush stained Jess's face at the praise. "Thanks. And yes, we do." A bit uncomfortable with the turn of the conversation, Jess moved back to more solid ground. "Well, I should get back to work if I ever want to get out of here," she said gesturing to the charts on her desk.

"Okay. I just came in to let you know I spoke to the woman from child protective services before she left with Tara. They're going to bring in a child psychologist to do a more comprehensive evaluation than I could here in the ER. I asked her to give me a call and let me know how Tara is doing."

Renewed anger surged through Jess at the thought of the little girl, alone among strangers, and scared. *You can't protect them all.* Jess wasn't sure she wanted to know about Tara. She saw too many hurt and abused children in the ER. Worrying about the fate of each and every one of them would tear her apart. "Okay. Thanks for letting me know. Have a good night."

"You too, Jess. I'll see you tomorrow."

"Night, Kim."

Jess stared at the door long after Kim had departed. A sense of loneliness she rarely acknowledged filled her. The scary part was that the few moments she had just spent with Kim had brightened her whole day and lifted that loneliness if only for a few minutes.

CHAPTER 6

Taking advantage of a lull in the action in the ER, Kim made her way to the cafeteria. It was hard to believe that tomorrow was the last day of her rotation. The two weeks had passed quickly. While she enjoyed working with psych patients in group sessions, in the past she found that she frequently missed the fast pace of the ER once she returned to psych.

Kim picked up a tray and began to make her selections. When the serving line started to bunch up, she noticed Cindy, one of the ER nurses just ahead of her. She was talking to another woman Kim didn't recognize.

The women were engrossed in their conversation and appeared unaware of her approach. As she moved closer she couldn't help but overhear their conversation.

"You should have seen Dr. Archer when his girlfriend showed up and bitched him out. Right in the middle of the waiting room too. Oh, man!"

Cindy laughed. "We haven't had that kind of fireworks in the ER since Dr. McKenna's ex stormed right up to her at the nurses' station and gave us all an earful."

Kim winced. *Poor Jess. She must have been humiliated. Maybe that's why her interactions with her staff are so guarded. Sure can't blame her.*

The nurse shook her head. "No way. McKenna's got an ex?"

"Shocked me too. But it's true," Cindy said. "Now this was awhile back, almost two years ago. Haven't seen or heard about her dating anyone since. Though after what I heard that day, I couldn't blame her. Phew, talk about more than you wanted to know about someone. I always thought she was stuck-up, but if even half of what her ex said about her is true it's—"

Anger surged through Kim. She pushed her tray forward and bumped it into Cindy's with enough force to jolt the other woman's tray. "Excuse me."

She had been feeling a bit guilty about eavesdropping, but it wasn't as if the women were trying to keep their conversation private. Despite her desire to learn more about Jess, this wasn't right. These women were professionals. They should not be gossiping in the cafeteria as if they were in high school.

Cindy turned. "Hey! Oh ... Dr. Donovan." A light blush spread across her face. Cindy's eyes darted over to her friend and then quickly back to Kim.

Kim resisted the urge to glare at the women. "I hope this isn't how you usually spend your lunch break, ladies." *That's right. I heard every word.*

Cindy's face flushed, this time with anger. "It was a private conversation."

"No. It wasn't." Kim struggled to keep her own temper. "There are people everywhere. And you weren't being quiet about it. I'm sure Dr. McKenna would not appreciate you gossiping about her—period. Much less doing so in the cafeteria where anyone, possibly even a patient, could hear you."

Cindy's expression changed swiftly from anger to panic. She jerked her tray off the counter and hurried away. Her friend quickly followed.

That's when Kim became aware of the presence behind her. She had been so focused on the two women that she had not realized that someone had walked up. She turned and came face to face with a stern-faced Jess.

A vivid blush burned across Kim's face. *Great. How much did she hear?* Kim knew she had not done anything wrong, but she was embarrassed by the situation, nonetheless.

Deciding to take the bull by the horns so to speak, Kim met Jess's gaze directly. She moved a bit closer to Jess and lowered her voice. "I hope I didn't overstep myself with your nurse? I just didn't think you'd appreciate her gossiping like that in such a public place."

"No, you didn't. Cindy is one of the worst offenders in ER when it comes to spreading rumors." Jess shrugged. "As far as gossip in general goes, I think it's unavoidable. As I'm sure you know, working in a hospital can be like living in a fishbowl. I try to ignore it. Doing anything else just seems to encourage it."

Kim could sense Jess's frustration despite her words. "I know what you mean, but in this case they were being so blatant about it I just couldn't keep quiet."

A resigned smile crossed Jess's face. "While I appreciate the sentiment, it's not necessary. I'm well aware of the things said about me."

Doesn't make it right or any less hurtful. Kim sighed in frustration. Although this wasn't the time or place to do so, she wanted so badly to reach out to Jess and comfort her. At the same time, she knew the gesture was not something Jess would ever acknowledge or accept. In fact, it would most likely drive her away.

A group of people came up behind Jess effectively ending their conversation.

Kim finished choosing her food and headed for the cashier. She waited for Jess to finish paying for her selections.

"Want to share a table?" Kim asked when Jess was done. This was a good chance to get to talk to Jess away from the hub-bub of the ER.

Jess hesitated and just for a moment Kim thought she was going to agree.

"Sorry, I can't. I have to get back to the residents," Jess said.

Kim wondered if it was just an excuse not to have lunch with her. *What do you expect? You know how she is about keeping people at arm's length. After hearing just the little bit Cindy said, she most likely has a damn good reason for that attitude.*

"Okay. I'll see you later in the ER," Kim said.

With a quick wave, Jess made for the exit.

Knowing what she did now, Kim wondered if she would ever get more than just a glimpse of the real woman beneath Jess's formidable ER chief persona.

CHAPTER 7

Jess returned to the ER from her meeting to find quite a few of the staff clustered at the nurses' station. She glanced at the patient board and was surprised to see only a few names listed. It was unusual for things to be so quiet on a Friday. She started to head for her office when she heard Bates's voice.

"What about you, Dr. Donovan? What are you up to this weekend?" Bates asked.

Jess hadn't noticed Kim sitting at the computer. She moved a bit closer but for the moment did not make her presence known. *He better not be bothering her again.*

Kim turned her chair to face the group. "Oh, not much, still settling in."

"A few of us are getting together tonight after work for a drink. Want to join us?" Bates asked.

"Maybe some other time. I just want to get home tonight and crash." Kim started to turn back to the computer.

"How about this weekend?" Bates persisted. "Let's go out for a drink and dinner. I'll show you around."

Several people snickered.

Bates glared at his co-workers.

Wonder what that's about? As realization dawned, a sense of satisfaction spread through Jess. What she had suspected from the start was true. *Ah ... I may be rusty when it comes to dating, but at least my gaydar still works.*

"No thanks. I used to live around here. I'm familiar with the area," Kim said.

Bates moved over to Kim and put a hand on her shoulder. "Come on. It'll be fun."

An unexpected surge of anger washed over Jess at the sight of Bates's hand on Kim. She strode into the center of the group.

Jess's gaze pinned several people as she looked around at the gathered staff. "Don't you people have something to do? There are patients to be seen. And if you don't have a patient, are all the drug carts stocked? Everyone's paperwork complete?"

Everyone scattered except for Bates and Kim.

Bates started to speak to Kim, but Jess cut him off.

"Dr. Bates, don't you have patients to see?" Jess struggled to keep the anger she was feeling out of her voice.

"I'm waiting for labs to come back on the guy in Bed Two," Bates said. He turned his back on Jess. "So, Dr. Donovan, maybe we could get together some other time?"

Jess quickly scanned the waiting charts, then plucked one from the rack. She smothered a self-satisfied smile. *This ought to keep you busy and cool your jets.*

Before Kim could respond, Jess marched over to Bates and shoved the chart into his hands. "Since you have so much time on your hands, you can take the guy in Bed Three. He's impacted and needs to be cleaned out."

Bates started to protest, but one look at Jess's face seemed to convince him otherwise and he hurried away.

"I'm sorry about him." Jess pulled over a chair and sat down next to Kim. "Obviously my talking to him hasn't made much of an impression. I'll talk to him again. This time I'll put a formal letter of counseling in his record."

Kim shook her head. "You don't need to do that.

I can handle him. He must have missed the hospital gossip about me. I'll be straight with him next time he asks." Kim laughed. "Well, maybe not straight, but I'll make sure he gets the message."

Gay and out. That's always a welcome combination. Jess met Kim's eyes and was surprised to see what looked like a bit of concern. *Huh ...maybe not so out? Then why did she ...* Realization dawned. *She's worried about how I'll react. I thought for sure big mouthed Cindy had clued her in after the incident in the cafeteria yesterday. Guess not.* She had not actually heard what Cindy had said, only Kim defending her.

The thought of Kim being upset or worried caused an inexplicable sick feeling in the pit of her stomach. She knew one sure way to put Kim at ease. Jess allowed a warm smile to grace her face. "Being straight is overrated." Arousal flashed through Jess and her heart rate soared when a brilliant smile blazed across Kim's face.

"Yes. It certainly is," Kim said.

A loud thump behind her made Jess jump. She jerked around in her chair and spotted Penny standing a few feet away with an angry scowl on her face. Several charts were lying on the counter in front of her. A quick glance around showed the nurses' station was deserted, except for Penny. *Still, it's hardly the place to be discussing your sexuality, no matter how obliquely.*

Jess turned back toward Kim. "I need to get back to work too. My paperwork is calling. I'll be in my office if you have any problems or just want a quiet place to work."

"Thanks," Kim said. "I may take you up on that later."

As Jess reviewed his chart, she kept a cautious eye on the patient sitting quietly on the gurney. He had been brought in from a local homeless shelter and appeared quite delusional. His responses to standard questions had been wildly inappropriate. After the patient had been cleared medically, Jess had sent the resident to find Kim.

Jess had not seen Kim since she had so blithely revealed her sexuality to her earlier in the day. Not only had she acted impulsively in telling Kim which was totally unlike her, more surprising was the fact that she didn't have any regrets. *Doesn't mean you should consider getting involved with her.* Although Jess knew that was true, the urge to do just that was getting stronger every day.

Looking over as the exam room door opened, Jess fought to keep the automatic smile off her face that appeared at the very sight of Kim.

"Dr. Bertucci fill you in?" Jess asked.

Kim walked up next to the patient's bed. "Yes. I'll take it from here. Thanks."

Jess hesitated to leave the room. While the patient had been calm so far, this guy seemed twitchy to her. She moved back and leaned against the door out of the patient's line of sight.

"Hello. I'm Dr. Donovan. How are you feeling today?" Kim asked.

"They took the cat, but they didn't get me."

"Can you tell me your name?"

The patient's gaze darted nervously around the room. He gripped the bedrails. "I can't tell you, because then they'll know," he said.

Faint alarm bells started to sound at the sudden shift in the patient's body language. Jess moved a bit closer to the foot of the gurney.

"Do you know where you are?" Kim asked calmly.

The man's eyes narrowed. "You're one of them. You can't fool me. All you women are."

Damn! I knew this guy was hinky. Jess took a step toward Kim and the patient.

He let out a blood-curdling scream. "Get away from me!"

Jess's body tensed. "Kim! Get back."

Kim stepped back but not quickly enough.

The man lunged against the bedrails and grabbed Kim by the shoulders. With an furious roar, he thrust her violently away.

No!

Jess rushed forward and grasped Kim from behind. She jerked her away from the patient and up close against her chest.

Jess's heart pounded fiercely in her chest and her arms tightened convulsively around Kim. A wave of nausea rippled through Jess at the prospect of something happening to Kim.

"Are you okay?" Jess asked breathlessly. She felt the rapid rise and fall of Kim's chest against her arm.

The patient glared at them but made no move to get off the gurney.

Kim appeared a bit rattled when she turned to look over her shoulder at Jess. "Yes. I am now." She offered a shaky smile. "Thanks for the quick save."

Now that she knew Kim was all right, Jess became acutely aware of the intimacy of their position. Arousal shot through her, making her nipples harden against Kim's back. *Oh God.* Jess was stunned by the strength of her wholly inappropriate reaction. Jerking her arms back, she quickly stepped away from Kim and put some distance between them.

Kim looked back at Jess with a strange expression on her face. "Are you okay?"

A vivid blush suffused Jess's face. She couldn't

bring herself to meet Kim's eyes. "Fine." Jess took a deep breath, trying to regain her composure.

She glanced over at the now quiet patient. Keeping a wary eye on him out of the corner of her eye, she forced herself to meet Kim's eyes briefly. "Since he seems to have issues with women, maybe it's time for some reinforcements. He was fine with the resident, Dr. Bertucci, earlier. You want to see if Dr. Kapoor is available to give us a hand? I'll watch our friend here while you're gone."

"Good idea. I'll call up to psych and see if he's available," Kim said.

The moment the door closed behind Kim, Jess began berating herself. *Damn, what the hell is the matter with you? Some psycho almost hurts Kim and you get all aroused by holding her in your arms.* Arousal soared anew at just the memory of Kim's body pressed against her and her arm pressed into Kim's breasts. *I've got to get this under control. This has got to stop.*

CHAPTER 8

Jess pulled into a parking space at her sister's apartment complex. The two sisters saw each other frequently. More often than not, she made the trip from Los Angeles to San Diego to visit her younger sister, Sam.

Originally, she had told Sam that she wouldn't be coming down to attend her softball game today. Jess had planned to spend the weekend working on an article she was submitting to an emergency medicine journal. After the events at work yesterday, as well as a sleepless night, she had changed her mind.

Now that she was here, she was having second thoughts. Jess scrubbed her hands across her face. *You know she's going to know something's up the minute she sees you.* Despite their four-year age difference, she and Sam had been very close growing up. They had remained so into adulthood. Her sister was the only person in the world who could read her easily. *Kim did a pretty good job the day you offered to share your office with her.* Jess grimaced. Kim was the last person she wanted to think about right now.

Going to Sam's game is just what you need. Watch some good softball and forget your troubles. Jess reached over and grabbed her duffle bag off the passenger seat.

She glanced into the rearview mirror. "Are you ready to go see Sam?" she asked her patiently waiting passenger. She laughed at the loud woo woo that immediately issued from the back of her Durango. Turning in her seat, she reached back and patted Thor, her Great Dane. "That's my good boy. Let's go."

Jess unloaded Thor and they headed for Sam's front door. She used her key to let them in, knowing Sam was more than likely still asleep.

"Go lay down," she said, pointing to the large dog bed in the corner of the living room. Once Thor was settled, she quietly walked down the hall to look in on Sam.

Peering into Sam's room, she was surprised to find it empty. *Where the heck is she at,* Jess glanced at her watch, *five o'clock in the morning? Hope she didn't get called back into work.* Due to Sam's profession, Jess always worried about her. She sighed. *Nothing to do but wait for her.*

Fatigue tugged at Jess. She refused to give in to the thought of sleep. During what little sleep she had managed to get last night, her dreams had been filled with disjointed images of Kim. She shook her head sharply as if she could dislodge the unsettling thoughts and feelings. *Coffee. I just need some coffee.*

Jess headed for Sam's kitchen.

She had just started to make coffee when she heard Thor's welcoming woof. Jess stuck her head out of the kitchen doorway in time to see Sam stagger back against the front door under the onslaught of Thor's welcome.

Thor stood up and put his paws on Sam's shoulders.

Jess shook her head as she made her way to the pair. "Hey, Sam."

"Now this is a welcome home." Sam wrapped her arms around the big dog and grinned at her. "I wasn't expecting you guys, or I would've been here."

Jess eyed her sister and her dog. "What happened to no jumping up? He does this to a stranger and someone could get hurt."

Sam looked suitably contrite. "Thor. Off."

Thor obediently dropped to the ground.

"Sorry." Sam pulled Jess into a one-armed hug.

Jess returned the hug. "I know he's never even tried to jump on anyone else like he does us, but I don't want to take a chance. He's such a big dog."

"No, you're right. I promise we'll be good. Won't we, big guy?" Sam said as she leaned down and hugged the big dog.

Thor woofed as if in agreement, making both sisters laugh.

As they moved back toward the living room, Jess asked, "Did you get called in to work?"

Sam shook her head and grinned. "Nope."

Jess took a closer look at Sam, noticing her rumpled clothing for the first time. Her short, dark hair was equally mussed. "When what—" Jess broke off when a little half smirk appeared on Sam's face and her blue eyes sparkled. She laughed when the clue bus arrived. "I thought you said you weren't going to see Gina anymore 'cause she was getting too clingy. Have a change of heart?"

Sam flopped down onto the couch. "Nah. I haven't seen her in over a month. She wanted a full-time girlfriend. I have no intention of getting tied down to one woman." Sam wiggled her eyebrows and grinned. "There are so many beautiful women out there and so little time to enjoy them."

Jess shoved at Sam's shoulder, knocking her over. "You're a dog, Samantha McKenna," she said as she joined her on the couch. Sam seemed to have an inborn aversion to commitment. Just the mention of the word made her twitch.

Sam pulled herself upright and scowled at Jess. "I am not. If I pretended to be something I'm not and led these women on ... Well, then I'd be a dog. I'm nothing if not honest about my intentions .... Or lack of them."

Jess shook her head. Sam would never change. She had never dated anyone seriously. *Like you're any different,* her more cynical side quickly noted. *I am too. I'd love to be seriously involved with someone. I'm just realistic enough to know it's not going to happen ... not to someone like me.* Jess pushed aside the depressing thoughts.

"So who's the latest?"

"Marina." Sam rubbed her hands together. "Picture: long black hair like silk, dark mesmerizing eyes, warm brown skin, and top it all off with a buff body. That's Marina." Sam wiped imaginary sweat from her brow. "And get her out of those blues and she is one sizzling hot Latina lady."

"Blues? She's a cop?"

"Yeah, she transferred in from another precinct a few weeks ago."

Jess shifted uncomfortably, her thoughts going to her situation with Kim. "Are you sure this is such a great idea? Gina at least worked in a different precinct. What if things go bad?"

Sam's expression turned serious. "Life can go bad, Jess. You know what I face every day as a cop. I could leave for work tomorrow and never come home again."

"Jesus, Sam. Don't say that!" The possibility of Sam being injured or even killed in the line of duty was something Jess tried very hard not to think about.

"It's the truth. So in my view, breaking things off with a woman is the least of my worries, even if we do work together." Sam shrugged. "Besides, it's not that kind of thing. We're just friends with fringe benefits."

A resigned sigh slipped from Jess's lips. While Sam was an avowed bachelor and loved playing the field, Jess had been involved with relatively few women. Although they both loved women, they had very different attitudes about relationships and sex. *Maybe that's 'cause there is one thing you've never told her about.* Jess ruthlessly slammed the door shut on those memories.

"Just seems like you're buying trouble." Jess could see Sam was getting exasperated with her. She gripped Sam's forearm and gave it a firm squeeze. "I'm just worried about you."

Sam sighed. "I know. Don't worry. I've got it under control."

That was wishful thinking. The very public meltdown of her relationship with Myra proved that. "But don't you think—"

"Come on, Jess," Sam said, cutting her off. "Enough already. Marina and I both know it's important to keep our personal life private."

Tension filled the room.

Sam slumped back against the couch cushions. "Look, I'm sorry. I'm just tired."

Jess brought her hands up and rubbed her stinging eyes. "Me too. Your life's your own. I shouldn't try and tell you how to live it. It's not like my personal life is any shining example to follow."

Neither woman spoke for several minutes.

"Hey." Sam sat up suddenly and peered at Jess with a questioning look. "Don't take this the wrong way, but I just realized ... What are you doing here? I thought you had that article you had to get ready."

Shit! Jess had hoped Sam had forgotten about that little fact. Struggling to keep her reluctance to discuss the topic off her face, Jess tried for casual nonchalance. "I just decided I wanted to see your game. No big deal. I can work on my article later."

Sam stared at her for a moment and then snorted. "You really don't expect me to buy that line of bull, do you? I got home a little after five this morning and you were already here. That means you had to have left LA at three o'clock in the morning." Sam leaned over and bumped shoulders with Jess. "Come on, sis. What's really going on?"

A mix of emotions buffeted her. Jess raked her hands through her hair. *You know you really want to talk. Otherwise, you wouldn't have come down here.* "It's some stuff at work. I needed to get away and relax."

The look on Sam's face made it clear she was less than convinced. "So what's happening at work—" A huge yawn caught Sam mid-sentence. She scrubbed her hands over her face. "Sorry."

"I'm pretty beat too." Jess yawned. "Tell you what. I was just getting ready to make some coffee when you came in. Why don't you grab a shower? I'll make coffee and whip us up some breakfast."

Sam looked ready to protest, then seemed to change her mind. Turning her gaze away, she stretched and then stood up. "All right. I'm too tired to argue with you."

Trying not to show how relieved she was at the reprieve, Jess stood up as well. Although she admitted that she did want to talk, she just wasn't ready yet.

Sam headed down the hall and stopped just outside her bedroom door. She turned back toward Jess and called out, "Don't think for a second I'm going to forget about this. We will finish this conversation."

"Yeah, yeah. I know." Jess headed for the kitchen, already wondering just what she was going to tell Sam. She couldn't explain her reaction to Kim to herself, much less to someone else.

Sam stepped out of the shower. She had been racking her brain trying to figure out what was up with Jess and work that she would feel the need to retreat to San Diego. Jess lived for her job. A niggling suspicion formed as she reached for her towel. *I wonder if it's that new doctor.* While she might talk about her cases in generic terms, Jess rarely spoke of her co-workers.

That had changed abruptly two weeks ago. After the third time Jess mentioned the new psychiatrist in less than a week, Sam had gotten the clue that something was different about ... *What was her name? Oh yeah. Kim.*

After making her way into the bedroom, she pulled out clean clothes. Sam sighed. *Not that Jess would ever let anything happen between them. Not after what that bitch did to her.* Anger burned through Sam at just the thought of Myra. She had never actually met her but hated her nonetheless. Jess had not let anyone get close since their breakup. *Not that she had ever let any woman really close to start with.* Sam knew Jess had real issues with trust. What she had never been able to figure out was why. Jess had a lot of bullshit rationalizations, but never one Sam truly believed.

Finished dressing, Sam headed for the kitchen to find out just what was up with Jess. *Maybe she's finally ready to move past Myra. She needs someone in her life. She might act like her job and Thor are enough, but I don't believe that. I may not want a girlfriend, but at least I have friends I go out and socialize with.*

Sam stopped in the doorway. What little floor space there was in the small kitchen was currently occupied by Thor, who was enjoying his breakfast.

Jess looked up and smiled. "He got tired of waiting for you."

"Just as long as he's not eating my breakfast." Sam leaned into the room and patted the only part of Thor she could easily reach, his butt.

Thor gave her a brief glance before going back to his food.

Jess picked up a plate and a mug off the counter.

Leaning over Thor, she handed them to Sam. "Lucky for you, he doesn't like coffee or bagels."

Sam laughed. "Thanks," she said, lifting up the items in her hands slightly.

Jess waved off the thanks. She picked up her own breakfast and carefully shuffled past Thor.

They both settled down at a small dinette table adjacent to the kitchen.

Sam took a large swig of her coffee. "Ah, just what I needed." Knowing Jess the way she did, she decided to ease her way into the conversation she really wanted to have with her. Sometimes getting Jess to open up about something was like pulling teeth. Not that she was any better. As she set her coffee back down she asked, "So what's up at work? New residents giving you problems?"

Jess took a moment to sip her coffee. "Had some trouble with one of the new ones, but I think she's got things worked out now. It's a lot more responsibility than they've ever had before, and it can be a tough adjustment."

Okay, not the residents. Sam knew the first few months after the new residents started were often a headache for Jess. She ate a few bites of her bagel. When Jess didn't offer any further comments, she tried again.

"Administrative problems, huh?"

Her mouth full of bagel, Jess shook her head no.

Running the ER was a lot more involved than most people realized. Sam had been amazed when Jess had explained all that her job entailed when she had taken over as Chief of the ER, in addition to being Program Director of the ER residency.

Okay that gets some of the usual problems out of the way. She really didn't believe it was any of the usual multitude of hassles at work that was bothering Jess anyway. Sam set down her coffee and turned her full attention to Jess, wanting to see her reaction. "So, how are things going with the new psychiatrist? Kim, right? She giving you problems?"

Jess choked on the mouthful of coffee she had just taken.

Ding, ding, ding. We have a winner. "You okay?"

Recovered from her coughing fit, Jess pushed back her chair and stood. "Yeah. I should go check on Thor."

Thor chose that moment to poke his head out of the kitchen.

"See he's fine," Sam said. "Come on, Jess. Talk to me. Tell me what's going on with this woman."

Jess shrugged, her gaze firmly locked on the table. "There's nothing to tell. Kim did a good job in the ER. She's done with her rotation and has gone back to psych." She began gathering up the dishes.

Sam stood and took the plates and cups out of Jess's hands and set them back on the table. "Leave these." She waited until Jess met her eyes. "You know I'm not going to let this go. So you might as well tell me."

"How can I tell you when I can't explain it to myself," Jess said.

Seeing the turmoil in Jess's eyes, Sam wrapped one arm around Jess's shoulders and squeezed. "Maybe we can make sense of it together, sis." She urged Jess toward the living room. "I'll grab us some more coffee. Then we'll talk."

Jess flopped gracelessly onto the couch. Her mind whirled as she tried to decide just what to tell Sam.

Thor lay down in front of the couch. He looked up and met Jess's eyes as if he could sense her jumbled emotions. He rested his head on her thigh and licked her hand, offering his own form of comfort.

Jess lovingly stroked the big dog's head. The peace and contentment she always felt at the simple act spread through her.

She glanced up when Sam set two mugs down on the coffee table.

Sam plopped down next to Jess on the couch. Reaching out, she began to gently pet Thor's neck.

"Tell me about Kim," Sam said quietly.

Jess's shoulders slumped. *I'm more attracted to her than I've ever been to anyone. She's a co-worker and off-limits. End of story.* She blew out a frustrated breath. "I—"

"I don't want to hear any of that," Sam said as if she could divine Jess's thoughts.

Jess scowled at Sam. She knew her too well.

"Don't think. Don't rationalize. Close your eyes and just tell me about Kim."

Jess leaned back and closed her eyes. A picture of Kim rapidly formed in her mind. Without giving herself a chance to think about it, she began to speak. "She's beautiful. Tall with a lithe build, shoulder-length curly blond hair, and warm blue eyes. I was taken with her the very first time I met her. Then she started working in the ER and I quickly discovered her beauty is much more than skin deep. Not only is she smart, but she's also a good person on the inside. Warm, caring, and compassionate with patients and families is just the start. She's great with the residents and staff. And a great teacher. I've enjoyed working with her more than anyone I can remember." Jess sighed. "Just being in the same room with her makes me feel good."

Jess's voice trailed off as the many images she had of Kim over the past two weeks paraded across her mind's eye. Kim laughing. Kim serious. Kim tenderly cradling a little girl in her arms.

No wonder she's invading my dreams. I don't remember experiencing that with Myra. An unexpected wave of longing washed over her. Jess's eyes popped open.

Sam was staring at her with a stunned expression on her face.

"Good God, Jess. She sounds wonderful. Why haven't you asked her out?" A grimace suddenly marred Sam's face. "Oh damn. She's not straight, is she?"

Jess shook her head. "You know why I can't ask her out."

"So she is gay?"

"Okay, fine. Yes, she's gay. I still can't ask her out." *No matter how much you want to.*

"Yeah. Yeah. I know. She's a colleague. So what! I understand about not dating someone who works directly for you. But she doesn't, she's a psychiatrist who consults in the ER." Sam raked her hands through her hair. "Damn it, Jess. Not every woman is going to be like that freak, Myra."

"Drop it, Sam." Jess's jaw clenched. "You don't know anything about Myra. It wasn't her fault things didn't work out."

"Only because you never let me meet her," Sam said in an aggrieved tone. "I know what you told me about her embarrassing you in the middle of your own ER. And I don't care whose fault it was; that's no excuse for what she did. But Christ, Jess, that was almost two years ago. You can't shut yourself off from everyone because of one woman."

Jess crossed her arms over her chest and scowled at Sam. "I'm not." *She's such a pain in the ass.* Despite her grousing, Jess knew there was truth to what Sam was saying. "I'd like to date someone ... just not someone I work with."

"Okay." Sam stared at Jess for a moment, then

a little half smirk appeared on her face. "Just one thing ..."

Ah shit. Jess braced herself. She knew that look, and it always meant trouble for whoever it was aimed at. "What?" Jess asked, unable to keep the trepidation out of her voice.

A full-fledged smirk danced across Sam's face. "Just where do you plan on meeting a woman if not at work?"

Jess racked her brain and quickly came up blank just as Sam apparently knew she would. She hadn't realized how cut off she had become from people in the last two years. She worked long hard hours at the ER. Most of her free time was spent in San Diego with Sam when Sam wasn't on duty. The rest of the time she spent with Thor or working at home, preparing lectures for residents and assorted ER administrative work. She couldn't remember the last time she had gone out to a movie or dinner with anyone other than Sam.

"Well?" Sam asked with a satisfied grin.

Jess's defenses kicked in. "Is this your way of telling me you're tired of my company?"

Sam stiffened and rounded on Jess with an angry glare. "Don't even think about trying to put this off on me. You know damn well that's not true."

Jess's shoulders slumped. "I know. I'm sorry." That had been a cheap shot. She knew Sam was just concerned about her.

The tension drained from Sam's face and she smiled. "Look, if you're worried, then don't ask her out on an 'official' date. Make it something casual, like lunch in the cafeteria or ... what's the name of that place across the street?"

"Charlie's."

"Yeah. Ask her to Charlie's. Just a friendly dinner between colleagues. Get to know her better."

Jess shook her head. "That would set the gossip

flying. I never go to lunch with anyone."

"Fuck 'em. Maybe it's time you started. You deserve to have a life."

"Sam," Jess said in a reproving tone.

"Come on, Jess. What do you care about what a bunch of people with nothing better to do say anyway? People are going to gossip no matter what you do."

"I know. I just don't want my personal life bandied about at work." *Any more than it already is. Hell, big mouth Cindy is still talking about something that happened almost two years ago.*

Sam's frustration at the impasse was readily apparent. She picked up her coffee and took a sip. "What about if you asked her to do something outside of work? It doesn't have to be a date. Ask her to go jogging with you or go Dutch treat to a movie. Even if you don't want anything else, wouldn't it be nice to have a friend to do things with?"

That's the real problem. I want a lot more than friendship. But I know I could never be what someone like Kim deserves in a lover. Hell, she's a psychiatrist. She'd head for the hills faster than Myra once she found out the truth about me.

"Jess?"

Jess shook away the troubling thoughts. "I don't know, Sam."

Sam's expression turned pleading. "I've never heard you talk about anyone as much as you have Kim in the last two weeks. And how you described her ... Wow. That must mean something," Sam said. "You said yourself you felt good just being in the same room with her. Do you really want to just let that go without even trying to see what might come of it?"

Fear and longing warred within Jess.

"Just think about it. That's all I'm asking," Sam said.

Jess looked over and met Sam's earnest gaze. "Maybe you're right. I'll think about it. I promise." Jess already knew in her heart what she wanted. She had known all along, she admitted. It just helped to hear Sam say the same things. Now she just had to convince her head to go along with the idea.

Thor, who had fallen asleep at Jess's feet, chose that moment to awaken. He stood and shook himself, then headed directly to the apartment's front door. He looked back over his shoulder at her.

Jess laughed. "Duty calls," she said as she stood. "After I take him out, do I have time for a shower before your game?"

Sam glanced at her watch. "Plenty of time. Why don't you go ahead and get a shower. I'll take him out."

"Thanks, Sam."

"Anytime," Sam said.

Jess watched as the duo headed out. She turned and made her way toward the bathroom feeling more light-hearted than she had when she arrived. For the first time in a long time she allowed a bit of hope for the future to fill her.

CHAPTER 9

Kim smiled her thanks at Darlene, Philip's receptionist, when she waved her toward the inner office. She had asked to meet with Philip to discuss the situation with the ER. After two weeks in the ER, Kim knew right where the majority of the blame for the problems between psych and the ER lay. *Philip is not going to be happy.*

Philip smiled warmly as she approached his desk. "Hey, Kim. Have a seat. How was the ER? Did the staff treat you well?"

Kim made herself comfortable in one of the chairs in front of his desk. "ER was fine. The staff down there was very friendly and helpful."

Surprise showed on Philip's face. "Well then, you must be the exception. I've heard nothing but complaints from the rest of the psychiatric staff."

I bet Chris Roberts is the chief complainer. Kim decided to keep that opinion to herself. "The complaints are justified."

"Ah. Well, that puts a different light on things," Philip said, clearly relieved. "I knew it couldn't be just our people causing the problems."

Kim shook her head. "You didn't let me finish. The complaints against psych are totally justified. The ones against the ER aren't."

"It can't all be on us," Philip said, his tone turning defensive. "I know for a fact that the residents call for consults for the most inane things. That should be better monitored by the ER staff."

"You're right. It probably should be," Kim said. *Tread carefully here.* While Philip had asked her to find out what the problems where between psych and the ER, he was the head of the department she was criticizing. "When was the last time you covered the ER?" Kim knew as chairman, Philip didn't cover the ER, but he would have as a staff psychiatrist.

Philip appeared confused by the non sequitur. "I haven't. I've always been the chairman of the department here."

"Well, unless you experienced it, you wouldn't believe the volume of patients that go in and out of that ER in a single shift." Even having worked in other ERs, Kim had been amazed at the number of patients seen every day. "So I'm not surprised some of the residents' requests for consults aren't cleared by one of the ER Attending. But the truth is the inappropriate consults are partly psych's fault as well."

"How do you figure that?" Philip asked, sounding shocked.

"Because psych isn't providing the residents with any lectures to teach them to evaluate patients correctly so they are able to judge when psychiatry needs to step in."

"No," Philip said, shaking his head sharply. "You can't put that off on psych. Those are ER residents. It's not our job."

Kim leaned forward, closer to Philip's desk. "Yes, it is. This is a teaching hospital. Just because there isn't a psychiatry residency doesn't mean the staff doesn't need to teach residents from other departments that interact with ours." Kim gripped the front of Philip's desk. "You hired me as a liaison between psych and the ER because of the staff conflicts. I thought you wanted me to find out where the problems were and try to correct them. So now I'm informing you ... this is one of the problems."

Philip's shoulders sagged a bit. "I can't make people give lectures." He cut her off when she started to interrupt. "Oh, I know. I could order the staff to give lectures, but I can't make them teach residents. And you know as well as I do that one without the other is useless. Just reciting a lecture verbatim from a syllabus doesn't teach anyone anything."

"All right." Kim sighed in frustration. "I don't like it but I understand." She relaxed back slightly in her chair. "Just so you know. I've agreed to provide an extended lecture series to the residents. The first series is for new incoming residents. I've also arranged to give an advanced set of lectures to the more senior residents. I'll need time away from psych floor duties when I'm not assigned to the ER."

"That's fine. I'm sure it will help improve things between the two departments," Philip said. "I'll see if I can find time to fit a couple of lectures in as well." A small smile touched Philip's face. "Maybe if it helps cut down on unnecessary consults, it will motivate the rest of the staff to participate more."

Kim smiled. "It's sure worth a try."

"You're right, you know," Philip said looking somewhat sheepish. "This is a teaching hospital, and it's time I remember that. The program director of the Family Practice residency approached me a while back. He wanted psych to provide lectures to his first-year residents. I said no, but I think it's time to reconsider that decision."

Philip leaned back and crossed his arms over his chest. He smiled slightly lessening the defensive nature of his posture. "Okay. What other problems did you find?"

"The teaching issue is a big one. The lectures are only a small part of it. I was more than a bit surprised to see how shocked the residents were when I invited them to work-up the patients with me."

"Come on, Kim. You can't blame the staff for that. They'll end up being in the ER all day if they have to hand hold the residents too. You know it's much easier and quicker to handle the case yourself."

"Fine." Kim shrugged. "Then they shouldn't complain when the residents request all sorts of unnecessary consults. How are they supposed to know what's necessary and what's not if the psych staff isn't willing to teach them?"

With a shake of his head, Philip chuckled. "You're relentless."

"That's why you hired me," Kim shot back.

Philip laughed. "Okay. I give," he said with a placating gesture. "I'll talk to everyone at the next staff meeting." Philip gave Kim a speculative look. "Is that it?"

Don't push your luck. You've made good progress. Kim smiled. "For now."

A dramatic sigh from Philip was his response, making Kim laugh.

"Hey, stranger. Welcome back." Kim heard as she opened her office door. She had just finished her meeting with Philip. Smiling warmly, she turned to greet Brenda. *Just who I need to see.* Brenda was the nurse-practitioner she would be proctoring for this week.

"Haven't seen hide nor hair of you in two weeks. I was beginning to think you'd been kidnapped by the ER."

With a laugh, Kim motioned Brenda into her office. "Come on in."

"Seriously, how did it go covering the ER?" Brenda asked as she settled herself on the leather couch in Kim's office.

"Really well," Kim said. She joined Brenda on the couch. "The staff was friendly and helpful. I especially liked working with residents."

Dark eyes wide, Brenda leaned over and felt Kim's forehead. "Nope, no fever. So that's not what's making you delusional." Her disbelief was apparent. "Are we talking the same ER staff that every other psychiatrist complains about incessantly?"

"I can't speak for the rest of the staff. But I found the ER to be an interesting and challenging place to work. I enjoyed my time there. And I look forward to going back."

"You'd be the first, then. Dr. McKenna has a reputation of running roughshod over our staff." Clearly Brenda was skeptical. "She didn't give you a hard time?"

"No. Jess and I worked very well together." Kim smiled as she remembered the night she worked with Jess taking care of the little girl, Tara.

Her eyebrows shot up. "Jess," Brenda mouthed incredulously.

Shit! Kim immediately realized she had made a mistake. *No one calls Jess by her first name.* "Anyway, enough about the ER. Bring me up to speed on your group. I'm working group sessions this week," Kim said.

"Hold on a sec," Brenda said, unwilling to let the subject go. "There're some things you need to know first."

"About what?" Kim didn't like where she thought this conversation was heading.

"I should've warned you about Dr. McKenna." Brenda sighed. "Don't get me wrong. She is gorgeous. But she's one of the most emotionally controlled women

I've ever met. And from all I've heard that—"

"Stop right there," Kim said, allowing her displeasure to leak into her voice. "Unless you have something to tell me about Dr. McKenna professionally, I don't want to hear another word."

Brenda's expression turned stubborn. "You need to hear this."

"If it's about Dr. McKenna's personal life, then no, I don't." It was hard enough working in, as Jess herself described it, a fishbowl. Sure, gossip was inevitable. And sometimes Kim used it to her advantage, like telling Chris she was a lesbian, knowing full well he would spread it around. But Kim felt strongly about talking about a co-worker's personal life behind his or her back. "You know how I feel about this kind of talk."

"I know and normally I'd agree with you, but this is different. It's important you know—"

"No," Kim said firmly, cutting her off. "You don't know any of it for a fact, do you?"

Brenda started to protest. The look on Kim's face dissuaded her. "No," she finally admitted.

"Right. It's just gossip. I'm not interested."

"I don't want to see you get hurt," Brenda said. Her eyes glistened with suppressed emotion. "I care about you."

You know she's not being malicious. She acts like a mother hen with all the staff. Kim had told Brenda early on that she was a lesbian, and Brenda had kept it to herself. She was not normally a gossip. Allowing her expression to soften, Kim offered a slight smile. She gave Brenda's forearm a quick squeeze. "I appreciate your concern. But there's nothing to worry about. Dr. McKenna and I are colleagues, nothing more." *And even if we were more than that I still wouldn't want to hear it. Jess will eventually tell me anything I need to know.* "I enjoyed working with her just like the rest of the ER staff."

Brenda eyed Kim, looking for any signs that she was being less than truthful.

Kim met Brenda's stare and carefully kept her expression neutral. *It's the truth. No matter how much you wish it wasn't.*

With a resigned sigh, Brenda gave in. "Okay. My group this month is all young adults dealing with situational depression," Brenda said.

Kim forced her thoughts away from Jess and to the business at hand as Brenda continued to fill her in on the individual patients in her group.

CHAPTER 10

Jess glanced at her watch. She was surprised to see Terrell still at the nurses' station waiting for Dr. Kapoor. He had been paged over an hour ago. Although not as prompt as she would have liked, he still usually appeared more quickly than some of the other psychiatrists. Unbidden the thought popped into her head, *Kim would have already been here.*

"Page Dr. Kapoor again," Jess said as she approached the waiting resident. She sighed to herself. Over the past week dealing with Dr. Kapoor, she had come to realize how quickly she had grown to depend on Kim's ready presence in the ER. Dr. Kapoor never stayed in the department any longer than he had to, which on busy days led to repeatedly having to page him.

"He's in the room with the patient," Terrell said, a dissatisfied look on his face.

Dr. Kapoor was good at treating patients, but he had shown no interest in teaching the residents. Although she suspected the answer, Jess asked anyway, "Why didn't you go with him?"

"He wouldn't let me. Told me I would be too distracting to the patient." Terrell scowled. "Dr. Donovan let me observe and even help with patient evals," he muttered just loud enough for Jess to hear.

Jess understood the resident's frustration. Now that they all knew how much better things could be with Kim covering the ER, the problems with psych seemed worse than ever. She had heard people complaining all week.

"Well, hopefully Dr. Donovan will be back in a few weeks," Jess said. A strange, but not unpleasant sensation skittered across the back of Jess's neck.

Terrell's attention was drawn to something behind Jess's back. A bright smile lit his face. "Hey, Dr. Donovan. When will you be covering the ER again?"

"Haven't seen next month's schedule yet. So I can't say exactly."

Jess willed away the automatic brilliant smile that wanted to grace her own face at the sound of Kim's voice. While she admittedly respected Kim professionally, Jess had been unprepared for the fact that she had missed her on a more personal level this past week. She turned to face her. "Dr. Donovan," she said, offering a brief nod and a subdued smile.

Jess had not expected Kim to continue her lecture series until she returned for her next rotation. As was becoming par for the course, Kim surprised her. Jess had arrived Monday morning prepared to give a replacement lecture to the residents. When she reached the conference room, Kim was already there talking to several of the residents. Kim had made it clear then that she planned to continue with the lectures she had promised even while not assigned to the ER.

"Good afternoon, Dr. McKenna. Could I talk to you for a few minutes?" Kim asked.

Now's your chance. Ask her! Sam had called several times to find out if she had asked Kim to go jogging or see a movie. Jess had struggled with this decision all week. Her brain insisted on presenting all the things that could go wrong, but one thing Sam said had stayed with her. Everyone, no matter how self-sufficient could use a friend. Jess was tired of being lonely. It was time to take a chance.

"Sure. Let's go to my office." Jess motioned for Kim to follow her. This was her opportunity to talk to her privately.

The words had barely left Jess's mouth when the ambulance bay doors swung open and a man staggered in. His chest and arms were covered in blood.

Jess yelled for a gurney and a gown. After a quick apologetic glance at Kim, she sprinted for the patient.

Kim nodded in greeting to several staff members as she made her way to Jess's office. She had finished her lecture and hoped to have the conversation with Jess that had been interrupted earlier. Remembering Jess's discomfort the last time she had come to her office made her hesitate. *This is different. It's business.* She knocked on Jess's door.

After a few moments Kim heard Jess's distinctive voice call out. "Come in."

She opened the office door to find Jess at her desk talking on the phone.

"Oh, sorry. I was just wondering if you had a few minutes, but I see you're busy."

"No problem. Have a seat," Jess said, gesturing toward the small couch against the back wall. "I'll be right with you," she said before turning her attention back to her caller.

Kim sat down on the couch. The room was very small. She couldn't help overhearing the conversation.

"Sorry for the interruption," Jess said. "Anyway, I won't be able to pick him up tonight. If you could give him his dinner and settle him for the night that would be great. I'll pick him up first thing in the morning ..." A loving smile spread across Jess's face. "Okay ... Give my boy a big hug for me ... Thanks. Bye."

Her boy? Jess has a son! The revelation was stunning. It brought home to Kim the fact that she knew next to nothing about Jess personally.

As Kim had seen Jess and interacted with her, she had begun to wonder if Jess might not be lonely too. Loneliness was new to her and something she thought they shared. *Guess you let your own emotions cloud your judgment.* Although she had gotten to know quite a few people at LA Metro casually in the six weeks she had been here, Kim had not let anyone into her personal life.

Normally she made friends easily at a new hospital, but not this time. Her experience at Memorial was still affecting her.

"Kim?"

Kim shook herself out of her morose thoughts. "Sorry. Was thinking about a case from earlier," she lied.

"Sorry to keep you waiting. I'm working a double shift, so I needed to let the daycare know I wouldn't be able to pick up Thor until tomorrow."

"Thor?" Kim blurted out before she could stop herself. *What kind of name is that for a kid?* Jess didn't strike her as the type to stick an offbeat name on a child. *Maybe her partner named the boy?* Kim glanced up at Jess to find her looking very uncomfortable. *Nice going, stupid. She shares something personal, and you question her kid's name.*

"Yeah ... He goes to doggie daycare three days a week. Whenever I work extra shifts, they keep him overnight."

Thor is her dog!

Jess shifted in her chair and looked down at her desk. "I know most people probably think it's weird to send your dog to daycare, but I work long hours and it's not fair to him to be cooped up in the house alone all that time."

Kim got up from the couch and moved over to sit in

the chair in front of Jess's desk. "I didn't know there was such a thing available. I think it's great. We had a dog when I was a kid, and I really miss that. I've wanted another dog but couldn't figure out a way to juggle my work schedule and still be fair to a dog's needs."

"Dogs are great companions. But they do require a lot of attention."

Jess looked up, and Kim's breath caught at the warmth in Jess's eyes. Jess hesitated and seemed to be debating something. Kim had no idea what. She tried not to let her disappointment show when Jess's expression turned businesslike.

"So what did you want to talk to me about?" Jess asked.

Kim forced her thoughts back to business. "As you know, Philip assigned me as liaison to help solve the problems between psych and the ER. I met with him on Monday to let him know what I had found. After working in the ER, it quickly became apparent where the problems lie." Kim hurried on when Jess's expression darkened. "The fault rests primarily with psych."

Surprise widened Jess's eyes.

Kim smiled. "Weren't expecting that, were you?"

"Honestly. No," Jess said with a smile of her own.

"Now the residents do request a number of unnecessary consults. But," Kim added quickly, overriding Jess when she started to object, "that's mainly psych's fault as well."

Jess nodded. "How do you propose we remedy this situation?"

"As I mentioned previously, I'm going to continue my lecture series. Philip has agreed to try and fit in a couple of lectures as well. I don't know if any of the other psychiatrists will be willing to lecture," Kim admitted.

"That's great. Philip giving lectures is an added bonus." Jess shrugged. "I wouldn't have expected the other psychiatrists to agree to lecture." As if to lessen the implied criticism, she quickly added, "Your lectures have been very appreciated by the residents. And me as well. Starting the new residents out right is going to be a big help in cutting down unnecessary consults."

Jess ran her hand through her hair. She offered a slight smile. "Not that I'm not grateful for all you've done so far, but do you think you might convince some of your fellow psychiatrists to let the residents into the exam room with them? I know it's a pain to babysit other departments' residents, but it would be another way to really help cut down on needless consults."

Kim laughed. "Great minds think alike." She could see Jess's confusion plainly written on her face. "That's the exact same thing I told Philip."

"Well, to be honest, the residents have been complaining since you returned to psych." Jess smiled sheepishly. "I think you've spoiled all of us in just two weeks. Everyone is asking when you'll be back in the ER."

A sense of satisfaction, out of proportion to the praise, filled Kim. The fact that Jess had included herself in that group meant a lot to her.

"Philip is going to talk to the other psychiatrists at the next staff meeting." Kim hated to end things on a down note but felt compelled to be honest. "No promises, of course."

"I understand that. I appreciate you going to bat for the ER regardless of the outcome."

Realizing her business with Jess was complete, and that she should let her get back to work, Kim stood. "Thanks for your time."

"Anytime," Jess said. *Now's your chance. Ask her*

before she leaves. Jess stood up as well. She had almost asked Kim earlier if she wanted to go jogging when they were talking about Thor, but she had lost her nerve. It had been a long time since she had invited anyone into her personal life. *You're just asking her as a friend. It doesn't have to be anything else.*

Distracted by her thoughts, Jess didn't find her voice until Kim had almost made it to the door. "Kim." Jess stepped out from behind her desk.

Kim turned back toward her with a questioning look.

Come on, you're a grown woman. You can do this. It's not like you're asking her on a date. With that little pep talk, Jess gathered her courage. "You mentioned earlier that you liked dogs. I usually go jogging on Saturdays with Thor. I was wondering if you'd be interested in meeting us at the park and jogging with us?"

Jess's spirits sank a bit when Kim stared at her with an incredulous expression on her face. *What did you expect? It isn't like she doesn't know by now that you don't socialize with anyone at the hospital.* Maybe a bit of levity would help. "Weren't expecting that, were you?" Jess asked with a smile, echoing Kim's earlier question.

Kim stepped back over to Jess's desk. A grin broke out on her face as she regained her composure. "Honestly. No."

The last thing Jess wanted to do was make Kim uncomfortable or damage their working relationship. "I know it's last minute. You probably already have plans for your Saturday," she said, offering Kim an easy out.

"Actually I don't have any plans. I've been meaning to find a good place to jog. I haven't kept up since I moved. So if you don't mind the company, going jogging would be great."

A knot of tension between her shoulders she had not

even been aware of eased at Kim's words. Jess smiled warmly. "Good. Do you know where Griffith Park is?"

Kim nodded. "The general area. I know there are several different sections of the park."

Jess pulled a piece of paper from a desk drawer. "Here. Let me give you directions on where to meet us." She wrote down directions to the dog park, figuring it would be a good place to meet. Handing the paper to Kim, she said, "Oh, I guess I should ask how you feel about big dogs. I have kind of a big dog."

Kim's face lit up. "I love big dogs! We had a lab when I was a kid. Daisy was the best."

Should I tell her just how big a dog I have? So long unused, it felt as if a rusty door was creaking open, Jess allowed a bit of her mischievous side to see the light of day. *Ah, what the heck. She'll find out soon enough what a big dog really is.* "All right then, we'll met you at the dog park at, say, nine tomorrow morning?"

"Works for me," Kim said. "Well, I should head back to psych." She walked over to the door and stopped just before opening it. She turned back toward Jess with a regretful look. "Oh, I just realized ..."

A shaft of disappointment struck. *I knew that went too well. She's already changed her mind.*

"You said you're working a double today. Are you sure you're going to feel like going jogging in the morning?"

Jess's breath almost whooshed out in relief. She hadn't realized just how much she really wanted this to happen. "I'm sure. It'll be fine." Jess met Kim's eyes and smiled. "I'm looking forward to it," she added a bit shyly.

Like the sun coming out from behind a cloud, a brilliant smile blazed across Kim's face. "Me too. I'll see you tomorrow."

God, she's beautiful. Jess pushed the intruding

thought away.

Jess flopped down into her desk chair as soon as the door closed behind Kim. She was both excited and nervous at the prospect of spending time with Kim outside the hospital.

CHAPTER 11

Entering the park, Kim followed the signs that lead to the dog run area. Jess had really managed to shock her yesterday. Having Jess ask her to meet with her outside the hospital was the last thing she had expected. While it was what she had been hoping for, Kim was still nervous. She wasn't sure what to expect. *I can do this.* Finally spotting what she was looking for, she headed for the large fenced-in area.

Dogs of all shapes and sizes were playing in the bright fall sunshine. She easily spotted Jess leaning against the fence just inside the dog run, near the gate. Kim stopped for a minute to admire the woman. Instead of the Dockers and button-down shirt or scrubs she was used to seeing Jess wear, she was dressed in Lycra shorts and a T-shirt. Kim's gaze ran appreciatively over her well-muscled body. Broad muscular shoulders, well defined biceps, and a flat stomach with trim hips led down to heavily muscled legs. Kim knew that Jess was a beautiful woman, but now, dressed like this... Kim shivered as a wash of arousal cascaded down her body. The strength of her response surprised her. *Friends,* she sternly reminded her wayward libido. *I'm going to be her friend.* She forced the distracting feelings away before heading over to Jess.

"Hey, Jess. Good morning."

Jess offered a tentative smile. "Hi, Kim. Glad you could make it." She opened the gate for Kim and motioned her inside the dog run.

The realization that Jess was a bit anxious made

Kim feel better about her own nervousness. To give them both a chance to get used to being together in a non-work situation, Kim took the time to look around. Excited dogs chased each other, nimbly dodging the park benches scattered throughout the area. A black lab was splashing in one of the large water bowls strategically placed around the run.

Several small dogs ran up. Their exuberant yipping pierced the crisp morning air. Kim knelt down and held out her hand to be sniffed. Once assured of their friendliness, she petted them. She smiled at Jess when she squatted down next to her and offered her own gentle ear rubs to the canine trio.

Kim stood as the small dogs scampered off. A lot of her tension had eased. Dogs were great stress relievers. She looked at Jess, pleased to see she appeared more relaxed as well. "They were cute, but I still like big dogs best."

"Well, luckily I can help you out there," Jess said. "Ready to meet my boy?"

Knowing Jess had a big dog, Kim checked out the dogs nearby. The only two dogs she saw that she considered big dogs were a German Shepard and a very large Doberman. "Which one is he?"

Jess quickly scanned the area, glancing right past both dogs Kim had spotted. "He must be down at the other end. See where those trees are? He'll come when I call."

That's when Kim noticed just how large the fenced area really was. "Great. I'm looking forward to meeting him." Kim glanced over at Jess. *Uh-oh. Never saw that look before.* Jess had a little half smirk on her face. The look screamed—look out; here comes trouble. Kim tried to brace herself for whatever was coming. At the same time, she was delighted to see Jess relaxing the tight control of her emotions she maintained at work.

Jess led them over toward a group of benches. Just as they reached the seats, Jess let out a piercing whistle, causing Kim to jump. "Sorry about that. I should've warned you." She pointed off to the left. "Here he comes." Jess slapped her palms against the tops of her thighs. "Come on, Thor. Come here, boy!"

Kim turned toward where Jess had pointed and nearly fainted. Charging straight at them was the biggest dog Kim had ever seen.

"Oh my God, Jess, that's not a dog. That's a horse!" Kim took a step back and moved slightly behind Jess.

Jess grinned as the big dog skidded to a halt in front of her. "I thought you said you liked big dogs."

Embarrassed that her bravado had slipped so badly, Kim mock-scowled at Jess. "Yeah, big dogs. You didn't say anything about a Clydesdale."

"Don't worry," Jess said, trying hard to control her laughter. Reaching out and stroking the big dog, Jess reassured Kim. "He's big, but he's harmless." Jess took Kim's hand and urged her to stand next to her. "Kim, this is my Great Dane, Thor."

Kim offered her hand to be sniffed.

"Thor, this is Kim. Be nice," Jess said.

Thor took a step forward to check her out. Kim swallowed a bit nervously when she realized the dog's head was almost chest height. And she was tall for a woman, she only missed by a couple of inches matching Jess's almost six-foot stature. He wagged his tail and proceeded to give her a thorough sniff. She smiled as her trepidation eased. Kim quickly saw what a gentle giant the big dog truly was and began to stroke his head and ears.

Thor made his approval known. He gazed into her eyes, and then laid his head against her breasts.

"I don't believe it," Jess muttered. She shook her head and stared.

"What?" Kim asked as she continued to pet Thor.

"I've never seen him do that with anyone except myself or my sister. He's not unfriendly, but he tends to be standoffish about offering affection to strangers. Usually he sniffs someone and then just walks away."

Thor suddenly leaned harder into Kim, forcing her to step back as his weight against her increased.

"Thor." Jess grabbed his collar. "Back up." She urged Thor back several steps. "Sorry."

Kim laughed. "It's okay. He's not bothering me." Pointing to the bench next to her, she said, "Why don't we sit down and you can tell me about this handsome boy."

Jess sat down, but kept a firm grip on Thor's collar.

"He's fine, really. Let him go," Kim said as she moved to a spot on the bench near Jess.

As soon as Jess let go of Thor's collar he headed for Kim.

Kim was a little taken aback when Thor stepped close. The huge dog's head was now level with hers. She met his eyes and was surprised by the intelligence that shone in his dark brown eyes.

Thor gently laid his head in Kim's lap. When she began to stroke his head, he closed his eyes and sighed in contentment.

"Come on, you big moose. Kim is not a cuddly toy." Jess reached for Thor's collar, intent on pulling the big dog off of Kim's lap.

Kim laughed. "Honestly, he's fine. Leave him." She stroked her hand down his shining black coat. "I've never seen a Great Dane that looked like this before." His black head and body shone in sharp contrast to his white neck and chest. "He looks like he's dressed in a top hat and tuxedo." Kim slid her hand down one of his strong front legs. "He even has the white spats to go along with his formal attire."

"He's what's called a Mantle Great Dane," Jess said. "Most people are more familiar with Fawn or Brindle Great Danes."

"I knew Great Danes were big," Kim reached down and tried to close her hand around Thor's front leg but couldn't, "but I never realized they were this huge," she said.

"They can get pretty big. Thor is larger than average. He's thirty-nine inches tall at the withers and just shy of two hundred pounds."

Kim gulped. It appeared to her that most of that two hundred pounds was solid muscle. "Good thing he's so docile."

"Yeah, they're big babies for the most part. But under the right circumstances they can be very protective of their owners." Jess stretched, arching her back.

Kim struggled to keep her eyes on Jess's face where they belonged. "Ready to go jogging?" *Either that or I'm going to need a cold shower.*

"Sure. Let's go." Jess snapped Thor's leash onto his collar.

Jess guided them back to where they had started before slowing down to a walk. Knowing Kim had not jogged in a few months, Jess had offered the one-mile route. Kim had opted for the two-mile trail. *Bet she's regretting that decision about now.* Kim was bent over at the waist with her hands resting on the top of her thighs as she tried to catch her breath.

Allowing her eyes to run over Kim's body for the first time, she took in the tall, slender figure before her. She had been so nervous earlier she had not really paid that much attention to Kim's attire. Kim had on short nylon running shorts and a T-shirt. Jess had suspected a gorgeous body lurked beneath the professionally tailored slacks and silk blouses she wore at work. The reality was much more than she had anticipated. *Your imagination sucks.* Drops of sweat trailed down Kim's well-defined arms and legs that seemed to go on forever. Her tight, sweat-soaked T-shirt clung to a flat stomach and hugged her breasts. Jess's libido immediately flared to life, and she pushed it down with difficulty. *Friends. Just friends,* she repeated what was becoming a mantra.

"You okay?" Jess asked.

Kim straightened up and started to shake out her arms and legs. "I'm fine. I know I'll probably be sore tomorrow, but it still felt good to get out and run. I need to get back to regular workouts."

"You're welcome to join Thor and me anytime on our runs." *What are you doing? This was supposed to be a one-time thing until you saw how she acted at work afterward.* Jess couldn't bring herself to retract the spontaneous offer. It felt right.

A quick glance at Kim proved she was just as stunned by the invitation as Jess was at having made it. A smile tugged at Jess's lips as Kim tried to regain her composure.

"I wouldn't want to intrude. I know you don't get to spend a lot of time with Thor," Kim said.

Beautiful and incredibly thoughtful. Jess knew Kim was offering her a graceful way out. "Thor really likes you." *And so do I.* "It's not an intrusion. We enjoy your company."

That beautiful, sun out from behind the clouds smile that Jess was coming to adore, blazed across Kim's face. "That would be great, Jess."

Thor bumped Jess's hip.

"Sorry, boy." She had been so distracted by Kim she had forgotten what she was supposed to be doing. "I need to get him some water. Walk over to my truck with us?"

"Sure."

On the way to the truck Jess couldn't help noticing the occasional sour look Kim was throwing at Thor. She looked him over but couldn't see any reason for Kim's apparent ire. Nothing untoward had happened on their run.

"Is something wrong?" *Oh I bet I know what the problem is.* Jess was so used to his drool she forgot that most people didn't appreciate being covered in Thor's slobber. Jess pulled the small white towel she had tucked in her waistband and wiped Thor's muzzle. "Sorry. Did he slime you?"

"No, he's fine." Kim glanced down at Thor, and a slight scowl once again marred her face.

Jess was getting a bit worried. Had Kim decided she didn't like Thor after all?

Kim looked up at Jess and laughed. "Don't mind me. I'm just jealous."

Huh? "Of what?"

Kim pointed at Thor.

"Of Thor? Why?" Jess asked. She looked back and forth between Kim and Thor, totally confused by this turn of the conversation.

"We just ran two miles and he wasn't even winded. He looks like he could go another two miles, easy, if not more. I'm jealous. I used to do five miles at a time and now look at me."

Jess did as instructed. Kim's hair was windblown and damp with sweat; her T-shirt was wet with perspiration, and her face was still flushed from exertion. *You're beautiful.* While undoubtedly true, Jess figured it was best to keep that observation to herself.

Pulling on her own damp T-shirt, Jess made a show of checking herself out. "I look pretty much the same.

I can't keep up with him either. I kept him by my side today. Normally he runs in front of me and zigzags back and forth to get some extra mileage. I think he runs twice as far as I do, and he's still not tired." She reached over Thor's back and patted Kim's shoulder. "Don't feel bad. He's a lot younger than we are."

Kim snorted. "Great. Thanks. I feel much better now." She looked down at Thor. "You just wait. Once I get back in shape then we'll see who gives out first."

Thor let out a deep-throated woof as if accepting the challenge.

Kim jumped and then laughed. She gently bumped Thor with her leg. "No comments from the peanut gallery."

Kim is so good with him. No wonder he likes her. She talks to him like Sam and I do. Watching the two interact, Jess had a feeling her quiet, solitary life was about to change. Her heart felt light at the prospect.

Thor's pace quickened, and he began to tug on the leash at the sight of Jess's vehicle.

Kim leaned against the side of Jess's Durango and sipped her water. Not only did Jess have a large container of water for Thor but also a cooler with small bottles of water. Thor was standing next to Jess, drinking his fill from a bowl she had placed in the open hatchback of her truck. Kim was still amazed by the big dog's size. He had no trouble whatsoever reaching the bowl to get his drink.

The day had turned out better than she had ever expected. Jess's standing invitation to join her and Thor whenever they went jogging had been a particularly amazing and welcome surprise.

Having enjoyed herself, Kim didn't want her time

with Jess to end so soon. While not completely sure she wasn't pushing too fast, too soon, Kim decided to take a chance. *What's the worst thing that can happen? If she says no, so be it. At least I tried.*

"Hey, Jess."

Jess looked up and smiled.

"Could I interest you and Thor in a trip to the local Del Java for a cup of coffee?"

The smile on Jess's face faltered for a moment and then quickly reappeared. "Sure. That sounds good."

Kim didn't miss the slight hesitancy on Jess's part. *But she agreed. That's what counts.* She was looking forward to the opportunity to sit and just talk with Jess. It was something they had never really gotten to do at work.

"Okay. Let me go get my Jeep and I'll follow you."

CHAPTER 12

" You got a saddle for that thing?"

Jess barely resisted the urge to roll her eyes. *Like I haven't heard that one a million times.* Since their arrival at the outdoor patio of the coffee shop, a steady stream of people had come by and ask about Thor. *Shouldn't have picked a table so close to the door.* Up until now, everyone had made friendly inquiries about the big dog. This was the first downright stupid comment. She quirked an eyebrow and flashed a half smirk at Kim before turning her attention to the middle-aged man standing next to a nearby table.

With her best deadpan delivery Jess said, "No. I'm waiting until he's full grown to get one."

It was hard to keep a straight face when she heard Kim smother her laughter with her hand.

At a quiet "hup" command from Jess, Thor leaped to his feet.

The man took a step back and seemed to be rethinking his decision to approach the big dog. "Well, you ladies have a nice day." The man gave Thor one last long look before turning to walk away.

As soon as the man was out of earshot, Kim started to laugh. "Did you see the look on his face?"

Jess grinned. "I don't mind answering questions about Thor. I know people don't often see a dog his size. People like that though ..." Jess shook her head. "They think they're being so clever. If I had a quarter for every time I heard that saddle comment, I'd have enough money to buy Thor food for the rest of his life."

Kim reached over and stroked Thor's back. "I understand people's fascination with him."

"It's been a while since I was out like this." Jess grimaced internally. *That sounded pathetic. She's probably out with friends all the time.* "With Thor I mean. I'd forgotten what a circus it can be. Sorry about that."

Jess swallowed heavily when Kim's vivid blue eyes turned in her direction and held her captive for a moment.

"Don't worry about it," Kim said. "This is actually the first time I've been out with someone from the hospital since I got here."

Anxiety twisted in Jess's stomach. *Shit. Did I make her think this was a date?* No matter how much Jess might want it to be a date, she knew she wasn't ready for that. She briefly wondered if she ever would be.

"It's nice to have a friend to go out with, to go jogging, out for coffee or whatever," Kim said with a warm smile.

Even as relief flowed through Jess, there was a tiny part of her that was disappointed. *You know it's for the best. Enjoy her friendship.* Jess offered her own smile in return. "Yeah, it is nice to have a friend to do things with."

The moment was broken by the excited squeal of a child. A little girl rushed toward Thor with a woman, most likely her mother, in hot pursuit.

"Carly Marie Ellis, you stop right this minute!"

Jess stood and stepped in front of Thor before the child could plow headlong into him.

The little girl managed to skid to a halt before running into Jess. She looked up at Jess with a big gap-toothed smile. Jess figured she must be all of six years old.

The woman arrived hot on her heels. "I'm so sorry." She took hold of the little girl's hand. "Carly, you know better than that. We've talked about this before. You can't rush up to strange dogs."

"Sorry, Mommy." Carly said, sparing her mother barely a glance before turning her attention back to Jess. "Hi. Can I pet your doggie? Please."

Jess couldn't help smiling. The little girl was adorable. Her blond hair fell to her shoulders in a riot of curls. Bright blue eyes shone with a child's innocent exuberance. Jess glanced over at Kim.

Turning her attention to the mother, Jess said, "He is friendly. She's more than welcome to pet him if it's okay with you."

The woman eyed Thor sitting quietly behind Jess. "All right. You can pet him."

Carly let out an excited squeal.

"But only if you stay calm and be gentle with him," her mother said.

Jess shot Kim a quick apologetic glance as she stepped out of the way. *This was not how I planned on spending our time together.* Her concern eased when Kim smiled. She kept a close watch on both Thor and the little girl as they interacted.

When the little girl and her mother finally departed, Jess decided to see if she could find a more secluded table. While she didn't mind people petting Thor, they had not even purchased their coffee yet. And it was beginning to look as if they were not going to get their coffee anytime soon unless they got out of the main traffic area of the patio.

She spotted a secluded table in the back corner of the patio near the retaining wall. "What do you say we change tables?" Jess asked. "Thor could use a break from the crowds."

"Would you rather just leave?" Kim asked.

"No!" Jess's face flushed at her abrupt denial. "I mean not unless you do?"

Kim smiled and shook her head. "That looks like a

good table back there," she said, pointing to the same table Jess had seen.

"Come on, Thor." Jess snagged the blanket off the chair. She had brought it for Thor and never gotten to lay it down. Taking his leash firmly in hand, she headed for the table before anyone else could claim it.

"Hang on to him for a minute, please," Jess said.

"Sure." It wasn't until the leash was in Kim's hand and Jess had turned away that realization stuck. *God, what do I do if he decides to take off or something?* Her hands clutched tightly around the leash. *You're being ridiculous. He's been nothing but well behaved all morning.* She looked down at Thor, and he calmly returned her gaze. Kim relaxed and turned her attention to what Jess was doing.

Jess moved the small cabaret-style table and chairs away from the retaining wall to make room for Thor's blanket. Once they were positioned, she bent over to spread out the blanket.

Kim's gaze was drawn like a magnet to Jess's backside. She bit her lip to stifle a groan as she watched the flex of Jess's superbly muscled gluts beneath her skin-tight shorts.

Pulling her gaze away with difficulty, Kim focused her attention on Thor until Jess stood up. *Friends don't ogle friends,* Kim berated herself.

The last thing she wanted was for Jess to realize just how attracted she was to her. Kim was sure it would end any chance of a friendship between them. She had not missed the brief look of panic on Jess's face when she had inadvertently given her the impression she thought this was a date. Kim was determined not to let her attraction get the best of her. *I could use a friend. I can enjoy her company and not expect anything else to come of it.*

"All set," Jess said as she reached for Thor's leash. She guided Thor around the barrier provided by the table and chairs. "Down. Stay," she said in a firm tone. She tied his leash around the arm of one of the chairs.

Thor obediently lay down.

Jess turned back toward Kim with a smile. "What kind of coffee would you like?"

"I'm a plain coffee with cream kind of girl. Never really got into drinking some of the more complicated concoctions. I know that's almost sacrilege considering where we are," Kim added with a laugh. "I planned on having the house blend."

"Plain coffee ... at Del Java? Oh, the horror!" Jess tried to hold an outraged expression but couldn't manage it. She grinned. "I prefer a strong cup of fresh brewed coffee without all that extra stuff added too."

"I won't tell if you don't," Kim said. She thoroughly enjoyed seeing this more lighthearted side of Jess's personality.

"What size do you want?"

That's when Kim realized Jess was offering to go get their coffee. "I can get it."

Jess shook her head. "Have a seat and get comfortable. I'll get the coffee."

"Okay. I'll have a grande. House blend with cream. Please." Kim unzipped the small pouch around her waist that held her money and pulled out a ten. "Here you go," she said, offering the money to Jess.

Waving off the money with a smile, Jess asked, "Would you like anything else?"

Kim hesitated. She was hungry but didn't want Jess to feel obliged to pay for anything else. "No. That's okay. Just the coffee is fine. Thanks." Kim flushed when her stomach chose that moment to growl, loudly.

Jess's eyebrow arched, but she didn't comment. She moved over next to Thor. "Thor. Stay. Watch!"

Kim's gaze darted nervously over to the big dog. *Please be a good boy.*

"He'll be fine. No one will bother you." Without a backward glance, Jess headed for the coffee shop's entrance.

Trying not to tense as she knew Thor would pick up on it, Kim kept a close eye on him waiting for his reaction to Jess walking away. Kim couldn't help being a little worried about being left in charge of the big dog. She was both honored and scared by the responsibility Jess was entrusting her with.

Thor peered past the table legs and watched his master enter the coffee shop. As soon as Jess was out of sight he laid his big head down on the blanket. He made no attempt to get up or move from the spot Jess had left him.

Kim quickly realized how well trained he was and relaxed. Now she understood why Jess had positioned the table and chairs in front of Thor's blanket. He was laying down with the retaining wall at his back, and the table and chairs in front of him. Despite the myriad of people coming and going in and around the busy coffee shop, Thor was not visible to the causal passerby.

The door to the coffee shop opened and Jess stepped out carrying a tray.

"Were you a good boy?" Jess asked Thor as she set the tray down on the table.

Thor's tail thumped a muffled beat against the blanket-covered concrete.

"He was the perfect gentleman," Kim said with a smile.

"Here you go," Jess said as she set a steaming cup of coffee and a small bag in front of Kim.

Kim took a moment to take an appreciative sip of the fragrant coffee. *Mm ...* Turning her attention to the bag, she peeked inside. "Oh, a chocolate croissant. One of my favorites. You didn't have to do that. Thanks."

Jess smiled, looking a little bashful. "Well, when you brought me a muffin, you mentioned you liked anything chocolate so..."

A delighted smile spread across Kim's face. *A treat and she remembered what I like.*

"You can never go wrong with me and chocolate," Kim said. She took the warm croissant from the bag and took a big bite. Her eyes fluttered shut and a moan slipped out as the flaky pastry and rich chocolate melted on her tongue.

Feeling eyes on her, Kim glanced over to find Jess staring at her with an intensity that immediately brought a flush to her body.

Jess quickly looked away but not before Kim saw a vivid blush suffuse her face.

What was that all about? Is she attracted to me after all? There had been a few instances at work that had made Kim wonder. She sighed. *Na. It's just wishful thinking on your part.*

For the first time since meeting earlier that morning, an uncomfortable silence settled between them.

Keeping her eyes on her breakfast, Kim searched for a topic of conversation to break the awkward moment. She didn't want to bring up work. While it was what they had in common, she wanted to move beyond that to other interests they might share.

Kim peeked at Jess through half-lidded eyes. Jess's gaze was firmly locked on her own pastry. *Come on, think! Say something before she starts to regret agreeing to have coffee with you.* As she picked up the last bit of her croissant, Kim was abruptly drawn out of her thoughts by a high-pitched chirping.

What the ...? Kim quickly looked around. When the sound repeated, her eyes were drawn to the source of the noise. *No way.* Kim's gaze jerked up at the sound of Jess's laughter.

"Hard to believe a dog that big could make that high-pitched sound, isn't it?" Jess asked.

Relief washed over Kim at the once again relaxed look on Jess's face. *Thank you, Thor.* Kim laughed. Even though she knew it was Thor, it was still hard to believe he had made the sound. "That was pathetic. He sounded like ... like ..." Kim couldn't think of an adequate description.

Jess laughed. "That's his tweety bird imitation."

"That's appropriate," Kim said with laugh. "I was actually looking for a bird when I first heard it." She picked up her forgotten bite of pastry, intent on popping it in her mouth.

Thor once again sounded off, this time louder and longer.

Pastry in hand, Kim looked down at the dog. "What?"

The strength of his "chirping" reached a fevered pitch. His tail beat a rapid tattoo against the blanket, but he never budged from his spot.

"That's enough, Thor," Jess said.

Sparing Kim one last pleading look, Thor immediately fell silent.

"Is he okay?" Kim asked. Although she didn't know Thor well, she was a little worried about him. Up until now he had been a very quiet dog. These were the first sounds she had heard from him all morning.

"He's fine." Jess picked up her scone and took a bite, leaving just the end of the pastry remaining.

Thor's head came up, and drool began to drip out of his mouth.

"Last bite," Jess said as she handed him the small bit of pastry.

As soon as Thor swallowed the bite, he turned to look beseechingly at Kim.

Kim shot Jess a questioning look.

"He thinks he is supposed to get the last bite. When he was younger, my sister and I used to take him out to Del Java all the time. It's a great place to socialize a puppy. Anyway, she taught him if he lay quietly while we ate, he would get the last bite of whatever we had. Now he expects it. But don't feel you have to give it to him. He's just being pushy."

"I don't mind," Kim said. She checked to make sure it was just a bite of pastry and no chocolate before she offered Thor her last bite. She smiled when he took it from her fingers with amazing gentleness. "He's a really good boy."

Kim pushed her chair back out from under the umbrella covering the table. She tilted her face up to soak in the warm California sunshine. "I should call my brother and tell him I'm outside, in shorts, working on my tan. He'd be green with envy. He's probably busy putting up our mom's storm windows."

"Where do they live?" Jess asked.

"Detroit."

Jess shivered. "Too cold for me. My parents live in Northern California. I left and headed for Southern California as soon as I graduated high school."

Pleasure filled Kim. Jess was starting to open up a little. "So you and your sister both live in Los Angeles?"

"No. Sam lives in San Diego." Jess shifted in her chair and stretched her long legs out in front of her. "You mentioned at work that you'd done your residency out here. Did you decide you didn't like the cold after all? Is that why you left Detroit?"

Kim had never mentioned her previous job to

anyone, not wanting to have to dodge uncomfortable questions. Anxiety gripped Kim and held her tight. She pushed away the irrational fear and forced herself to be calm. *You didn't do anything wrong. And it's not like it's a big secret.*

Still that lingering caution remained. *Just say yes, it was the cold, and be done with it.* No matter how tempting, Kim knew she couldn't do that. She wanted a friendship with Jess. Starting that friendship with a lie would doom it before it ever got started.

"No. It wasn't the cold," Kim said. Despite her resolve, Kim's response came across sharper than she intended. She dammed Pruitt and Anna for the millionth time.

Jess's relaxed posture disappeared. Like a flower closing in on itself, she sat up straight and pulled in her legs, then crossed her arms over her chest. "Sorry. Didn't mean to pry," Jess said, her voice flat and devoid of emotion.

Kim's heart sank at Jess's defensive posture.

Things had gone well today, and she had enjoyed her time with Jess immensely. Now this. *Just tell her. They may share a job title, but she's not Anna.* Jess had proven that in just the short time they had been working together. It was time to move past what had happened in Detroit.

Determined to take the chance, Kim reached across the table and laid her hand on Jess's forearm. The muscles felt like granite. "You're not prying. I had some problems at Memorial. I guess I'm still kind of defensive." The tight knot in her stomach eased when the muscles under her fingers lost their stiff rigidity. She gave Jess's arm a quick squeeze before retreating back to her own side of the table.

"I understand." Silvery-blue eyes filled with the weight of Jess's own pain and secrets met Kim's.

Brimming with a yearning she knew that she could never act on, Kim longed to wrap Jess up in her arms and soothe the hurt so readily apparent in her eyes. While she couldn't provide that comfort, she could offer Jess something important to both of them: her trust.

"About six months ago, I saw a young woman in the ER who presented as an attempted suicide." Keeping her eyes locked on Jess's, Kim began to share her story. "Her mother had caught her in bed the month before with another girl and made her life a living hell. She was admitted to psych, and I took her on as a patient."

Jess winced. "That would be tough on anyone, no matter what age."

Kim nodded and they shared a sympathetic look.

"Her mother wasn't happy with me from the start, because I wouldn't divulge anything her daughter told me in therapy. She claimed because her daughter just turned eighteen and was still living at home that made her a minor." Kim held Jess's gaze. "Even if she had been a minor, I'd still never breach someone's trust like that."

"I know you wouldn't," Jess said.

Kim took comfort from the certainty in Jess's voice. "Anyway, her mother also worked at Memorial. I guess she decided to ask around about me, and someone informed her that I'm a lesbian. She flipped out." Kim shook her head, remembering that scene. "She stormed into my office and demanded that her daughter be assigned to a different psychiatrist. One that would 'cure' her, not indoctrinate her in a deviant lifestyle. She ordered me to stop treating her daughter."

"Christ!" Jess rolled her eyes.

"Yeah. Tell me about it. I thought I was going to have to call security."

Jess's expression darkened. "She didn't hurt you, did she?"

"No. Nothing like that." Kim instinctively reached out to lay a comforting hand on top of Jess's.

Flipping her hand over, Jess cradled Kim's palm in hers. "So what happened next?"

Gritting her teeth, Kim pushed away the anger that thinking about this always brought. "When I wouldn't agree to stop treating her daughter, she went to my boss, Dr. Pruitt."

"He back you up?" Jess asked hopefully.

Kim snorted. "Not likely. I didn't find out until I'd been at Memorial for a few months that the only reason he hired me was because of pressure from the hospital administration to add a woman to his staff. Seems Pruitt thinks women are too emotionally volatile to be psychiatrists."

Anger deepened Jess's voice. "I wish I could say I'm surprised." She raked her hand through her hair. "What did he do?"

"I was coming up for my one-year review. I still had two years left on my contract, so Pruitt decided the situation would be a good excuse to get rid of me." Kim swallowed hard as the emotions of that time threatened to overwhelm her. She was brought back to the here and now when Jess gently squeezed her hand.

Drawing strength from the hand warmly clasping hers, Kim continued, "He called me into his office and explained that the young woman's mother had just come to see him and was extremely upset. She stated that she had spoken to her daughter and claimed that I had not only told her daughter I was a lesbian, but actively encouraged her to participate in deviant activities by extolling the joys of pursuing a gay lifestyle."

"That bitch!" Jess blurted.

"My sentiments exactly," Kim said. "That wasn't the worst of it. Pruitt didn't bother to investigate or even talk to the patient. After telling me about the complaint, he put on this patronizing father act as if he was looking out for me. That's when he dropped the bomb. He would make it all go away if I would quietly resign. I was to submit my resignation and state it was for personal reasons. That way there was no need for this 'unfortunate incident' to ever be reported."

A growl rumbled from deep within Jess's chest. "And if you didn't?"

"Well, then as much as he didn't want to see me embarrassed or have my professional reputation damaged, for the good of the patient, he would have to file a breach-of-ethics complaint against me."

"Bastard." Jess scowled fiercely. "We may have only worked together for a short while, but I know there is no way in hell you did anything you were accused of." Her anger fairly vibrated from her. "Please tell me you didn't resign. Or better yet that you sued the shit out of him for filing an unsubstantiated complaint."

A tidal wave of emotion washed over Kim. With the exception of one brother, the rest of her family and her lover had been adamant that she quietly resign. Jess's staunch defense meant the world to her. Moisture prickled at the corners of her eyes as she struggled not to be swamped by the rising tide of her emotions. It was a losing battle. Tears began to trail down her face.

Jess reached across the table and captured Kim's other hand. Taking both hands in hers, she began to softly run her thumbs across the backs of Kim's hands.

A loud mournful woo woo emanated from Thor.

Several people turned toward their table, reminding Kim that they were in a very public place. Mortification stained her cheeks. She dashed her tears away. "I'm so sorry," she muttered, too embarrassed to meet Jess's eyes.

Jess looked over her shoulder and glared at several people who were staring. "Nothing to be sorry for. Don't worry about it."

In an attempt to give herself some time to regain her composure, Kim leaned down and stroked Thor.

Thor's big tongue swiped several times across Kim's tear-streaked face before she could react.

"Blech." Kim sputtered. "I appreciate the sympathy, big guy, but your technique leaves a lot to be desired." She used her shirt sleeve to wipe the slobber off her face.

Jess worked hard to smother her laughter. "He should at least get an A for effort." All evidence of humor fled from her expression. "Seriously, he usually doesn't express that kind of empathy. He really likes you."

Warm, understanding blue eyes met hers. Kim swore she could almost hear the "and I do too" that Jess didn't give voice to. Kim bent over and hugged Thor's neck. "He's very sweet." She captured Jess's gaze and added silently, *And so are you.*

A faint blush painted Jess's face, and she glanced away for a moment. Shifting uncomfortably in her chair, Jess once again brought her gaze back to Kim. "I ... I'm sorry I upset you." A heavy sigh escaped her lips. "If you felt resigning was appropriate, it was totally your decision and I respect that."

"That wasn't why I was crying." Kim reached for Jess's hand and curled her fingers around her palm. "It was that you actually defended me. My own mother was more concerned that it might come out in the local newspaper that her daughter was a lesbian than she was about what a complaint like that could do to my career."

Jess's hand tightened in Kim's. "I'm sorry your family didn't support you. That must have been awful."

"Oh, it gets worse." Kim knew she sounded bitter but couldn't stop herself. "When I refused to resign and complained to Human Resources and the hospital administration, I suddenly became a pariah." Kim's free hand clenched into a stiff fist. "No one at the hospital supported me. Not my friends, not even my lover. Anna, my ex, was furious with me that I didn't resign immediately. Her only concern was that while investigating the complaint against me, someone might find out about us. She didn't even work in the psych department. It didn't have anything to do with her, but all she cared about was how it might affect her. She was more afraid of getting dragged out of the closet than what the whole affair could do to my professional reputation."

Jess reached out and gently brushed her tears away.

Kim hadn't even been aware of the fact that she had started to cry again. She ducked her head and began to silently berate herself. *Way to go, Kim. This will really make Jess want to have anything to do with you. The first time you get together you pour out your pitiful sob story, and just to top it off tell her about your closeted ex-girlfriend.*

"Look at me. Please," Jess said.

Although she was shamed by her emotional breakdown, Kim forced herself to look at Jess. A gaze filled with a combination of anger and compassion met hers.

"I'm sorry you had to go through something like that. I've seen you with patients. You're a great psychiatrist. You didn't deserve that kind of treatment. Not professionally or personally," Jess added, giving Kim's hand a firm squeeze.

Kim immediately started to choke up again.

"Hey now. No more of that. Forget that homophobic prick, Pruitt. He didn't get away with it. Right?"

"Once HR got involved, Pruitt totally backed off. I really think he believed I would resign and hadn't thought about what would happen if I didn't. There was no formal complaint ever filed against me. Even the mother recanted her statement. The official word was that it was all just a big misunderstanding."

Kim scrubbed her hands over her face. "The truly ironic part is Pruitt has a gay son, and he and his dad get along fine. Pruitt didn't care I was a lesbian. He didn't like that I was a woman psychiatrist, or maybe he just didn't like me. And in the end, he did get his way. I left. Under my own terms, but I did leave."

"Well, if I should ever cross paths with Pruitt, I'll be sure to thank him," Jess said.

"What!" Kim was so shocked she didn't even care that people were once again staring.

Jess grinned. "That's better. And yes, I said thank him. If he hadn't been such a total bastard, you wouldn't be here, working at LA Metro." Jess turned a bit shy. "And we would never have met."

Maybe there is something to that old adage "every cloud has a silver lining." A lightness she hadn't felt in months filled Kim's heart. It was matched by the brilliant smile that spread across her face.

"I'm glad I met you, Jess."

A loud woo woo from Thor made both women jump.

Carefree laughter bubbled up. Kim slid out of her chair and dropped to her knees. She wrapped her arms around Thor and gave him a big hug. "I'm glad I met you too, big guy."

CHAPTER 13

Jess pushed her chair away from the desk. She had retreated into her office to get some paperwork done, but had lost her usual relentless focus. Earlier in the week, she had experienced some trepidation about seeing Kim in a work situation following their outing. Those feelings had changed as the week progressed. It was Friday afternoon and she had not gotten so much as a glimpse of Kim all week. Now a part of her longed to see her, if just for a few minutes.

A quick glance at her watch confirmed what Jess already knew: Kim was in the department for noon conference. She was lecturing the first-years. *She should be done by now. Just go out and say hello. That's what a friend would do.* Jess still resisted.

Her emotional insecurities plagued her. As much as she wanted to see Kim, past experience reared its ugly head and made her leery. Jess did not trust her own judgment. Myra had made her extremely gun-shy. Right from the start, Myra had not understood the need to keep their professional and personal lives separate.

You're not dating Kim. Besides, she has already proven she's not like that. She hasn't been down here trying to be your best buddy at work. You haven't seen her all week, Jess's more logical side reminded.

A knock on the door interrupted her musings. "Come in," Jess said.

The door swung open and the focus of all her thoughts stood in the doorway. Surprised pleasure showered Jess at the sight. It was like unexpectedly coming around a corner and finding a beautiful rainbow painting the sky in vivid hues.

"Hi, Dr. McKenna. Got a minute?" Kim asked.

Jess was surprised by the use of her title until she spotted the two residents conversing in the hall just outside her door. *See, she's not even using your first name, because there's a chance of someone overhearing her. She knows no one calls you Jess at work.*

Jess stood and came around her desk. With a friendly smile, she said, "Sure. Come on in."

Kim smiled and stepped inside, then pushed the door shut behind her.

"What's up?" Jess asked. "Is there a problem with the residents?"

"No." Kim glanced over at the pile of charts on Jess's desk. "I don't want to interrupt if you're busy." She hesitated. "This is more personal than professional."

Springing to alert, Jess's defenses slammed up before she even had a chance to think about it. Her cool and distant ER chief persona came to the fore.

"I am bothering you," Kim said. "I'll go." Resignation dripped from her voice.

You're overreacting. Give her a chance. Jess's gaze darted to Kim's face. Worry and disappointment were easy to read. *Now look what you did!*

Three quick steps brought her over to Kim. Without conscious thought, she reached out and gently put her hand on Kim's shoulder. "Wait. Don't go." Jess motioned toward the couch. "Have a seat. As long as I don't get paged, I've got time."

Kim still looked uncertain but at Jess's reassuring smile finally moved toward the couch and sat down.

Jess joined her. "So, what did you want to talk to me about?"

"I was just wondering if you and Thor were going jogging tomorrow morning? I thought if you wouldn't mind, I'd join you."

"Oh." Jess's expression fell. *Damn. It would have been fun to go jogging with her again.* "I'm sorry. I already have plans for tomorrow."

The words had barely left Jess's mouth and Kim was on her feet.

"Maybe some other time," Kim said. Her tone said something totally different. She headed for the door.

An unaccustomed feeling of anxiety gripped Jess. *You're screwing this up!* She stood. "What about tonight?" Jess asked before Kim could open the office door.

Kim turned to look at Jess. "You want to go jogging tonight?"

Jess shook her head. "Not really." Swallowing nervously, Jess forged ahead before she could lose her nerve. She offered the first thing that popped into her head. "Could I interest you in going to see Colleen Bryce's new movie?"

The brilliant smile that lit up Kim's face made Jess's heart pound. *Ah, that's more like it.*

"Oh! I love her Deven Masters movies. Who can resist a take-charge kind of woman? Much less a gorgeous one who wears leather," Kim said, her expression going dreamy.

Jess's libido stood up and took notice. She didn't know what happy place Kim had just disappeared to, but she would sure as hell love to join her there. *Down girl! None of that.*

It was time to steer the conversation back to safer waters. "We could stop and get some dinner first. I know a good Mexican restaurant not far from the theater." *Now that sounds like we're making a date.* A sliver of apprehension touched Jess. She forced away the almost automatic response.

"That sounds great. I love Mexican." Kim gave Jess

a knowing look. "Dutch treat, of course."

How does she do that? Jess was not used to anyone being able to read her quite so easily. Pushing that thought aside to contemplate at a later time, Jess turned her attention to the here and now. She was already looking forward to an enjoyable evening spent in Kim's company.

Twinkling white lights and colorful decorations were hung around the restaurant's large patio. The area resounded with the sounds of conversation and laughter. Muted strains of mariachi music from inside the restaurant added to the festive air.

Kim sat at the outside bar, sipping a glass of wine while waiting for a table. Since the restaurant didn't accept reservations, she had offered to head for the eatery and secure a table while Jess made a quick trip home to take care of Thor.

While making the plans on where to meet, it had been a pleasant surprise to learn that the condo she was renting was only twenty minutes away from Jess's home. It made the logistics of doing things together that much easier, especially taking Thor into consideration.

Jess's initial reaction to her overture this afternoon had, at the time, filled Kim with doubt that she would be spending any more time with Jess outside of work. Happy that she hadn't scared Jess off with her emotional breakdown on their last outing, she silently vowed this time would be different. *No matter what, no tears this time.*

Feeling a presence behind her back, Kim smiled. She knew who it was before she even turned around.

"Hey, Jess," Kim said as she turned to face her. Kim took a moment to admire the dark blue sweater Jess had added over her shirt. It deepened the color of her already striking blue eyes.

"Hi." Jess reached past Kim and snagged a tortilla chip from the basket on the bar. "Sorry. I'm starving. I didn't get any lunch."

"Help yourself." Kim pushed a bowl of salsa closer to Jess. "I think I've already had half a basket." Moving over on the bar stool, Kim made room for Jess to squeeze in next to her at the crowded bar. "Get Thor all settled?"

Jess nodded, her mouth full.

Kim grinned, pleased by Jess's relaxed attitude. The pager Kim had been given when she arrived at the restaurant began to flash. "Table's ready. Let's eat."

Kim pushed her plate away with a satisfied sigh.

"Was it okay?" Jess asked.

"It was wonderful. I spent the year I was in Detroit looking for a good Mexican restaurant. I tried quite a few of them, but nothing even came close to comparing to this meal."

Jess smiled. "Well, that sure won't be a problem around here."

Conversation had been sporadic during dinner, confined to the weather and neutral topics. The interspersed silences had been comfortable ones as they each concentrated on the meal.

Now that they had relaxed and eaten, Kim allowed her curiosity to come to the fore. She was still feeling a little emotionally exposed after their previous outing. Not only had she shared with Jess her less than stellar experiences at Memorial Medical, but her family's lack of support as well.

Kim hoped to not only learn more about Jess but share more positive aspects of her own life with Jess.

Although she would rather talk about something besides work, it was a major part of both their lives. *It's a good place to start.*

"So, how long have you worked at LA Metro?" Kim asked.

Jess's eyebrow quirked at the change of subject. "Almost seven years."

"But you haven't been in charge of the ER all that time ... right?"

"No."

"How long have you been chief?"

"Two years," Jess said.

"Do you like it?" Kim asked. She wondered at Jess's short-worded answers. Jess didn't seem to be intentionally unfriendly, just not particularly forthcoming.

"For the most part."

Kim waited, hoping Jess would expound some on that answer.

Jess didn't.

She groaned to herself. *God, this is like pulling teeth.*

That's when Kim stopped and took a closer look at Jess. She realized her body posture had changed. Jess was leaning back in her chair with her arms pulled in close to her body. Kim mentally compared it to Jess's relaxed stance when talking about Thor. *She's not used to talking about herself.*

"How about you?" Jess leaned forward and placed her arms on the table. "Now that you've had a chance to see what working at LA Metro is like, do you think you'll stay?"

"Yes. I think the hospital is a good fit for me," Kim said.

Further conversation was halted by the arrival of the waiter. He was carrying a tray filled with sweets. "Could I interest you ladies in some dessert? The specialty of the house is our own freshly made flan."

Yum! Kim didn't even have to think about it. "I'll have the flan and a cup of coffee."

"Not for me," Jess said. "I'll just have a cup of coffee."

The waiter set a piece of flan in front of Kim, then left to get their coffee.

"You don't know what you're missing. I love this stuff. I haven't had any since I've been back in California." Kim picked up her spoon and dug in. The rich, thick custard and caramel sauce melted in her mouth. The combination of flavors inundated her taste buds, creating a sensory bliss.

"Oh God. This is incredible. You have to try some." Kim scooped some of the custard up on her spoon to offer it to Jess. Her hand was halfway across the table when the realization of the intimacy of the gesture struck her. *What are you doing?* She flushed and started to draw her spoon back.

"Hey," Jess reached over and gently took hold of Kim's wrist and guided her hand back across the table. Jess grinned and quickly leaned forward to capture the offered treat. She smacked her lips. "That is good."

Kim froze in place, her spoon hanging in mid-air. Heat rushed through her. Her brain frantically tried to catch up with her body's reaction to the sight of Jess's lips closing around her spoon.

Jess waved a hand in front of Kim's face and laughed. "Earth to Kim. You okay?"

"Sure. Fine." Kim was sure Jess could feel the heat radiating off her skin all the way across the table. She was saved any further embarrassment by the arrival of the waiter.

He served each of them a cup of coffee and then placed an extra spoon in front of Jess. When Jess looked at him questioningly, his gaze darted to Kim's dessert and he winked.

Jess blushed.

Kim felt her own face heat.

The humor of the situation hit them both at the same time. They burst out laughing.

The dazzling full moon hung suspended in the crystal clear night sky. Combined with the bright overhead lighting, it chased away the darkness, painting the parking lot in vivid relief. The huge lot served not only the multiplex theater but the shopping mall as well. It was a sea of cars.

"Sorry about the movie," Jess said as they made their way across the parking lot. They had not seen the Deven Masters movie as originally planned.

"You had no way of knowing it would be sold out," Kim said.

"I should have checked online. But I wasn't talking about that. I meant the movie we ended up seeing." *Could it have been any more idiotic?* Jess shook her head. "Should have just skipped it."

Kim moved close enough to Jess to gently bump shoulders with her. "It wasn't that bad," she said with a smile.

Jess's eyebrows arched. "Oh, so you weren't the woman sitting next to me bemoaning the inane dialogue?" Jess grinned at the endearing blush that rapidly covered Kim's face.

"Well, my brother, Patrick, always used to say, no matter what the reviews were, going to see a movie is always a crap shoot," Kim said. "So in this case—"

Jess snickered. "We stepped right in it?"

Kim grinned. "Pretty much."

"Next time, we'll stick with Deven Masters. She never disappoints." Jess was getting a big kick out of the playful banter. She had never experienced this type of interaction with the women she had dated. *This friend thing is even better than I thought it could be. Now, if I can just learn to ignore the attraction, I'll be all set.*

A sudden sharp breeze cut Kim's laughter short. She shivered. Her long-sleeved oxford shirt provided no real protection against the chilly night air. "Guess I misjudged. My Michigan blood isn't as thick as I thought." Kim rubbed her hands up and down her arms.

"It's so warm during the day it's easy to forget just how cold it can get at night." Jess instinctively stepped close and wrapped her arm around Kim's shoulder. It was only when Kim's body came to rest against her side that she realized what she had done. *What are you doing?* Her first impulse was to pull away, but she managed to stop herself. After all, it really had been an innocent gesture of comfort. She darted a quick glance at Kim to gauge her reaction.

"Thanks. I hate being cold." Kim smiled at Jess and inched a little closer.

"And you still moved back to Michigan?" A quick stiffening of Kim's muscles made Jess regret the question.

"What can I say." Kim momentarily ducked her head, then looked at Jess and shrugged. "I caved to pressure from my mother. Big mistake, as usual."

Jess gave Kim's shoulder a gentle squeeze. "I know how that goes. Mothers can be relentless."

Before Kim could comment, they arrived back at their vehicles.

"Finally," Jess said. The lot had been packed when they arrived. They ended up parking on the outer reaches of the giant lot.

Jess dropped her arm from around Kim's shoulder and motioned for her to step between the vehicles and out of the wind. "We might not have gone jogging, but we still got a good walk in."

Kim laughed. "I needed it after that big dinner, not to mention the huge popcorn we ate."

"That wasn't my fault. The popcorn only came in huge, extra huge, and monstrous," Jess said with a laugh. "Oh, speaking of jogging. How about we go next Saturday? I'm sorry about this week, but I promised my sister I'd come down for her softball game." She wanted to make sure Kim didn't think she was reneging on the offer to jog together. Thinking of Sam's game, Jess was struck by the sudden urge to invite Kim to go with her. She pushed it firmly away. *No. It's too much, too soon. At least for me.*

"Oh." Kim frowned. "I have a hair appointment at nine next week."

"No problem. Maybe some other time." Jess struggled not to let her disappointment show. *It's no big deal. You can always go some other time.*

"Wait." Kim touched Jess's arm. "Would you mind going later, say eleven? Then maybe catch some lunch afterwards?"

Jess smiled brightly. "That would be great. Thor and I will meet you at the park."

"I—" A sudden gust of wind whipped between the cars. Kim gasped. She wrapped her arms around herself and shuddered.

Jess moved close to block the worst of the wind. "You better get going before you freeze." Even with her shirt and sweater, Jess was starting to feel the cold.

Kim's teeth chattered. "Okay." She opened the door to her Jeep and climbed in. "If I don't see you at work, I'll see you and Thor next Saturday at the park."

"See you," Jess said before closing Kim's door.

Jess had enjoyed herself tonight. It had been fun and relaxing to spend time with Kim. She was already looking forward to next weekend.

CHAPTER 14

W *hat a waste of time.* Kim massaged her temples as she made her way to her office. She had a pounding headache. Marcus, the psychiatric nurse-practitioner she was proctoring this week, had a family emergency. She had taken over his group counseling session, or at least tried to. Her session with Marcus's boys had been an exercise in frustration. Thankfully, it was her last group of the day. *I can't wait to get back to the ER. Only one more week to go.*

A raised voice echoed down the hall drawing Kim out of her thoughts. *Now what?* She quickened her pace.

Standing in the center of the nurses' station was Chris Roberts, ranting to anyone who would listen.

Slowing her stride, Kim stopped at the far side of the nurses' desk. She leaned against the counter and listened.

"I can't work with that woman. I'm a staff psychiatrist, damn it, not one of her residents. Where does she get off lecturing me in front of residents? You need to arrive in a timely manner for your psych consults, Dr. Roberts." Chris mimicked Jess's husky voice and stern posture. "It's not like I don't have other things to do besides cater to her damn ER."

Chris stalked over to Kim when he spotted her.

"You're the ER liaison, Kim. You have to talk to that woman. I won't be treated like some flunky."

Then act like a professional and do your job, Kim resisted saying. Chris might be willing to air this issue at the nurses' station, but Kim was not. "Let's go into my office and talk." Kim turned and headed toward her office without giving Chris time to protest.

Catching up to her, Chris huffed loud enough to make sure Kim heard but followed her nonetheless.

Kim opened her office door. She stepped inside with Chris right on her heels.

Chris strode across the room and flopped onto her couch. "I mean it, Kim," he said pointing a finger at her. "That woman is impossible."

I so don't need this right now! Kim was still smarting from her failed encounter with Marcus's group. The patients, all in their twenties, were without exception: over-indulged, unmotivated, self-serving whiners. To make matters worse, the men—boys really—had spent their time trying to one-up each other with increasingly vulgar innuendo. Kim knew it for the defensive behavior it was, but it was frustrating to deal with nonetheless. *You can't help people who aren't ready to be helped.*

Kim rubbed the back of her neck as she made her way toward her desk. She grabbed the chair in front of it and pulled it over to where Chris was ensconced on her sofa.

Chris glanced at the chair, then over at the empty space next to him on the large couch. He quirked an eyebrow at Kim.

Kim ignored the look and sat down in the chair. She had originally planned on sitting behind her desk. This was not a conversation between friends. "What happened in the ER?"

"I went down for a consult, and McKenna berated me in front of two residents. It was totally inappropriate!"

Yeah. Sort of like you ranting about the head of the ER at the nurses' station in the psych department? She was certainly surprised by Jess's behavior. In her experience, Jess didn't normally confront people with other staff members present. It just wasn't like her.

Kim pushed way the irrelevant thoughts. *Jess can take care of herself and her department.*

"Why weren't you in the ER? Philip talked to everyone about this last week." Kim gave Chris a hard look. "When the ER pages, you need to get down there as quickly as possible. How long did it take you to answer the page?"

Chris's chin jutted out. "I was busy."

"Come on, Chris. You know as well as I do that you don't have any other duties when assigned to the ER. How long did you make them wait?"

Shifting, Chris suddenly found his shoes interesting. "Over an hour," he finally admitted.

Damn it. So much for all the fence mending I did while I was in the ER. Barely resisting the urge to strangle him, Kim asked, "What was the patient doing all that time?"

"He was in restraints, sort of ranting about the things he was seeing," Chris said.

What the? Sedating a violent, hallucinating patient was standard protocol. "Why didn't they sedate him?"

"Well…" Chris flushed and he looked down. "I might've hollered at them last time for sedating someone before I got there. I told them if they wanted my help, they weren't to sedate a patient 'til I arrived."

No wonder Jess was pissed. Kim shook her head in disgust. "And you're mad that Dr. McKenna called you on leaving a screaming patient in her ER for over an hour? What exactly do you want me to talk to her about?" she asked.

"Come on, Kim. You've worked down there. You get tossed into a room with a patient with little or no history. It's chaotic at the best of times. Total bedlam at its worst." He slammed his fist into the couch cushion. "I hate it. I don't want to be assigned to the ER anymore."

Kim wasn't surprised by Chris's attitude. She knew

several psychiatrists who disliked covering the ER. Like Chris, they found the unstructured atmosphere intimidating. Ironically, that was the thing Kim liked best about the ER. It was a challenge. You never knew what was going to come through the doors next. She occasionally struggled with boredom seeing the same patients week in and week out.

So his problem isn't with Jess after all. In spite of her anger at his behavior, Chris's sudden bout of honesty made Kim willing to help him. "Okay, Chris, tell you what, tomorrow is Friday. You finish out this week and I'll take your ER rotation for next week. You take my group sessions."

"Can't you take tomorrow too?" Chris asked with a pathetic whine.

The disastrous session with Marcus's group flashed through Kim's mind. Despite trying several different approaches, she had been unable to make any headway with the group and finally ended the session prematurely. *Maybe he'll have better luck.*

"All right, but I'm covering for Marcus. You'll need to hold a session with his group as well."

Chris grimaced and looked ready to protest.

Ah, so it isn't just me that had trouble. That took a little of the sting out of her failure with the group. "It's that or the ER," Kim said. She had no intention of covering both Marcus's patients and the ER.

"Fine. Anything is better than the ER. I'll cover your groups and Marcus's."

The sudden strident beep of a pager filled the room.

Chris pulled the pager off his belt and looked at the screen. "Damn it."

"ER?" Kim asked.

"Who else?" Chris glanced at the clock on the wall behind Kim's desk. "Harland is on-call. He can answer it."

The end of the day shift was coming up. "His duty call doesn't start for half an hour."

Chris shrugged.

Kim clenched her fists, trying to rein in her temper. She failed.

"Damn it, Chris! This is exactly why Dr. McKenna was pissed at you. And rightly so. What about the patient that needs your help?"

Crossing his arms over his chest, Chris remained mute.

Deciding not to waste any more time, Kim held out her hand. "Give me the pager. I'll answer it."

Chris started to hand over the pager, then hesitated. He sighed. "I'll go."

Kim plucked the pager from his fingers. "Forget it. I'll take care of it." She knew that she would do a much better job than he would. It wasn't ego. It was fact. *And you'll get to see Jess.* While that was true, it was an added bonus, not the motivating factor for Kim.

The whole situation cemented for Kim the ideas that had been percolating through her mind for the past three weeks. The next quarterly staff meeting was only a week away. She would find time tomorrow to meet with Philip and talk him into her plan. He could make the announcement at the meeting.

"Who paged psych?"

Jess's head jerked up at the sound of Kim's voice. *Thank God,* came the unbidden thought. She didn't know why Kim was answering the page when Roberts was covering the ER but was grateful nonetheless.

"I did, Dr. Donovan." Bates called out above the din of the bustling nurses' station.

Jess scowled as she stepped out from behind the

nurses' station. She was just in time to see Bates make a beeline for Kim. *Damn it. I told him to page psych, not take over the case.*

Jess snatched the patient's chart off the counter. She strode up to Kim and Bates.

Bates was not discussing the case with Kim. He was busy trying to chat her up.

Irritation warring with outright anger, Jess cut him off mid-sentence. "Thank you, Dr. Bates. Dr. Donovan and I have this under control."

Jess motioned down the hall. "Dr. Donovan, if you'd follow me." She turned on her heel and quickly walked away, pleased when Kim followed without a word.

This case was going to take a skilled clinician and someone good with children. Jess couldn't think of anyone better qualified than Kim.

Jess stopped opposite the door to one of the private treatment rooms.

"Sorry about Bates."

Kim waved off the apology. "What have you got?"

The release of a tension she had not even been aware of eased the set of Jess's shoulders. *Right to business. And she's not even supposed to be here. Too bad she doesn't cover the ER all the time.*

Reaching up and rubbing the back of her neck, Jess sighed. This case had her worried. "Patient is a nine-year-old female. She presented as an accidental poisoning. According to the mother, the girl mistakenly took a whole bottle of the mother's sleeping pills. The mother claims her daughter mistook the red pills for candy."

A frown marred Kim's face. "Is she developmentally delayed?" She pulled a notebook from her pocket to record the salient facts.

"Not that I've been able to determine."

"Who found her?"

"Her father. Apparently, she didn't come down for dinner and he went up to her room. She was sitting in bed. The empty pill bottle was sitting on her nightstand. He asked her about the bottle and she admitted to—in his words—eating them."

"So she was awake and alert when he found her?" Kim asked.

Jess nodded. "And she was still alert and responsive upon arrival in the ER. Best I've been able to establish there was about ten minutes between her swallowing the pills and her father discovering she had taken them." Jess raked her fingers through her hair. "We did a gastric lavage, followed up by activated charcoal." She hated having to subject a young child to such an invasive procedure but had not had any choice. "There were approximately twenty pills in her stomach contents." While she knew the scenario presented by the parents was possible, it wasn't very believable.

As if reading her thoughts, Kim said, "Doesn't sound very plausible to me, especially considering the patient's age. A nine-year-old would know what a pill bottle is versus a package of candy. Not to mention the obvious, a child of nine can or should be able to read." Kim stared at the door of the treatment room as if she could see inside. Her brow furrowed. "How did the parents present?"

"That's what bothered me, aside from the obviously less than believable story," Jess said. "The mother appeared distraught, but her behavior was off. She fawned all over her daughter, but it came across as just going through the motions. There was no genuine emotion behind it that I could see."

"What about the father?" Kim asked as she continued to scribble notes.

"The father seemed truly upset and scared. The other thing that struck me was the little girl. The whole time her mother was holding her, she never took her eyes off her father. She didn't seem to take any comfort from the mother at all. Her body posture was stiff and distancing."

Jess shook her head. "I don't know, maybe I'm seeing something that isn't there." She blew out a breath and stuffed her hands in the pockets of her lab coat. "But I can't get past the gut feeling that this was if not an outright suicide attempt, it was certainly a cry for help."

Kim lightly touched Jess's arm. "I trust your instincts." She shoved her notebook in her pocket and then scrubbed her hands over her face. "Which begs the question, what would drive such a young child to do something like this?"

"Exactly. I'm concerned that she may be actively suicidal." Jess sighed. "I tried talking to the little girl but got nowhere." Jess had seen for herself how good Kim was with children. "Would you evaluate her and see if you can get the real story?"

"Sure," Kim said with a smile.

"Let me know what you find out." Jess rubbed her neck. "Fair warning. I've already told the parents that I'm requesting that pediatrics admit the girl overnight for observation. The mother was not happy." Having the girl admitted to pediatrics was the only option at this point. "Unless you decide she needs to be on a psych hold, then we'll need to get her transferred to a hospital that has psych facilities for children."

"Okay, I'll—"

"Dr. McKenna!"

Terrell rushed toward them.

"We just got the call. We have multiple traumas coming in. First ones are five minutes out. Cement truck versus a bus."

Adrenaline pumped through Jess. "Call everyone

together. Get both trauma bays set up," Jess said. They were most likely in for a long night.

Terrell raced off to do Jess's bidding.

Jess glanced at the treatment room door, where the little girl and her parents waited, and then back at Kim.

"Go. I've got this under control," Kim said.

"Find me when you're done," Jess said. She turned and sprinted down the hall.

Brightly painted animals chased across the walls of the small room. The muted light above the bed illuminated the diminutive figure in the bed. In stark contrast to the glaringly lit, harsh, sterile ER, the pediatric floor room was warm and welcoming.

Kim was sitting on the edge of the hospital bed. "Now you're never going to do something like that again ... right?"

"I promise, Dr. Kim."

"Good girl." Kim gently patted Charlene's leg. "You're really going to like Dr. Kate."

Tears welled in Charlene's eyes. "But I like you, Dr. Kim."

"I know, sweetie, and I like you too. But remember what we talked about? How Dr. Kate is a special doctor that only takes care of children? I promise, she's going to take good care of you. You can talk to her and tell her anything that is bothering you. Okay?"

Charlene sniffed. "Okay." Her gaze darted toward the door. Tension suddenly radiated from her.

Kim turned to see what had caused the reaction. She smiled when she spotted Jess standing in the doorway.

"Oh good. You got my note." Motioning Jess in, Kim said, "Charlene, do you remember Dr. McKenna?"

Charlene inched closer to Kim. She nodded slowly,

fear written clearly on her face.

A brief flash of dismay marred Jess's face. She quickly replaced it with a smile. "Hi, Charlene." Her tone was calm and soothing. She reached into the pocket of her lab coat and pulled out a small, stuffed frog. "I brought a friend along. I'm really busy downstairs and I was wondering if you could keep him company for me?"

Ah, Jess. You act emotionally distant, but what a soft heart. Kim knew how difficult it must be treating children in the ER. The invasive procedure Jess had performed on Charlene, although for her own good, had to have been emotionally hard on Jess.

The smile started small but quickly grew when Jess handed over the stuffed animal. Charlene ducked her head not quite willing to meet Jess's eyes. "Thank you," she said in a quiet voice.

Jess smiled. "You're very welcome." She turned her attention to Kim. "Can I talk to you?"

Kim stood and moved around Charlene's bed. "Why don't we step outside?"

Charlene clutched the frog in both hands. Tears trembled at the edge of her lashes.

The reaction was not lost on Kim. She sat back down on the girl's bed and took a much smaller hand in one of hers. "Hey now, none of that." Kim gently stroked the girl's hair. "It's okay. I'll be right outside the door with Dr. McKenna for a few minutes. I won't leave until your dad gets back. Okay?"

Charlene gave her a watery smile and nodded.

"Good girl."

"How's she doing?" Jess asked as soon as they were out of earshot. Her gaze darted around the area, checking to make sure they would not be over heard.

Kim positioned herself where she could keep an eye

on Charlene through the open doorway. "She's scared and confused. But she's going to be okay. I contacted a colleague, Dr. Kate Dean.

She's part of a private practice group. Her specialty is working with children in crisis. Kate agreed to see Charlene tomorrow."

Jess's eyebrows shot up. "How did you get the parents to agree to that?" Having dealt with the parents, the mother specifically, Jess knew what a hard sell that must have been. Especially since the mother claimed it was an accidental poisoning.

Kim let out a heavy sigh. "It wasn't easy. Mrs. Kessler kept insisting it was all much ado about nothing. It was just an accident." Kim nodded at Jess's disbelieving grunt. "I couldn't make a dent with Mrs. Kessler and Charlene wouldn't talk with her mother there. I finally managed to convince Mr. Kessler to talk to me alone." Kim met Jess's gaze. "You called it right. He was really scared. I told him this was a cry for help from his daughter. Once I started talking about what might happen next time if he wasn't lucky enough to be there ... he crumbled and told me what really happened. I got the rest of the story from Charlene."

"I knew it wasn't an accident," Jess said. "Why the hell did they make up that story?"

"Mrs. Kessler convinced her husband that family services would take Charlene away if they found out she took the pills on purpose."

Jess scowled. "Damn. So she is actively suicidal?" It was so hard to believe with such a young girl. *What the hell is going on with this family?* She shifted position so she could look into Charlene's room. The little girl was lying quietly in the bed, playing with the frog.

"No. It wasn't an accident," Kim said with a shake of her head. "But it wasn't a true suicide attempt either. Charlene took the pills knowing that her father would come looking for her in a few minutes when she didn't come down for dinner."

"But why? Why would she do that?" Jess blew out a breath. "It's not something I would expect a nine-year-old to even think of."

Kim's scowl matched Jess's earlier one. "That's because she didn't. Charlene's best friend's older sister gave her the idea. Told her it was a way to make her parents pay attention to her."

Jess scrubbed her hands over her face. "Maybe you better start from the beginning. What the hell is going on with this family?"

"Okay. It's complicated. Parents are getting a divorce. They didn't think Charlene knew—she does. Mom has a boyfriend, and so does Dad. They—"

"Whoa ... wait, back up. Mother has a boyfriend and Dad has a girlfriend ..."

Blond curls bounced when Kim shook her head. "Nope. I told you it was complicated. Mom has a boyfriend and Dad has a boyfriend. Though not the same man," Kim added with a slight grin.

Jess rolled her eyes. *Cripes. Complicated indeed.* "Okay, I'm with you so far."

"Long story short ..." Kim snorted. "Or as short as I can make it. Mrs. Kessler wants a divorce, money, no responsibility, and plans on sending Charlene to boarding school. Mr. Kessler wants Charlene but is petrified that if his wife finds out about his boyfriend, he'll never get to see her again. Charlene is caught in the middle. She wants to be with her dad. She's terrified of being sent to boarding school. She is totally dominated and controlled by her mother. Mrs. Kessler is using Charlene as a pawn to manipulate her husband."

Wow. She got all that in less than two hours? "What a mess!" Although appalled by the situation, Jess was very impressed by Kim's expert handling of a bad situation. Despite the parents' problems, Kim had convinced them to get Charlene the treatment she needed. *She's good. Though, obviously not the person to try and keep secrets around.* A shaft of apprehension struck. Jess shook the troubling feeling away.

"Tell me about it," Kim said. "Cases like this are why I know I would never make a good child psychiatrist. I'd be too focused on strangling the parents."

Jess gave Kim's shoulder a quick squeeze. "You're a great psychiatrist—period. I didn't get a chance to say anything earlier. I don't know how you ended up covering the ER this afternoon instead of Roberts, but thank you. I really appreciate your help."

Kim smiled brightly. "Thanks, Jess. But I have to admit in this particular situation, it was easier than usual. Mr. Kessler was desperate for someone to talk to. Usually it would take weeks to pry out this kind of information."

Jess nodded and offered a warm smile. "Well, I better let you get back to Charlene. Where are the parents anyway?"

"Mrs. Kessler went home. Mr. Kessler is getting something to eat. He's going to stay the night with Charlene. I promised I'd stick around until he got back." Kim glanced at her watch. It was well past shift change. "Are you working a double again?"

"No. Thankfully, all the patients we got from the crash were minor injuries. I just wanted to follow up with you before I headed out."

Kim hesitated just a moment before asking, "Thor at daycare today?"

"Yeah. I need to get him before they close." Jess grinned. "I'll tell him you asked about him. He's looking forward to our jog on Saturday." *And so am I.*

A delighted smile lit Kim's face. "Me too."

Jess spotted Mr. Kessler heading for them. "I better go. Thanks again." With a quick wave, Jess turned and walked away. *I wonder if I could convince her to cover the ER full-time?*

CHAPTER 15

Stepping back into the ER proper, Jess let the sights and sounds ease her lingering tension. A brief smile played across her face when she spotted what had become a familiar sight in the ER over the last week. *Kim.* She was sitting at the computer workstation. Just the thought of her was enough to wash away Jess's remaining stress.

Jess stopped and leaned against the counter of the nurses' station. "Dr. Donovan," she said by way of greeting.

Kim looked up from the chart she was working on and smiled. "I was beginning to think you weren't working today."

"Believe me, I'd have much rather been here than where I was."

Eyebrow quirked in question, Kim asked, "And where was that?"

"Quarterly budget meeting ... chaired by Dr. Rodman."

Kim's face scrunched up as if she had bitten into a lemon. "You have my sympathy."

Jess knew that Kim's initial encounter with Rodman had left her with a less than stellar impression of the man. A small laugh escaped. Jess quickly squelched it when she noticed Penny watching from farther down the counter.

Jess glanced up at the patient status board. "Have things been pretty quiet?"

"So far." Kim mock scowled at Jess. "Nothing

compared to last Friday."

"That did get a little out of hand," Jess said with a grimace. Kim had never explained why she covered the ER in Roberts's place last Friday, but Jess had been grateful for her presence.

Kim's hands went to her hips. Her eyebrows shot up. "A little!"

Jess held up her hands in surrender. "Okay, it was total pandemonium." After a fraternity initiation gone bad, the ER had been swamped with inebriated college students, their parents, and the police. It was not something that psych would have normally been called to the ER for, but Kim had pitched right in. Her help in keeping the chaos under control and counseling parents and students alike had been invaluable. *Get her off this subject, or you'll never convince her to cover the ER full-time.* "Are you busy right now?"

"I need to finish up this chart, then I'm free. What can I do for you?"

"I have something I'd like to talk to you about," Jess said.

"Okay." Kim smiled. "I want to discuss something with you as well. Give me a minute to finish up here, and I'll be right with you."

"We can talk in my office as soon as you're done." Jess forced herself to stand still and not fidget while she waited for Kim to finish up. *If she wanted a job like this, she would have taken a position in a psychiatric ER.* Jess pushed away the pessimistic thought. *Just ask her.* Part of Jess's anxiety stemmed from not wanting to damage their blossoming friendship. Not only did they work very well together, but the time they spent together outside the hospital was also coming to mean more to Jess than she had ever expected. She didn't want Kim to feel obliged to accept her request because they were friends.

∞

Jess led the way down the hall to her office. She was just opening the door when a loud rumbling sound intruded. She turned to look at Kim with a raised eyebrow.

"I was running late this morning and didn't get any breakfast." Another loud rumble issued from her stomach. Kim blushed. "I haven't had lunch yet either."

"We can talk later." Jess stepped just inside her office doorway and turned back to face Kim. "You want to meet back here after you get some lunch?"

Kim started to speak, then hesitated.

Jess tensed in anticipation. *She's going to want us to go to lunch together.*

The smile dropped off Kim's face. Shoulders drooping, she took a step away from Jess. "I can just grab something from the vending machines and eat in your office. That is if you don't mind me eating while we talk?"

With an inward scowl, Jess forced herself to relax. *Would going to lunch be such a bad thing?* The sight of Kim's withdrawal filled her with a sense of determination. Sam was right. People were going to gossip no matter what she did. *To hell with them. I can have lunch with a colleague if I want.* "I haven't eaten either. Why don't we head to the cafeteria? We can talk while we have lunch."

Kim's mouth dropped open. She stared at Jess for several moments.

Jess quirked her mouth in a little half smirk. "You okay? Do I need to get the crash cart?"

Eyes sparkling, Kim grinned. "Maybe just a little jolt to get my heart going again." She playfully shoved Jess's shoulder. Her eyes widened at the realization of what she had just done. She quickly pulled back and cautiously glanced around. Kim's expression turned serious. "Are you sure? I don't want to start any gossip."

Beautiful and thoughtful. Jess smiled. *That wasn't so hard.* With each passing day, her trust of Kim grew. "Yes. I'm sure. Let's go."

Kim followed Jess, allowing her to choose their table in the cafeteria. Realizing what a big step Jess had taken in asking her to lunch at work, Kim wanted her to be as comfortable as possible.

It was lunchtime and the cafeteria was rapidly filling up. Jess set her tray down on a table on the outskirts of the main seating area, but well within view and hearing of nearby tables.

Wonder why she didn't pick one of the more secluded corners so we could talk without worrying about being overheard. Kim set her tray down and then glanced at one of the tables tucked in the corner. She realized why Jess had not chosen to sit there. The tables were small, meant for two people. The hospital workers currently occupying the space were holding hands and seemed oblivious to anything but each other. Despite the hospital setting, it looked very romantic. *That's all we need to set the gossip flying.*

As she situated herself at the table, Kim realized their presence had already attracted some attention. Feeling eyes on her, Kim looked around.

Cindy, the ER nurse who had been gossiping about Jess a few weeks ago, was sitting off to her left with several other women. When Kim met her gaze, Cindy smirked at her. *Ah, crap. I bet she can't wait to get back to the ER and blab that she saw us together.*

"Just ignore her," Jess said.

Kim jumped, startled out of her thoughts. Her head

snapped back around to face Jess. "I'm sorry. Maybe we should just go back—"

"No." Jess gently cut her off. "There's nothing to be sorry for. People are going to gossip no matter what we do. There is nothing wrong with two colleagues having lunch together." While Jess's words were calm and logical, her hands clenched on the sides of her tray belied her words.

She's trying so hard. Barely resisting the urge to reach out and touch Jess's arm, Kim resigned herself to offering a warm smile instead. "You're right, it's best to ignore it. So what did you want to talk to me about?" she asked, knowing Jess would be more at ease discussing work.

Jess took a deep breath. She let go of her tray and clasped her hands together in her lap. "I wanted to ask you to consider coming to work in the ER full-time. You're a great asset to the department. You work well with the staff and residents. We could really use someone of your caliber working in the ER on a daily basis. I wanted to see how you felt about it before I approached Philip."

Kim knew her mouth was hanging open. Jess had managed to floor her twice today, once with the invitation to lunch and now this. *So much for your worry about asking her what she thought of you working full-time in the ER.*

Mistaking Kim's silence, Jess shifted uncomfortably. "Um ... I want you to know that you are under absolutely no obligation to agree. If you're not interested, it won't change anything as far as I'm concerned either in the ER," Jess hesitated, visibly struggling for words, then continued, "or anywhere else for that matter."

Huh? Anywhere else. Realization hit Kim like a ton of bricks. *Jess is worried I'll think she's pressuring me to agree because we're friends.* Kim could only wonder once again about Jess's past. *Who made you so unsure of yourself? Your ex?* Pushing away the irrelevant thought, Kim turned her attention to the matter at hand.

"I understand if you'd rather not," Jess said. Her voice had taken on the more reserved tone she frequently used in the ER.

Kim silently cursed herself. Her lack of immediate response had made Jess assume the worst. Kim smiled. "Actually, working in the ER is what I wanted to talk to you about."

Jess's brow furrowed. "It was?" she finally managed.

Nodding, Kim said, "I spoke to Philip on Monday. I planned on talking to you about it to make sure you were okay with it before he announced the change at our next staff meeting."

"You really want to come work in the ER full-time?" Jess asked.

"You look so surprised." *Turn about is fair play. You surprised the hell out of me today.* "That's what you want ... Right?"

"Yes. Of course," Jess said. She ran her fingers through her hair. "I just thought it would be a harder sell."

"Well, it did take me a while to sell it to Philip." Kim smiled warmly. "Personally I very much enjoy working in the ER. As I told Philip, I actually considered a position at a psychiatric ER before accepting the job here."

"So when can you start?" Jess asked.

"I've got another week on my current rotation. Our monthly staff meeting is the Monday after the end of my rotation. Philip will announce at that meeting that I'll be officially taking over covering the ER exclusively." Kim grinned. "So I guess that means you're stuck with me from here on out."

A brilliant smile flashed across Jess's face. "Works for me."

A sense of satisfaction filled Kim. Although she understood intellectually that she had not been to blame for what happened at Memorial, emotionally her confidence had taken a blow. That Jess had approached her with the request to work in the ER gave her a much appreciated boost to her confidence.

CHAPTER 16

Kim walked into the conference room bright and early Monday morning. The quarterly psych staff meeting was held half an hour before morning shift change to allow as many staff as possible to attend.

Philip waved her over to the lectern.

"What's up?"

"Are you sure about this?" Philip asked. "It's not too late to change your mind."

Kim smiled. "I'm sure." The last two weeks working alongside Jess in the ER had only strengthened Kim's belief that she had made the right decision.

"All right then, once I cover the other items on the agenda, you can make the announcement. I'm sure it will be met with enthusiasm."

"I'm sure it will." Kim started to walk away.

"Kim."

She turned back toward Philip.

"If you should ever change your mind, just let me know. This doesn't have to be permanent."

"Thanks, Philip." She nodded to several people before taking a seat next to Chris Roberts. Philip called the meeting to order. Kim sat back and listened while she waited for her turn.

"Now for the last item on our agenda, Kim has an announcement to make," Philip said. "Kim."

Kim approached the lectern. Philip stepped aside, allowing her to take his place. "As you all know, I am the liaison with the ER. I've had numerous complaints about psych coverage from the ER."

"That's because they're totally unreasonable," Chris called out.

Kim glared at him before continuing, "As Philip has previously discussed when staff are assigned to the ER, they aren't remaining in the department as they should. In addition, they are slow responding to pages."

"There's no office to use when assigned down there," Harland interrupted. "And even if there were, I still wouldn't want to be down there. McKenna treats us like residents." He tipped his nose up with a haughty air. "I personally prefer to work on the psych floor. I'm a psychiatrist, not an ER doctor."

Kim held up her hand before anyone else could complain. "I understand that not everyone is comfortable working in the ER. With Philip's approval, I've come up with a solution that I think will be acceptable to everyone. I will be taking over coverage of the ER on a permanent basis."

Cheering broke out in the room.

Philip clapped his hands. "Settle down."

When the room quieted, Kim continued, "The only time any of you will be required to cover the ER is when you are the staff on-call after-hours. Also someone will need to cover my days off. But starting today, there will be no more two-week rotations in the ER."

The room erupted with clapping and whistles.

"All right. That's enough," Philip said. He opened a folder. "Grab a copy of the updated assignment schedule on your way out."

"Who has the duty pager?" Kim asked the departing group.

"I do." Harland pulled the pager off his belt.

Kim glanced at the pager as he handed it over. *Damn it!* "Harland, this is turned off."

He looked down his nose at Kim. "Well... Of course. We were in a meeting."

Grinding her teeth together to keep from letting her temper loose, Kim spun on her heel and headed for the ER at a fast clip. *I just hope like hell things were quiet in the ER.*

"Don't page them again," Jess said. "Call the psych department. Tell them to get someone down here now. I don't care who."

Kim skidded to a quick halt. The nurses' station counter separated her from Jess. "I'm here," she said, still slightly out of breath from her rapid descent down the stairs. She had forsaken the elevator in her rush to reach the ER.

Jess turned to face her.

Kim flinched at the expression on Jess's face. She expected her to be angry. The look of deep disappointment on Jess's face was far worse. It struck her hard. *Damn you, Harland!* "Sorry. There was a meeting—"

Jess cut her off before she could continue. Her voice was as cold as an arctic winter. "Psych meetings are not my concern, Dr. Donovan. I expect you to answer your pages, meeting or not." Jess's gaze bore into Kim's. "We needed you down here."

While she knew it was unrealistic to think that she and Jess would never come into conflict on the job, in this case, it was not her fault. As much as she wanted to explain, now was not the time. "What have you got?"

Jess blew out a breath and scrubbed her hands over her face. "Patient is a twenty-five-year-old male: diagnosed schizophrenic—off his meds. He was combative and paranoid. We sedated him, but he's still very agitated. Dr. Johnson is with him in Exam Two."

"I'll take care of him right away," Kim said. As she

headed toward the exam room, Bates came scurrying up.

"I'll help with him, Kim. Don't let that bitch get you down." He offered a sympathetic smile. "When we're done we can go get a cup of coffee."

Great. Just what I need. Kim scowled. *And I never told you that you could use my first name.* She didn't have time to deal with Peter's behavior right now. "Is he your patient?"

"Well, no. He's Terrell's, but—"

"I've got this." Kim pulled open the exam room door. "I'm sure there are other patients waiting to be seen, Dr. Bates." She stepped inside and pushed the door shut in his face.

Kim sighed as she sank down onto the couch in the staff lounge. This was her first real break since stepping foot in the ER today. The pace had been relentless. She took the opportunity to grab a cup of coffee and relax for a few minutes. Kim had hoped for a chance to explain to Jess about what happened earlier but had not seen her except in passing all morning.

The door to the lounge swung open. Jess stepped inside.

A little unsure of her reception, Kim offered a professional greeting. "Dr. McKenna," she said with a slight nod.

Jess winced. She nodded in return and then moved over to the coffee pot. After getting a cup of coffee, she returned to stand next to the couch. "You mind?" Jess asked, gesturing to the opposite end of the couch.

Okay. So maybe it's not as bad as I thought. "Have a seat."

Jess settled onto the couch and laid her head back

against the cushion. A heavy sigh escaped her lips.

"Tough day, huh?" Kim asked.

"I've definitely had better," Jess said. She sat up and took a sip of her coffee.

"I'm sorry about earlier. I didn't get the duty pager until after our meeting was over." Kim's hand clenched around her cup. "I had no idea Harland had turned it off for the meeting," she said, her voice tight with renewed anger.

"I owe you an apology as well." Jess shifted around until she was facing Kim. "I'm sorry. It was really crazy this morning, but I still should've given you a chance to explain. You've always been here when we needed you."

The gray cloud that had hung over Kim all morning finally dissipated. "On the bright side, it's official. I'm permanently assigned to cover the ER." Kim smiled. "I'll make sure everyone knows from now on to use my personal pager number so they can reach me at all times."

"Thanks." Jess reached over and lightly touched Kim's forearm. "And welcome to the ER."

Quiet reigned as they enjoyed their coffee. The momentary peace was broken by the sound of Kim's stomach growling.

Jess grinned. "Missed breakfast again, huh?"

A second louder rumble was her answer.

Although Kim wanted to, she hesitated to ask Jess to lunch. They had eaten lunch together last week in Jess's office, but that was a private setting. Other than the day Jess asked her to work in the ER, they had not been to the cafeteria together again. Kim decided to take a chance. *After all, I work here every day. It shouldn't seem that noteworthy for people to see us together.* "Could I interest you in going to lunch?" Kim didn't miss the sudden tension radiating from Jess. *Oh well, it was worth a try.* She tried not to let her disappointment show. "Well, I guess I'll just go grab myself something from—"

Jess bolted from the couch startling Kim. "No. Let's go to the cafeteria. My treat ... as a welcome to the ER."

Peering up at Jess, Kim looked for any sign of hesitation. Jess held her gaze and smiled. Kim sucked in a breath at the warmth emanating from Jess's vivid blue eyes. She rose from the couch. "Great. I'm starved."

"What's new," Jess said with a laugh.

Kim playfully elbowed Jess in the ribs. *Yeah, the day is definitely looking up.*

CHAPTER 17

Jess applied the finishing touches to a dressing on the patient's arm. She leaned over and watched Terrell suture the man's other arm. The patient had suffered an unfortunate run-in with a power saw. "Nice suturing job, Dr. Johnson."

Terrell looked up with a smile. "Thanks, Dr. McKenna."

"Okay, Mr. Merrill, Dr. Johnson will take care of anything else you need."

"Thanks, Dr. McKenna."

Jess pulled off her soiled gown and tossed it into the marked trash bin. "I'll be in my office if you need me." She moved over to the door and pushed it open. "Don't forget to have the nurse give him the wound care handout and make sure he gets a tetanus shot before he leaves."

"Sure thing, Dr. McKenna," Terrell said.

Stepping outside the door, Jess allowed her fatigue to surface. She stretched her tight back. A quick glance at her watch made Jess groan. *God, only three o'clock. Seems later.* Jess's stomach growled, reminding her of her interrupted lunch with Kim. They had no more than sat down with their trays when she got paged back to the ER.

This week had been a turning point for Jess. She had gone to lunch with Kim several times. It had been hard. Jess had cut herself off from everyone at work for so long it was difficult to change. The gossip had been flying, but Jess had done her best to ignore it. *We're just friends.* Jess's rumbling stomach brought her back to the here and now.

Jess turned toward her office and then stopped. She remembered seeing some bagels in the lounge earlier. Changing course, she headed for the staff lounge. She pushed the door open and stepped inside. The sight before her stopped her dead in her tracks. Kim was sitting at the table with a pile of charts in front of her. Rodman was standing directly behind her, leaning over her shoulder. His eyes appeared locked on her cleavage.

Kim looked up. An expression of relief washed across her face.

A rush of anger so strong it took her breath away roared through Jess.

She didn't think. She just reacted.

Three long strides brought her across the room.

Rodman's eyes went wide at Jess's headlong rush.

He took an involuntary step back.

Kim used his momentary distraction. She pushed her chair back sharply and caught him in the groin.

"Watch it!" He growled, stumbling back several steps.

"Sorry," Kim said, sounding anything but. She stood and quickly stepped into the space between Jess and Rodman.

Jess gazed into Kim's worried blue eyes. She had been within seconds of shoving Rodman away from Kim. *Christ! Are you out of your mind?* She blew out a breath and forced herself to calm down. Donning her ER persona like a protective suit of armor, Jess once again turned her attention to Rodman. "What brings you to the ER, Dr. Rodman?"

Rodman glared at them before turning his attention to Jess. "As usual the quarterly patient numbers from the ER are late. They were due on Monday—today is Friday." He jutted his chest out and sneered. "Maybe it's time for a new ER chief ... one who can actually do the job."

"The report was delivered to your office last Monday," Jess said in a calm measured voice.

"Good. Make sure it's on time next quarter."

Grinding her teeth, Jess resisted the urge to retort. She knew Rodman was just trying to get her goat. "Was there anything else?"

Rodman looked them both up and down.

Jess instinctively stepped closer to Kim. Their arms brushed.

"Figures," Rodman said, an ugly sneer twisting his face.

"Excuse me?" Jess said.

Rodman waved the question away. He turned away and headed for the door. "Great. Just what we need, another queer doctor. Like there aren't enough of them around here already," he muttered just loud enough for them to hear.

The door swung shut behind Rodman.

"How the hell does that man keep his job?" Kim asked.

Jess glanced over at Kim and realized just how close to her she was standing. She stepped away and propped her hip against the table. "Not that I'm defending him with this whole homophobic," Jess waved her hands vaguely in the air, "letch thing he has going on." She shook her head. "But he wasn't always like this."

"What happened to him?" Kim asked.

The door to the lounge swung open.

Bates stepped inside. His face lit up and he smiled widely when he spotted Kim. The smile vanished at the sight of Jess.

Jess struggled not to smile when Kim looked over and rolled her eyes. She quickly gathered up the charts on the table and offered half of them to Kim.

Kim took the charts without question.

Bates moved over to the coffee pot but continued to watch them.

"Dr. Donovan." Jess motioned toward the door. "After you."

They quickly made their escape.

Kim plopped the charts down on Jess's desk. She was grateful for the chance to avoid having to deal with Bates. The man just did not seem to understand that she was not interested in him. "Is the day over yet?"

"Soon." Jess motioned her toward the couch. "Relax while you can."

Kim dropped down onto the couch with an exaggerated sigh. "Thanks for the escape route."

Jess laughed. She put the charts she was carrying down on the desk. She leaned over and rummaged in the center desk drawer before joining Kim on the couch.

"Speaking of escapes," Jess said. She offered Kim a single key.

Eyebrow raised, Kim accepted the key. *Is this what I think it is? Wow.*

"That unlocks my office door. This way you can let yourself in when I'm tied up in a trauma or whatever." Jess shifted on the couch and looked away. "You won't have to put up with people bothering you in the lounge while you're working on charts."

Kim's brow furrowed. *Does she feel guilty about what happened with Rodman? That wasn't her fault.* Kim put her hand on Jess's arm. "Thank you."

Jess jumped, her eyes darting back to Kim.

Before Kim could pull her hand back, Jess covered it with one of her own and gave Kim's hand a quick squeeze.

Kim smiled. "So what is the deal with Rodman? I remember Philip mentioning that Rodman wasn't always as bad as he is now."

"I don't know much. It all started about two and a half years ago." Jess flushed and looked away again. "I was kind of busy with my own issues at the time." She scrubbed her hands over her face and looked back at Kim. "Anyway, up until then, Rodman had the typical arrogant surgeon personality. A driven go-getter. But he didn't chase anything in a skirt like he does now. And while not overly gay friendly, he was at least tolerant. Nothing like his current homophobic attitude."

"So what changed?" Kim asked.

"He separated from his second wife after only six months of marriage. I don't know who broke it off. It wasn't long after they split that he started hitting on every woman in sight." Jess raked her hand through her hair. "You know his brother is on the hospital board?"

Kim nodded.

"Well, his brother has done a great job of sweeping any complaints under the rug before they reach the formal stage. It's always a he said, she said type of thing."

"You mentioned before he wasn't so openly homophobic. What did that have to do with his divorce?" Although she disliked the man intensely, Kim couldn't help but be interested. Maybe if she could understand what motivated him, it would help make ignoring his behavior easier.

"That part never made sense, but it happened around the same time." Jess scowled. "All the sudden he started going out of his way to make my life difficult. And I've heard the same thing from other gay staff."

Kim leaned back and contemplated all Jess had told her. She sat up suddenly when the pieces came together. *Could it be? Would sure explain his behavior.*

"What?" Jess asked.

"I was just thinking. Maybe his wife left him for a woman. That would explain his need to chase women—to prove is masculinity."

Jess's eyebrows rose. "And explains why he hates gays all the sudden." She shook her head. "I'll be damned. I never put it together." Jess met Kim's gaze. Her eyes held respect with just a hint of trepidation. "Damn. You're good."

"Thank you." Kim smiled and buffed her nails on her shirt. "It's just a theory, but you have to admit—it fits."

"I—" The loud grumbling of her stomach interrupted Jess.

"You didn't get anything to eat after our lunch got interrupted?" Kim asked.

"Nope. Too busy."

"Don't let me keep you. You should get something now while it's quiet."

Jess looked at her watch. "Shift is over in an hour. I'll just grab something out of the vending machines to hold me over." She stood and stretched. "You want anything?"

"No. I'm good. Thanks." Kim stood and moved over to the desk to gather up her charts.

Jess motioned Kim toward her desk chair. "Make yourself at home," she said with a smile.

Kim settled into Jess's chair. She looked up at Jess and smiled. *I still can't believe she gave me a key to her office.* "Thanks again for the key."

"No problem." Jess reached for the door and then stopped. She turned back to Kim. "I know it's Friday night and short notice, but would you be interested in going to dinner after work?"

Wow. Two invitations to lunch this week and now this. She is getting more comfortable. Didn't even hesitate. "That would be great. Want to hit that Mexican place again?"

Jess laughed. "You're just addicted to their flan."

Kim stuck out her tongue. "And that would be bad—why?" Curiosity piqued when Jess blushed. *What was blush-worthy about that comment?*

Momentarily flustered, it took Jess a moment to regain her composure. She cleared her throat. "Mexican it is."

"I can head over there and put our names on the wait list while you take care of Thor."

"Not necessary. Thor's with Sam this weekend. She's off today, so she drove up and got him," Jess said.

She's never mentioned him spending time at Sam's before, at least not without her. Kim waited, wondering if Jess would offer any further explanation.

Jess shifted, looking a little uncomfortable, then straightened and met Kim's gaze. "I um ... really get a kick out of Halloween and all the kids dressed up. I get a lot of trick-or-treaters in my neighborhood. Thor gets kind of spun up with all the people coming to the door." Jess looked down. "He's not used to people coming to the house." She shrugged. "I don't like to have to confine him to my bedroom. He thinks he's being punished. So he goes and stays with Sam on Halloween."

Kim moved out from behind the desk and over close to Jess. *Yep, definitely a softie.* "I think it's great that you consider his feelings. Too many people don't give their companions that type of consideration." Meeting Jess's gaze, she smiled warmly. "Dogs have feelings too."

"Thanks," Jess said. An endearing blush covered her face. "So what do you have planned for Halloween? Going to the party at Blane's?" The ER department staff got together for a costume party at the local bar and grill every year.

"Kids in costumes are cute." Kim shook her head. "But adults in costumes, drinking too much and acting out—not my thing at all."

Jess laughed. "I'm with you on that one. So are you going to pass out candy at your place?"

Blond curls bounced when Kim shook her head. "One of the neighbors already let me know they don't do that at my complex. That was one of the things I enjoyed in Michigan. I spent Halloween at my mom's place. Her neighborhood gets a ton of kids on Halloween."

Indecision rippled across Jess's face.

Silence that quickly started to become uncomfortable surrounded them.

Kim ended the stalemate. "You should get something to eat while you've got the chance." She turned back toward Jess's desk.

"Kim." Jess reached out and touched Kim's arm, stopping her in her tracks.

Eyebrow raised in question, Kim turned back toward Jess.

Jess took a deep breath. "Why don't you come over to my place and help me pass out candy."

Things really are changing! Although they had met outside work quite a few times, they always met up at the park or wherever they were going. Kim searched Jess's eyes. She knew what a big step this was for Jess. And for herself if she was honest. "That would be great, Jess."

A delighted smile spread across Jess's face. "It'll be fun. I'll give you directions at dinner." Jess's pager shrilled. "Duty calls. I'll meet you after shift," she said before hurrying out.

Kim sank into Jess's chair. She had never expected Jess to invite her into her home. As much as she looked forward to spending the time with Jess, she was nervous as well. Her attraction to Jess continued to grow by leaps and bounds. It was getting harder and harder to ignore. Kim sighed. She had come to value their friendship too much to risk it with an ill-timed display of her desire. *Don't screw things up now.*

CHAPTER 18

Ding, dong.

Jess froze, a ball of ice solidifying in her stomach. Her gaze darted around the living room, making sure everything was in place. It had been almost two years since anyone other than Sam had been in her home. *Come on. This is Kim. It'll be fine.* A vision of warm, caring blue eyes flashed through her mind, melting the icy feeling in her belly. She blew out a breath and headed for the door.

"Hey, Kim." Jess smiled at Kim through the screen door. A single porch light draped with cobwebs cast a pallid swath of light across the covered porch.

"Hi. Wow. The decorations look great," Kim said. "I love the carved pumpkins on the steps. They look spooky all lit up. And the skeletons and bats hanging from the eves are a great touch."

"Thanks. I loved Halloween as a kid and I guess I never grew out of it. It's still one of my favorite holidays." She couldn't help but compare Kim's genuine enjoyment of the decorations to Myra's more jaded reaction. Not to mention her patronizing comments.

Should I? Jess debated with herself ... for about half a second. Her mouth quirked up in a lop-sided smile as she unobtrusively reached for a switch next to the door.

Kim's expression turned wary. Her eyes flittered around the porch.

Ah. She's getting too good at reading me. Jess slowly pushed open the screen door that separated her from

Kim.

The hanging skeletons lurched to life.

The bats' wings fluttered.

An eerie high-pitched cry emanated from overhead.

Kim ducked and did a little backward hop.

The bag in her hand dropped to the porch with a resounding thump.

Quickly regaining her composure, Kim mock scowled at Jess. Her hands went to her hips. "Very funny."

Jess grinned as she stepped out onto the porch to join Kim. "Happy Halloween."

Kim laughed. "Happy Halloween to you too." She reached down and picked up the bag she had dropped. Opening it, she peered inside. "You got lucky." She reached into the bag and pulled out a six pack of beer. "Your trick didn't break your treat."

Reaching out to accept the beer, Jess smiled warmly. "My favorite. Thank you." Jess was once again reminded of Kim's thoughtfulness. She had ordered the beer twice at their favorite Mexican restaurant. Kim had obviously taken note of that and gone out of her way to buy the beer for her. It wasn't available in local stores and had to be purchased directly from the microbrewery.

"You're welcome. I was going to bring a bottle of wine, but I thought the beer would go better with pizza."

At dinner the previous evening, Jess had invited Kim to stay for pizza after they handed out candy.

Childish laughter sounded. Jess glanced down the street and spotted a group of young children with several adults accompanying them heading their way. "Ah. Here they come." Jess set the beer down on the half wall surrounding the porch. "Hang on a sec." She headed down the steps. She turned on the luminaries positioned along the walkway, then returned to the porch. Jess picked up the beer. "All set. Let's head inside. I've already got the candy ready to go."

"The luminaries are a great idea with all the little kids running around." Kim looked down at the lighted bags lining the walkway. "I've seen ones with small LEDs in them, but those look like they have real candles burning inside even though I know that's not the case."

"They do have candles in them. But you're right they aren't real. They're battery powered." Jess reached for the screen door.

As the door swung open, the skeletons and bats once again sprang to life.

Kim walked close to one of the cardboard skeletons hanging from the covered porch roof and looked up. "Are they attached to a motion sensor?"

Jess reached in the door and flipped the switch. The dancing skeletons and fluttering bats stilled. "Yeah. It's rigged to the screen door. I normally don't turn it on until after all the really young children have gone in for the night. I want their introduction to Halloween to be fun and not scary." Jess grinned. "The older kids love it, though."

Shaking her head, Kim laughed. "I bet they do."

"After you," Jess said, motioning into the house.

"That was fun," Kim said as she flopped down onto the overstuffed leather couch. It was surprising just how quickly she had gotten comfortable in Jess's living room. The warm and cozy setting had drawn her in immediately. "When I saw all the candy you had, I thought for sure you'd be eating it for weeks. I still can't believe we gave all of it out." Kim grinned up at Jess. "Of course, being the good friend that I am, I would've offered to help you finish it off."

Jess snorted, her mouth pulling up in a smile. "Oh.

I'm sure it would have been a terrible imposition." She sank down into the padded chair opposite Kim.

Kim tipped her head back as laughter bubbled up. The evening had been wonderful so far. Kim knew that had a lot to do with being with Jess. It was hard to figure, but she enjoyed spending time with Jess more than she had the women she dated. The Jess that she had seen tonight was a far cry from the overly emotionally controlled ER chief at work. Even compared to their other outings, tonight had been different. By being invited into Jess's home, Kim felt as if she had finally been allowed into the life of the real Jess McKenna. It was a heady experience.

"Well, since the candy is gone, could I interest you in a pepperoni and black olive pizza and a beer?" Jess asked.

She remembered. Warmth filled Kim at Jess's thoughtfulness. They had gone out for pizza only once, and that was what Kim had ordered. "That sounds great. Now all we need is a scary movie and we'd be all set."

"Actually I have some movies ..." Jess's gaze flittered away from Kim. She ducked her head, and her right leg began to bounce up and down.

Brows furrowed, Kim studied Jess. *What's going on here?* Not wanting Jess to be uncomfortable, Kim said, "Pizza and a beer would hit the spot. It's getting kind of late for a movie anyway."

The breath left Jess in a blast hard enough to ruffle the hair hanging in her face. Kim could almost see her squaring her mental shoulders. *Huh?* Confusion reigned.

"It's not that late." Jess popped up from her chair and walked over to one of the oak bookcases next to the fireplace. After lifting the leaded glass door, she reached in and pulled out three DVD cases. "Take your pick," Jess said as she set them down on the coffee table before resuming her seat.

While still unsure just what was causing Jess's unusual behavior, Kim did as asked. She surveyed the DVD boxes. The first was a vampire movie. The second, a classic monster flick. It was the third one that made her grin. 'Under The Stairs'. Kim laughed. "I love it. Where did you find it? I didn't know her early movies were even available." Colleen Bryce had begun her career making B grade horror movies before hitting it big as the action-hero, Deven Masters. Kim had raved about the actress after they had finally managed to see her latest movie.

The corner of Jess's eyes crinkled with the brightness of her smile. "I thought you might like that one. I found a place online that has all sorts of eclectic titles. I don't watch much TV, but I do love movies. I have a pretty big movie collection."

"I haven't seen one of her scream queen movies in years," Kim said as she picked up the DVD and handed it to Jess. She rubbed her hands together in anticipation. "I can't wait to see it again."

Jess's earlier awkward demeanor immediately returned. "Um ... well, the thing is ..." Jess turned the DVD case over and over in her hands. "The living room really isn't that big ..."

At this point, Kim was beyond puzzled by Jess's confounding behavior. She had no idea what Jess was trying to get at. Kim looked around the room. The room was on the small side but typical of a Craftsman bungalow. A fireplace with a deep stone hearth dominated the far wall. Built-in oak bookcases flanked the fireplace. The remainder of the room was taken up with the overstuffed leather couch where she was sitting, a low set coffee table, the antique Morris chair Jess was sitting in, and a large dog bed tucked in the corner. One more glance around the room and the obvious finally hit Kim. There was no TV in the room. *So where is it that she's so uncomfortable?* The answer hit Kim right between the eyes. *Oh shit.* Her gaze darted to Jess.

The flush on Jess's face substantiated what Kim suspected. She confirmed it a moment later. "The television is in my bedroom."

A flash of Jess and her entwined on Jess's bed seared through Kim's mind. Heat flooded her face and body. *Oh God.* Kim quickly scrubbed her hands over her face, willing the blush to fade. *You're a grown woman. Act like it. Get your hormones under control. You can share a bed with a friend to watch a movie.* She glanced over at Jess.

While Jess met Kim's gaze, her leg was once again bouncing up and down in an apparently unconscious gesture.

Kim was sure that Jess could sense her arousal. It was the last thing she wanted. Jess had made it quite clear right from the start, in action, if not words, that she was only interested in being friends. And she respected that and Jess.

Acting on impulse, Kim rose from the couch and moved over to stand next to Jess's chair. "It's okay." She gently squeezed Jess's shoulder. "Maybe we could save the movie for another time? We could just call it a night?"

Jess's gaze locked with hers. Kim's breath caught. Jess's eyes turned a dark, bluish silver. Emotion Kim couldn't decipher churned in those striking depths.

Jess cleared her throat and broke the spell. "I promised you pizza and a beer." She stood and offered a shy smile. "I'd like to see the movie too. So if you really wouldn't mind hanging out in my bedroom ..."

Kim had no doubt that this was well outside of

Jess's comfort zone, but she was doing it anyway. "I don't mind if you don't." *This is one special woman. Too bad I have such a lousy track record with women.* Kim stifled a sigh. *Not that Jess is interested in me that way anyway.*

"Pizza and a movie it is, then," Jess said.

Kim blew out a breath, which was echoed by Jess. She grinned and Jess laughed, banishing the last of the tension.

"Want a beer while we wait for the pizza?" Jess asked.

"Sure."

"Come on in the kitchen. I'll call for the pizza and you can grab us each one of the beers you brought."

Kim smiled. "Lead the way."

Slowly drifting to awareness, Jess sleepily blinked open her eyes as she tried to orientate herself. The first thing she became aware of was Kim's head resting on her shoulder. The TV mounted on the wall opposite the foot of the bed was displaying the screensaver. *Guess we fell asleep. Too much pizza and beer.*

Jess's thoughts went back to earlier in the evening. When she picked out some movies for them to watch before Kim arrived, she had been so nervous about Kim coming over, she had totally forgotten about the television being in her bedroom. Then, as soon as Kim had mentioned the movies, realization struck along with a swift surge of arousal at the thought of Kim in her bed. A resigned sigh escaped. *It can never happen. Not like that. She would never respect you again.*

Turning her attention back to Kim, Jess took the opportunity to study her face in repose. It just reinforced what she was already well aware of. *God, she's beautiful.* Resisting the temptation to stroke Kim's face, instead she gently shook her shoulder. "Kim. Time to wake up."

A sleepy little smile appeared. With an unintelligible murmur, Kim rolled closer and threw her arm across Jess's belly. She sighed deeply as she settled herself snuggly against Jess's body.

Jess bit back a groan. The feel of Kim's body intimately pressed to hers was exquisite torture. Without conscious intent, her hand moved up to stroke silky blond hair. Regret at what could never be darkened Jess's thoughts. She forcibly pushed the longing away.

"Kim. Time to wake up," Jess said again, putting a bit more force behind her words. Despite the situation, she couldn't bring herself to physically push Kim away.

With a protesting whimper, Kim tightened her hold on Jess. Her eyes fluttered open. Jess could see the confusion in them. "We fell asleep," Jess said.

That's when Kim seemed to realize just where she was lying. Her body stiffened against Jess's. "Shit!" she blurted as she rolled away.

Jess couldn't help but laugh. "It's no big deal."

Kim sat up on the side of the bed. Her head dropped into her hands with an embarrassed groan.

Shaking her head, Jess got off the bed. She moved around to the other side where Kim sat. "Hey," Jess said softly. When Kim finally looked up, Jess offered a warm smile.

"Sorry for falling asleep on you ... literally," Kim said. A smile twisted her lips even as a blush colored her cheeks.

"No biggie. I fell asleep too." Jess was determined not to make Kim feel any more awkward than she already did. "Guess it's time to call it a night. Are you okay to drive?"

"I'm good." Kim stood and moved toward the bedroom door. "I'll get out of your hair and let you get some rest."

"Kim."

Kim turned back toward Jess.

Butterflies danced in Jess's belly. It was important to her that Kim know how much tonight meant. She didn't want any lingering awkwardness between them. "I had a great time tonight. I'm really glad you came over."

"I am too, Jess."

They made their way to the front door in companionable silence.

Kim followed Jess as she moved down the porch steps. Kim stopped on the middle step. Leaning down, she once again admired the jack-o'-lanterns. Jess had left the lights illuminating the pumpkins earlier when she extinguished the luminaries. "Did you carve these?"

A smile lit Jess's face. "Yeah. Sam and I usually do them, but she couldn't get away earlier in the week. So I was on my own this year."

"You did a great job. I especially like this one." Kim pointed to a pumpkin with an intricately carved face. "It looks like it could come alive at any moment. I always loved making jack-o'-lanterns with my dad when I was a kid." Painful memories swirled close to the surface. Kim pushed them away. She didn't know what had made her mention her father. She never talked about him.

"Thanks." Jess glanced at Kim through lowered lashes. "Maybe next year, if you wanted, you could help."

Next year! Kim's heart leaped in anticipation. Jess was coming to mean more to her with each passing day. "That would be great, Jess." Kim's heart was light as she walked with Jess toward her Jeep. However, that did not stop the part of her, deep down inside that yearned for more than friendship with Jess.

CHAPTER 19

"Do you want to stop and get something to eat before we drop off the car or wait and eat at the hotel?" Sam asked. They were headed to San Francisco to spend the night before flying out the following morning for Los Angeles.

Silence reigned.

Sam took her eyes off the road long enough to glance at her sister.

The lights of a passing car splashed across her face. Her brow deeply furrowed, Jess stared morosely out the window. She had not done more than grunt in response to Sam's attempts at conversation since leaving their parents' house an hour ago.

"Earth to Jess," Sam said as she gently touched Jess's shoulder.

Jess's head swung around. "What?"

"No need to bite my head off."

"Sorry." Jess arched her back and stretched as best she could within the confines of the rental car. "I'm just tired. What were you saying?"

"Did you want to stop and get something to eat or wait until we get to the hotel?"

"Either way is fine with me." Jess resumed her contemplation of the windshield.

Reaching up to knead tight neck muscles, Sam sighed. Jess had been subdued during the visit home to celebrate Thanksgiving with the family. She had put on a happy face for the relatives, but her smile had never quite reached her eyes. With the crowd that had been at their folks' house, Sam had not been able to get Jess alone and find out what was bothering her. "What's going on with you?"

Jess shrugged.

"Come on. Talk to me, sis. Why are you so down all the sudden? I thought things were going well for you. You've seemed happier than you have been in a long time, especially these last few weeks." Sam had only seen Jess once since Halloween. Jess had been spending all her time off with Kim.

Raking her hands through her hair, Jess said, "I've got some things on my mind, that's all."

Like maybe a beautiful psychiatrist? Kim was all Jess talked about these days. Sam had never heard her talk so much or so enthusiastically about any woman. Even more unusual was the fact that Jess appeared totally unaware that she was doing it. That was what made it so strange that she had not mentioned Kim once since leaving Los Angeles three days ago. "So tell me what's bugging you and—"

"Look, there's our exit," Jess said. She opened the glove box and pulled out the rental papers. "We should go ahead and drop off the car. We can grab something to eat at the hotel."

Sam shot Jess a sharp look before taking the indicated exit. Jess was doing her best to appear totally engrossed in the rental car documents. *This conversation is so not over!*

Lying on one of the beds in their hotel room, Sam waited for Jess to finish her shower. She was bound and determined to get Jess to open up about what was bothering her. Keeping things bottled up inside was a trait they shared.

The bathroom door swung open and a cloud of steam wafted into the room. Jess stepped out, wearing scrub pants and a T-shirt.

"I thought we were going to go out and get something to eat?" Sam asked.

Jess walked over and picked up the room service menu. "Heads up." She tossed it toward Sam. "Order what you want. My treat." She flopped down on the empty bed. "And you can pick a pay-per-view movie too."

"Cool!" As Sam flipped open the menu, she caught a glimpse of the satisfied expression on Jess's face. That's when she recognized the offer for what it was—a subtle bribe. Or at the very least, an attempt to keep her mind off their earlier conversation. *Nice try, Jess.* "Great, if we're staying in, then we'll have lots of time and privacy to talk about what's been bothering you."

Eyes narrowing to slits, Jess sat up on the side of the bed. "You're not going to let this go—are you?"

Sam sat up directly opposite Jess. She met Jess's eyes and held her gaze. "I love ya, sis."

Jess muttered something that sounded like "no fair" as she dropped backward onto the bed. She flung her arm over her eyes. "You'll think I'm being stupid ... and pathetic."

"I won't." Sam slid her foot across the distance between them and nudged Jess's foot. "When have I ever told you I thought you were stupid?"

With an exaggerated huff, Jess sat up again. She closed her eyes and her face contorted.

"What are you doing?"

"I'm thinking. Hush."

"You're a nut." Sam laughed.

"Shh ..." Jess's eyes popped open. "Ah ..." A little half smirk twitched at the corner of her mouth. "We were at Dovers for your birthday, and you told me I was stupid."

Racking her brain, Sam tried to remember the incident Jess was talking about. When the memory hit, she burst out laughing. "Jess, I was eight!"

Crossing her arms over her chest, Jess said, "Still. You did call me stupid." The struggle to keep up the stern demeanor clearly showed on Jess's face.

Sam tried to put as much righteous indignation into her voice as she could, which wasn't much. "I did not." Sam mirrored Jess's stance. "I called you a stupidhead because you wouldn't let me use my birthday money to buy that five pound block of chocolate."

They both dissolved into laughter.

Sam wiped tears of laughter from her eyes. "Seriously. What's got you so down?"

Jess's gaze dropped. The bedspread was suddenly fascinating. She picked at a loose thread. "I miss her," she said, her voice almost a whisper.

There was no need for Sam to pretend she didn't know Jess was talking about Kim. "What's wrong with that? You guys have become good friends. Right?"

"Yeah. I just ..." Jess looked up, her expression open and vulnerable. "I just didn't expect it to be this hard." She sighed. "I hate the fact that I wasn't there to spend Thanksgiving with Kim. She said she didn't mind. And that she was just going to hang out and catch up on her journals. But still, I keep thinking about her, wondering how she's doing."

Shock rendered Sam momentarily speechless. If Jess could see the look on her own face, she would freak. Sam knew despite Jess's continued insistence that it could never happen, she wanted more than friendship with Kim. She just hadn't realized until this moment how far gone Jess was. This went way beyond friendship. *I hope like hell Kim feels the same way about Jess. I've got to talk Jess into introducing us.* Sam was thrilled that her sister was finally opening her heart to someone, whether Jess realized it or not.

"There is nothing wrong with caring about someone, Jess. It feels good, doesn't it?"

A bright smile spread across Jess's face. "You're right. It does."

"So call her and see how she's doing. Have you called her at all while we've been gone?"

Jess's smile dimmed. "I tried twice on Thanksgiving." Her brow furrowed. "She wasn't home."

"Maybe she got a last-minute invitation."

"That's kind of what I figured."

"Did you try her cell?"

"No." Jess's shoulders slumped. "I didn't want to be ... I mean if she ... I thought ..." She scrubbed her hands over her face.

It took a minute to sink in just what Jess was trying to avoid admitting, but Sam was pretty sure she had figured it out. "You're worried she was out with another woman, because you weren't there."

Jess's head snapped up. "That's not true. I have no claim like that on Kim. She can see whoever she wants. We're just friends."

"Whoa. Easy." Sam held up her hands. "My mistake." *You are so gone on this woman, Jess.*

"I'm sorry, Sam." Her breath blasted from her in an audible huff as Jess flopped back onto the bed. "I don't know what the hell is wrong with me."

I do. The question was how could she help Jess realize the depth of her feelings for Kim without making her panic and run for the hills. She would have to think on that one. Right now, she would be happy just to get Jess's mind off her troubles for a little while. "Well, I don't know about you but I'm starving. Let's go out and hit Chinatown. It'll be fun. We haven't spent much time together recently."

"Okay." Jess stood, her expression contrite. She offered Sam her hand. Sam clasped her wrist, and Jess tugged her off the bed. "I'm sorry about that too. I know I haven't been around much, especially lately. I'll start making more frequent trips to San Diego again. I promise."

Sam bumped shoulders with Jess. "Don't worry about it. Maybe you and Kim could come down and we'll hit the zoo or, better yet, the botanical gardens. That way the big guy can come too."

Some of the tension left Jess's face and she smiled. "Maybe we'll do that."

Sam tried hard to hide her shock. She never expected Jess to agree so readily.

Jess walked across the room to her suitcase and pulled out a pair of jeans. "You still remember any good places in Chinatown? It's been years since you lived here."

Rubbing her hands together, Sam said, "I know just the place."

Jess sat at a small table in a dark corner and sipped her beer. *How in the hell did I let Sam talk me into this?* After leaving the restaurant in Chinatown, Sam had led them to a bar she remembered from her college days. A heavy bass beat pulsed through the room. Strobe lights overhead bathed the gyrating bodies on the dance floor in random patterns of shadow and light.

Sam was out on the dance floor. Jess had already turned down several invitations to dance. She wasn't even vaguely tempted. Sighing, she leaned back in her chair, determined to finish her beer and then find Sam. When she spotted Sam making her way toward the table, Jess pushed to her feet.

Sam stepped out of the crowd, carrying two beers.

"I thought we agreed to one beer," Jess said when Sam reached the table.

"One more round, then we'll go." Sam's cheeks were flushed, and sweat glistened on her forehead. She took a big swig of one beer and offered the second to Jess.

Jess grumbled under her breath, then accepted the beer.

Sam glanced over Jess's shoulder, and her eyes widened. "Wow," she mouthed.

A hand landed on Jess's shoulder.

Jess turned and her breath caught in her throat. The woman standing before her was beautiful—tall and lithe with long blond hair.

The blonde looked Jess up and down and, judging by her wide smile, liked what she saw. "Dance with me?"

Jess hesitated.

Sam bumped her arm. She leaned close and whispered, "Go on. What will one dance hurt?"

The fact that the woman's coloring and body type bore a resemblance to Kim's was not lost on Jess. *What the hell. Why not?* Jess could not remember the last time she had danced with a woman. She nodded and held out her hand to the blonde.

The woman led them to the dance floor. Without preamble, she stepped into Jess's arms and pressed their bodies together.

As they moved against each other, Jess's arousal soared. It had been way too long since she had felt a woman against her like this. Heat rushed through her. When the woman tightened her arms around Jess's neck, she gave in to her rapidly growing excitement and pressed her leg between the woman's thighs. Jess slid her hands down and squeezed the woman's ass, drawing her closer.

The blonde groaned and began to move against her.

Jess moved her own hips in counter point. The woman's hand came up and palmed her breast, then gave it a firm squeeze. *Whoa!* She grasped the offending hand and removed it from her breast. *Oh, no, you don't.*

The woman leaned close and whispered in her ear, "Let's go in the back."

Huh? The woman's hot breath against her sensitive ear added to the already pounding pulse between Jess's thighs and made it hard to think clearly. She allowed the blonde to lead her toward the back of the room.

They stepped into a hallway that had doors lining each side. One of the doors opened, and a couple stumbled out laughing and hastily straightening their clothes.

Realization dawned.

Jess's feet felt as if they were suddenly glued to the floor.

The woman tugged at her hand. Her dark brown eyes were filled with desire. "Come on, baby." She cupped her own breast.

Jess's long-denied libido surged. *Fuck it. I'm not hurting anyone. We're both adults.* Jess grinned. She grasped the woman's hand and pulled her into the first open doorway she found. It turned out to be a small bathroom.

Once inside, Jess began to fondle the woman's breasts. After Jess pulled the woman's hand off her breast again, she seemed to get the hint and allowed Jess to lead. Finally unleashed, Jess's libido was firmly in control. Continuing to kiss the blonde's neck, she quickly unzipped the woman's pants. Jess closed her eyes as she slipped her hand inside the woman's underwear. *Oh yeah.* Her hand stroked down a tight abdomen, heading for her heat. Just before Jess reached her goal, an image formed in her mind's eye.

Warm caring blue eyes held her captive.

Oh God. Kim.

Jess froze.

"Don't stop."

The woman's voice brought her back to reality.

A wave of nausea washed away every trace of arousal. Jess jerked her hand out of the woman's pants. "I'm sorry. I can't—" Heartsick at what she had almost done, Jess fled.

Sam stepped out of the bathroom just in time to see Jess do the same a little farther up the hall. "Hey, Jess!"

Jess glanced back.

Sam got a brief glimpse of her stricken expression before Jess turned and took off at a trot. Before Sam could react, the door opened again and the woman Jess had danced with stepped out, tucking her shirt into her pants. The implications were staggering. *Holy shit! No way!* Sam took off after Jess.

Sam scanned the bar, trying to spot Jess. She moved to the back corner where they had been sitting. The table was occupied, but not by Jess. *Where the hell did she go?* Worry ratcheted up a notch.

Going on a hunch, Sam headed for the bar entrance. She stepped outside and quickly spotted Jess. She was sitting on the short concrete wall that separated the bar's parking lot from the one next door. Jess's head was down, and she had her face buried in her hands.

"Hey, sis," Sam said as she moved to sit next to her. "What's wrong?"

Jess remained immobile.

"I saw the blonde."

With a heavy sigh, Jess looked up.

Oh Jess. Shock rippled through Sam at the despair etched on Jess's face. Sam wrapped a consoling arm across Jess's shoulders. "Hey now. It can't be that bad. What happened?"

"It doesn't make any sense. It's stupid." Jess's hands dropped to her thighs. She kneaded the material of her jeans.

Giving Jess's shoulder a comforting squeeze, Sam said, "Let's not go there again." Relief loosened the tightness of her chest when a smile ghosted across Jess's face. "You know you can tell me anything."

"I know." Jess sighed. She straightened up, and Sam removed her arm. "I got hot dancing with the blonde. We went into one of the bathrooms." Jess rubbed her face. "Christ, Sam, I had my hand in the woman's pants!" She shot her sister an embarrassed look.

"And?"

"Just before I touched her, I got this picture of Kim in my mind. It was so clear it was like she was in the room with us. I couldn't go through with it." Jess shook her head roughly. "It felt like I was cheating."

"But, Jess, you're not—"

"You think I don't know that?" Jess fisted the hair at her temples. "I know it's ridiculous. We're just friends."

"But you want to be more," Sam said.

Jess slumped. "You know I can't ..." She sighed heavily.

The defeated look in Jess's eyes kept Sam from protesting. *There has got to be more to it than the fact that they work together holding Jess back.* As she had many times in the past, Sam wondered about Jess's trust issues. "What are you going to do, Jess?"

A single tear trailed down Jess's face. "I wish to God I knew."

CHAPTER 20

" Hey Dr. Donovan. You're here early," Penny said as Kim walked by the nurses' station.

Kim approached the counter where Penny stood. She set down a cardboard tray with coffee and pastries "Good morning. Did you have a nice holiday?" She glanced around, hoping to spot Jess.

"Yes." Penny beamed. "How about you, did you spend Thanksgiving with anyone special?"

Oh, here we go again. Penny frequently attempted to find out if she was involved with anyone. Well aware of Penny's interest in her, Kim tried to discourage it. Normally, she would have ignored the question since all of her free time these days was spent with Jess. And there was no way in hell she would ever tell anyone that. But in this case, she didn't think it would hurt to give out a little information about her private life. "I spent my day serving meals at a homeless shelter."

"Oh." Penny looked a bit stymied, then she smiled brightly. "Well, of course, I would do something like that in a minute if I could. But with my family over for the holiday and all, my mom needed me."

Right. Sure you would. Kim had been surprised when she learned that Penny was only a few years her junior. She acted much younger. Penny wasn't shy about discussing her personal life. In conversations around the nurses' station, Kim had discovered that Penny still lived with her parents. More remarkably to Kim, Penny didn't seem the least bit embarrassed that her mother still did her laundry, cleaned her room, and cooked her meals. Kim was willing to bet Penny had not lifted a finger to help out at Thanksgiving.

Kim picked up her tray off the counter. "Well, page me if you need me." With that she turned and headed toward Jess's office.

Finding Jess's door locked, Kim let herself in with the key Jess had given her. She glanced around the office that had over the last few weeks come to feel like her office as much as Jess's. She set the tray down on the desk. A sigh escaped. There was no sign that Jess had arrived yet.

Okay. I'm anxious to see my friend. So what? There's nothing wrong with that. She blew out a breath. *Be honest with yourself, Kim, if no one else.* One thing their time apart had made crystal clear to Kim was that she could no longer delude herself as to the depth of her feelings for Jess. She had missed Jess with an intensity that had shocked her. It was as if a vital part of herself had been missing.

Kim was startled out of her thoughts by the opening of the office door. Her heart soared at the sight of Jess.

Jess stepped into the room. A bright smile blossomed when she spotted Kim. "Hi." The door swung shut behind her.

All the loneliness and longing Kim had struggled with for the past four days overwhelmed her. Kim crossed the room, and before she realized what she was doing, she enveloped Jess in a hug. "Welcome back." Reality struck like lightening when she came into contact with Jess's stiff body. *You idiot!* "Sorry," Kim stammered and pulled back.

Jess's arms wrapped around her, stopping Kim's retreat.

Kim's heart rate shot into overdrive when Jess pulled her close and returned the hug. The warmth of Jess's body drew her in. When Jess didn't immediately let go, Kim had to fight the urge to bury her face in Jess's neck. A tantalizing scent she couldn't put a name to teased her senses. Her arms instinctively tightened around Jess's back. A single powerful thought filled her mind. *Home.*

The hug lingered for much longer than a quick greeting between friends.

"Good to see you too," Jess said, near her ear before finally releasing her. Her voice was a husky whisper that sent shivers down Kim's spine.

Thoroughly flustered by the embrace, Kim stepped back. Although Jess had more than returned the hug, which in itself was unexpected, Kim was still nervous about her reaction. She met Jess's gaze hesitantly.

Jess's eyes were silvery-blue pools of emotion.

Unspoken longing hung between them like a palpable presence.

Kim's world tilted, then righted itself as a new understanding dawned. *She does want me.* Drawn like a humming bird to a tempting flower, Kim reached out to stroke Jess's flushed cheek. Her fingers trembled.

The rap of knuckles on the office door shattered the moment.

Jess hastily pulled back before Kim's fingers made contact.

Oh God. Kim mentally shook herself. She had been seconds from kissing Jess.

A second louder knock sounded. "Dr. McKenna?" Penny called.

Kim quickly moved away from Jess.

Jess spun around and jerked open the door. "Yes?"

"Here are the files you wanted," Penny said. She peered past Jess as she handed over the files. Her gaze darted back and forth between Jess and Kim. A frown marred her face.

"Was there something else?" Jess asked.

Penny shook her head.

"Thanks for the files," Jess said and then promptly shut the door in Penny's face.

Damn. Jess was shaking. With a white-knuckled grip on the doorknob, she struggled to regain her composure. She knew she should be grateful to Penny for the interruption. But if she was honest with herself— she wasn't. Kim's impromptu hug had shocked her at first, but the feeling had immediately turned to guilty pleasure at the feel of Kim pressed against her. The intoxicating scent of Kim's perfume had made her head swim. Or at least that was what she was telling herself to excuse letting the embrace go on for as long as she had. *You are so pathetic.*

The expression on Kim's face afterward had been as thrilling as the embrace itself. Her beautiful face had been painted with arousal. *You know how fast that would change if you ever acted on those feelings.* Jess sighed, all too aware of just how true that was. For a moment, Jess had been sure Kim was going to kiss her. She still wasn't sure she would have had the willpower to refuse, no matter how bad an idea. She mentally shook herself and turned to face Kim.

Kim had moved away. She was standing by the desk.

Jess joined her. A rosy flush still colored Kim's cheeks. Jess wanted to pull her back into her arms and never let go. Unwilling to openly acknowledge the emotions that still tinged the air so strongly between them, Jess struggled for something to say. Her gaze landed on the coffee sitting on her desk. She propped her hip on the desk, then picked up one of the Del Java coffee cups. "For me?" Jess asked with a pleased smile.

An answering smile flitted across Kim's face. "Of

course."

Jess picked up the bag and held it up to her forehead. "I, Swami, predict that this contains a chocolate croissant and a maple scone."

Laughing, Kim pulled the bag out of her hand. "You know me too well."

Not even close to how well I'd like to know you. If only things could be different. Jess forced a smile. "Thanks for the coffee."

"You're welcome. So how was your Thanksgiving?" Kim asked.

"Not bad. I enjoyed seeing my family, but it's good to be home." Jess was almost afraid to ask, but she had to know. "How was your holiday?"

"Busier than I planned. Do you remember the teenage boy you saw a few weeks ago who presented as a suspected overdose?"

"Vaguely." Jess saw so many patients that after a while they all tended to blur together. Her brow furrowed. *What's that got to do with Thanksgiving?*

"Well, my name was on his hospital paperwork as the consulting psychiatrist. It was really an amazing coincidence. Turns out, the director of the group foster home for teens where he lives is an old friend from college. She called me the day before Thanksgiving."

I knew I shouldn't have left. An emotion so foreign she almost didn't recognize it claimed Jess. "Oh, were you good friends?" She tried hard to keep her tone neutral.

Kim's gaze darted away. She picked up her coffee and took a swallow.

Jealousy clawed at Jess. *She's an ex.*

Setting her cup down, Kim said, "I haven't seen Sid since I left Michigan to go to medical school." She shook her head. "She's really changed. Anyway, she called to catch up and I ended up spending Thanksgiving with her."

Dread replaced jealousy, knotting Jess's stomach. *Does Kim want to get back together with her?* The very thought was enough to make Jess sick to her stomach. *You knew this would eventually happen. Someone as wonderful as Kim doesn't stay single forever.* It didn't make the reality of it any easier to take.

Tilting her head, Kim regarded Jess curiously. "What's wrong?"

Realizing her expression had betrayed her, Jess fought to hide her rising emotions. She shook her head. "Nothing. Sorry. You were saying?"

Kim's eyebrow arched, and she held Jess's gaze for a moment. She seemed about to question Jess further, then changed her mind. She brushed her hair over her shoulder before moving back to lean against Jess's desk. "Sid's group volunteers every year at a local homeless shelter on Thanksgiving. When Sid asked if I'd be willing to help out supervising the teens and serving meals, I couldn't say no. Afterward, we went back to the group home and I met Sid's partner, Alan." Kim laughed. "Shocked me when I met him. In college, Sid swore men were the root of all evil in the world."

Relief almost buckled Jess's knees. She grabbed the side of the desk. For the first time since this conversation started Jess didn't have to force a smile. "I'm glad you didn't spend the day alone. I felt bad that I had already committed to going to my parents before I knew you weren't going home."

Kim briefly squeezed Jess's arm. "I'm sorry I missed your call on Thanksgiving. Next time you don't reach me at home, call my cell. I always want to hear from you."

Jess met Kim's emotion-filled eyes and saw her own feelings reflected back at her. Jess tensed, expecting the familiar fear to strike that such an emotionally vulnerable moment always brought. Equal parts relief and surprise flowed through her when it didn't happen. Something had definitely shifted between them.

CHAPTER 21

A subtle awareness nudged the edge of Kim's senses. She looked up from the patient's chart she was reviewing. At the sight of Jess approaching the nurses' station, a smile tugged at the corners of her lips. In the days since they had shared a hug in Jess's office, things had changed between them. Kim had expected Jess to retreat behind her formidable emotional walls. That had not happened.

While neither had made any conscious effort to change the nature of their relationship from friends to lovers, a new anticipation hung in the air between them whenever they were together in private.

The mournful wail of a siren growing rapidly louder caused Jess to veer off and head for the ambulance bay doors.

The pace in the ER had been nothing short of frantic all week. Kim didn't know how Jess and her staff kept up with the unrelenting stream of patients.

Kim moved to the end of the counter closest to the swinging double doors that led to the ambulance bay—close enough to be of help if she was needed while at the same time, out of the way.

The doors swung open with a whoosh.

Jess grabbed the head of the gurney as soon as it cleared the doorway. "What have you got?"

"White male, GSW to the chest."

"Trauma One," Jess said, already moving toward the room—gurney in tow.

The paramedic rattled off the patient's stats.

"Bates, Armstrong, you're with me," Jess called over her shoulder.

Glancing down at her watch, Kim frowned. It was fifteen minutes to shift change. *Almost made it.* It wasn't an uncommon occurrence for Jess to work overtime, and while Kim respected her work ethic, she couldn't help sighing as she saw their dinner plans going out the window.

The second paramedic stepped up to the nurses' station.

Terrell strode over to greet him.

"The other team is bringing in the shooter. They were right behind us."

The wail of a siren punctuated his words.

"What're his injuries?" Terrell asked.

"Don't know about the son. We were concentrating on the father."

Kim raked her hands through her hair. *A father and son. What is this world coming to?* Even with all she had seen so far in her career these violent family conflicts still affected her.

The ambulance bay doors swooshed open.

Her attention was once again drawn to the incoming patient.

A paramedic pushed a gurney through the doors.

The patient struggled weakly against restraining straps across his chest and thighs. "I didn't want to. Please ... I didn't mean it."

"Settle down now. Let the docs help you," the paramedic said.

"He made me. I swear." The patient whimpered.

Where have I heard that voice before? Frowning, Kim took a step forward as Terrell and the paramedic pushed the gurney past her.

"Do you need a hand?" Kim asked. She glanced down at the patient.

A young man with a bloody, battered face looked back at her through eyes swollen to thin slits. "Mom?" He strained toward her. "Oh, Mom."

Kim quickly moved to the side of the gurney. "Take it easy." Her nose wrinkled at the pungent smell of urine that wafted up from the patient's bloody, torn clothing.

His mangled features defied recognition for a moment, then it hit.

Oh my God. "Brian." He had been part of one of her therapy groups.

"Please. Help me." Brian clutched the front of Kim's shirt.

"Hey!" Terrell's hand shot out and grabbed Brian's wrist.

Keeping her eyes on Brian, Kim said, "It's okay. Let him go, Terrell." When he didn't immediately comply, she glanced up at Terrell.

Terrell met her eyes, and Kim nodded. He slowly and somewhat reluctantly released Brian's wrist.

"You need to let go, Brian." Kim kept her voice calm and as soothing as she could make it.

"I didn't mean it!"

Brian's hand tightened on her shirt.

Kim grabbed his forearm. *Don't panic. He's hurt and scared.* The muscles turned to granite under her fingers.

With a low undulating moan, Brian's body arched against the gurney's restraining straps.

"Brian!" *God. What's happening?*

As if pulled by a marionette's strings, his body began to jerk.

"Damn it. He's seizing," Terrell said. "Get him into Trauma Two."

Kim struggled to pry her shirt out of Brian's hand as the paramedic grasped the stretcher and started to pull.

She gripped the side of the gurney with one hand to keep from falling as she was dragged along.

Two arms wrapped around Kim from behind.

One hand grabbed Brian's wrist; the other grasped Kim's shirt.

The fabric was wrenched from his grip.

Kim let go of the gurney as she was jerked back against an instantly familiar body. *Jess.*

Unthinking, Kim turned within the circle of Jess's arms.

Scared silvery-blue eyes met hers.

"You okay?" Jess asked.

Not sure if she really was okay, but aware enough to know Jess needed to do her job, Kim nodded. From the look on Jess's face, she wasn't going anywhere until she made sure Kim was all right.

"I'm good," Kim finally managed. "Go."

Jess hesitated for just a second, then turned and sprinted down the hall in hot pursuit of the gurney carrying Brian.

A hand landing on her shoulder made Kim jump. She turned to find Penny standing behind her.

"Are you all righ—" Penny's gaze dropped to Kim's chest and she gulped heavily.

Glancing down, Kim spied the lurid red stain that saturated her blouse directly over her heart. Now aware of the blood, the cold, clammy feel of it against her skin made her stomach roil.

Kim bolted for the nearest restroom.

The door to Jess's office flew open with enough force to slam it against the wall.

Kim jumped, fumbling to keep from dropping the journal she had been trying to read.

Jess blew into the room.

She paused long enough to kick the door shut, then stormed over to her desk.

"Damn it." Jess struggled to free herself from her lab coat. Her anger made her movements jerky and uncoordinated. Once free of the coat, she balled it up and threw it on her desk. "What a fucking waste."

Whoa. Kim had never seen Jess so openly emotional. A sinking feeling filled the pit of her stomach. *She doesn't realize I'm here.* She couldn't help but dread Jess's reaction to being observed unaware. Kim knew how important Jess's need to feel in control emotionally was to her.

"Hey, Jess."

Jess spun around. Her glare pinned Kim in place on the couch. "What are you still doing here?"

Flinching at Jess's harsh tone, she quickly stood. "I waited to see how Brian was doing." That was the truth—just not the whole truth. Seeing a patient, even one she had only seen a few times in group, bloody and broken like that had shaken her up. However, a large part of Kim wanted—no, needed to be with Jess. Just being in the same room with Jess gave her a sense of comfort and safety she had never experienced with anyone else. *Well, you ruined any possibility of that happening now.* Knowing how Jess must feel about her having witnessed her loss of control, Kim had no doubt that her presence was not welcome at the moment. "I'm sorry. I'll go."

Like a balloon losing its air, Jess deflated. She made her way over to the couch. "No. Wait." Jess sat down on the couch, then reached up and tentatively clasped Kim's hand. "Please."

Kim allowed herself to be tugged down to sit next to Jess. She smiled when Jess didn't let go of her hand. That was one of the things that had changed between them. They each seemed to find any excuse to touch the other—however casually.

"I'm sorry. You startled me." Jess blew out a breath. "But that's no excuse." She ducked her head. "You're welcome to be in this office any time you want. I hope you know that."

Kim used just the tips of her fingers to urge Jess's head up. "You don't have to hide your feelings from me, Jess. Everyone gets angry. You want to talk about what made you mad?"

Jess shook her head. "It's just work ..." Her eyes widened suddenly. "Um, what patient were you waiting to find out about? It wasn't the one in the hall was it? Who had a hold of you?"

"Yes, that's Brian. He was in one of my therapy groups a couple of months ago."

"Oh," Jess said.

A trickle of dread crept down Kim's spine at the look on Jess's face.

Jess took hold of Kim's other hand. She cradled both of Kim's hands within hers. "I'm so sorry."

No. It can't be. Jess's expression made it clear that it was, but Kim needed to hear it out loud. Her throat constricted. She struggled to force the words out. "He's dead?"

Jess nodded. "Yes. I'm sorry."

Kim's stomach churned. *God, no. It's not fair. He's just a boy.* She leaned forward over their joined hands. When Jess pulled her hands free and wrapped her arms around her, Kim sank into Jess's embrace.

Jess gently stroked her back.

The strong beat of Jess's heart under her ear soothed Kim. She soaked in the comfort of Jess's strong arms wrapped securely around her for several long moments while she regained her composure. Although it was the last thing she wanted to do, she knew she should break the embrace. They were at work and anyone could walk in. She forced herself to ease out of the warmth of Jess's arms.

"Better now?" Jess asked quietly.

"Yeah. Sorry."

"No reason to be sorry. It's tough to lose a patient." Jess took one of Kim's hands in hers. She rubbed her thumb over the back of Kim's hand.

"It's just so hard to believe. He was confused, but he was talking and ..." Kim shook her head. "What happened?"

"It's like that sometimes with head trauma. After having a second seizure, he arrested." Jess's shoulders slumped. "I couldn't get him back."

Oh Jess. "I know you did everything you could."

"It wasn't enough." Anger flared across Jess's face. "He was just a kid."

"I know. I'm sorry." Kim took Jess's other hand in hers and gave them both a strong squeeze.

Jess pulled away, clearly uncomfortable with even that small show of sympathy. "Let's get out of here." She stood and walked over to her desk.

Kim followed in her wake. Now she understood Jess's earlier outburst. Her anger was a shield to protect her against more painful emotions. Anger was a safe emotion to feel. She longed to pull Jess into her arms and soothe away her hurt. *If only you would let me.*

Their eyes met over Jess's crumpled lab coat.

A blush stained Jess's cheeks. She gathered up the rumpled coat and tossed it over the back of her desk chair. Jess turned back toward Kim and her eyes dropped to the scrub shirt Kim was wearing. Jess's eyebrow arched. "I didn't damage your shirt, did I?"

"No." Looking down at her shirt, Kim shuddered. She swore she could still feel the blood on her skin although she had scrubbed herself raw in the locker room. "It had blood on it. I tossed it in the trash."

Jess's eyebrows shot up. "Where did you get ...?" Realization dawned. "Oh. Right."

Kim rubbed her hand over the spot on her chest where the blood had been. She tried to push away the memory of the lurid stain on her shirt.

A glance at her watch made Jess frown.

Looking at her own watch, Kim mirrored her expression. "Are you going to be able to make it to pick up Thor?" While Kim knew that Thor stayed at doggie daycare three days a week, she didn't know their hours or exactly where the kennel was located.

"No. They close in twenty minutes." Jess shuffled together some of the scattered papers on her desk. "I hate for him to have to stay again." She sighed. "But it's better than him being home alone for hours on end. I'll give them a call and let them know I'll get him first thing tomorrow morning." A halfhearted smile appeared. "At least tomorrow is Saturday."

"I'm so ready for the weekend," Kim said. After the hectic week in the ER and then what happened with Brian, she was more than ready for a break. *God, Brian.* Ambushed by the vivid memory of Brian's bloody, mangled face, Kim's eyes started to sting. *Shit.* She turned her back on Jess. *Get hold of yourself.*

Jess was around the desk before Kim finished the thought. She stepped close. Without a word, her hand began to move up and down Kim's back in slow, comforting strokes.

Looking up, Kim gazed into caring blue eyes. Touched by the warmth and understanding in Jess's gaze, she felt a single tear slide down her face.

Using her thumb, Jess gently wiped away the tear. "Let me take you home."

Conflicting emotions pulled at Kim. On one hand,

she didn't want Jess to think she was helpless or weak. On the other, she craved the comfort Jess offered. She couldn't bear the thought of going home alone to her empty condo. A second gentle stroke of Jess's thumb across her cheek made the decision for her. Leaning into the touch, she stared into Jess's eyes for just a moment, then nodded. "Thank you."

The ringing of the phone made them both jump.

Growling under her breath, Jess moved to answer the phone. "Dr. McKenna." Jess listened, her scowl growing. "I already talked to her—" She rubbed the back of her neck. "Fine. Put her in the main conference room. I'll be there shortly." Jess smacked the desk with her palm after hanging up the phone.

"What's wrong?" Kim asked.

Jess started as if she had forgotten Kim was there. She tugged at the bottom of her scrub shirt. "The police detective wants to talk to me. I spoke to her after," Jess hesitated, then continued, "after Brian. I told her I don't know anything. Now she's insisting on talking to me about the father."

Kim blanched. "God. I was so upset about Brian, I didn't even think about his father's condition. He's not ..." She couldn't bring herself to say it.

"He was in bad shape, but still alive when he left the ER. Craig Peterson, one of our trauma surgeons took him straight to the OR." Jess picked up her lab coat and smoothed it out before pulling it on. She checked her pockets and then straightened some papers on her desk.

"I guess you should get going. The detective is waiting," Kim said.

Shoving her hands into her pockets, Jess looked up. "Yeah. I'm sorry about this. I'll be as quick as I can, then I'll take you home."

Hearing the weariness in Jess's voice made Kim

take a closer look at her. She had been so caught up in her own emotions she hadn't realized until now just how tired and stressed Jess looked. Guilt washed over Kim. *This isn't just about you. Jess not only took care of his dad, but Brian as well and had to pronounce him. God.* "I have a better idea. Why don't you go talk to the detective and I'll head out and pick us up something to eat on the way home? When you get done, come on over and we'll eat and share a bottle of wine." Kim moved over close to Jess. "We could both use a break. What do you say?"

"I don't mind—"

Kim reached up and placed a finger on Jess's lips to stop any further protest. "I appreciate that. Let me do this. It will help take my mind off—things. Unless you're too tired?"

Jess shook her head. "Are you sure?"

"Positive."

Some of the tension seemed to ease from around Jess's eyes. "Okay. You're right. I could use a break too. I better go meet with the detective." She walked to the door, then turned back to face Kim. "I'll be over as soon as I can." She pulled open the door and was about to step out, then stopped. "Damn."

"What is it?" Kim asked.

Jess walked back to her desk and tugged open the center drawer. She pulled a business card from inside. "I hate to ask this, but could you call the kennel and let them know I won't be picking up Thor tonight?" She held out the card to Kim. "Please tell them I'll pick him up first thing tomorrow."

"Sure. I'd be glad—"

Jess's pager shrilled. She glanced down at the display and grimaced. "Looks like the detective is getting restless. I better go." Jess stopped in the doorway. "Thanks for calling the kennel, and I'll be at your place as soon as I can." Jess seemed reluctant to leave.

"Go," Kim said.

Jess offered a half-salute, then turned and hurried down the hallway.

Kim picked up the phone and dialed the kennel. That Jess was trusting her with this meant a lot.

CHAPTER 22

" Hey, Jess. Come on in." Kim stepped back to allow Jess inside.

Some of the day's tension melted away at the warm, welcoming smile on Kim's face. It never ceased to amaze Jess how a simple smile from Kim could have such an effect on her. Kim's damp hair made it apparent that she had not only had time to change but to shower as well.

"Sorry for holding up your dinner. Traffic was a mess with the rain." The storm that had been threatening all day had finally let loose just as Jess left the hospital.

"Don't worry about it. I'm just glad you got here safe and sound." Kim led her to an already set table. "Let's eat." She quickly pulled the food containers from the oven and poured the wine.

Companionable silence held as both women concentrated on the meal.

As Jess pushed her chair back from the table, a contented sigh escaped her lips. "Thanks. That hit the spot." This was the first meal she had shared with Kim at her condo. Most of the time they went out to eat. Any other time spent together was at Jess's home because of Thor. Kim's complex did not allow pets—not even visiting ones.

"Hardly a gourmet meal, just some takeout Chinese." Kim smiled from across the table. "But you're welcome nonetheless."

The lack of conversation during dinner had been a relief. It gave her a little time to decompress before she had to face telling Kim about Brian's father. She was not looking forward to once again being the bearer of bad news. It was hard enough at work dealing with a patient's family when delivering distressing news. At least with strangers she was able to keep an emotional distance. She didn't seem to be able to close off her feelings anymore where Kim was concerned. And if she was honest with herself—she didn't want to.

"Ready to tell me now?" Kim asked, startling Jess out of her thoughts.

Ah, shit. Jess found it disconcerting just how good Kim had become at reading her. She briefly considered dissembling. A single glance at Kim's open expression promptly quashed that idea. Still, Jess wasn't quite ready to face the inevitable. Picking up her wine glass, she asked, "Could I have a refill?"

Kim opened her mouth, then closed it. She rose from her chair and took Jess's glass from her hand. "Sure." A few steps took Kim into the kitchen area.

Jess gathered up the cardboard containers that held the remains of their dinner.

After refilling Jess's glass, Kim held it out to her. She motioned with her free hand toward the living room. "Have a seat. I'll take care of this."

"Thanks," Jess said as she accepted her wine. She set the glass on the table. "You got dinner. Least I can do is help you clean up."

"That's okay. Relax. It'll just take me a minute to toss these plates in the dishwasher." Kim set the plates on the kitchen counter before turning back to Jess. "Besides, my kitchen isn't meant for two people."

A glance over at the narrow kitchen bracketed by a stove and sink on one side and a refrigerator and cabinets on the other confirmed Kim's contention. Jess smiled. "Okay. I see your point."

A gust of wind rattled the glass patio door.

"Storm is really picking up," Jess said.

"Yeah, it's getting cold and damp in here." Kim shivered. She scrubbed her hands up and down her goose bump covered arms.

Jess's gaze followed the path of Kim's hands and inadvertently grazed her chest. The sight of Kim's taut nipples poking through her T-shirt momentarily froze Jess in place. The chilly room suddenly seemed much warmer. She swallowed heavily. *God ... she's not wearing a bra.* She immediately berated herself for the thought. *You're here to comfort her, not ogle her.* Jess jerked her gaze back where it belonged. Thankfully, Kim did not seem to have noticed her wandering eyes.

"Tell you what you can do. Would you turn on the gas fireplace? There's a wall switch next to the sliding glass door," Kim said.

Looking across the room at the fireplace tucked in the corner, Jess was easily able to spot the switch in question. "Sure." Kim's condo consisted of a large room that encompassed the living room, dining nook, and kitchen. Although Jess had never seen either room, she knew the short hallway off the living room led to a bedroom and a bath.

"That's the only thing I don't like about this place," Kim said as she finished cleaning up the remnants of their dinner. "A single electric wall heater is the only other source of heat besides the fireplace." Kim laughed. "And you know me—I hate being cold."

Jess snorted as she flipped the switch. "No kidding." The flames leaped to life. The way Kim reacted to the cool, rainy December weather you would have thought she was the native Californian—not Jess. She walked back toward Kim. "I don't know how you ever survived Michigan."

Kim looked up and her expression darkened for just a moment. "I don't know how I did either."

It was not lost on Jess that Kim wasn't referring to the weather. Two quick steps brought her to Kim's side. She gave Kim's shoulder an understanding squeeze. "Come on." Jess picked up both their wine glasses. "Let's go warm up by the fire."

A smile reappeared on Kim's face.

Together they moved toward the fireplace.

Kim detoured to grab two large couch cushions off the back of the couch. She laid them on the carpet in front of the fireplace. Sinking down to the floor, she stretched out on her side and used the cushion to support her upper body.

Jess smiled down at Kim. She handed Kim her wine glass, then carefully set her own glass down on the narrow fireplace hearth. Jess lay down opposite Kim, using the second cushion.

"Ah, this is more like it," Kim said. A contented sigh left her lips as her eyes slid closed.

Jess allowed herself the guilty pleasure of letting her gaze roam Kim's beautiful profile. Barely resisting the urge to reach out and touch, Jess rolled onto her stomach and faced the fire. She blew out a breath as the serenity of the moment washed away some of the stress of her day. *I needed this.* Normally after a day like today, Jess would have worked out until she was ready to drop. *This is so much better.* Surprise rippled through her that the thought of another person being the source of her sense of comfort did not scare her as it would have in the past. *But then, Kim isn't like anyone I've ever known.* That thought in and of itself was oddly soothing.

A comfortable silence prevailed as they enjoyed their wine. The fireplace, while small, put out a relaxing heat.

The peaceful interlude was broken when Kim audibly blew out a breath.

Jess rolled onto her side and faced Kim.

"I hate to even bring this up ... but it's not going to go away by ignoring it." Kim tugged at her ponytail. "What happened with the detective? How about Brian's dad—was there any news about him?"

It was Jess's turn to sigh. She really did not want to have this conversation. "The detective wanted to clear up some things so she could close the case. Once I was able to convince her I didn't have anything to add, that was the end of it." *Tell her the rest and get it over with.* "I spoke to Craig Peterson before I left and asked about the father." Jess raked her hand through her hair.

By the look on Kim's face, she knew what was coming.

Jess forced herself to say the words anyway. "He never made it off the table. I'm sorry."

Kim's expression crumbled. "My God. It's all just so hard to believe. First, Brian, now this." Tears sprang into her eyes. "Their whole family gone in six months."

Jess tried to make sense of what Kim was saying. Her confusion must have shown on her face.

"That's why Brian was in my group. He was having trouble dealing with his mother's death." A smattering of tears leaked out. "I only saw him for a couple of sessions before Dr. Kapoor took over, but I thought I was getting through to him."

"I'm sure you did everything you could."

Looking away, Kim focused her gaze on the fireplace log. "Not enough," she said, sorrow evident in her tone.

A sense of helplessness flowed over Jess in the face of Kim's pain. Not knowing what to say to make her feel better, Jess offered comfort the only way she could. She wrapped Kim in her arms and drew her against her chest in a body-hugging embrace. The feel of Kim trembling made her heart ache. She placed a lingering kiss on Kim's forehead.

Kim raised her head. Tears glistened on her cheeks.

Wanting nothing more than to ease her pain, Jess began to kiss away Kim's tears. She feathered her cheeks with touches as soft as a butterfly's. A soft whimper from Kim drew Jess's gaze to her mouth. Jess's insides clenched at the sight of the parted, inviting lips. Without a thought to the consequences, Jess pressed her lips to Kim's.

Surging forward, Kim tried to deepen the contact.

A groan was wrenched from deep in Jess's chest. Her tongue slipped out to lick Kim's bottom lip, silently urging her to open to her.

When Kim's lips opened and readily accepted her inside, Jess moaned into her mouth. *So soft. So sweet.*

The need for air finally caused them to part.

With Kim's lips no longer on hers, Jess's passion-hazed thought process began to clear. Reality hit like a dash of cold water in the face. *What the hell's the matter with you? You can't do this.*

Jess started to pull away only to be stopped by Kim's hand clutching at her shirt, trying to draw her close again.

"No. Don't. Don't stop," Kim said.

Their gazes locked.

Long repressed need and yearning burned in the depths of Kim's brilliant blue eyes. The sight struck Jess like a physical blow. Her body thrummed. She moved forward, then stopped, her lips scant inches from Kim's. A small part of her resisted still. *There's no going back after this.*

"Please," Kim whispered, her breath brushing Jess's lips. "I need this ..." She guided Jess's hand to her breast. "I need you."

Jess's heart answered the call. Her resistance was blown away like a wisp of smoke on the wind. She dipped her head and reclaimed Kim's lips.

Electricity sizzled between them as long restrained passions flared.

Kim clung to Jess as if trying to merge their bodies into one.

"Easy." Jess pressed forward, and guided Kim onto her back.

A throaty groan of protest tumbled from Kim's lips when Jess removed her hand from her breast.

"I'll take care of you," Jess whispered into Kim's ear. She tasted the skin of Kim's neck before making her way down to the hollow of her throat. She placed a kiss on the delicate spot, feeling the thump of Kim's pulse beneath her lips.

As she moved back to Kim's lips, her hand slid down to pull Kim's T-shirt from her sweats. Warm, soft skin met her fingers. Jess slid her hand up and gently caressed the underside of Kim's bare breast.

Kim whimpered and clutched at Jess's arm.

Pulling herself away from Kim's sweet mouth was an exercise in willpower. Jess moved down, needing to see what she was touching. Her breath caught. *So perfect.* She reverently stroked the soft, pliant flesh in her hand, then leaned down to lave the enticing nipple with her tongue.

Kim's hand came up and cupped the back of Jess's head, urging her closer to her breast.

When Jess took the now rock-hard nipple into her mouth and began to suckle, Kim's back arched.

"Yes. Just like that." Kim moaned.

Alternating between each breast, Jess lavished them with equal attention. Her arousal soared. She had wanted this for so long. Being able to touch Kim's silken skin and caress her beautiful body was beyond anything Jess had dared imagine. An insistent inner voice intruded. *But what are you going to do when she wants to make love to you?*

Jess ruthlessly thrust the thought aside, banishing it from her mind. Nothing was going to spoil this moment with Kim.

Leaving Kim's breasts, she shifted to lay claim to her mouth once again. When she felt the press of Kim's tongue against her lips, Jess groaned. She opened willingly for the welcome invader. Their tongues wrestled together in an erotic dance.

Panting for air, Jess pulled back. She met Kim's gaze and fell into eyes gone indigo with arousal. Keeping her gaze locked with Kim's, Jess slid her hand down Kim's firm abdomen and into her sweats. She fondled the baby soft skin of Kim's lower belly before moving down to her heat. *Oh, God.* Jess moaned as her fingers slipped into the soaking wet folds waiting for her. Her own hips jerked against Kim's side. Jess fought the rising tide. This wasn't about her.

Kim hissed through her teeth. "Yes." Her hips bucked sharply.

Jess's fingers dipped low, then back up, drawing the abundant moisture with her. She used just the tip of her fingers to stroke across Kim's engorged clit, matching her rhythm to the rocking of Kim's hips. She savored the sight of Kim's impending climax. "So beautiful," Jess whispered.

Kim's eyes slammed shut and an inarticulate cry was torn from her throat. Her back arched as she released. With her climax came the tears, pouring down her face in a torrent.

Oh, sweetheart. After gently removing her fingers from their warm haven, Jess drew Kim against her chest.

Kim pressed her face into Jess's breasts. She wrapped her arm around Jess's back and clung to her.

Jess placed a tender kiss on the crown of Kim's head. "Shh ... it's okay. I've got you." While Jess still felt a bit helpless in the face of Kim's tears, she knew the powerful physical and emotional release was what Kim needed. She ran her hand up and down Kim's back in languid strokes. "Let it all out."

Slowly Kim's tears trailed off and she relaxed against Jess's body.

Jess continued to gently rub Kim's back. It took her a few minutes to realize Kim had fallen asleep. She debated with herself the wisdom of waking her up and sending her to bed. *The hell with that.* She reveled in the feeling of Kim nestled in her arms. She wasn't about to give that up any sooner than she had to. Jess shifted them into a more comfortable position.

Kim murmured in her sleep and snuggled closer but didn't wake.

Jess closed her eyes but knew she wouldn't fall asleep. She was never able to sleep with anyone touching her. *I just want to enjoy this for a little while longer, then I'll wake her up.*

CHAPTER 23

Sunlight streamed through a gap in the blinds and made Kim squeeze her eyes shut. Not completely awake, she rolled over to escape the piercing light. A sharp pain in her lower back brought her to full alertness. *Ugh.* She sat up and rubbed her hands over her face. *I'm getting too old to fall asleep on the floor.*

Looking around the room, Kim only took a moment to register several things. It was no longer night, and the wine glasses had been removed from the hearth. What pierced her heart was the realization that Jess had left without waking her.

What did you expect? You know damn well how hesitant Jess is to get romantically involved. Kim drew her knees up to her chest. *Damn it. Why did you do that? If you'd just been patient for once in your life you could've had it all: a friend and a lover.* She wrapped her arms around her legs and buried her face in her upraised knees. *But no, you had to throw yourself at her. Of course she's gone. She didn't want to face you after you forced her into having pity sex. And then sobbed in her arms like a baby.* Crushing regret overwhelmed her. *You've ruined the best friendship you ever had.*

A warm hand touching her back almost sent Kim into orbit.

It can't be.

Kim's head whipped up. *You didn't leave me.* Her relief was so intense it rendered her momentarily speechless.

"Hey, Kim. You okay?" Jess asked.

"Yeah. You just startled me."

"Sorry. Didn't mean to scare you. I had to use the bathroom." Jess offered her hand.

Kim clasped it and allowed Jess to pull her off the floor.

Face to face with Jess, she was suddenly tongue-tied. *Now what? Should I even mention what happened last night?* She ran her hands over her rumpled T-shirt and sweats. *I must look a mess.*

Jess's smile seemed a bit unsure. She cocked her head.

The gesture reminded Kim of Thor when he was trying to figure something out. That thought brought a smile to her face. *Relax. Just let things happen in their own time.*

"How about I make us some breakfast?" Kim said.

"Oh. Sorry," Jess said. Her smile disappeared. "I can't—"

Kim's insecurities roared back. *I should've realized. She just stayed to be polite.* "That's okay. No problem. I've taken enough of your time. I won't hold you up any longer." She turned away, intent on heading to the front door to let Jess out.

Jess's hand on her arm stopped her. "You didn't let me finish," she said. "I'd like to stay, but I need to go pick up Thor. On the weekends, the kennel is open from seven to nine in the morning, then not again until the afternoon. If I don't go get him now, I won't be able to pick him up until five o'clock."

God, Kim. Get hold of yourself. Don't jump to conclusions. Jess doesn't seem to be freaking out. She put aside the astonishment that observation caused for later contemplation. "I understand. Go pick up the big guy," Kim said, her fears temporarily laid to rest. She turned once more and walked to the front door.

Jess followed in her wake. She grabbed her jacket

off the back of a dining room chair and shrugged into it. "Looks like it's going to be a nice day, now that the rain has stopped." Jess cleared her throat. "I was wondering … um. Would you like to go out to lunch later?"

See, have a little faith. "Sure. Where did you want to go?"

"I was thinking of our favorite Mexican place since they have an outdoor patio."

"Why outside?" Kim wasn't thrilled with the idea of eating outside. Even though the sun was out, it was still cool and damp.

"Well." Jess shifted and looked at her feet. "I was hoping you wouldn't mind if I brought Thor along. I don't want to leave him home alone so soon after he's been at the kennel overnight."

You are such a big softie. Kim was pleased when Jess showed her softhearted side. It was such a contrast to her tough-as-nails work persona. That Jess was comfortable enough to let her see what Kim felt was the real Jess McKenna meant a lot to her.

She grasped Jess's hand and gave it a firm squeeze. "Of course I don't mind. Bring Thor. You know I love the big guy."

When Jess looked up, her vivid blue eyes were filled with warmth.

"What time do you want to meet at the restaurant?" Kim asked.

"Thor and I will pick you up at noon?" It sounded more like question than a statement. Jess peered at her from under half-lidded eyes. "If that would be okay?"

Kim studied Jess for just a moment, intrigued by her body language. *What's this?* Jess looked almost— shy. She quickly thought of how Jess had worded her invitation to lunch and now the offer to pick her up.

Oh … is she asking me on a date? They normally went

to restaurants and other places in separate vehicles.

Only one way to be sure. "I'd love to go out on a date with you and Thor. I'll be waiting for you at noon."

The dazzling smile that blazed across Jess's face assured Kim that she had been right. *A date with Jess.* Even after what they had shared last night, the thought was both thrilling and scary.

"Maybe after lunch, we could go for a walk, then back to my place ... for a movie or something?" Jess asked, with a bit of an uncharacteristic stammer.

Wow. She's inviting me to her house? Even after what happened last night? Kim wondered what all this meant for their relationship. *Worry about that later.*

"That would be great." She glanced at the clock in the kitchen. *Damn.* "You better get going."

Jess raked a hand through her hair. "Yeah."

Kim flipped open the dead bolt and put her hand on the doorknob.

"Kim." Jess stepped close, but didn't touch her.

Something in Jess's voice caught Kim's attention. She met Jess's gaze and froze.

Jess's eyes had turned silvery-blue. She moved forward, closing the distance between them.

Oh, yes. Please.

Jess's lips brushed hers in a soft, tender kiss.

Kim leaned into the kiss. Relief mingled with pleasure. She hadn't messed up things between them after all.

"I'll see you later," Jess whispered, her voice gone husky. She started to move away, then swept back in for a second kiss.

Arousal washed over Kim like a wave at high tide.

When Jess attempted to deepen the kiss, she eagerly opened for her.

Jess's tongue slid into her mouth.

Kim groaned deep in her chest. She clutched at

Jess's jacket as her knees turned weak.

Strong arms wrapped around Kim and pulled her close.

Everything ceased to exist for Kim—except Jess. The feel of her body pressed against the length of hers, Jess's scent filling her senses, the press of her tongue in Kim's mouth.

Panting, Jess pulled back from the torrid kiss.

Kim whimpered. *My God.* She had kissed her share of women but had never experienced anything so powerful.

Jess pressed her forehead against Kim's. Her breath hitched in her chest. "Wow," she muttered.

Kim's heart soared with the knowledge that Jess had been just as affected by the kiss.

"I better go," Jess said. She didn't sound very thrilled with the idea.

The last thing Kim wanted was for Jess to leave. *If she doesn't pick up Thor now, she'll feel guilty later and so will you.*

"Go get our boy and I'll see you both in a little while," Kim said.

A brilliant smile made Jess's face glow. She looked as if she was considering kissing Kim again. With a rough shake of her head, she apparently thought better of it.

Although disappointed, Kim knew it was for the best. Her body was still thrumming with arousal. One more kiss and she would drag Jess off to her bed.

"Okay. Later," Jess said before slipping out the door.

It wasn't until the door closed behind Jess that Kim realized what she had said. *Our boy.* Kim shook her head. *Oh boy!*

Jess pulled into a parking spot outside Kim's condo complex but made no move to get out of her SUV. "I can do this." She wiped her sweaty palms on her pants. "It's just like all the other times I've been out with Kim. We've been going out together for months." Even as Jess said it, she knew it wasn't true.

Last night had changed everything.

Now that she had touched Kim so intimately, she could not hide the depth of what she felt—from herself or Kim.

Add to that the shock she had gotten this morning when she woke up with Kim in her arms. She had tried to write it off as both of them being overstressed and tired. After all, they had slept on the floor. Then she remembered Halloween. *You claimed that time it was too much pizza and beer. There's more to it than that and you know it.*

Jess sighed. The thought of spending the night with Kim wrapped in her arms was an appealing one. It was not something she had wanted to do with either of her exes. Both had complained about her rarely spending the night and never cuddling up to sleep when she did. *But Kim's different. You've known that for a while.*

Despite her lingering fears about how she was going to react when Kim took control and wanted to make love to her, Jess was determined to make this relationship work. She had already stepped well outside her comfort zone a number of times where Kim was concerned. *She's worth it.*

"Okay. Enough of this." She looked into the back seat. "Time for me to go pick up our date."

Thor's tail thumped against the seat.

Jess reached for the bouquet of flowers lying on the passenger seat. She picked them up, set them back down, then picked them up again. Shaking her head, she blew out a breath. "Make up your damn mind."

The flowers had seemed like a good idea, but now she wasn't sure. "She's already your friend. You don't have to impress her."

Turning slightly, she held up the flowers to Thor. "What do you think? Take them?"

Thor yawned.

"You're no help." Jess laughed. "Great, I really am losing it. Now I'm asking a dog for advice." She shook her head. What she really wanted was for Kim to feel special. *Flowers it is, then.*

She took a moment to make sure at least two of the windows where cracked open for Thor. Her mind made up, Jess climbed out of the truck, flowers in hand. She leaned back inside and met Thor's eyes. "I'll be right back. Thor. Stay. Watch," she said before closing the door.

A fire blazed in the fireplace. The logs crackled and popped. Kim sighed when warmth crept back into her chilled limbs. The morning sunshine had given way to clouds. Another storm loomed on the horizon.

Kim kicked off her shoes. She pulled her legs up onto the couch and tucked them under her. She had grown quite comfortable in Jess's home.

Thor was stretched out in front of the fire like a huge furry rug.

"Hot chocolate as promised," Jess said, returning from the kitchen. "Hope you like it with marshmallows."

Looking up, she smiled. "Yes, I do. Thanks." She accepted the mug Jess offered.

Jess settled onto the couch next to her.

I could get used to this.

A sense of contentment filled Kim as she sipped her chocolate.

It had been a very long time since a woman made her feel as special as Jess had today.

It still amazed her that she had not realized Jess had feelings for her beyond friendship until recently. Maybe it was because she still did not trust her own judgment after Anna, who was admittedly the last in a long line of mistakes. Or maybe it was the fact that Jess was so good at hiding her feelings.

Either way, Kim was very glad that things had turned out the way they did. She had a wonderful friendship with Jess that could only make their growing relationship stronger. With the deepening of her relationship with Jess old fears had surfaced, but Kim refused to give in to them. *Not everyone you let yourself care about will lie to you. This time will be different. I know it will.*

Kim turned sideways so she was facing Jess. Her knees pressed against Jess's thigh. "I can't believe it's almost Christmas. Less than three weeks to go." She bounced a little in place. "Are you going to put up a tree?"

Jess's gaze darted away from Kim for a moment. "Since I work on Christmas, I don't put up a tree."

"So you've always covered on Christmas Eve and Christmas Day?" Kim had been dismayed to find out that Jess planned to work back to back twelve-hour shifts. She had hoped they could spend at least part of the holiday together.

"I always volunteered to work the holidays when I was an attending. Now that I'm head of the department, I feel if I provide a good example, it will encourage other single doctors to do the same. I know most people celebrate the holidays but I've always believed that staff with young children should get Christmas Day off. Same with the residents. The ones with children get excused from the duty schedule—if at all possible."

Ernest blue eyes met Kim's. "This is the first year I've ever wished I didn't have to work."

Kim fought to hide her surprise. *I can't believe you admitted that to me.* "I wish we could spend the holidays together, but I understand." She rubbed her hand over Jess's shoulder. "I think it's a wonderful thing you're doing. Christmas is such a special time for families, especially those with young kids."

Jess's face went dark. With a shake of her head, Jess's expression cleared. "Thank you for understanding."

That wasn't a happy memory. Does her family give her a hard time?

"Do you celebrate beforehand with Sam?" Kim knew that Jess was going to San Diego tomorrow to go Christmas shopping with her sister.

"Oh yeah. We celebrate. Sam wouldn't have it any other way." Jess laughed. "She loves Christmas. But we usually don't get together until the weekend after Christmas." An indulgent smile spread across Jess's face. "I'm sure she already has a tree up and her apartment decorated."

"So does she go home to your family on Christmas Day?" Kim asked.

"No. Sam volunteers to work both days of the holiday as well. She feels the same way I do about that."

"How about you? I didn't see a tree at your place either." Jess's brows furrowed. "Or have you changed your mind about going home for Christmas?"

Her mother had called and tried to guilt her in to coming home. One Christmas with her mother shoving eligible men at her every chance she got had been enough to remind Kim why she never went home for the holidays. Even if it meant spending Christmas alone, she would not go back to Michigan.

"No. Definitely not," Kim said, unable to keep the bitter tone from her voice. That wasn't the only reason she wouldn't go home for Christmas. She refused to let her mother taint what were some of the best memories of her father. Despite the painful emotions thinking of him stirred, his love of Christmas and everything associated with it was something she had chosen to keep alive.

Kim laughed, trying to lighten the mood. "Fair warning. I'm with the 'you have to have a tree for it to really feel like Christmas' camp." *Come on, ask her.* "I've been meaning to ask you if you'd be interested in going with me to pick one out."

Jess smiled. "Sure. I'd like that. It would be fun."

Go all the way. Ask her for what you really want but have been too chicken to ask. "And decorate it ... if you wanted."

"Really?" Jess's eyes sparkled and her face lit up.

So maybe it isn't just Sam who loves Christmas. I don't know just how, but I'm going to make this special for you. "Of course. How can Santa bring you presents without a tree to put them under?"

Jess grinned. "Now you sound like Sam."

"Well, then obviously, she's a very smart woman." Kim laughed.

"Um ..." Jess lowered her gaze. She picked at the seam of a couch cushion before finally looking up. "Would you like to meet her sometime?"

Kim's jaw dropped. *This is huge.* She had wondered if Jess would ever feel comfortable enough to introduce her to Sam. It wasn't hard to see how nervous Jess was about making the invitation. *Help her out.*

"I'd like to meet your sister." She put her hand on Jess's leg. "Whenever you're ready."

"She wants to meet you too," Jess said.

She's talked to her sister about me? It had not occurred to Kim that Jess would talk about her. Other than the fact that Sam was a police officer, up until today Jess had told her next to nothing about her sister. *What has she told her? About Memorial? Or just that we're friends?*

When the muscles under her hand tensed, Kim was pulled out of her musings. She looked down at her hand, surprised to find herself stroking Jess's thigh.

She started to pull away only to be stopped by Jess sliding her own hand over and entwining their fingers.

Passion-darkened silvery-blue eyes met hers.

Arousal shot through Kim at the look of want on Jess's face. Kim leaned forward to claim Jess's lips.

Jess met her halfway.

Her tongue slid into Jess's mouth. *Mm, I could kiss her all day.*

The kiss deepened as Jess's tongue wrestled with hers.

Breathlessly, they broke apart.

Kim pressed her forehead against Jess's collarbone. "You are such a good kisser," she said, trying to catch her breath.

"You're not so bad yourself."

"Not so bad." Kim lifted her head to mock scowl at Jess. "What kind of compliment is that?"

"A not so bad one?" Jess laughed.

She poked Jess in the side. "I'll show you not so bad."

A little half smirk twisted Jess's lips.

Kim swooped in and captured Jess's lips in a searing kiss.

She smiled into the kiss when Jess moaned. *Oh yeah. Much better.* Kim rose up on her knees and pressed their breasts together. Her long held yearning to touch Jess would no longer be denied.

Jess's arms wrapped around her waist.

Using her dominant position, she pressed Jess back on the couch as she continued to kiss her hungrily.

Kim groaned into the kiss when she settled firmly on top of Jess.

The warm, pliant softness of Jess's body turned to stone underneath her.

Jess wrenched her mouth away from the kiss.

Her heart pounded in her chest.

She pushed the oppressive weight off her chest and sprang off the couch.

Once free, it only took a second for Jess's brain to catch up with her wayward body.

No. Not with Kim.

Kim's stunned face looked up at her from the couch. She pushed herself back into a sitting position.

A red wave of anger flowed over Jess. Her fists clenched to her sides, she moved away from the couch.

Goddammit! One day. One day and you've already fucked it up. The reaction had become ingrained over the years. At this point, it was purely instinctive. It had nothing to do with Kim. *You shouldn't be in this relationship. Kim deserves better than you.*

Kim gently touched her arm. "Jess. Are you okay?"

Jess jumped. She was so intent on beating herself up, she hadn't noticed Kim approach.

Her anger drained away. She forced herself to meet Kim's gaze. Shame weighted her shoulders. "Yeah. Sorry."

Jess could see the questions in Kim's eyes but she didn't have any answers for her. At least not any she was willing to give. *You have to tell her something. She's a smart woman. And don't forget a psychiatrist. A damn good one.*

She offered her hand and waited for Kim to take it, then entwined their fingers. "Would you sit back down with me?"

Kim nodded. She sat down next to Jess on the couch.

Blowing out a breath, Jess tried to come up with something to say. "I'm sorry about that. You caught me by surprise. Um ... I don't like to be on my back."

Kim's eyebrows shot up. She started to say something, then seemed to reconsider. She took a deep breath. "I'm sorry I did something that made you uncomfortable." Kim squeezed her hands. "Would you like to talk about it?"

"No. There's nothing to talk about." The lie tasted bitter in her mouth.

"All right, Jess." Kim pulled her hands back and clasped them together in her lap.

Shit. Shit. Shit.

Jess knifed her fingers through her hair. "Listen, would you mind if we skipped the movie tonight?" Feeling exposed and vulnerable, Jess didn't think she could deal with Kim in her bed tonight—no matter how innocently. "I was thinking it might be better if I went ahead and drove down to San Diego tonight. It would give Sam and me more time in the stores tomorrow."

Coward.

"Whatever you want." Kim hesitated. "Would you prefer I called a cab?"

What? Pain stabbed her heart that Kim would think her capable of doing something so low. "God no. Of course I don't want you to call a cab. I'll take you home."

Unsure of her reception, Jess reached out tentatively. Her hand trembled. When Kim didn't pull away, she gently cupped her cheek. She stroked Kim's face with her thumb.

Kim offered a timid smile.

Jess made a slow approach, giving Kim plenty of time to refuse the kiss. She sighed as their lips gently brushed.

"I'm so sorry," Jess whispered.

She kissed Kim again, both of them sighing into the contact.

Jess pulled back and looked deeply into Kim's soft blue eyes. "Are we okay?" she asked, her voice trembling.

"Always." Kim sealed her declaration with a gentle kiss.

CHAPTER 24

Kim walked toward the nurses' station, chart in hand. She needed to complete Mrs. Ingram's discharge summary.

Penny smiled brightly at her as she approached. "Hi, Dr. Donovan."

Nodding distractedly, Kim set the chart on the counter. She flipped it open and began to work on her discharge note.

"Finished with your case?"

Obviously not, since I'm working on the chart. "Not quite." *I should've gone into the staff lounge or Jess's office.* While Penny tended to try and chat Kim up whenever she got a chance, she had been particularly persistent this morning. Kim didn't have the mental energy to fend her off today. *Don't take your anxiety and insecurities out on her.*

But there was a reason Kim had chosen to work at the nurses' station. She didn't want to take a chance of missing Jess—if she ever showed up. She glanced up from the chart and scanned the surrounding area— again. *Where the heck is she?*

Kim had not seen or spoken to Jess since their date on Saturday. In retrospect, she should have realized that Jess's need for emotional control would transfer over into her intimate encounters. But at the time, Kim had not been thinking at all.

After the incident on Jess's couch, a myriad of questions had swirled through her mind over the remainder of the weekend. The big unanswered question was what or rather who had hurt Jess so deeply. None of the answers she came up with were pleasant ones. Panic had been clearly evident on Jess's face when she bolted from the couch. Jess's need to be in control obviously stemmed from a trauma much deeper than a bad breakup.

Now, on their first day back at work, Jess was nowhere to be found. Not finding Jess in her office when she arrived, Kim had asked Penny if she had seen her. Apparently Jess had been in the department before she arrived and then left. Penny didn't know where she had gone, only that Dr. Franklin was covering for her. Jess was frequently absent from the department for meetings, but as far as Kim knew she had nothing scheduled for this morning. The longer Jess was absent from the ER, the more Kim's anxiety escalated. *Did she change shifts so she didn't have to work with me?* Memories of Anna floated through her mind. She bit her lip when an even worse possibility occurred to her. *Has she changed her mind about us?*

Kim was brought back to the here and now when someone stepped close, well into her personal space. Hope flared for an instant, then vanished. Without looking, she knew it wasn't Jess. The tingling sensation on the nape of her neck that always signaled Jess's presence was missing. She stepped to the side, away from whoever it was. She turned to find Penny.

"Hey, Dr. Donovan," Penny said with an exuberant smile. "Didn't mean to startle you."

Penny was still standing too close for Kim's comfort. She moved back a step. "What can I do for you, Penny?" she asked, making sure to keep her tone and manner professional.

The smile on Penny's face faltered a bit. "Could I talk to you?" Her gazed darted around the nurses' station. "Alone."

A warning bell sounded loud and clear. *Now what?* She had a feeling whatever Penny wanted she wasn't going to like it. Kim now realized her repeated excuses to avoid accepting Penny's off-hand invitations to lunch had been a mistake. As was her hope that Penny would get over what seemed like a school girl crush. She should have just told her, thanks, but no thanks, right from the start.

"Sure. Why don't we go into the lounge?" No way was she going to be alone with Penny in Jess's office. She really did not want to alienate the woman. Penny was an integral part of the smooth running of the ER, and Kim was sure Penny could make her life miserable if she put her mind to it.

"Great," Penny said, an expectant smile on her face. "Come on." She reached for Kim's hand.

Shit! Acting as if she had not seen the gesture, Kim snapped her fingers and then spun back toward the counter. "Forgot my chart." She grabbed the chart off the counter and hugged it to her chest like a shield.

Penny held open the door to the lounge for Kim.

Looking around as she stepped inside, Kim was disappointed to find the lounge empty. *Time to face the music.* "What did you want to talk to me about?" She walked over to the couch that rested against the back wall. Kim intentionally bypassed the round table in the center of the room. The chairs could be pulled too close together. She sat down on one end of the couch and placed her chart on the center cushion. Her hand rested on the chart to keep Penny from moving it.

Penny looked down at the chart and hesitated. With a sigh, she moved to sit down on the opposite end of the couch. She tugged at her pants, then the bottom of her knit shirt. Her hands twisted together in her lap.

An uncomfortable silence filled the space between them.

Kim was more convinced than ever that Penny was trying to work up the nerve to ask her out. *Let's get this over with.* "Penny?" She was already preparing herself for what to say to let Penny down gently.

Penny's gaze darted toward the door, then back to Kim. She took a deep breath. "My BFF scored tickets to the Bed Heads." She grinned, peering at Kim expectantly as if waiting for an excited reaction.

Who or what the hell are the Bed Heads? "That's nice," Kim said with all the enthusiasm she could muster. Which wasn't much.

Penny's expression fell. "You don't like them?"

"Honestly, I have no idea who they are."

"Oh." Penny looked at Kim for just a moment as if she was seeing her in a different light. She shook her head. "Well, I know you'd love them. They are just the bomb. And Beba's voice is so ..." A dreamy expression filled Penny's face.

BFF? The bomb? What adult talks like that? This was not how Penny talked when conducting ER business.

Kim shifted on the couch, drawing Penny's attention back to her.

"Anyway, my girl's boss wouldn't let her off on Saturday." Penny scowled, then her expression brightened and she smiled. "Would you go to the concert with me? We'll have a blast."

Keep it simple and concise. "Thank you, but no," Kim said.

"No?" Penny echoed.

Kim shook her head. "No, thanks."

Penny's shoulders slumped. "Oh ... okay. I guess it is last minute. I should have asked you sooner."

Wouldn't have mattered a bit, but you don't need to

know that. The tight knot in Kim's stomach started to ease. *That wasn't so bad.* "I should get back to work." Kim reached for her chart.

"Wait!" Penny slid across the couch. Her progress was stopped when her knee hit the chart on the cushion between them.

Kim removed her hand from the chart and crossed her arms over her chest. She didn't want to give Penny an opening to try and take her hand again. *I knew that was too easy.* She sighed.

"Are you free next weekend? How about dinner?" Penny's eyes lit up. "Afterward, we can go clubbing."

Kim glanced toward the door. Normally, the staff lounge was a busy place. Today, of course, had to be the exception. *No help for it. Just get it over with. You tell people things they don't want to hear every day.* Problem was, she knew Penny well enough by now to know that no matter what she said it was not going to be well received.

"I appreciate you putting yourself out there to ask. But my answer is still no."

"But I thought ..." Penny flushed. "You're not gay?"

"Yes. I'm a lesbian."

Penny flinched at the word lesbian. Her gaze darted away from Kim for just a moment before returning to hesitantly meet her eyes.

Kim was curious about the strange reaction but remained focused on the issue at hand. She chose her words carefully. While she didn't want to hurt Penny, she didn't want her to continue to ask her out either. "I respect the job you do here in the ER. I think we work well together. But I'm not interested in anything else. I'd prefer to keep our interactions on a professional level."

Tears filled Penny's eyes. She sprang from the couch and bolted for the door.

Ah, damn. Kim stood but resisted the urge to call her back and try to comfort her. She knew it would just make things worse.

The door to the lounge swung open just as Penny reached it.

Unable to stop her forward momentum, Penny plowed into the person coming through the door.

Bates grabbed her biceps to keep them both from falling. "Watch where the hell you're going," he snarled.

Penny wrenched away from him and ran out the door.

"Stupid cow," Bates said. He started when he spotted Kim, then smiled. He stepped into the room and let the door swing shut behind him. "Hey, Kim."

Kim gritted her teeth. Although she knew she should call him on using her first name without her permission, she decided to ignore him. After the confrontation with Penny and continued worry about the situation with Jess, she was not up to dealing with Bates at the moment. She moved toward the door. "Excuse me. I've got work to do."

Bates remained in place, effectively blocking the only exit.

Great. Just when I thought this day couldn't get any worse.

"What's got Penny's panties in a twist?" A speculative look filled his face, and then he laughed. "You finally tell her you're not a freaking queer like her?"

His words landed like a spark on dry tinder. Kim's temper flared. "Dr. Bates—"

"It's okay, Kim." Bates smirked. "I knew all along it was just a ruse to keep a bunch of loser guys from pestering you." His eyes swept down her body. "You're way too gorgeous to be a dyke."

The flare burst into flames, rendering Kim momentarily speechless. Her hands clenched at her sides.

Bates slithered closer. "Don't worry. It'll be our secret." He tried to touch her face.

Kim batted his hand away. It took every ounce of her professional training to mask her blazing anger. She had to handle this calmly. An emotional outburst would put her in the wrong. "Do not ever touch me again," she said in a flat, ice-cold voice that would have done Jess proud.

Bates backpedaled. His retreat was stopped by the wall next to the lounge door. He raised his hands beseechingly. "Come on, Kim. Don't be like that—"

"Stop right there." *This ends here and now.* "First: You will address me as Dr. Donovan."

Bates's face turned red and he started to interrupt.

Kim cut him off. "Quiet. Second: I am not your friend, nor am I interested in dating you. Not now—" she pinned him with a hard stare, "not—ever. Don't ask me again. If you persist, I will file a comp—"

The lounge door started to swing open.

Terrell slid to a halt. His gaze bounced between Kim and Bates.

Bates hissed. "Get lost, Terry."

Terrell shot Bates a sharp look. He pushed the door open fully and blocked it from swinging shut with his foot. "Dr. Donovan?"

Great, an audience. Just what I don't need. She spared a glance at Bates. He looked like he was about to rupture something. *Okay, maybe a strategic exit wouldn't be such a bad idea. He definitely got the point.*

"What can I do for you, Dr. Johnson?" Kim asked, dropping the icy tone she had used with Bates.

"I've got a patient I could really use your help with if you're not busy."

"Sure. I'd be more than happy to help you. Lead the way," Kim said.

Without so much as a glance at Bates, she followed Terrell. As Kim stepped through the door, she heard Bates mutter something under his breath. She was glad she had not heard him clearly because she would not have been able to let it go if it was something derogatory. Which she knew more than likely it was.

Terrell led the way toward the back of the ER department. He stopped in the hallway just down from Jess's office.

Kim quirked an eyebrow. "What's going on? Where's your patient?" There were no patient rooms back here.

"I just …" Terrell shuffled his feet. He dug the tip of his shoe into the linoleum and refused to meet Kim's gaze. He looked like a little boy who knew he was in trouble. "I lied. There isn't any patient."

More curious than angry, Kim asked, "Why did you do that?" Even as she asked, Kim realized why—Bates. *He was trying to rescue me.*

"It's just … I know how Peter can be," Terrell said, his gaze firmly locked on his shoes.

"You didn't need to do that." Kim lightly touched the sleeve of Terrell's crisp white lab coat.

He looked up and finally met her gaze.

"While I appreciate what you were trying to do, I can handle Dr. Bates. Please don't interfere."

"I know. I just really like you a lot," Terrell said in a rush. His gaze darted away with the admission. "And—"

Although his blush was hidden by his dark complexion, Kim had no doubt it was there. *God. What is this—ask Kim out day?* She had never suspected Terrell was attracted to her. Unlike how she had dealt with Bates, Kim wanted to let Terrell down gently. "Thank you, but I'm really not interested in—"

"No. I wasn't." Terrell started to stammer. "I mean you're beautiful and everything, but I'm not ...." He scrubbed his hands over his face as if trying to wash away his embarrassment. "I'll just shut up now."

Kim's face went hot. *That's what you get for assuming. You know better.* "No. I'm sorry. I misunderstood. Go ahead, tell me what you wanted to say."

Terrell blew out a breath. His dark-eyed gaze settled firmly on Kim. "I've learned so much from you. I don't want you to stop working in the ER because Peter is such a jackass. That's why I butted in when I shouldn't have. Sorry."

"Don't worry. I'm not going anywhere. I like working in the ER. As far as Dr. Bates goes, let me take care of the situation. Okay?" She smiled, trying to ease both their discomfiture.

Terrell returned the smile. "Okay. I better get back to work."

"Me too." *And please let the rest of the day be quiet. I've had quite enough drama for one day.*

Kim turned to follow him when the sound of footsteps behind her drew her attention. She glanced over her shoulder. A wave of relief washed over her at the sight of Jess opening her office door.

"Go ahead. I'll see you later," Kim said.

As soon as he was out of sight, she headed for Jess's office.

Kim's hand hovered over the door knob. Her insecurities gripped her once again. *Just go in. You've done it plenty of times before.* Still, she hesitated. She settled for knocking before she opened the door.

Kim stuck her head into the office. "Hi."

Jess was already halfway out of her chair. What

Kim thought of as Jess's ER mask was already firmly in place on her face.

"Hey, Kim." Jess plopped back down into her chair with a grunt. Her mask dropped and she allowed Kim to see the stressed woman underneath.

Recrimination stung Kim. *Instead of giving in to your own insecurities, you should have been more worried about Jess and given her the benefit of the doubt. Everything is not about you.* Anxieties forgotten, Kim moved over to stand next to Jess's chair. "Are you okay?"

Jess rubbed her temples. "Long morning. And I've got a killer headache." She opened her desk drawer and pulled out a bottle of aspirin. Popping the cap, she tossed two into her mouth and swallowed them dry.

Kim grimaced. "How can you stand to do that?"

"Lots of practice." Jess went back to rubbing her temples.

"I missed you this morning." It was as close as Kim could come to admitting her earlier anxiety.

Jess looked up. She offered a tired smile. "Believe me, I would have much rather been here with you instead of the GME meeting I was stuck in."

Surprise rippled through Kim. The Graduate Medical Education Committee met quarterly. The next meeting wasn't supposed to be until next month. Procedural and program specific problems could wait for the next meeting. If the committee was meeting outside its normal schedule, something serious must have occurred concerning one of the residents.

"It wasn't an ER resident, was it?" Kim asked. She knew Jess couldn't get into specifics, but worried that a wayward resident could be a black eye for her program.

"No. Thank God." Jess rubbed her neck.

Kim moved behind Jess's chair. Wanting to help, but taking into account Jess's need for both emotional and physical control, Kim held her hands just above Jess's shoulders. "This okay?"

"Yes. Please." Jess whimpered as Kim began to knead her shoulders.

The muscles under Kim's hands were rock hard. She increased the pressure of her massage.

"Oh. Yes." Jess's head dropped forward and she moaned, long and low.

The sound shot through Kim's body. Arousal pulsed insistently.

The ringing of the phone on Jess's desk made them both jump.

The noise acted like dash of a cold water on Kim's libido and reminded her just where they were. She let her hands drop and stepped away from Jess's chair. She propped her hip against the edge of Jess's desk.

"Thank you," Jess said before picking up the phone. Her voice was soft and warm. Jess sat up straight in her chair. "This is Dr. McKenna."

In the fleeting seconds between picking up the phone and answering it, all trace of the previous warmth in Jess's voice was gone. The ER chief was back.

Jess's jaw tensed almost immediately. Whatever was being said was not good news.

"Just like that she left? Without waiting for a replacement?" Jess's hand went back to her temple. "Did anyone in the department examine her?" She blew out a breath. "Contact Mrs. Gotti, and let her know what's happened and that we need coverage at the nurses' station ...Thanks."

Kim's stomach sank. She had a bad feeling about this. Was her already rotten day about to get worse? *Please don't let this be about Penny.*

"What's going on?" Kim asked. Mrs. Gotti was the nurse-manager responsible for the nurses and ER clerks.

Jess started as if she had forgotten Kim was there. The mask dropped once again, and Kim looked down into Jess's face, seeing the tight stress lines around her eyes. "That was Henry."

Damn, it is about Penny. Henry was one of the ER clerks that worked at the admission desk.

"He was at the nurses' station dropping off patient intakes. Penny came up to him and said 'I'm sick, cover the desk.' According to Henry, she already had her purse in her hand and her coat on. And looked like she had been crying." Jess shook her head. "I don't know whether to be worried or angry. This isn't like her. She's always been very reliable. She should have at least let one of the doctors check her out."

This is really going to add to her already crappy day ... and mine. You have to tell her what happened.

"I did this. It's all my fault," Kim said before her brain had a chance to censor her mouth. *Smooth, really smooth. That made total sense. And you talk to people for a living. Shit.*

Jess blinked several times. Her brow furrowed. "What?"

Needing some distance, Kim moved to sit in the chair in front of Jess's desk. "Penny taking off is my fault. She asked me out a little while ago, and I turned her down—twice." Kim sighed. "I tried to be as gentle as I could, but she didn't take it very well. I'm sorry. I know you don't need the extra hassle, especially today." She clasped her hands in her lap. Guilt tugged her gaze down. The last thing she wanted was to add to Jess's stress or burdens at work.

"That's bull and you know it," Jess said.

Kim's head whipped up.

Jess's eyes had turned silvery and sparked with emotion. "You, of all people, know that you aren't responsible for another person's behavior. This is

Penny's doing—not yours."

"But if I had handled her better—"

"No." Jess's hand slashed sideways in negation. "Remember, I've worked with Penny much longer than you have. I'm well aware of her strengths ... and her weaknesses. Don't worry about it. I'll talk to her tomorrow."

Then Penny will feel that I talked about her behind her back. And it wasn't like that. This is going to make things worse. "Jess. I don't think—"

Jess held up her hand, stopping her. "I won't mention you telling me about her asking you out. It would just make things worse."

Took the words right out of my mouth. Jess was right. She wasn't thinking clearly about the whole situation. "Which one of us is the psychiatrist again?" Kim asked, her tone light and teasing.

Jess laughed. She rose from her chair and came around the desk to perch on the edge next to Kim's chair. "I could never do what you do every day. But I do have lots of practice handling ER personnel."

"And you're very good at it." *And at reading me apparently.*

"Thank you, ma'am," Jess said and gave a little bow, making Kim laugh. "Seriously, Penny's not the first staff member to run out of the ER because they had their feelings hurt. I appreciate you telling me so I wasn't worried all day that she was really sick."

Stuffing her hands into her lab coat pockets, Jess stood. A shy smile graced her face. "I um." She shuffled her feet. "I missed you on Sunday."

With those simple words, the tension and anxiety that had plagued Kim all morning vanished as if they had never existed at all.

CHAPTER 25

Jess's head jerked up when her office door flew open.

Kim, dressed in blue scrubs and paper slippers, marched into the office. Sparing Jess a single glance, she headed straight for the couch. She dropped the plastic bag in her hand on the floor and flopped face-first onto the couch. She muttered something ominous-sounding into the cushion.

Oh. This is not good. Jess walked over to the couch. When she looked down at Kim's scrub-covered back, she noticed Kim wasn't wearing a bra. She winced. *Got her underwear too.*

The sight of Kim coming out of the exam room was one Jess would not soon forget. Kim had been in the direct line of fire when the activated charcoal a patient had been given made an explosive exit, along with the rest of his stomach's contents. Her shirt had taken the brunt of the nasty black slurry, but it had run down over her pants and into her shoes.

"Kim?"

"She's not here. She quit."

"You don't mean that." Jess nudged Kim's hip. "Scoot over."

Grumbling under her breath, Kim rolled onto her side and made room for Jess. "I hate Bates."

As Jess joined her on the couch, she bit the inside of her cheek to keep a straight face.

Kim glared.

Oops. Remember how well she reads you. Apparently, Kim was not in the frame of mind to see any humor in the situation. Of course, it didn't help matters any that the culprit had been Bates. After Kim laid down the law to him on Monday, he appeared to have given up on his infatuation. In fact, he had been conspicuously avoiding Kim—until this. Had it been anyone else, Kim would probably have laughed it off.

She took a chance and gently stroked Kim's arm. "I'm sure he didn't do it on purpose. ER doctors just have a finely developed 'anti-puke' reflex."

"I've dodged my share of puke." Kim growled. "You weren't there. I hadn't even greeted the patient yet. I had just walked up to the gurney. Bates didn't say a word. He just smirked as he stepped behind me. Then—bam."

Kim smacked her open palm against the couch cushion. "He could've warned me. He knew what was coming." Her eyes narrowed. "I just know that little snake did."

Jess looked down into blue eyes that seemed to glow from within. *Whoa. I've never seen her so pissed.*

Now is not the time to suggest again that she wear a lab coat. After the last insult Kim's clothes had taken, Jess had asked her why she insisted on not wearing a lab coat. According to Kim, it intimidated her patients and made them less likely to confide in her.

Hoping to soothe her ruffled feathers, Jess stroked Kim's silky curls. "I'm sorry."

Kim leaned into the touch and sighed. "It's not your fault. But I still hate Bates."

Ah. I know. "I could assign him a bunch of really nasty, smelly patients if you want."

A smile ghosted across Kim's face, gone as quickly as it had appeared.

That's better.

Kim huffed. "Don't tempt me." She dropped her arm over her eyes with an exaggerated sigh. "Is it Friday yet?"

"I wish," Jess said. "Only one more day to go."

It had been a hellish week in the ER. The situation with a wayward surgical resident had turned into a public relations fiasco. The press had been running loose in the hospital all week, wreaking havoc. Jess had been so tied up with the GMEC and the continuing repercussions of the incident, as well as the upcoming quarterly ER budget, that she and Kim had not managed dinner together even once all week. *We could both use a break.*

Jess smiled. "I know just what you need."

Kim lifted her arm and peered at Jess. "A stiff drink."

"Well, that's a possibility too. But I was thinking more along the lines of a glass of wine." Jess arched an eyebrow at Kim's somewhat dubious expression. "Okay, maybe two glasses of wine and a nice dinner." Kim still didn't look completely convinced. "Ah ... did I forget to mention, a back massage and a long soak in a bubbling Jacuzzi to go along with it."

"That sounds heavenly, especially a good long soak." Kim tilted her head to the side. "You have a Jacuzzi tub?"

"I sure do." Jess had avoided taking Kim outside and showing her around the back deck, where the tub was located. *'Cause you couldn't deal with the thought of her in a swimsuit ... but now.* Jess grinned. "A big one with lots of jets. Guaranteed to fix what ails you. It's heavenly." *Or it will be when I'm in it with you.*

"You've got a date." Kim sat up and placed a soft kiss on Jess's lips. "And thank you."

"More wine?" Jess held up the bottle of Merlot.

"Maybe just a little," Kim said. This was the first time Kim had been at Jess's since the incident on her couch the previous Saturday. She had worried that things would be awkward, but that had not been the case. After sharing a quiet dinner, they had crashed on the couch to relax while the spa heated.

Jess poured while trying to stifle a yawn.

"Are you sure you still feel like getting in the spa?" When Jess had mentioned it at work, Kim had envisioned a Jacuzzi bathtub. She had been amazed earlier when Jess took her outside onto the back deck for the first time. There, tucked in a corner and surrounded by slatted privacy fencing, was a large hot tub.

Jess glanced at the clock on the mantle. "Absolutely. Should be up to temperature by now." She had turned the spa on before dinner.

The ringing of the phone pierced the air.

Jess picked up the portable from the table. She looked at the screen, then tossed the phone back onto the table. "Harold is the most persistent of the jackals. I'll give him that."

Several reporters had begun calling Jess when her membership on the GME committee became known. Watching Jess have to deal with them at work had been bad enough. Thankfully, so far none of them had tried to ambush her at home.

"What a mess," Kim said. "Who would have thought a single punch in a bar would lead to all of this." Although Dr. Woods had made a mistake, her heart went out to him. A mental shiver shook her. She pressed her arm against her stomach. *This could have been you.* Had the wrong person gotten wind of her situation at Memorial, she could have had her life and career shredded by the media. The truth would not have mattered.

Jess snorted. "Tell me about it. These reporters are driving everyone to distraction. And the negative press is killing LA Metro." She shook her head. "All because some bozo captured the punch on his cell phone and decided to seek his fifteen minutes of fame. It was that damn reporter." Her hand stiffened on her wine glass. "Once he found out Woods was a doctor, he couldn't wait to splash some sensational bullshit all over the media." Jess took a healthy drink of her wine. "I can still see that video clip and damn headline. 'Violent doctors in our hospitals. Could your loved one be next?' Christ."

Kim set down her wine and moved closer to Jess. She started a gentle massage of her neck. Jess whimpered, and Kim increased the pressure.

Blowing out a breath, Jess pulled away. "I'm supposed to be giving you a back rub." She grimaced. "Sorry. I'm not doing a very good job of taking care of you."

You always find a reason not to let me comfort you for long. Who made you think you don't deserve to be comforted? "You're doing just fine." Kim placed a soft kiss on Jess's lips but made sure to keep her hands to herself. "Now how about that soak you promised?"

Jess smiled. "You got it." She jumped off the couch and offered Kim her hand.

She allowed Jess to pull her off the couch.

Anticipation and nervousness rippled through Kim. The thought of Jess in a bathing suit made her head swim and other parts of her body leap to life. The nervousness sprang from the expectation of just how this evening might end. As much as she wanted to be Jess's lover, she didn't want to make another mistake and ruin their first time together. Not knowing what other landmines might await in an intimate encounter with Jess was nerve-racking. *Just remember to let her make the first move.*

Shit. Something else occurred to her. "Oh. Wait, Jess. I wasn't thinking. I don't have a suit."

A familiar little half smirk made an appearance on

Jess's face.

Kim would have given her next month's pay to know exactly what Jess was thinking.

"Not a problem." Jess grinned. A sparkle lit her eyes.

God. Is she going to suggest we go naked? Kim wasn't sure her heart could take it. And she sure as hell wouldn't be able to manage to keep her hands to herself.

Jess started to speak, then seemed to change her mind about what she had been about to say.

Kim didn't know whether she should be relieved or disappointed.

"I have a spare suit." Jess ran her gaze down, then slowly back up Kim's body.

Kim felt the look all the way to her core.

"It should fit you." Jess turned toward the hall. "Come with me."

I can only hope.

Jess pulled the bathroom door shut. *Coward.* When Kim said she didn't have a suit, Jess had almost suggested they both skip them, but she had chickened out. Then, when it came time to change, she had retreated into the bathroom. Seeing Kim naked in her bedroom was not something she was ready for just yet. Not that she didn't want to see her naked. She longed to make love to Kim. Her dreams were filled with the memories of that all too brief encounter in front of Kim's fireplace.

She started pulling off her clothes. *What are you going to do when Kim wants to make love to you?* And Jess knew that Kim would want to. In the past, Jess had been upfront with her lovers. She got her pleasure from touching them, not from them touching her. And both her exes had been willing to go along with that—at least for a while.

But things were different with Kim. Jess was ashamed to admit to her that she needed to be in control. But that wasn't all of it. *You want her to touch you.* That was the real crux of the matter. The thought of Kim touching her intimately filled her with longing—and apprehension.

Jess jerked her suit into place. *Enough of this. It's too late to go back now. And you don't really want to anyway.* That much was true. Kim already meant too much to Jess to not at least try. She just prayed she didn't disappoint her too deeply or worse yet, drive her away.

She opened the bathroom door and took a single step into the room, then froze.

Kim was standing next to the bed, dressed in a dark blue tank suit. It molded to her lush curves and full breasts like a second skin.

"You are absolutely stunning." The sound of Jess's own voice startled her and she flushed. She had not meant to say the words out loud.

A pleased smile graced Kim's face as she moved to stand near Jess. "Thank you." She appraised Jess's matching black suit. "So are you."

As Kim's gaze moved down her body, Jess felt it like a caress. Flustered, she blurted out the first thing she could think of. "Water should be nice and hot." *But not as hot as I am.* She was thankful she managed to keep that second part to herself.

Kim lifted darkened blue eyes and gazed at Jess. "Then we should jump in." Her eyes held a world of promise.

Dreams do come true.

Jess peeked at Kim through half-lidded eyes. She had urged Kim to try out the special lounge seat that was lined with jets. Kim's head was resting against the small pillow and her eyes were closed. In the muted lighting, Jess could only see a vague outline of her body under the water. But the sight of the tops of her breasts bobbing at the water line was enough to stir Jess's already simmering libido. She forced her gaze back to Kim's face. It was calm and smooth in repose.

I'm glad she's calm. This is killing me. She slid off the seat. Sinking farther down into the hot water, Jess tried to relax. She braced her feet in the corner to keep her head above water. It was no use. After seeing Kim in her swimsuit, every time she closed her eyes, her mind kept insisting on going back to that night at Kim's. Her eyes drifted shut. *Oh yeah* ...The feel of Kim's silky smooth skin. The taste of her nipples as they filled her mouth. The heat between Kim's thighs as her fingers—

"Jess?"

Jess yelped, startled out of her fantasy.

Her feet slipped and she went under.

She came back up sputtering.

"Are you okay?" Kim slid over next to her in the water and lightly touched her back. "I didn't mean to startle you."

Damn. Jess hoped like hell Kim mistook her flushed face for a reaction to being in the hot water. She slicked her hands over her wet hair, then tucked it behind her ears. "I'm okay. I must have been nodding off." *Better her think that than what I was really doing.*

"You want to get out?"

With Kim so close, Jess could not resist touching. She trailed her fingers through the droplets on Kim's upper arm. "I still owe you a back rub."

Kim edged closer, and their thighs pressed together beneath the water.

Their eyes met and held.

"Where do you want me?" Kim's voice held a rich throaty tone that sent shivers through Jess's body.

Underneath me. Jess bit her tongue to keep the words from tumbling out. She clenched her thighs together.

Kim whimpered as if she had actually heard the words.

It was too much for Jess. She surged forward, desperate to taste Kim's sweet lips. Her arms wrapped snugly around Kim's back.

As she thrust her tongue into Kim's mouth, she pressed forward and, just for a moment, forgot where she was.

That was all it took.

She felt them both start to slide on the polished acrylic surface.

Before she could catch her balance, they went under.

Jess came up sputtering for the second time that night. *Damn it. God. I've never been such a klutz with a woman.* Then again she had never wanted any woman as she did Kim. *Just relax before you kill her or yourself.*

Kim rose out of the water next to her and stood. Despite her dripping hair, she looked like a goddess.

Shoving her hair back from her face, Jess said, "I'm sorry."

Kim laughed and sat back down next to her. "Don't worry about it. It always seems so sexy in books when the characters make out in the hot tub." She wrung her hair out over her shoulder. "Guess that's creative writing for you."

I dunked her and she still tries to make me feel better. Jess smiled. "Why don't we adjourn to someplace," she shook her wet head like a dog, "drier."

"Hmm ..." Kim ran her fingers lightly up and down

Jess's arm. "Where did you have in mind?"

The words were out before Jess could even think of stopping them. "My bed."

After grabbing towels and quickly drying off, they didn't stop until they reached the side of Jess's bed.

Jess thought she saw a bit of hesitancy mixed in with the arousal in Kim's eyes. *How can you blame her after you flew off the couch when she kissed you.* Jess pushed away the memory. She refused to let anything spoil this moment between them.

She leaned forward and softly kissed Kim's neck. When Kim tilted her head, she smiled into the kiss. Trailing kisses down Kim's neck, she stopped to nip at her pulse point.

"God, Jess. Kiss me." Kim pressed closer and put her hands on Jess's towel-covered hips.

"I am."

Kim pulled her neck away from Jess's mouth. "Kiss me. Please."

Jess opened her stance and drew Kim against her body. She pressed her lips to Kim's and groaned when Kim opened to her.

She wasn't sure how long they stood by the bed and kissed. As wonderful as it was, she wanted more. After denying for so long that she could have this type of relationship with Kim, now that she could, she wanted it all. Her hands roamed restlessly up and down Kim's back. She broke away from Kim's mouth and kissed her way up to her ear. "I need to touch you. Please let me touch you?"

Kim took Jess's face between her palms. Her passion-dark eyes bore into Jess's. "Make love to me."

Her heart soared at the trust in Kim's gaze. Jess

reached for the towel wrapped around Kim and gently tugged it loose. It dropped to the floor, already forgotten.

Jess reached for the strap of Kim's suit, then hesitated. "May I?"

Kim nodded.

Slowly peeling the suit down Kim's body as if she was unwrapping a precious gift, Jess admired every inch of bared skin. She paused often along the way to brush her fingers over a tantalizing soft spot or along a tempting curve.

Kim's breath hitched with each feathery touch.

The suit joined the towel and Kim stepped out of it.

Jess softly ran her fingers down the midline of Kim's body. Kim arched into the touch. "You are exquisite," Jess said, her voice low and husky with arousal.

A beautiful flush worked its way down Kim's chest to her rosy nipples.

"Sit on the side of the bed for me?" Jess asked.

Kim sat down and looked up at Jess.

Jess pulled off her towel and let it fall to floor but kept on her suit. She dropped to her knees in front of Kim. "I've wanted this ... wanted you, for months," Jess said. She could see the surprise in Kim's eyes and smiled. "It's true." Laying warm hands on Kim's thighs, she began to stroke the silky-smooth skin.

Kim ran her fingers tenderly through Jess's hair. "I've wanted you too, Jess." She allowed Jess to spread her legs.

Jess's heart tripped double time at the sight of the treasure laid bare before her. She moved between Kim's legs. Her hands slid up and cupped full breasts. She ran her thumbs back and forth over the already taut nipples. *So beautiful.*

Kim leaned forward and pressed herself into Jess's hands, her pulse already skyrocketing.

This is heaven. Jess lavished Kim's breasts with

kisses before taking one of her nipples into her mouth and suckling.

"God." Kim put her hand on the back of Jess's head. She tugged Jess's hand off her other breast and pressed it between her legs.

Jess moaned at the slick heat that greeted her fingers. Stroking through the soaking wetness, she struggled to stave off her rising passions. Her own hips surged forward and pushed her hand more firmly against Kim.

Kim gasped and her pelvis began to rock.

Jess pulled back.

"Why did you stop?" Kim whimpered and tried to guide Jess's hand back between her legs.

She looked into Kim's wide pleading eyes. "I'll take care of you. I promise." Jess moved back a little more and urged Kim to spread her legs farther open.

"Let me taste you?" Jess asked. Her own thighs clenched at the very thought. "Please."

Kim's response was a throaty groan. Her hands gripped the comforter as if she was hanging on for dear life.

Using her thumbs, Jess opened Kim and then dipped her head for her first taste. *Perfect. Just perfect.* Kim's hips bucked in her face. Never ceasing her explorations, she used her forearms to press down on Kim's thighs. Kim was close. Jess could feel it in the pulsing of her clit against her tongue. She closed her lips around Kim's clit and gently sucked.

Kim let out an inarticulate cry and dropped backward onto the bed. Her climax struck a moment later. Her back arched bowstring tight for just a moment, then she slumped.

Jess continued to lick her gently until Kim's body went completely limp and the tension left her thighs. Her own arousal was beating an insistent pulse between her legs, but she refused to give in to it.

A soft warm smile graced Kim's flushed face when she finally lifted her head. She held out her hand to Jess. "Join me?"

Jess nodded. She stood and started to take Kim's hand, then hesitated. *Go the rest of the way. Don't be a coward and ruin things now.*

Kim's expression fell and she sat up.

This is Kim. You can do this. Jess smiled, trying to ease Kim's mind. Taking a deep breath, she reached for the straps of her suit. Hyperaware of Kim's gaze on her, she quickly pulled the suit off.

She joined Kim on the bed, and together they scooted into the middle. Jess lay on her back and opened her arms. Kim snuggled against her side and let out a long sigh.

Despite the renewed throb between her thighs at the feel of Kim's nude body pressed to hers, Jess was filled with a contentment she could not remember ever experiencing before.

After several minutes of contented bliss, Kim roused herself. Jess's hand stroking slowly up and down her back was lulling her to sleep.

Wouldn't do to fall asleep. Very déclassé. Especially after Jess got down on her knees and fairly worshiped you. It had been a unique experience. Never had a lover been so solicitous and careful with her. The look in Jess's eyes and her soft, tender touches had made Kim feel wanted down to her very soul.

Lifting up, Kim gazed down at Jess's beautiful face. Jess's eyes slowly opened. She smiled into silvery-blue eyes. Unable to resist, she leaned in and kissed Jess's soft lips.

Jess hummed into the kiss and opened to Kim.

Kim shifted closer as she pressed her tongue into Jess's mouth. The taste of herself on Jess's lips sent her arousal soaring. She put her hand on Jess's bare belly and started to slide her hand up.

Jess stiffened.

Damn. You know you can't treat her like your other lovers. Kim pulled back, breaking the kiss. She remained on her side but moved far enough away to break all body contact between them. "Sorry."

"No." Jess turned on her side and drew her knees up. She draped one arm across her breasts. "You didn't do anything wrong. I'm sorry. I ... I want you to touch me ... but ..." Jess glanced away. "I don't know if I can let you," she whispered.

Oh Jess. Seeing Jess, normally so confident, looking so unsure and vulnerable broke Kim's heart. *How can I fix this?* She wanted their first time together to be as special for Jess as Jess had made it for her.

That was when inspiration struck. Jess had given her the clue she needed when she made love to her. *I can give her this.* "It's okay, Jess."

Jess's gaze remained fixed on the comforter. "No. It isn't—"

Kim put her finger on Jess's lips. "Yes, it is." She stroked Jess's cheek. "Please look at me." It took a moment, but Jess finally looked up. Kim gazed deep into her eyes, willing Jess to believe her. "I understand. Whatever you need. It's okay. Trust me." She sat up and positioned herself so that she was on her knees near Jess, but not touching her.

"Sit up against the headboard for me. Please." She could read the confusion on Jess's face, but she did as Kim asked. "If you'll let me, I'd like to try something. If you get the least bit uncomfortable, I'll stop. Okay?"

Blowing out a breath, Jess nodded hesitantly.

Not a ringing endorsement, but she didn't say no. Kim moved closer until she was kneeling next to Jess. She sat back on her heels. Her thigh lightly touched Jess's hip. "Can I kiss you?"

This time the nod was not at all tentative. Jess smiled.

Keeping her hands on her own thighs, Kim leaned in and softly kissed Jess. She took her time, making sure just their lips touched at first. Then she trailed kisses down her neck and over her collarbone, never going lower than the upper swell of Jess's breasts.

It wasn't long before Jess started to respond. She captured Kim's lips in a deep kiss.

So far, so good. Kim could see the rapid beat at Jess's pulse point. "Feel good?"

"Yes. More," Jess said, in a breathy voice.

Kim picked up one of Jess's hands and put it over the top of hers. She gently placed her hand on one of Jess's breasts. Scooting closer, she said, "Show me what you like, how to touch you."

Jess groaned. She applied pressure to Kim's hand, guiding it. She pressed Kim's palm firmly to her breast and used it to knead the pliant globe. Then she used Kim's fingers to roll her nipple.

That's it. Show me. Kim smiled into Jess's eyes when her breath hitched. Kim brought up her other hand and began to caress the opposite breast the same way.

Soon Jess's eyes closed and her head went back. She removed her hand, leaving Kim's in place.

Kim placed kisses across Jess's breasts before going lower to take one of her taut nipples into her mouth. When her mouth made contact with Jess's nipple, Jess moaned loudly. Her hand came up to cup the back of Kim's head, pressing her into her breast.

She continued to pleasure Jess's breasts until she

felt Jess's hips begin to rock. Her own arousal was rising again, but she concentrated on Jess. She eased away from her breasts.

A desperate groan escaped Jess's lips. "Don't stop." She tried to urge Kim back to her breast.

"I'm not stopping. I promise." *That's it. Don't think about anything but how good you feel.*

Kim waited until Jess opened her eyes before going any further. She wanted to make sure Jess was seeing her. *I don't want anything to ruin this.* Holding out her hand to Jess, she was ecstatic when Jess eagerly took her hand. She linked their fingers together and slowly guided their entwined hands down Jess's abdomen. She bent forward and delicately licked Jess's ear. "Spread your legs for me, Jess."

Jess moaned, long and low. There was no hesitation. Her legs spread open.

Arousal skittered down Kim's spine. "Show me, Jess. Make me touch you," she said.

Jess's hips bucked as she guided Kim's fingers to stroke through her heat, working herself closer to release. She threw her head back, her eyes tightly clenched as she panted for breath.

Kim felt Jess start to tremble. She picked up the motion Jess had started, sliding her fingers faster over her throbbing clit. Kim could feel the increased tremors. She knew Jess was close.

"Come for me, Jess," Kim whispered, close to her ear.

"Oh my God, Kim!" Jess climaxed, her whole body going rigid. Her back arched off the bed.

When Jess finally went limp, Kim slid up next to her. She was dismayed to see tears trickling out from between Jess's tightly closed eyelids.

"Jess, what's wrong? Oh, sweetheart, did I hurt you?" *Please, tell me I didn't.* She placed soft kisses on

Jess's face.

Slowly Jess opened her eyes and looked at Kim.

"Did I hurt you?" Kim asked again. Jess looked more dazed than hurt. She took a chance and stroked Jess's belly in small comforting circles.

Jess covered Kim's hand and squeezed it. "No, you didn't hurt me. That was... that was... amazing." Jess still had a slightly glazed look in her eyes. "No one has ever done that for me before." She shook her head as if she could not quite believe what had happened.

Huh? "No one has ever brought you to climax?" Kim asked, still not quite sure she understood correctly. *That can't be true. Can it?*

"No. Never. Not by touching me. And when someone tried ..." Jess blushed. "I could never come."

Oh my God. Kim thought her heart would burst with the strength of her feelings. "Oh, Jess, thank you, sweetheart."

Jess rubbed her hands over her face as if to wipe away the blush. She finally met Kim's eyes. "What are you thanking me for? I should be thanking you."

Kim placed a soft kiss on Jess's lips. "For trusting me. For letting me pleasure you."

"You're welcome. It was my pleasure, believe me." Jess laughed.

It thrilled Kim beyond measure to hear Jess's easy laughter and see the shadows lifted from her eyes. She knew one night of lovemaking could never banish all the dark memories that plagued Jess, but they had made a good start—together.

CHAPTER 26

Jess drifted up from sleep. Something felt very strange, but she wasn't awake enough to figure it out. She opened her eyes to find her face buried in a mass of blond curls. *Kim.* She was spooned behind Kim, her arm draped over Kim's belly. Their naked bodies were pressed snugly together. She remembered them cuddling after they made love but not falling asleep. *This is getting to be a habit.* She couldn't get over the fact that she was able to sleep naked with Kim plastered against her. *She's the first one—ever.* Myra had complained bitterly, on the rare occasions Jess allowed her to stay, when Jess insisted on putting on her pajamas.

That's not the only thing Kim was first at. Images from last night paraded past her mind's eye. Kim was opening a whole new world for her. First, with her unwavering friendship, and now as her lover. Not only had Kim made her feel cherished, but safe, to the point where she had been able to let Kim touch her. Even more amazing was Kim bringing her to orgasm. Jess had long ago given up on that ever happening from a lover's touch. Kim had given her that and so much more. It had been an incredible experience. *And you want her to do it again.*

With the realization of just how deeply she had opened herself to Kim, Jess braced herself, waiting for fear to strike. She was determined to fight it.

It never came.

Jess's chest grew tight with the strength of the emotions Kim stirred in her. A sense of peace and contentment filled her. She stroked her hand along the curve of Kim's hip.

"Good morning," Kim said in a sleep-roughened voice. "Sleep well?"

Jess lifted up and kissed her temple, inhaling the scent of her hair. "Yes, I sure did … thanks to you."

Kim rolled over in Jess's arms and faced her. "So last night was really … okay?"

"More than okay." She kissed Kim, loving the feel of her soft lips under hers. "Much, much more than okay," Jess said, interspersing each word with a feather-light kiss. The feel of Kim's breasts against hers roused her desire. She wrapped her arm around Kim's back and drew her closer. As the kiss deepened, a moan was torn from her throat.

Jess started when Kim rolled onto her back and tried to take Jess with her. She braced an arm on the opposite side of Kim to keep her weight off of her.

Kim grumbled in protest. "I want to feel you on top of me."

A shiver of anticipation rippled through Jess. "Are you sure?"

Holding Jess's gaze, Kim said, "Very sure." She pushed the covers off, baring her body. "Come over here. Please," she said as her legs spread to make room for Jess.

Jess needed no further encouragement. The thought of Kim underneath her like that was sending her arousal into overdrive. She slid into position between Kim's thighs and settled on top of her. *Oh God.* Her hips jerked, pressing her belly against Kim's center.

They both groaned.

Jess lifted up, supporting her weight on her arms. She looked down into Kim's loving eyes. "Touch me."

Kim's eyes went wide. She brought her hands up slowly and cupped Jess's breasts.

Jess's hips bucked. "Yes. Just like that." She ducked down and took Kim's lips in a searing kiss. Kim's pelvis began to rock and Jess picked up the rhythm.

The blaring of an alarm clock shattered the moment.

Jess slumped down on top of Kim. *No. Not now.* She rolled off Kim with a frustrated growl and moved to the side of the bed. "I'm sorry," she said as she shut off the alarm. "I have an early meeting."

She looked back at Kim, all warm and soft and naked in her bed. Her libido flared anew. Unable to resist, she slid back over to Kim and kissed her. She pressed her tongue into Kim's mouth. When Kim's tongue entwined with hers, she moaned. "I want you so much."

"God. Jess. I want you too, but you have to go."

Jess pulled away from Kim and sat on the side of the bed. The rapid beating of her heart was matched by the insistent pulse between her thighs. *Work. Think about work.*

Kim moved to sit next to her. "I should get going too."

The thought of leaving Kim sleeping in her bed was strangely appealing. "It's early. Let me reset the alarm for you." Jess reached out and stroked a silky thigh. She lost herself in the vivid blue depths of Kim's eyes. She didn't realize how high her hand had gone until her fingers slipped into wet heat.

Kim grabbed her wrist. "God. We have to stop. Work ... shower ... late." She panted.

This was something Jess had never dealt with before, the need to control her libido. Blowing out a breath, she removed her fingers from their warm haven. It took every ounce of willpower she could muster to make herself stand and move away from Kim. "Right. I'll go grab a shower. Relax. You don't have to run off." She scrubbed her hands over her face and groaned.

"Shower, work, late," Jess muttered as she turned to walk away.

Kim flopped back onto the bed with a frustrated growl. She refused to watch Jess walk away. The temptation of seeing that firm ass flex was more than she could take.

Now that her brain was clearer, she was thrilled by how comfortable Jess had been this morning in allowing her to touch her, even encouraging her. *And very comfortable touching you.* The memory of the brief touch of Jess's fingers between her thighs sent her pulse higher.

Enough of that. You have to get through all day at work without touching her.

The thought of work gave Kim an idea. *Jess has been taking such good care of you, now it's your turn.* She got out of the bed and glanced around the room. She grabbed her shirt and pants from the night before and slipped them on.

She padded barefoot toward the kitchen.

When Thor spotted her, he jumped out of his bed and trotted over, tail wagging.

"Hey, there." Kim gave the big dog a warm hug. She managed to dodge a tongue in the mouth when he greeted her. "Come on. I'm going to make your mom some coffee and a bagel. You can show me where everything is."

Thor followed her into the kitchen but was no help whatsoever in pointing out where things were. Kim searched the kitchen for what she needed. She knew that she didn't have a lot of time.

She had the coffee brewing and the bagels in the toaster when Thor approached and bumped her arm. "What? No coffee or bagels for you."

He bumped her again and woofed.

Kim jumped. "I'm sorry. I don't know what you want."

Thor stared into her eyes as if he was trying to communicate what he wanted.

"Help me out here."

Thor took several steps away from Kim, then looked back over his shoulder.

Taking the hint, Kim followed him. He led her to the sliding glass door. She had seen Jess let him out this door previously. Hoping she was doing the right thing, Kim opened the door.

Thor woofed softly as if in thanks and trotted out onto the deck.

Kim followed him out onto the deck, her toes curled at the feel of the ice-cold wood under her bare feet.

He crossed the deck and went down a set of steps Kim had not noticed last night. The steps led to a small fenced area.

Satisfied that he was safe, she scampered back into the warm house.

In the process of putting the lid on Jess's travel mug, Kim's hands froze mid-turn. *Ah, shit.* Her gazed darted around the kitchen. She had been so focused on doing something nice for Jess, she had not stopped to think about how Jess would view it. *This is Jess's kitchen and you just took over.*

A subtle tingling of her senses alerted her to Jess's presence. She looked up to find Jess standing in the doorway of the kitchen with an unreadable expression on her face.

As Jess walked across the kitchen, Kim formulated and discarded apologies. *Sorry, didn't mean to play*

Susie homemaker. Sorry for invading your kitchen without asking. Sorry, I'm an idiot.

Jess stopped opposite her with the center island between them.

Kim was so caught up in trying to come up with an apology, it took her a moment to realize Jess wasn't looking at her face.

She looked down to see what had garnered Jess's attention. It wasn't her breakfast. She grinned and her knees went weak with relief. When she had grabbed her clothes, she had forgone her bra. What she hadn't realized was in her hurry to dress, she had left quite a few shirt buttons undone.

Jess's gaze was locked on her exposed cleavage. She chose that moment to finally look up.

Kim gulped. The desire in Jess's gaze sent a flood of warmth to her core. *Work. She has to go to work.* As much as Kim wanted to step around the counter that separated them and answer the call in Jess's eyes, she knew she couldn't. They would both regret it. Her earlier nervousness returned. "I know you don't have a lot of time. So, I made you some coffee and a bagel to take with you."

Jess blinked rapidly several times, then shook her head as if trying to clear it. She smiled. "You didn't have to do that. Thank you." She looked around the kitchen and her brow furrowed. "Thor's not in here with you?"

"I let him outside. I hope that was okay?" Kim asked.

A brilliant smile blazed across Jess's face.

Huh? Okay. I guess it was all right to let him out. But it's not that big a deal.

"He didn't give you a hard time about going out?"

"No. Actually, he kind of asked." She explained to Jess what had happened.

Jess's eyes sparkled with pleasure. "That's great." As if noticing Kim's confusion, she said, "He never listened to Myra ..." Her face contorted for just an instant. "My ex. She used to get furious with him. He wouldn't go out for her or even stay in the same room with her if I wasn't present." Her mouth twisted with chagrin. "Guess I should have trusted his judgment, instead of my own." Jess's expression turned serious. "He knows you belong here." The words were barely out of her mouth when she seemed to realize the significance of what she had said. A deep blush suffused her face.

Kim came around the counter to stand before Jess. She gently cupped her face. Meeting Jess's gaze, she let her own emotions show. "That makes me very happy to hear." And it wasn't just about Thor. This was the first time Jess had shared any details of her past.

"Me too," Jess whispered. She brushed her lips gently over Kim's, then pulled back. "I don't want to, but I have to get moving." She glanced at her watch. "I still need to feed Thor."

"I could do that. If you wanted," Kim said. Her heart sank a little at Jess's wide-eyed reaction. *That was pushing too much.*

"You would? You really wouldn't mind?" Jess asked, her amazement clear in her tone.

Oh ... that's it. Wow. Myra must have given her an incredibly hard time about Thor. "Of course, I don't mind. I love the big guy. You know that."

"Yeah. I do." Jess's smile returned. "Okay. His food is in that bin over there." She pointed to a large lidded bin. "The scoop is inside. He only gets one." Jess wagged her finger. "Don't let him convince you otherwise."

Kim laughed. "Only one scoop. Got it."

Another glance at her watch made Jess grimace. "Damn. Okay. I'm out of here." She snapped her fingers. "Oh wait." Turning on her heel, she scurried out of the room.

What is she doing?

Jess returned several moments later with Thor right behind her. "Here you go." She extended her closed fist.

Kim held out her hand. She stared in disbelief at the keys Jess placed in her hand. *She's giving me a set of keys.* Her more pragmatic side spoke up. *No way. She's going to want them back.*

"I really have to go. Please, make yourself at home." Jess scooped up her travel mug and the bagel. "Thank you again for this and for taking care of Thor." She gave Kim a quick kiss. "I'll see you later at work." Taking a moment, Jess patted Thor. "You be a good boy for Kim."

A quick wave and she was gone.

Kim stood where she was for several moments. A sense of elation washed over her that Jess felt at ease enough to leave her alone in her house. This was a big step for both of them. She had to admit, after all it had taken for them to get to this point, it was a much more comfortable morning-after than she would have imagined. Or that she had ever shared with anyone else.

Although she couldn't help being a little apprehensive with the responsibility Jess was entrusting her with. She looked down at Thor when he leaned against her. He met her gaze with calm confidence. She hugged him around the neck and got a kiss for her efforts. "Well, it's just you and me, big guy. How would you like some breakfast?"

Jess lengthened her strides as she neared the ER. The meeting had gone on longer than expected. She was anxious to get back to her ER. *And see Kim.* Just the thought of Kim made her heart feel light.

This morning had been surprising on many fronts. Seeing Kim ensconced in her kitchen had not bothered her in the least. *You were much more interested in her cleavage.* The thought brought a flush to her cheeks. But it was much more than that and Jess knew it. She had come to trust Kim during the months they had spent building a friendship. Being cared for felt amazing.

Wonder how she did with Thor? She had no doubt that Kim loved the big dog and was confident she would keep him safe. Unlike Myra, who had alternated between faking affection for him and barely tolerating his presence.

"Good morning, Dr. McKenna."

Jess's heart sped up at the sight of Kim standing at the nurses' station. *Face it. You are so gone on this woman.* She smiled. "Good morning, Dr. Donovan." She stopped at the counter, opposite Kim.

Penny peered at them from farther down the counter.

"I have that article I told you about in my office," Jess said. "If you're not too busy, why don't you come and get it." She could see the momentary confusion in Kim's eyes before she got it.

"Great. I've been looking forward to reading it." Kim walked out from behind the nurses' station and joined Jess. She turned back to Penny. "Penny. Psych will be down to pick up Mr. Gale. If they don't arrive within the next half an hour, please page me."

Penny grunted an acknowledgment.

Kim shook her head and then smiled at Jess. "Lead the way."

Neither spoke as they made their way to Jess's office.

Jess held open the door for Kim. "After you." She was being polite, but it was also nice to be able to enjoy the view without guilt.

As soon as the office door closed, she made her way over to Kim and enveloped her in her arms. "I missed you." She groaned at the sight of Kim's enticing lips so close to her own. Unmindful of where they were, she gave in to the urge to kiss Kim. It quickly turned passionate and she moaned into Kim's mouth. Her hands went down to grasp Kim's ass.

They broke apart, gasping for air.

"God. We can't do this here," Kim said.

Are you crazy? Anyone could walk in. Jess pulled away. "I'm sorry. I don't—"

"Stop." Kim put her finger to Jess's lips and smiled. "There's nothing to be sorry about. I wanted to kiss you the second I saw you at the nurses' station."

Jess grimaced. *Rodman would go apeshit.* "That would have sent the gossip flying at warp speed." She scrubbed her hands over her face. "We need to be very careful." *What's this we stuff? You're the one who can't keep her lips to herself.*

Kim moved back a step and her expression closed off.

Shit. Of course, that would remind Kim of how her ex acted after they were lovers. Jess closed the distance between them. "New rules. No matter how much I might want to. No making out at work. Other than that, nothing is going to change. We work together. We go to lunch together. We share an office."

Tears glimmered at the edge of Kim's eyes.

Jess cupped Kim's face in her hands and kissed the corner of each eye. Then placed a gentle kiss on her lips.

Kim smiled. "I thought there was no kissing at work."

"Special exception," Jess said. "Better?" A tight hug was her answer. "Good."

When Kim released her, Jess moved away and perched on the edge of her desk to avoid further temptation.

Jess bit her lip. *Ask her.* She readied herself to be disappointed, determined not to show it. "So did you get your tree?"

Kim shook her head, making her blond curls bounce. "No. You promised you'd help me pick it out."

She waited for me. They had planned on picking out the tree earlier in the week, but work demands on Jess had precluded that. "Tomorrow. I promise. We'll go tree shopping first and then the festival of lights in the evening." Jess grinned, unable to hide her eagerness.

Moving to lean against Jess's desk, Kim said, "Sounds like a plan."

"Well ... I was just thinking ..." Jess shoved her hands into her lab coat pockets. *Come on. The worst she can say is no.* "If you wanted, you could stay over tonight. So we could get an early start on Christmas tree shopping. And then maybe we could decorate it before going to the light festival." *Please say yes.*

"I'd like that, Jess ..." Kim's voice dropped, becoming soft and husky. "A lot."

Jess was blindsided by a flash of Kim, lying naked under her that morning. She met Kim's eyes and flushed. *It's going to be a long day.* "Well, I guess I better get back to work."

"Me too." Kim moved toward the door and then stopped. "I almost forgot." She reached into her pocket and pulled out a set of keys. "I got Thor all settled and made sure the house was locked up." She offered the keys to Jess.

Jess shook her head. "Keep them. You never know when you might need them again." She smiled when Kim clutched the keys to her chest as if she had been given a special gift.

Kim's shocked expression had been hard to miss when she had given the keys to her earlier. And the fact that she was offering them back to her was reason enough to let her keep them. Myra had repeatedly asked for a set of keys from almost the first night they spent together. Jess had never given them to her. Just as it had when she had given them to Kim that morning, it felt right to let her keep them.

She gave Kim's hand a quick squeeze. "Let's go to work."

CHAPTER 27

Kim propped up a four-foot tall Douglas fir and walked around it. *Perfect.* She didn't have a lot of room for a tree in her condo. As it was, she was going to have to wedge her dining room table against the wall unit that held the TV. She looked around for Jess, eager to show her the tree. *Where did she go?*

"Hey, Kim. Over here. I found it."

She could hear the excitement in Jess's voice. *I'm so glad I waited until she could come with me.* After laying her tree back on the pile, Kim walked to the next aisle over that held the larger trees.

Jess was standing next to a tree at least a foot taller than she was. Considering Jess was just an inch shy of six feet, the tree was huge. Its base spread out at least five feet, if not more. "How about this one?"

There was no way the tree would fit in her condo. *How the hell am I going to tell her no?* Jess had that same look on her face that she had earlier when she asked her if she had gotten her tree. Eager, but waiting to be disappointed. *What in the hell did that bitch Myra do to you?*

"It's really a beautiful tree, Jess. But there's no way it'll fit in my dinky condo."

"Oh." Jess's shoulders sagged. "Okay." She put the tree back.

Damn. Kim thought fast. "You could get a tree too. I'm sure this one would fit in your place. I'd help you decorate it."

Jess's expression brightened. She started to stand

the tree back up. Her face fell and she let it go. "I forgot. I don't have any decorations."

"We could get you some." Inspiration struck. *Take a chance.* Kim spent most of her time at Jess's. "Or how about this ... We could share the tree. You buy the tree and I'll provide the decorations."

"You would really want to do that?" Jess asked.

Her tentative manner made Kim more determined than ever to make this a special Christmas for Jess. "Sure. Why not? It'll be fun."

Jess shook her head. "Of course you would," she said, sounding as if she was talking to herself. When she met Kim's gaze, the sparkle was back in her eyes. "Thank you."

"No need to thank me. It's been a while since I had someone to share Christmas with." She bumped shoulders with Jess. "I'm really looking forward to it."

"Me too." Jess wrapped one arm around Kim's shoulders in a brief hug.

Wow. Wasn't expecting that.

"Have you ladies decided on a tree?"

Thought we dumped him. The overeager salesman had followed them around when they first arrived. After Jess turned the full force of her ER Chief persona on him, he had made himself scarce.

Kim looked over at Jess. "Have we decided?"

With a broad grin, Jess pointed to the seven-foot tree she had chosen. "That one."

The salesman put on his gloves and hefted the tree.

"Can you deliver it today?" Kim asked.

"Yep. Cost you twenty-five extra, though."

"We don't need—"

Kim cut Jess off. "That'll be fine. Thanks." When the salesman was out of earshot, she turned to Jess. "I'll pay for the delivery."

"I could have taken it home."

"Do you really want to drive on the freeway with a huge tree tied to the roof of your truck? And have tree sap stuck to your paint job? Plus trying to get that monster in the house?"

Jess deflated. "Oh. Guess I should have picked a smaller tree."

Kim bumped Jess's hip. "I love the tree. It's perfect. Come on. Let's set up to have it delivered, then we can buzz by my place and get the decorations."

They were just getting ready to leave the Christmas tree lot when Jess's phone rang. She pulled her phone off her belt and glanced at the screen. "It's my sister. I can call her back later."

"No. It's okay. Go ahead and answer it if you want." Kim was curious to see what the interaction on the phone was like between Sam and Jess.

Smiling, Jess pressed the phone to her ear. "Hey, Sam. What's up?" She listened for a moment, then laughed. "That's not a very subtle hint." Tilting the phone away from her mouth, she said, "She's telling me where the video game she wants for Christmas is on sale." She turned her attention back to the phone. "I was talking to Kim …" She rolled her eyes. "No. We just bought a Christmas tree for my place." Jess's eyes grew wide. "No. I will not tell her that."

Kim was dying to hear the other side of the conversation. She caught herself leaning closer to Jess. *If she wants you to know, she'll tell you.*

"I have to go, Sam. I'll talk to you later … Okay … Bye."

When Jess set her phone on the center console, Kim noticed a crack in the screen. "What happened to your phone?"

"Um ..." Jess looked everywhere but at her. "It got knocked off the coffee table. Thor stepped on it." She shoved the phone back into its holder on her belt and glanced at Kim.

Kim quirked an eyebrow at Jess. *Come on. Tell me.* There was more to this story, she just knew it.

Jess blushed. She shifted in her seat and then seemed to come to a decision. "Well ... Sam and I were playing video games and sort of arguing over whose turn it was." She stuffed her hands into the pockets of her leather jacket. "We started wrestling over the game controller. Thor rushed over and tried to join in." She looked down. "One of us either sat on my phone or Thor stepped on it ... I'm not sure," she finished in a rush.

Kim had to bite her lip to keep from laughing. *I wish I could have seen that.* She hoped she would get a chance to meet Sam soon. She had a feeling she would get to see a whole other side of Jess when she did.

"So did you win?" Kim asked.

"Huh?" Jess looked up.

"Did you win at the video game?"

Jess grinned. "I got two levels farther than Sam. Without killing her once."

Kim was having too much fun to let this go. "Sam?"

"No." Jess laughed. "Adara."

I should have known. "Ah. The intrepid explorer of exotic lands." *Who just happens to be incredibly stacked. Now I have an idea of what to get Jess for Christmas.*

Jess's eyebrows shot up. "You know the games?"

"I haven't played in a while." Kim grinned. "But yeah. I might have played some of the earlier ones ... a time or two."

"All right. Sam is going to be so jealous. She hasn't dated a woman yet who likes Adara."

Kim's jaw dropped. *No way.* "Your sister is a lesbian?" she blurted before she could stop herself.

"Oh. I thought I mentioned that." Jess arched an eyebrow and grinned. "Is that a problem?"

Kim snorted. "Hardly." Her stomach chose that moment to growl loudly. "I'm starving. What do you say we get some lunch before they deliver the tree?"

Jess laughed. "What's new?" She dodged Kim's playful poke. "Okay. I give." She started the engine. "Mexican?"

"Of course," Kim said.

"Ready?" Kim bent toward the outlet.

"No. Wait. Let me turn off the lights." Jess doused the room lights. "Okay. Go."

Kim smiled. Jess's exuberance as they decorated the tree had been heartwarming. It was the most fun that Kim had had decorating a tree in more years than she could count. She plugged in the Christmas tree lights.

When she stepped from behind the tree, she saw Jess staring at the tree with an awestruck expression. Moving close to her side, Kim asked, "Like it?"

"It's perfect." Jess cradled Kim's face in her hands. "Just like you."

Kim flushed from the heat of Jess's gaze. "I'm not even close to perfect."

"You are to me," Jess said. She drew Kim into her arms and kissed her long and lovingly.

Pressing herself against Jess, Kim whimpered as Jess's tongue slid into her mouth. *Oh, what you do to me with just a kiss.* She wrapped her arms around Jess's back. The press of their breasts ratcheted her arousal higher.

Jess grasped her ass and pulled Kim tightly into the space between her spread legs.

Unable to stop herself, Kim ground herself against Jess's pelvis. She pulled away from the torrid kiss, panting. "God, Jess." When Jess began to tug at her clothes, Kim groaned in relief. "Yes." She lifted her arms and allowed Jess to pull her sweater over her head.

Jess's eyes sparked fire at the sight of Kim's bra-clad form. "Just perfect." Her hands came up and cupped full breasts, then squeezed.

Her legs going weak, Kim latched onto Jess's shoulders. "I'm going to fall."

"I've got you." Jess guided Kim to the couch and urged her down onto it.

The lights from the Christmas tree formed a multicolored aura around Jess.

Unwilling to wait a moment longer to feel Jess on her, Kim reached up and tugged at Jess's belt. "Come here."

Jess resisted. "Wait," she said, her voice velvety soft with arousal. She pulled her shirt from her pants and struggled with the buttons. Growling, Jess jerked the shirt over her head. She pulled off her sports bra and then leaned down and slid her hands behind Kim's back to unlatch her bra. "Take this off."

Kim lifted up enough for Jess to complete her task. As soon as her bra was undone, she pulled it off and tossed it to the floor. She looked up at Jess. "I need to feel you on me. Now."

A whimper escaped Jess's throat. She moved into place on top of Kim.

They both groaned at the feel of their bare breasts pressed together.

Jess slid one leg between Kim's thighs and pushed against her center.

Kim's hips bucked up into Jess, trying to deepen the contact.

Jess took Kim's lips in another deep kiss, keeping

pressure against her center as she rocked her hips.

The seam of Kim's jeans rubbed against her clit. Arousal skyrocketing, she grabbed the firm globes of Jess's ass and urged her on. "Harder."

Jess lifted up enough to grasp the armrest behind Kim's head. Shifting position, she straddled Kim's thigh. Her eyes locked with Kim's. Jess's hips began to pump, hard and fast.

"God. Yes. That's it." Kim growled. She squeezed Jess's ass in rhythm with her thrusts. Pleasure coiled in her belly and shot down her legs. Her eyes slammed shut and she cried out. Her hips arched with enough force to lift them both off the couch.

Jess thrust one final time. An inarticulate sound was torn from her lips as she slumped down onto Kim.

Her chest heaving, Jess tried to move her shaking body off of Kim. *My God.* The force of her orgasm had been mind-blowing.

Kim's arms wrapped around her back. "Don't go."

"I'm not going anywhere. Just don't want to squash you," Jess said.

They shifted positions until Jess was lying behind Kim on the couch. Jess traced languid patterns in the sweat on Kim's bare stomach. She had never considered her libido particularly strong. As with so many things in Jess's life, Kim was rapidly changing that notion. Jess couldn't seem to keep her hands off her.

Kim sighed and snuggled back against Jess. "That was a unique tree-lighting ritual."

"I found it particularly enjoyable." Her hand slid up to stroke a soft breast. "We should make it a tradition."

"Mm ... that could be arranged." Kim captured Jess's hand. "So you like the tree?"

Jess gazed at the tree. Multicolored lights twinkled in the darkened room. "Best tree I've ever had."

Kim laughed. "Well, you mentioned before that you didn't put up a tree. So since it's the first tree you've had, that's not saying much. But I'm glad you like it."

It was easier for Jess to tell the truth without having to face Kim directly. "Well, actually that wasn't quite the whole truth. I've had a tree here before … just not for the last several years." Jess smiled when Kim interlaced their fingers and hugged them against her belly.

"Why did you stop putting up a tree?" Kim asked.

Her defenses down, the words came tumbling out. "Myra didn't believe in Christmas. She made me feel stupid and childish for being excited about the holiday. And a total heathen for killing a tree." She scowled. "But she made sure she let me know exactly what she wanted for a winter solstice gift. And after she left …" Jess shrugged. *Note to self: Incredible sex makes your brain mush and turns you into a big blabbermouth. Could you sound any more pathetic?* "Sorry. I shouldn't be telling you all this. I'm ruining our day. You don't want to hear about me and my ex."

"That's where you're wrong." Kim cradled their entwined hands between her breasts. "I want to know everything about you that affects you—good or bad."

The declaration simultaneously thrilled and scared the hell out of Jess. She buried her face in Kim's silky hair. *Please don't let me screw up the best thing that has ever happened to me.*

"It's incredible," Kim said. This was a wonderful way to end an already amazing day. *Well, spending another night in Jess's bed would make a perfect ending to the*

day. But this is an excellent second choice.

They were strolling down the main thoroughfare of the fairgrounds. A sea of Christmas lights sparkled in every hue. A multitude of festive holiday displays competed for attention. The excited laughter and delighted smiles of children and adults alike abounded.

"And it gets more elaborate every year." The lights reflected off Jess's face, highlighting her exuberance. "We'll have to make this part of our Christmas tradition."

Kim barely resisted the urge to hug Jess. Joy filled her heart as she heard Jess talking about their future.

Old fears surfaced to dim her happiness. A future together was something she had not allowed herself to contemplate with any of her lovers. *You let yourself care for someone too deeply and they leave you. One way or the other.* Kim forced the thought away. *No. Not this time. Things are different with Jess.*

"Kim," Jess said, sounding a bit worried.

She pulled herself out of her morose thoughts and smiled at Jess. *Don't ruin the day.* "Sounds like a wonderful tradition." Leaning close to make sure she wasn't overheard, she added, "But not as wonderful as our tree-lighting tradition."

Jess grinned. "How about we head over to the pavilion? They've got a vendor that comes in specially for this event. They serve fantastic hot chocolate and cinnamon rolls."

"Oh. My kind of place. Lead on, Macduff," Kim said, making Jess laugh.

Jess held the door for Kim and she stepped inside. Kim took a deep breath. The air was awash in heavenly smells. Chocolate and cinnamon dominated. A man walked by with a large cinnamon roll smothered in icing.

Her mouth watered. "Oh yeah. I need one of those."

She started when Jess leaned close to her ear.

"You're killing me. Mercy," Jess whispered, her voice low and deep.

Kim looked into silvery-blue eyes. *Oh. God.* The desire burning brightly in Jess's eyes sent a shaft of desire straight to her center. Kim swallowed heavily. Without thinking, she stepped closer to Jess.

A group coming in the door behind them jostled them and brought her back to earth.

Jesus. Kim flushed. She pulled Jess out of the flow of traffic and over next to the wall. "You're dangerous," she said.

Jess's gaze darted around, then returned to Kim.

That little half smirk Kim had come to learn meant trouble made an appearance. *Uh-oh.* She tensed when Jess leaned close, but Jess didn't touch her.

"I wasn't the one who looked like I wanted to make lo—"

"Ah ..." She wagged her finger at Jess. "Don't even say it," Kim said, trying to hold back her laughter.

Laughter burst from Jess. She dodged the poke Kim sent her way. "I'll buy you a cinnamon roll and a hot chocolate. If you promise not to torture me."

Wow. Although Jess had shown her more mischievous side as their friendship had grown, Kim had not thought she would be so open and playful when it came to expressing her sexuality. This was a totally unexpected side of Jess's personality. *I love it.*

A saucy smile quirked Kim's lips. "No promises."

"I'm a dead woman," Jess muttered.

Kim laughed. "Come on. Let's go get in line. I'm hungry."

Jess led the way toward the two lines snaking out from the vendor's booth.

As they took their place in line, Kim scanned the

area. There were a number of booths selling food. A large section of the room was filled with tables.

Her ears perked when she thought she heard a familiar voice from a nearby table. She turned to look and froze. *Oh, shit! Jess is going to freak.* A short distance away, Penny sat at a table with an older man and woman.

Kim spun around and grabbed the sleeve of Jess's jacket. Her heart beat frantically in her chest. "We need to leave. Right now."

Jess's brow furrowed. "What's wrong?" she asked even as she turned to leave.

"Not in here. Outside." Dodging people right and left, Kim didn't stop until they got outside. She leaned against the building and blew out a breath.

"What was that all about?" Jess asked.

"I saw Penny sitting at a table, not four feet from where we were standing." Dark memories from her time with Anna threatened to overwhelm her. *It's not the same. Jess just wants to keep her personal life personal, not hide you.*

Jess blinked a couple of times as the information sunk in. "I knew it was just a matter of time. Didn't figure on it being quite this soon, but oh well."

Kim sighed. *Not the end of our day I was hoping for.* "We should go, before she comes out."

"No," Jess said, her voice firm and clear.

No? "But you know she'll blab all over LA Metro that she saw us together. It won't take much of a leap to figure out we're together." *And I don't want you to ever regret becoming involved with me.*

Jess took Kim's hand. She led her over to a bench against the building's wall. "Sit down for a minute."

Kim's gaze darted toward the doors to the building when Jess took both her hands in hers.

"Please, look at me."

She forced her gaze back to Jess.

"Do I wish we didn't have to deal with this? Yes. Our personal life isn't anyone's business." She tightened her grip when Kim tried to pull her hands back. "But are we going to hide? Absolutely not."

A lump formed in Kim's throat and tears prickled at the corner of her eyes. *She is not Anna. Get that through your head.* "I'm sorry. I don't want ...." She looked at Jess just in time to see her expression close down.

Jess pulled her hands away and stuffed them in her pockets. "I know you've heard the stories about Myra and what happened in the ER. I don't have the greatest reputation at work. So I understand if you don't want people to know you're involved with me."

Oh, Jess. No. She's been so open and honest with you. It's time to do the same.

Kim put her hand on Jess's thigh. Her heart sank when she felt her flinch. "Please, look at me."

Shadowed blue eyes lifted to hers.

Ah, Jess. Aren't we a pair?

"I'm sorry. You misunderstood me. You're not the only one with an ex from hell." Kim blew out a breath. "You know Anna didn't want to be seen with me at work. But what you don't know is she acted the same way away from work. If I even leaned too close to her in public, she would have a fit." Kim met Jess's gaze and held it. "She was more than happy to fuck me in private, but otherwise treated me like her dirty little secret." *Tell her the rest.* "I didn't realize it until much later, but I think she really got off on it."

A growl rumbled from deep within Jess's chest. "That bitch."

"My sentiments exactly." Kim winced. "And the other thing I might not have mentioned." *Might not? You know you haven't.* "She was the Chief of the ER."

Jess's eyes went impossibly wide. "Fuck." She

shook her head. "And you still took a chance on me and became my lover? You are one incredibly special woman."

Warmth flowed through Kim, healing another piece of her psyche damaged by Anna. "So are you." *God, I lov ... Whoa. Where did that come from? Let's not get carried away.*

A bright blush covered Jess's cheeks. "We're a pair, huh?" Jess asked, unknowingly echoing Kim's earlier thought.

"That we are." Kim's stomach growled. "Can I have my hot chocolate and cinnamon roll now?"

Jess laughed. "Some things never change." She stood and reached for Kim's hand. "Come on."

Kim had no more than stepped back into the building when she came face to face with Penny, accompanied by the older couple she had been sitting with. *Damn.* She had hoped Penny had left by now.

Penny stared. Her gaze went over Kim's shoulder, and her mouth formed an "oh" when she spotted Jess.

"Penny," Kim said by way of greeting. She worked not to let her trepidation show on her face. The last thing she needed was for Penny to realize how uncomfortable this made her. It would only add fuel to the fire.

She felt Jess step up next to her but didn't look at her.

"Dr. Donovan." Penny shot a look at Jess and scowled. "Dr. McKenna."

Kim chanced a glance at Jess to see her reaction. Her face was perfectly calm. She had her ER Chief mask firmly in place.

"Good evening," Jess said.

"Penelope, where are your manners?" the woman standing next to Penny asked.

"Mom," she whined like a petulant teenager.

Her mother arched an eyebrow.

Penny blew out a breath, ruffling her bangs. "This is Dr. Donovan and Dr. McKenna. I work with them."

Penny's mother offered her hand to each of them. "It's so nice to finally meet Penelope's co-workers." She shook her head as she let go of Jess's hand. "Oh my ... my manners. I'm Cynthia Graham, and this is my husband, Gerald. We're Penelope's parents."

Mr. Graham nodded but didn't offer his hand.

"It's nice to meet you both," Kim said. She could feel Penny's gaze on her. *Be pleasant, but brief. Get this over with.*

Jess spoke up before Kim had a chance to. "Well, if you'll excuse us, we were just on our way to get some of the wonderful cinnamon buns they have here before the stand closes."

Nice segue, Jess.

"Oh. You'll love them. It's a family tradition. We get them every year," Mrs. Graham said.

Oh great. So we can look forward to running into them again next year. Kim plastered a smile on her face. "Have a nice evening." She started to edge away.

"You too, dear," Mrs. Graham said. "Merry Christmas."

"Yeah. Merry Christmas," Penny said. She glanced at Jess and then threw Kim a hard look. "I'll see you ... both—at work."

Ah, crap. "Merry Christmas."

CHAPTER 28

Kim turned the corner.

Two nurses standing outside an exam room abruptly stopped talking. One of them threw a smirk her way.

Kim barely resisted the urge to scowl at the man. The same thing had been happening all morning. Obviously, Penny had wasted no time in spreading the news of seeing her and Jess. *The way everyone is acting who knows how the hell she embellished the story.*

Although Kim knew Jess was more than capable of taking care of herself, the situation still stirred her protective instincts. *Why can't they just leave us alone? Jess's job is hard enough. She doesn't need this.* She was thankful Jess was tied up in a quarterly budget meeting. Maybe everyone would get the childish behavior out of their system before Jess got back. *Yeah. And pigs can fly.*

Ignoring the nurses, Kim continued down the hall to the exam room she had been in earlier. She had misplaced her small notepad and was backtracking her movements in hope of finding it.

She smiled when she spotted her pad sticking out from under the edge of the gurney's base. The notebook contained drug references and dosage tables. *Glad I don't have to start all over.*

As she squatted down to pick the notepad up, she heard feminine voices and laughter from outside the exam room door.

Kim grabbed for her notebook as the door swung

open.

A loud familiar voice became crystal clear when the women entered the room.

"I'm telling you. They were hot and heavy." Cindy snorted. "Talk about beauty and the beast. I wonder what Donovan calls her when they—"

Kim stood, making the women aware of her presence. *Bitch. Jess has never treated you anything but fairly and this is how you repay her?*

Nancy, one of the nurses' aides, had the grace to look embarrassed.

Cindy met Kim's gaze with a gloating expression that dared her to comment on what she had overheard. Ever since she had berated the woman a few months ago for gossiping about Jess, Cindy disliked her.

Kim met the look head on and refused to look away. Cindy seemed to have forgotten an important fact about the lack of privacy in a hospital—it went both ways.

As Kim moved toward the door, she paused close to Cindy. She pitched her voice for Cindy's ears alone. "This is just the kind of behavior that got you transferred out of pediatrics. It would be a shame if that happened again."

Kim tried not to take too much satisfaction from the woman's stunned face. *Leave Jess alone.* She made her exit before Cindy had a chance to respond.

Jess became aware of the speculative looks being thrown her way as soon as she stepped foot in the ER. *Great. Penny didn't waste any time.* She glanced around, hoping to spot Kim. *Wonder how she's weathering the storm?* Jess didn't like it, but she was used to the gossip. People knew so little about her, they made things up to fill the gap or, like Cindy, talked about the only thing they knew about—the Myra incident. The thought of people talking disparagingly about Kim set her teeth on edge.

She made her way to the nurses' station.

Several nurses as well as Bates and Aimee were gathered around Terrell near the status board. Penny was at the counter on the phone.

"You should have seen the look on Dr. Donovan's face when this guy—" Terrell stopped mid-sentence when he caught sight of Jess.

A spike of alarm hit as she flashed back to Kim with Brian. *Calm down. Kim can take care of herself. And Terrell doesn't look upset.*

"Morning, Dr. McKenna," Terrell said. "Dr. D—"

Penny cut him off. "So, did you have a ... pleasurable weekend, Dr. McKenna?" she asked, her voice brimming with innuendo.

Jess turned to face Penny. She could feel the shift of everyone's attention to their conversation.

Penny tossed a smug look past Jess at the apparently rapt audience behind her.

You may have seen me with Kim. But I'm still your boss. Don't test me. "Yes. I did. Did you enjoy the holiday light festival?"

Penny's eyes went wide.

Weren't expecting that, were you? Jess could almost hear the 'oh shit' from Penny. "It was nice meeting your parents."

Someone snickered behind Jess.

A bright blush suffused Penny's face. "I'm ah ..."

Not the story you told them, was it? Jess had suspected as much.

The phone rang, saving Penny further embarrassment. She dove for it.

Jess turned on her heel.

Everyone scattered like rats from a sinking ship

except Terrell.

"As I was trying to tell you before, Dr. Donovan asked me to let you know as soon as you got here that she wanted to consult with you about her patient," Terrell said. He shook his head and grinned, then pointed to the status board. "He's one for the books."

Jess scanned the board, looking for what room Kim was in. Her eyebrows shot up when she found the entry. The patient's name was listed as Cat Guy. *What the hell?*

"Thanks." She spun around and headed for the exam room.

Jess heard the sound before she even reached the door.

It sounded like a cat meowing. *Okay. That explains the Cat Guy.*

She pushed open the exam room door and winced at the increase in the volume. Kim and Karen Armstrong flanked a gurney. A little man with delicate, surprisingly catlike features was crouched on his haunches at the head of the gurney. His greasy hair was slicked back so tightly it resembled a skullcap. He was meowing incessantly. What looked like the remains of a saucer of milk was on the bed tray in front of him.

Jess strode up to the end of the stretcher. "Dr. Donovan, what do we have here?"

Cat Guy hissed like an angry feline.

Jess took a half step back and shot a look at Kim. *What's this, an early start on the full moon tonight?*

Kim bit her lip and struggled to keep a straight face. "I don't think he likes you, Dr. McKenna."

Karen laughed, then slapped her hand over her mouth.

Cat Guy resumed meowing.

"Let's step out into the hall," Jess said. She headed for the door.

Kim followed. Karen remained at the patient's bedside.

"Is he okay alone in here?"

"Sure. He should be as long as I can keep an eye on him through the door," Kim said.

Jess pulled open the door. "Join us, Dr. Armstrong."

Karen threw Jess a relieved look and hurried after them.

As soon as the door closed behind them, the meowing turned to yowling. He sounded like a tomcat in rut.

"What's his story?" Jess asked.

"Police brought him in. They picked him up in the park. He was approaching people and rubbing himself against them and meowing." Kim glanced in the exam room window. "He's been meowing or yowling like that since they brought him in. I haven't gotten anything from him. No name, nothing."

"And he tries to rub against you if you get too close," Karen said with a shudder.

"Any injuries?" Jess asked, directing her question to Karen.

"Small cut on his palm. I cleaned it." Karen's face twisted. "He kept trying to lick me and the cut. It was nothing. Didn't even need stitches."

"Did you do a complete physical exam?" Jess asked. The man was dirty and smelled bad. She knew the resident might have been tempted to skimp on the exam.

Karen nodded. It was clear from her expression it had not been a pleasant experience. "I didn't find anything else of significance on exam. He does have some fungus on his toenails. And lots of dirt," she added under her breath.

"Good job," Jess said. After a rough start to her residency, Karen had really turned things around. She was becoming one of the best of the first-year residents.

Karen beamed at the praise.

Jess turned back to Kim. "So why didn't the police take him straight to Gateway? They have the facilities for dealing with this type of thing. He doesn't need to be in the ER."

"I asked that too. They claimed it was because he was bleeding." Kim scowled. "I think they dumped him on us because they didn't want to deal with him and we were the closest place."

God. Jess rubbed her ears as the yowling continued unabated. "How long can he keep that up?"

"He's been here almost two hours," Kim said.

Oh great. She had only been here a few minutes and was already getting a headache. "So what can I do? Is there a problem with Gateway taking him? Do I need to contact them?"

"No. I wanted to find out if you'd seen him in the ER before. I'm convinced this guy is playing us. The tox screen came back negative. And as far as I've been able to tell, he doesn't fully meet the criteria for an axis I or axis II disorder." Kim rubbed her neck. "He's done this before. I'm sure of it. I'm willing to bet he's using this as a way to get a couple of days rest and some hot meals. He doesn't fit what I would expect to see with a furry gone too far either."

Jess peered in the window. "Well, he looks kind of catlike to me."

Kim laughed. "I noticed that. But I still don't believe that's what we're dealing with. You can almost see the calculation in his eyes."

"Excuse me, but what the heck is a furry?" Karen asked.

Jess made a go-ahead motion to Kim.

"It's not seen as a true psychiatric disorder. 'Furries' is an umbrella term that covers a group of people who prefer to interact with others as animals rather than as human beings. It feels safer for them."

"Seriously?" Karen shook her head. "So they what ... dress up like animals or something?"

"They can. At the extreme end of the spectrum, some people modify their physical appearance with tattoos and implants to better match their 'inner' animal."

"Wow."

"So back to Cat Guy," Jess said. He still had not shut up and her headache was getting worse. "I haven't seen him in the ER before. And I'm sure I would have heard about it if he had come in while I wasn't here. What do you want to do with him?"

Kim shrugged. "I'd like to just street him. Maybe it would convince him to give up on this." Kim raked her fingers through her hair. "There are lots of ways to get shelter and a hot meal without draining an ER's limited resources. But as long as he's like that, I can't take the chance, in case I'm wrong."

Jess racked her brain, then grinned to herself when inspiration struck. *Oh, yeah. This will flush you out, buddy.* "So you're sure he's faking?"

"As sure as I can be. Nothing in psychiatry is a hundred percent," Kim said.

"Okay. I've got an idea." Jess looked at Karen. "Now, don't ever try something like this on your own without consulting Dr. Donovan or myself first. Understood?"

Karen nodded. Jess could see the questions in her eyes, but Karen resisted asking.

"When we get inside, I need you to follow my lead, no questions asked."

"I can do that," Karen said.

"What are you going to do?" Kim asked.

Jess smiled at Kim. *I knew you'd ask.* Although Kim thought the patient was faking, he was still her first concern.

She hadn't missed Karen's shocked expression

on seeing her smile. *Maybe it is time to loosen up a little.* Kim was showing her that it was possible to be professional without keeping everyone at arm's length. *Myra has claimed enough of your life. It's time to let all that go.*

Turning her focus back to the business at hand, Jess said, "Sometimes an unusual situation calls for a unique solution." She pushed open the door and entered the room before Kim could question her further. For this to work, she needed the patient to see Kim's and Karen's shocked reactions.

As soon as they entered the room, Cat Guy ceased to yowl and began to meow again.

Jess strode up to the side of the gurney and met the patient's eyes. He stared right back and hissed. There was none of the gaze avoidance or any of the other behaviors she would have expected to see in a patient this dissociated from reality. Kim was right. This guy knew exactly what he was doing.

Karen took up position on the opposite side of the gurney.

"Dr. Armstrong, would you get a suture kit, please."

Karen's eyebrows shot up, but she turned and headed for the cabinet holding the trays.

Totally ignoring the patient, Jess turned to Kim. "This is a very interesting case. I've read studies about this. Once they devolve into their pure animal state, there is no going back."

Cat Guy's meowing got quieter with longer pauses. He was clearly worried about where Jess was going with this.

Karen returned with the requested suture tray.

"Ah, good. Thank you." Jess pushed the over-the-bed table away. She grabbed a stand and placed the instrument tray on it and then opened the tray, exposing the contents.

Kim's expression grew wide-eyed. "Ah ... Dr. McKenna?"

Perfect. Kim sounded honestly concerned.

A glance out of the corner of her eye showed Cat Guy looking nervous. Jess could see sweat beginning to form on his forehead. *Not such a great gimmick now, is it, bud?*

"Don't worry, Dr. Donovan. It's a very simple procedure to neuter him. Believe me, it's the best thing for him. It will make him much calmer ... and quieter."

Cat Guy squeaked, then his meowing stopped. Sweat ran down the sides of his face.

"But ... don't you need permission," Karen asked. Her eyes sparkled with interest.

Good job, Karen. Jess sent her an impressed look.

"Well. I would, Dr. Armstrong, if he was a person. But as he has clearly demonstrated to us, he's a cat." *Come on, guy. Break. I can't go much further with this.* "A person could speak up and refuse the procedure."

Jess took her time setting up the tray before pulling on sterile latex gloves. *Shit. He's not going for it.* There was one more thing she could try. She moved over to a nearby drawer and pulled out a disposable scalpel. On her way back to the bed, she pulled off the outer wrapper, but left the sheath on the blade.

She faced Cat Guy. "Ready?"

Kim and Karen gasped simultaneously.

"Wait. No. You can't do that. I refuse." The words burst rapid fire from Cat Guy. He pressed himself against the opposite side of the gurney, as far away from Jess as he could get.

About time! Jess didn't relent. "People give their names when asked. Cats don't. What's your name?"

"Donny. Donny Nowicki. I swear. I'll give you my social security number. You can check."

Jess turned her back on Donny and Karen to hide

her grin. "All yours, Dr. Donovan."

She tossed the scalpel in and then scooped up the open suture kit. As she moved past Kim, she lowered her voice, "Good luck with your cat. As you know, I'm much more a dog person myself."

Jess pulled off her gown and tossed it into the marked hamper near the door. She glanced back at one of the nurses. "Check the pulses in that leg every five minutes until ortho arrives to take him to the OR. If there is any change before they get here, page me."

"Sure thing, Dr. McKenna."

Jess's stomach growled, reminding her it was time for lunch. She had gotten pulled into a trauma right after leaving Kim and Karen.

Wonder how Kim did with her cat.

She turned the corner and headed for her office. An automatic smile blossomed when she spotted Kim ahead of her in the corridor. "Dr. Donovan."

Kim stopped and waited for her to catch up.

"How did it go with Donny?" Jess asked as they resumed walking.

"I can't believe you did that," Kim said, nudging her with an elbow.

"Hey. I never touched him."

"True." Kim shook her head. "Well, it was certainly effective, I'll give you that. Once he started talking, I didn't think I was ever going to get him to quit."

"Did you street him?" Jess asked.

"No. He's not a bad guy. He lost his mother and then their apartment. He just made bad choices."

Ah. I'm not surprised. You always go that extra mile for your patients.

"I contacted the Homeless Services Authority," Kim

said. "They'll get him situated temporarily and then find a therapist to work with him."

The sound of raised voices interrupted.

What the? Jess lengthened her stride.

As Jess neared the junction of the two corridors, Karen's voice became clear. "Knock it off, Peter. No one wants to hear that garbage. Who cares if they're together? More power to them."

"You're just pissed 'cause Donovan wouldn't give you the time of day," Terrell said.

Jess stopped just short of the corner. She glanced back at Kim and could tell from her expression she had heard what had been said.

Without a word, they quickly backtracked down the hall and took a different route to Jess's office.

Kim spoke up as soon as the office door closed behind them. "I'm sorry. I wish you didn't have to put up with all this." She sighed. "But I don't see any way to stop it."

"It's not just about me. I don't want you to have to put up with this either." Jess gave Kim's arm a gentle squeeze. "Once everyone figures out that we're not making any attempt to hide the fact that you're my girlfriend, it'll be no big deal anymore. They'll move on to the next hot gossip."

Kim stared at Jess for several stunned seconds. A brilliant smile lit her face. "Your girlfriend?"

Jess realized she had talked about their future, but never actually told Kim that was how she thought of her. She knew her smile rivaled Kim's. "If you'll have me?" *She's a lot more than your girlfriend. You need to tell her how you feel.*

Moving close, Kim said, "Girlfriend. I like that."

Jess closed the small distance between them. "Me too." She brushed her lips softly against Kim's, then stepped back before she gave in to temptation. Jess wondered if Kim had any idea the power she held over her. *If she knew how much I lov—no.* Jess cut the thought short; she wasn't ready to acknowledge that just yet.

Kim walked over to the couch and flopped down gracelessly. "We still have to deal with this crap until word spreads throughout the hospital."

"Well, we know the word is out in the ER." Jess joined Kim on the couch. "Heck, two of my residents are even sticking up for us." She nudged Kim in the side and smiled. "How I feel about you wouldn't change even if they weren't, but it's still nice."

"You're right. I just don't want you to get sick of dealing with this," Kim said. She met Jess's gaze.

Jess could see the worry and vulnerability in her eyes. "I won't." After finding out the full extent of Anna's mistreatment of Kim, anger and sorrow warred within Jess. She did not want Kim to ever feel like that again, not even for a moment. She tipped her head back and closed her eyes.

What else can I do?

Her eyes popped open. "Come on." Jess stood and held her hand out.

"Where are we going?" Kim asked even as she put her hand in Jess's.

"The cafeteria."

As they approached the entrance to the cafeteria, Kim's stomach fluttered. This was a big step for both of them. It was almost like coming out at work all over again. She glanced over at Jess. The resolved but calm look on her face helped Kim's nerves settle. *This is what you wanted.*

Jess pushed open the swinging door. "Ready?"

"You don't have a scalpel, do you?"

Laughing, they stepped into the cafeteria together. Their entrance immediately attracted attention.

As they made their way through the food line, heads turned and people started to whisper.

Jess paid for their lunch. "Come on."

Kim's steps faltered for a moment when she realized where Jess planned for them to sit. The two-person tables in the back corner of the room were routinely used by couples seeking a little privacy.

"Are you sure about this?" Kim asked quietly.

"Yes." Jess's gaze and voice were rock-solid. She set the tray on the small table and sat down. She smiled at Kim as she joined her. "This should pretty much assure that word gets out to the greatest number of people."

You are amazing. Just when I think I have you figured out, you surprise the hell out of me. Kim shook her head.

"What?" Jess asked.

"You never cease to surprise me."

"That's a good thing ... right?"

Kim gave Jess's arm a quick squeeze. "So far."

"Well, then let's see if I can keep my streak going."

Kim tensed. She had learned to be a little wary of just what Jess might do when that little half smirk appeared.

Jess laughed. "Gotcha."

Scowling, Kim looked around. As she suspected several people were staring.

A tug on her sleeve brought her attention back to Jess.

"Ignore them." Jess suddenly looked a little nervous. "I did have something I wanted to ask you." She cleared her throat. "Will you come with me to San Diego to meet Sam?"

You are just full of surprises today. "Sure. When?"

Jess fiddled with the tray. "Well, Christmas is on a

Friday, and as you know I'm working. But I'm going to Sam's on Saturday. Come with me?"

Wow. Christmas? "Are you sure you want me to go then? I mean won't Sam mind me barging in on your Christmas celebration?"

"Heck, no. She's been pestering me to meet you." Jess clasped her hands together. "Unless you have other plans?"

Kim smiled. "You know I don't. I'd really like to meet Sam."

"Then it's settled."

As if on cue, Jess's pager shrilled. She glanced down at it. "Back to the trenches."

CHAPTER 29

Jess rested her chin on Kim's shoulder. "It really is a beautiful tree."

"Yes, it is." Kim patted Jess's hand that was resting on her belly. *I can't wait to see your face when you find your present from Santa under it.*

After an early Christmas Eve dinner, they had retired to the couch to relax until Jess had to leave. Kim was on her side with Jess spooned behind her. A dancing fire provided the only illumination besides the tree.

Kim looked over at Thor. She could just make out his form in the darkened room. He was curled up in a tight ball on his bed. "Although I don't think Thor is very fond of it."

Thor's tail had hit a glass ornament earlier. It exploded with a resounding pop when it hit the wood floor.

"Are you sure he's okay?" Kim asked. Jess had checked him out to make sure he had not cut his tail or his pads. But he had not moved out of his bed since the ornament broke.

"He's fine." Jess lifted up. "Come here, you big baby."

Thor jumped up and charged across the room. He tried to push his way onto the couch in front of Kim, all the while licking any spot he could reach on both women.

Laughing, they tried to fend him off.

He scored a direct hit on Kim's lips.

"Blech." Kim pushed on his broad chest. "Thor, off."

He got off the couch but stood right in front of Kim, panting in her face, his tail wagging non-stop.

"Okay. I believe you," Kim said.

Jess laughed. "Thor, down."

He flopped down right next to the couch.

Kim leaned down and patted him.

Jess settled in place behind Kim again and sighed.

"What's wrong?" Kim asked.

"Wish I didn't have to work."

That makes two of us. But she was determined not to make this any harder on Jess than it had to be. Kim captured Jess's hand and hugged it to her chest. "We'll celebrate after."

Jess lifted up and placed a kiss on Kim's temple. "Are you sure you don't mind looking after Thor? I could probably still get him in at the kennel."

It was a big responsibility. Kim knew Jess had never left Thor with anyone except Sam or at the kennel. Although she felt up to the task, maybe Jess was still uncertain of leaving him with her for an extended period alone in her house.

"I'm more than happy to have his company. But if you'd feel better with him at the kennel—"

"No." Jess's arm tightened across Kim's belly, pulling her more snuggly against her. "I just didn't want you to feel obligated. He loves you and would be much happier here with you. And I'd feel better too, knowing both of you are here together."

"Good. I shouldn't be more than a couple of hours helping out Sid and Alan tonight. They really try hard to make Christmas special for the teens at the halfway house." Kim tugged Jess's hand up to her lips and placed a kiss on her palm. "Then Thor and I are going to hang out the rest of the time and wait for you to come home."

Home? The realization shocked Kim. There was no denying it. *Yes. Home.* Her heart stilled as she waited for Jess's reaction.

Seconds ticked by like minutes.

Jess touched Kim's chin and urged her to look back at her.

Kim met warm silvery-blue eyes, and her heart started to beat again.

"I'll be counting the hours until I can come home to you," Jess said.

I'll be waiting. Kim leaned in and kissed Jess's lips. Her heart was filled with love and hope for their future.

CHAPTER 30

After shifting the bag in her arms to one side, Kim used her free hand to press the freight elevator button for the first floor. She had come into the hospital via the front entrance and ridden the main elevators to the second floor. That was the closest access point to the freight elevators.

When the doors opened and revealed an empty ER hallway, she sighed in relief. She gave herself a pep talk as she used the back hallways to make her way toward Jess's office. *It's Christmas morning. Jess will be glad to see you. She didn't want to leave yesterday afternoon.*

Nervousness made her stomach jittery. This had seemed like a much better idea when she was making breakfast for Jess. Kim had never come into the ER while Jess was working when she was not on call herself.

The door to Jess's office was unlocked. She quietly opened the door and smiled at the sight that met her eyes.

The light spilling in from the hallway showed a blanket-draped Jess, curled up on her side, asleep on the couch. Her long legs were pulled up almost to her chest to fit in the small space.

Kim stepped inside and eased the door shut. She stood still for a few moments until her eyes adjusted to the dim room. A nightlight near the couch provided the only illumination. Once sure that she wouldn't run into anything, Kim walked over and set the bag with breakfast on Jess's desk.

She made her way over to the couch and gazed down into Jess's face. Kim extended her hand to touch Jess, then thought better of it. She squatted down next to the couch. "Jess."

Jess's eyes flickered, but she didn't waken.

"Jess," Kim said, a little louder. "Time to wake up."

When Jess's eyes fluttered open, Kim couldn't resist the urge to touch any longer. She stroked Jess's arm through the blanket.

"Good morning."

A pleasure-filled smile blossomed on Jess's face. "Hi. What time is it?"

"A little after seven," Kim said.

Jess untangled herself from the blanket and sat up. She reached out a hand and tugged Kim onto the couch with her and into her arms.

Kim sighed into the warm embrace. "Merry Christmas, Jess."

Pulling back a little, Jess met Kim's gaze. "Merry Christmas to you," she said and then kissed her.

When the kiss broke, Kim snuggled against Jess. *This was a good idea. A very good idea.*

The rumble of Jess's stomach broke the quiet moment.

Jess pulled back and rubbed her belly. "Sorry. We were swamped last night. By the time we got everything cleared out, it was almost three a.m. and the cafeteria was closed. It's not much, but could I interest you in Christmas breakfast in the cafeteria?"

Kim smiled and ran her fingers through Jess's sleep-disheveled hair. "I have a better idea."

Jess sighed and leaned into the touch. "What?"

"Look on your desk."

Tilting her head, Jess peered at Kim and then over at her desk. "You brought me something?"

You sound so surprised. I need to start doing more

little things for you to make you feel cared for. "I sure did."

"Thank you." Jess untangled herself from Kim and headed for her desk. She took a detour and turned on the overhead lights.

They blinked in the sudden brightness.

Pulling open the bag, Jess inhaled the escaping aromas. Her stomach growled louder than before.

Kim moved over to the desk and tugged the bag toward herself. "One official Christmas breakfast coming up."

Jess set their empty plates on her desk and then returned to the couch. She sat down close enough to Kim that their thighs brushed. She patted her stomach and sighed. "That was wonderful. Thank you again."

It was wonderful that you let me take care of you for a change without protest. Kim stroked Jess's thigh. "I'm glad you liked it."

The office door flew open.

Fuck. No. Kim jerked her hand off Jess's leg.

Rodman barged into the room.

He stared at them for a moment, then sneered. "Well, isn't this cozy."

Kim resisted the urge to move away from Jess. *We aren't doing anything wrong.* Clasping her hands in her lap, she projected a calm demeanor, as if it was a normal thing for Rodman to find them together.

Jess took her time standing. "What can I do for you?" she asked, her voice totally devoid of the warmth present just moments before.

"My sister is bringing my niece in. She's got a hot appendix. Make sure she gets taken care of as soon as she arrives. Don't do anything except get her checked in and her paperwork done." Rodman pointed a finger at Jess. "And keep your residents away from her. I'm going up to alert the OR. I'll be back down to get consent." After one last withering look, he spun on his heel and headed for the door. He stopped short and turned back. "Have her ready to go to the OR by the time I get back."

The door slammed shut behind him with a resounding boom.

The sound brought Kim off the couch like a shot. Dread settled like a lead weight in her stomach. People knowing that they were dating was one thing, but having Rodman find them together in Jess's office when Kim wasn't working was quite another. *So much for my discreet visit to the ER.*

Kim chanced a glance at Jess and winced. Jess's hands were clenched at her sides, and Kim swore she could hear Jess's teeth grinding together. *Damn it.*

"I should go," Kim said. She couldn't keep the sadness out of her voice. *That's the end of what was a great first Christmas morning together. It was nice while it lasted.*

Jess turned and faced her. The warmth rapidly returned to Jess's eyes. "No. Stay. I'll be back as soon as I take care of this."

"But Rodman ..."

"Rodman can shove it. We weren't doing anything wrong." Jess stepped close and wrapped her arms around Kim. She brought their lips together in a sweet, gentle kiss. When the kiss broke, she stroked Kim's cheek. "Wait for me."

Scanning the intake sheet, Jess made her way to the exam room. She didn't care what Rodman said. He might be Chief of Staff, but his niece was on her turf now. There was no way she was going to send anyone to the OR without, at a minimum, a complete history and physical. Anything less was substandard patient care, and she would not be part of that.

Jess entered the room and did a double take. *Did I get the room number wrong?*

A young Asian woman was lying on the gurney. An impeccably dressed, white-haired Caucasian woman stood next to her, holding her hand. She looked old enough to be Rodman's mother.

Jess moved next to the gurney. "Beatrice Hartford?"

The young woman nodded.

Beatrice looked younger than her listed age of twenty-two.

"I'm Dr. McKenna. I'll be taking care of you this morning." She met the older woman's gaze. "Mrs. Hartford?"

"Eleanor Hartford," she said with an unexpectedly strong New England accent. She politely offered her hand to Jess across the gurney. "I am Beatrice's mother." When Jess took her hand, Mrs. Hartford clasped Jess's hand in both of hers. "Thank you for seeing to Beatrice so promptly. I've been terribly worried."

What a pleasant surprise. Jess had been bracing herself for the female version of Rodman.

Beatrice cried out and clutched her abdomen.

Jess placed a gentle hand on Beatrice's shoulder. "Is the pain getting worse?"

Beatrice nodded.

"How long has this been going on?" Jess asked.

Beatrice glanced at her mother, then back at Jess. "Off and on for a couple of days ... I guess."

"Have you had a fever? Or any nausea or vomiting?"

She darted a look at her mother before answering. "I've been sick to my stomach and stuff ..."

Jess frowned. *Does she not want her mother in the room?* Before Jess could suggest Mrs. Hartford step out, Beatrice cried out again.

"Can you show me where the pain is?" Jess asked.

Beatrice rubbed her hand in a circular motion over her lower abdomen.

"Okay. Let me take a look." Jess pulled the sheet back. She reached for Beatrice's gown.

The exam room door banged open.

Rodman stomped into the room. He took a white-knuckled grip on the end of the gurney. "What the hell are you doing?"

"My job," Jess said. She met Rodman's angry glare with calm confidence. "Now, if you'll step out, please. I haven't completed my history and physical yet."

Rodman growled. "I will not. You're done here, McKenna. Out." He patted Beatrice's leg. "Don't you worry, sweetheart. I'll take good care of you."

"Richie," Mrs. Hartford said, in a warning tone.

Rodman froze. He shot a glare at Jess as if daring her to comment.

Richie?

"Let Dr. McKenna do her job."

Rodman turned to his sister. "I'm a doctor too," he said, sounding like a petulant little boy.

"Yes, dear," Mrs. Hartford said as if placating a stubborn child. She walked over to him. "Come on. We can come back once Dr. McKenna is finished."

"I know what's wrong with Bea. She," Rodman jutted his chin out toward Jess, "works for me."

"Yes, dear. I know." His sister patted his arm. "Let's go. You can show me your big office."

Mrs. Hartman tugged Rodman to the door. He whined all the way—but went anyway.

Jess bit the inside of her cheek to keep from laughing. *I'll be damned. Wouldn't have believed it if I hadn't seen it with my own eyes.*

Once the door closed behind them, Jess turned her attention back to her patient.

Shit. I so don't need this. Especially with Rodman breathing down my neck. Jess stepped out of the exam room. She glanced around, relieved to not find Rodman waiting to pounce.

Jess made her way to her office and pushed open the door.

"Hey, Jess. How did it go with Rodman's niece?" Kim asked.

Jess walked over to the couch where Kim was sitting but was too agitated to sit down. "Not so good. With the help of his sister, I managed to get Rodman out of the exam room so I could do a history and physical."

Kim's eyebrow shot up.

"I'll tell you all about that later, but right now I have a problem."

"With Rodman's niece?"

"Yeah. She's obviously in pain, but she's not cooperating or answering questions. I thought at first it was because her mother was in the room. Beatrice was giving these nebulous answers and saying things like 'I guess.' But once we were alone, things went downhill. Every question I asked, she responded with, 'Uncle Richie says I have appendicitis.'"

"Richie," Kim mouthed.

Jess quirked a smile. "Later."

"Sorry. Go ahead," Kim said.

"I asked if there was any possibility she might be pregnant. She looked completely panicked and didn't answer. When I pressed her, she muttered an unconvincing no, then refused to speak to me any further. I did examine her before all this, and while her belly pain could be appendicitis, it could also be an ectopic pregnancy." Jess raked her hands through her hair. "She refuses to have blood drawn or allow me to do a pelvic exam or even an ultrasound."

"What can I do?" Kim asked.

"I was just hoping you had some bright idea of how to get her to realize how serious this is. Otherwise, I'm going to have to involve her mother and Rodman. Beatrice is an adult, so if Rodman gets her consent, he can take her to the OR." Jess shoved her hands into her lab coat pockets. "There is no way I will allow Rodman to do that without adequate pre-op blood work and an ultrasound—especially if there is a chance she's pregnant."

"And you think Rodman will have a fit if you insist on a pregnancy test?"

"It's a good assumption considering how she's acting. I figure that's what she's afraid of. Either Rodman or her mother finding out that she might be pregnant." Jess started to pace. "Plus the fact that she looks about twelve." She blew out a breath. "I bet that's how Rodman sees her."

"Do you want me to try and talk to her?" Kim asked.

Jess stopped in her tracks. *Is that why I came in here?* Had she wanted Kim to take over with the girl? Guilt flooded Jess. *She comes on Christmas and brings you breakfast and this is how you thank her, by dumping your problems on her?* "No. That's okay. You're not on-call today. It's Christmas."

Kim rose from the couch and walked to Jess. "I really don't mind." She tugged at her shirt. "Only I'm not sure I'm dressed appropriately."

Jess took a moment to admire Kim's form. She was wearing a long-sleeved Henley shirt and jeans that hugged her curves. She put her hands on Kim's hips.

"You look like you'd fit right in with the college crowd. Maybe that will help." She gently squeezed the soft flesh under her hands. "You sure you don't mind?"

Kim gave Jess's lips a quick peck. "I'll let you know how it goes." She took a moment to grab her ID badge out of her purse, then headed for the door.

Jess wrote up Beatrice's chart while she waited for Kim. *Hope she has better luck than I did.* That wasn't an unreasonable expectation. Kim had a way with people that Jess had never possessed. Something about Kim made people feel safe confiding in her.

The door to her office blew open with enough force to slam it against the wall.

Jess jumped. *Damn it.*

She glared at Rodman.

He stormed over and stood next to her chair, glaring down at her. "What the hell is Donovan doing in the room with Bea?"

Jess grasped the edge of her desk and shoved her chair back, forcing Rodman to step away or have his toes run over. She stood. "I'm providing your niece with the best possible care." *Unlike you, who wants to whisk her off to the OR without a workup.*

Rodman got right in Jess's face. "She doesn't need to talk to some dyke psychiatrist. She needs a real doctor."

Her hands clenched at her sides as Jess struggled for control.

Kim heard raised voices from down the hall. She quickened her pace toward Jess's office. The voices suddenly became clear.

"Don't ever let me hear you talk about Kim like that again. She's the best psychiatrist this place has ever had."

Who the hell is in there with her? Kim had never heard Jess sound so furious. Realization struck. *Rodman.*

"What's the matter?" came Rodman's sneering response. "Did I hurt your feelings? I insulted your little dyke girlfriend?"

"Mine and Kim's personal life has nothing to do with this and is none of your business."

"Now I know why you wanted her to work down here, so you could have your puss—"

"Get out of my office!" Jess's voice vibrated with rage.

You bastard.

Kim broke into a sprint. She slid to a halt outside Jess's door.

The sight before her froze her in place.

No, Jess. Don't! She gripped the door frame.

Jess and Rodman were standing toe to toe and looked as if they would come to blows any second.

"Dr. McKenna," Kim called sharply.

Jess's head whipped around.

Rodman sneered. "Speak of the dev—"

"Shut up," Jess snarled.

Shut the fuck up, Rodman. Kim could see the tendons in Jess's neck standing out. Her fists were clenched at her side. She was barely holding it together.

"Dr. McKenna. I need to speak with you," Kim said, trying to keep Jess's attention on her. She had to break this up but wasn't sure Jess would walk away. She took a single step into the room. "Please," she said.

Jess blew out a breath. She walked away from Rodman without a glance.

Kim's knees went weak. *Thank, God.*

When Jess's body blocked her view of Rodman, Kim

smiled at her.

The tense set of Jess's face eased a notch.

Just as Jess reached Kim, Rodman spoke up. "Release Beatrice and get her up to the OR. Right now."

Jess stiffened.

Kim grabbed the front of Jess's lab coat before she could turn back to Rodman. "Let it go. Come on." She tugged on Jess's coat. "Beatrice needs you."

She breathed a sigh of relief when Jess allowed herself to be pulled out the door.

Kim tried to focus on a psych journal while she waited for Jess.

After taking Jess in to see Beatrice, she had returned to Jess's office while Jess ran the tests Beatrice had finally agreed to. Rodman had tried to interfere, but quickly backed off in the face of his sister's disapproval. His sister had been an unexpected surprise, and Kim had liked her immediately.

Already on edge, Kim jumped when Jess's office door opened.

Jess stepped inside and closed the door behind her.

Kim couldn't help smiling when Jess made a point of locking the door. She moved off the couch and approached Jess. When Jess opened her arms, Kim willingly fell into them.

"You okay?" Kim asked.

"Yeah. You?"

"Better now." Kim leaned back in Jess's arms until she could look into her eyes. She caressed her cheek. "You scared me earlier. I thought for sure you were going to hit Rodman." *Or stroke out.*

"Scared myself a little," Jess said. "But when he started bad-mouthing you and then our relationship ..."

I just kind of lost it."

Kim rubbed her hands soothingly up and down Jess's back. "He's not worth it ... No matter how tempting." Jess's staunch defense had been like a soothing balm over a still tender wound. Her eyes misted up as her throat grew tight with emotion. "It meant a lot to me that you stood up for me." *More than you will ever know.*

Jess cradled Kim's face in her hands and used her thumb to gently wipe away a tear. She held Kim's gaze. "I would never deny you. Not professionally. Not personally. Never."

"I love you." The words were out before Kim could stop them. Her heart tripped double time. But once the words were out, she couldn't bring herself to regret them.

A tremor rippled through Jess's body. She pulled Kim into an almost painfully tight embrace. "I love you," she whispered, her voice cracking with emotion.

The admission made Kim's heart soar.

When Jess pulled back, tears shone in her eyes.

Kim smiled and tenderly brush away Jess's tears. "We're quite the pair."

A loving smile spread across Jess's face and she nodded.

The phone on Jess's desk rang, shattering the moment.

"Damn it." Jess winced. "Sorry."

With a warm smile, Kim stepped back, breaking their embrace. "Duty calls."

Jess smiled and headed for the phone. "Dr. McKenna ... Yes ... Thank you." She hung up the phone and then walked back to Kim.

Kim took her hand and together they moved to the couch.

"That was OB. Beatrice is on her way to the OR." Jess sank back against the cushions. She rubbed her neck and groaned.

Kim tugged Jess's hand away from her neck. *You need to relax.* "Sit up and scoot forward a little."

Jess readily did as instructed. She gave Kim an endearing, lopsided smile.

Kim laid her hands on Jess's shoulders and kneaded the stiff muscles.

A whimper escaped from Jess. "Oh yeah. That's wonderful."

"So what happened with Beatrice?"

"Oh ..." Jess seemed to be having a hard time concentrating. "You did a great job with her. Getting her to tell the truth and agree to the tests, you saved her from an unnecessary appendectomy and possibly having an ectopic pregnancy rupture."

"What did Rodman say?" Kim asked.

"What could he say with the test results right in front of him?"

"Don't suppose he apologized?"

Jess snorted. "No. Hell has not frozen over." She pulled away and turned around to face Kim. "But Mrs. Hartford thinks you are an absolutely wonderful doctor." Jess's eyes sparkled. "And ... told Rodman he should give you a big raise."

Their laughter filled the air.

CHAPTER 31

Jess eased the front door closed. *Home at last.*

Despite her exhaustion after her twenty-four hour shift, Jess's spirit was light. Kim's declaration of love had filled a place in Jess's soul she had not even known was empty.

She glanced into the living room when Thor did not make an immediate appearance. The light from a fire created flickering shadows that danced around the room. The Christmas tree was a shimmering beacon of light.

Jess kicked off her shoes and made her way into the living room.

Kim was asleep on the couch. Thor was stretched out in front of it. One of Kim's arms hung over the side of the couch, her hand resting on his chest.

She found the domestic scene unexpectedly soothing. Smiling, Jess approached the pair.

Thor lifted his head.

Jess quickly gave him the hand signals for quiet and stay. That didn't stop the thumping of his tail against the couch.

Kim blinked. Sleepy blue eyes opened, and she smiled. "You're home."

Jess moved to the side of the couch, leaned down, and kissed Kim softly. "Merry Christmas."

Thor took that as an invitation and jumped up to offer his own greeting.

Fending him off, Jess laughed. "Merry Christmas to you too, my boy."

Kim sat up and patted the spot next to her.

A big yawn escaped before Jess could stop it. She flopped down on the couch next to Kim.

Kim scooted closer. She slid her hand along the nape of Jess's neck and began a light massage.

Jess relaxed into the gentle, loving touch. "Feels good," she murmured. Her eyelids drooped.

She jerked, startling Kim. *Great. Falling asleep on Christmas.* Jess scrubbed her hands over her face. She was sinking fast but determined to fight it. "Sorry about that."

"You just got off of a twenty-four hour shift. Don't worry about it." Kim leaned close and kissed her. "Are you hungry?"

Jess's stomach growled right on cue.

Kim chuckled. "I'll take that as a yes." She stood and offered Jess a hand. "Come sit at the table. I've got plates in the oven already made."

Kim disappeared into the kitchen.

Jess headed for the table. She was too tired to protest; besides, if she was honest, it felt good to know Kim wanted to take care of her after a long shift.

Kim watched as Jess chased the last bit of gravy around her plate.

"That was excellent. Thank you. Two home-cooked meals in one day." Jess smiled. "You're spoiling me."

"I'm glad you enjoyed it." Taking Jess breakfast had been one thing, but she had surprised herself when the urge to have a meal prepared and waiting for Jess had struck. *You're getting very domestic these days.* Normally, Kim avoided anything that even hinted at domesticity with her girlfriends. Then again, none of her previous relationships had prepared her for Jess.

When Jess had returned her spontaneous declaration of love without hesitation, another fragile piece of her heart had mended.

Jess stood and began to stack the plates.

"Go sit down. I'll get this," Kim said.

"You cooked. I should clean up."

Kim stood and pointed toward the living room. "Go." She had seen Jess trying to stifle a yawn several times during dinner. She knew she had to be nearing the end of her endurance.

Jess followed her instructions without protest, proving how tired she really was.

Having cleaned up everything else earlier, Kim made quick work of the plates and then returned to the living room. She softened her steps when she realized Jess's eyes were closed. Bypassing the couch, she sat down in the Morris chair, not wanting to take the chance of waking Jess.

Jess roused. "I'm awake."

"I should get going and let you get some rest," Kim said.

Jess sat up straight and rubbed her face. "No. It's Christmas day. Time to open presents."

Kim moved over to the couch and sat next to Jess. She stroked Jess's hair. "We can open them tomorrow."

"No. Don't want to." Jess's lower lip stuck out and she knuckled her eyes like an overly tired child.

The juxtaposition of that image with the one of the usually stoic ER Chief was endearing to say the least.

Kim turned sideways and ran her fingers into Jess's thick black hair. Using just the pads of her fingers, she gently massaged her scalp.

Jess's blink rate got slower, and even though she

was obviously fighting it, her eyes slid shut.

"Sleep tonight. Presents tomorrow," Kim said, her voice soft and low.

Jess sighed. Her eyes slowly opened. "Stay with me?"

Kim's heart clenched at the open, love-filled look on Jess's face.

"Always," Kim said.

CHAPTER 32

The butterflies in Kim's stomach were rapidly morphing into bats the closer they got to San Diego and Sam's apartment. Kim had wanted to meet Sam for months, and she still did, but yesterday had changed things.

Now that she and Jess had exchanged "I love you," it upped the ante of this meeting significantly. Instead of simply meeting the sister of someone she was dating, this had become about being introduced to her girlfriend's family. And that was something well outside her comfort zone. *You can do this. How many times has Jess gone outside her comfort zone for you?*

Jess's warm hand landing on her thigh made Kim jump.

"You okay?" Jess asked, glancing at Kim before turning her attention back to the road.

"Yeah. Just a little nervous." Kim put her hand on her stomach. *Okay, maybe more than a little.*

"Don't be. I'm sure you'll like Sam."

Kim put her hand on top of Jess's. "I was more worried about her liking me actually."

Jess squeezed Kim's thigh. "I promise. You have nothing to worry about."

Hope you're right. Knowing what she did about Jess's past, Kim expected Sam to be skeptical of her until she proved herself. *Once Sam sees you're nothing like that bitch, she'll be fine. I hope.*

Jess turned into an apartment complex. She parked and then turned to face Kim. "Hey." She leaned across the console and cupped Kim's face. Jess placed soft kisses across her cheeks, along her jaw line, and finally kissed her lips.

Kim sighed into the gentle kiss.

"Better?" Jess asked when the kiss broke.

Kim nodded.

"All right then." She turned toward the backseat. "Ready to go see Sam?"

Thor woofed, and his tail began to beat against the seat.

Jess knocked on Sam's apartment door.

Kim's stomach fluttered as the bats attempted to escape.

Her nervousness turned to amazement at her first sight of Sam. Her resemblance to Jess was uncanny. Sam's thick, black hair was shorter than Jess's but they shared the same tall, broad shouldered build. Sam's striking blue eyes were an exact match to Jess's. She glanced back and forth between them. Although Kim knew better, she couldn't help but be amazed. *They could pass for twins.*

Jess grinned. "Hey, sis."

Kim turned her attention back to Sam. Sam looked as stunned as she felt.

Sam's gaze slid down Kim's body and back up to her face. "Holy smokes, Batman. She's gorgeous," she muttered under her breath.

Heat suffused Kim's face at the open appraisal.

Sam's gaze darted to Jess and she flushed. Apparently the comment had come out louder than she planned. She met Kim's eyes and smiled sheepishly. "Sorry."

Jess shifted the bag in her arms to one side and then

shoved Sam's shoulder. "If you're through drooling over my girlfriend, how about letting us in?"

Sam's eyebrows shot up. "Girlfriend?" she mouthed.

"Sam. Anytime," Jess said, hefting the bag.

"Come on in." Sam stepped back and let them into the apartment.

As soon as Jess let Thor off the leash, he raced to Sam and greeted her enthusiastically. She hugged him, then sent him off to the large dog bed in the corner of the living room.

Sam settled on the loveseat. Her gaze bounced back and forth between Kim and Jess.

Jess put the bag on the coffee table, then chose the couch situated catty-corner to the loveseat. She offered her hand to Kim and drew her down next to her side. Jess smiled at Kim and rested their joined hands on her thigh.

Sam stared at her sister as if she had grown an extra head.

Kim wasn't sure what to make of Sam's reaction. *Jess brought Myra to meet Sam—didn't she?*

"This usually much more articulate person is my sister, Sam."

"Hey." Sam mock-scowled at Jess.

"Sam. I'd like you to meet Kim Donovan, my girlfriend."

"All right." Sam threw up her hands. "Who are you and what have you done with my sister?"

Laughing, Jess turned to Kim. "I've never brought a woman home to meet any of my family before."

Wow. The bats were back, stronger than ever. The admission filled her heart with joy and fear. This was even bigger than she had imagined—for both of them.

Kim smiled at Jess. "Well, I've never been brought home to meet anyone's family. So I guess we're even."

Jess's eyes sparkled. "Really? Never?"

The delighted look on Jess's face pushed the fear from Kim's heart. She leaned over and placed a kiss on Jess's cheek. "Never."

"Holy smokes," Sam said in an awe-filled tone.

Sam admired the spectacularly lit poinsettia trees that lined the walkway as she made her way back to where Kim and Jess waited. The botanical garden was wreathed in thousands of Christmas lights, turning its rainforests and bamboo gardens into a holiday wonderland.

Sam rounded the corner and spotted Jess and Kim sitting on a bench together. Jess's arm was draped around Kim's shoulders. Thor lay at Kim's feet with his big head resting on her knee. Sam grinned. Jess wasn't the only one enamored of Kim. Not that Sam could blame the big dog or her sister for that matter. Kim had turned out to be a delightful surprise.

Despite Jess's glowing praise of Kim, Sam had been a little worried. *You should have known when Jess agreed to you meeting her.* Kim had quickly put her fears to rest. It was clear that Kim cared deeply for Jess. While she was thrilled for her sister, Sam was a bit surprised at the envy that niggled at her. *You're not girlfriend material, forget it.* But now, seeing Jess with Kim, a small part of Sam began to wonder if that might not have to be true.

Sam pushed the thoughts away as she approached Kim and Jess. She smiled and passed out the cups of hot cider she was carrying.

"Thanks," Kim said.

"Yeah. Thanks, sis."

Sam nodded and sat down next to Jess.

Conversation lagged while they enjoyed their cider

and the beautiful plants around them.

Sam got up and tossed her empty cup into a nearby trashcan and then sat back down next to Jess. "So what did Jess get you for Christmas? She never did say."

"A mini-fridge and—"

"You've got to be kidding?" Sam snorted. "She bought you a refrigerator ... for Christmas?" She rolled her eyes at Jess and nudged her in the side. "Kim got you a cool portable video game console and you got her a refrigerator. What were you thinking?"

Jess's head dropped, and she muttered something under her breath.

Kim put her hand on Jess's thigh. She leaned forward and caught Sam's gaze and glared.

Sam flinched. She could swear she had seen Kim's eye spark flames. *Whoa. Okay, I got it. No picking on Jess.*

"Actually, it was an incredibly thoughtful gift," Kim said. "Every time I put food in the refrigerator in the staff lounge, it disappears. Then I'm stuck with food from the vending machine." Kim grimaced. "Or going hungry. It's very busy in the ER and not always possible to get to the cafeteria. So a mini-fridge for the office was the perfect gift."

Jess shot Sam a "so there" look.

You're a lucky woman, Jess. Sam grinned at Jess and gave her a thumbs-up.

A gust of wind swirled the leaves on the ground around their feet.

Kim shivered.

Jess glanced up into the darkening sky. "We should probably head back to your place, Sam. Kim and I still have a two-hour drive home."

"Why don't you stay the night? You guys can help me eat all the goodies Mom and Aunt Edna sent. And we haven't gotten to play my new video game yet." She looked at Kim beseechingly. "Please."

"Jess?" Kim met Jess's gaze and raised an eyebrow.

Before Jess could reply, Sam took Thor's leash out of Kim's hand. "Talk it over. Thor and I are going to check out the lights," she pointed to an area about twenty feet away, "over there."

Sam walked over to the lighted display with Thor. She turned back and could see Kim and Jess in conversation but not hear what was being said.

She patted Thor. "Looks like you've got yourself a second mom."

Thor woofed as if agreeing, making Sam laugh.

Finally, Kim nodded and Jess leaned forward and kissed her.

Sam had noticed the easy physical intimacy between them earlier. She had been surprised to see it. The ease with which Kim breached Jess's personal space was one more thing that convinced her how very special Kim was. Sam had been out many times with Jess over the years in social situations. Jess always had an aura about her that seemed almost a physical barrier, keeping women at arm's length, literally and figuratively.

"So what's the verdict?" Sam asked when they walked up.

"We're staying," Jess said.

"Great." Sam turned to Kim. "Wait until you try the double chocolate fudge brownies Aunt Edna sent."

Kim's eyes lit up.

"You just said Kim's favorite word, chocolate," Jess said. She wrapped her arm around Kim's shoulders and hugged her.

Sam grinned at Jess. *That's where you're wrong, sis. It's clear as day that her favorite word is "Jess."*

CHAPTER 33

Hanging in limbo between waking and sleep, Kim moaned as pleasure skittered along her nerve endings. She woke, luxuriating in the slowly building pressure between her legs. Jess's warm body pressed against her back. Her hand was under her T-shirt and Jess gently stroked her breasts and belly. She attempted to turn over, but Jess's arm tightened around her, holding her in place. "Good morning," she said, turning her head to meet Jess's gaze.

Jess's pupils were dilated, her arousal apparent. "Good morning to you," she murmured. Her caresses turned purposeful. She tweaked Kim's already rock-hard nipple.

Clenching her thighs together, Kim groaned. She wondered how long Jess had been touching her. She was so wet and ready for her.

"Shh ... you need to be quiet. Sam's right across the hall."

Kim growled under her breath. *Easy for you to say.* Unlike Jess, who rarely made a sound louder than a whimper, Kim tended to be very vocal in bed.

Jess's hand slid into Kim's underwear. She petted her mound but went no lower.

Biting her lip, Kim buried her face in the pillow. She lifted her knee, hoping Jess would take the hint.

Jess lifted up enough to nip Kim's pulse point.

Kim jerked. A loud gasp escaped her lips.

"Shh," Jess said, her hot breath blowing against Kim's ear.

"Quit playing already." Kim grabbed Jess's wrist and pushed her hand farther between her thighs. She lifted her leg and planted her foot behind Jess's knee.

Jess's fingers moved down and stroked through abundant moisture.

Much to Kim's frustration, Jess avoided her clit.

Kim's hand tightened on Jess's arm. "Jess." Her thighs shook as the fire built in her core.

Jess hovered outside Kim's entrance. "What do you want?" she asked, her voice low and deep. She nipped at Kim's earlobe.

Heat shot down her belly. "Inside. Now."

Jess whimpered. She pressed home. "So wet." Her hips bucked against Kim's ass.

Groaning in relief, Kim tried to draw Jess deeper. Her inner muscles clutched at Jess's fingers.

Jess thrust deep: once, twice, three times.

Kim grabbed the pillow and pressed it to her face as her body went bow-tight with the force of her orgasm.

She slumped back into Jess, breathing hard.

Jess cradled Kim's body against hers while Kim regained her composure. "Okay?" she asked.

Kim nodded. Aftershocks rippled through her as Jess gently eased out of her. She lifted her leg from behind Jess's and then looked over her shoulder into Jess's grinning face.

"That was an ambush."

Jess laughed. "Are you complaining?"

"No. But ..." Kim rolled over and kept going, forcing Jess onto her back. "Now it's my turn."

Before Jess could react, Kim straddled her hips. She put her hands on Jess's shoulders, pinning her to the bed.

Jess's body turned to stone underneath her.

Ah, shit. In the heat of the moment, Kim had forgotten. She scampered off Jess. "I'm sorry, Jess."

Jess sat up on the side of the bed, her back to Kim. "Forget it. It's no big deal."

That was a lie, and they both knew it.

This was not the first time Jess had withdrawn when Kim tried to take control during their lovemaking.

Nor the first time Jess had lied.

Kim touched Jess's back. Hurt blasted through her when Jess flinched. "Maybe it would help if you talked about it."

"There's nothing to talk about," Jess said.

Another lie. Painful memories swirled through Kim's mind.

"I'm going to go grab a shower," Jess said. She bolted from the room.

Kim stared at the door for long minutes after Jess left. An ache grew in her chest. She had hoped that now that they had admitted the depth of their feeling for each other, Jess would finally confide in her.

It wasn't as if Kim didn't have a very good idea what had befallen Jess. But she needed Jess to trust her enough to share what haunted her.

This wasn't about Jess's intimacy issues. They could work through those. This was about Jess's repeated lies and unwillingness to even admit there was anything wrong. *I can't go through that again.*

Jess gripped the sink so hard her fingers ached. She stared at her reflection in the mirror. Red-rimmed, wounded blue eyes looked back at her. *Coward.*

Every time, she swore this would be the time she would tell Kim. And each time, her mouth grew as dry as the desert. It felt as if sand filled her throat, choking off the words. Jess couldn't bear the thought of seeing the look of disdain in Kim's eyes and knowing she had lost her respect.

And you made it worse this time, by bolting out of there like your ass was on fire.

A knock on the door sent her heart into overdrive. She wasn't ready to face Kim.

"Hey, Jess."

It's only Sam. Jess grabbed the counter as her knees threatened to buckle.

"Yeah?"

"I've got coffee made. Is Kim up? Should I start breakfast?"

"She's awake. Why don't you ask her?" *Especially since I don't know if she even wants to talk to me.*

"Okay," Sam said.

Jess listened to the sound of Sam's steps down the hall, then the knock on the door, but she couldn't make out their conversation.

Fear lodged like a fist in Jess's stomach. How long would it be before Kim gave up on her? She gazed at her reflection but didn't find any answers.

Jess's hands fisted in her hair. *No. Not this time. I have to tell her the truth about me.*

What the hell is going on? Sam glanced over at Jess. She was staring at her plate as if it held the secrets of the universe.

Jess and Kim had been trying to act as if everything was fine, but neither of them was doing a very good job.

Everything had been fine when they went to bed last night. *What happened?*

"Would you like some more coffee?" Sam asked Kim.

Kim smiled, but her eyes were missing the sparkle that had been there yesterday. "Sure. Just a little."

"I'll get it." Jess shot out of her chair before Sam

could move.

Jess poured Kim's coffee. She reached out to touch her, then pulled back, as if she was afraid her touch would be rejected.

Kim took Jess's hand and held it to her cheek for a moment.

Jess looked as if she was going to pass out from relief.

Sam met her sister's eyes over Kim's head. *What did you do, Jess?*

"I just need to take a bathroom break, then I'll be ready to go," Jess said.

"Okay." Kim stood next to Thor and stroked her hand down his back.

Sam had tried several times to take Jess aside and find out what was wrong, but Jess managed to avoid her.

She joined Kim by the door. "It was really great to meet you. I hope you'll come down with Jess again soon."

Kim met her eyes. "Thanks, Sam. I enjoyed meeting you too."

Sam glanced down the hall to make sure Jess was still in the bathroom. She bumped shoulders with Kim. "I know she's hard to handle sometimes. But please be patient with her. She really cares about you."

Tears filled Kim's eyes. "I will. I care about her a lot too."

Sam wrapped her arm around Kim's shoulder and squeezed. *I don't know what you did, Jess, but fix it. Kim is one very special woman. You need her in your life.*

CHAPTER 34

Jess gazed down into the woman's pale, emotionless face. Her eyes had a vacant look as if she had retreated to somewhere no one could touch her.

Her stomach roiling, Jess gripped the rails of the gurney with white-knuckle intensity. She had not reacted like this to a sexual assault case in years. The stress of trying to confess to Kim over the past month had stirred Jess's own dark memories.

She forced her gaze away from the patient and focused on Caroline Beck, a third-year resident, standing on the other side of the gurney. Jess inclined her head toward the door.

When Caroline joined her near the door, Jess spoke in a low voice. "Have you done a ..." Jess silently cursed the tremor in her voice, "kit before?"

Caroline peered at Jess. "Yes. I know the procedure." Her brow furrowed. "I can do this."

Jess stuffed her hands in her lab coat pockets to still their shaking. *Do your damn job.* Years of practice allowed Jess to don her ER chief persona like a protective mantle. Once again firmly in control, she said, "I know you can. Get one of the female nurses to assist you." Her eyes bore into Caroline's. "Just the two of you in the room. No one else."

"Of course, Dr. McKenna." Caroline moved back to her patient.

Jess opened the exam room door and stepped out into the corridor. Humiliation tinged the relief she felt at being out of the room.

Caught up in her churning emotions, Jess didn't realize she wasn't alone.

"Hey, Jess." Kim was leaning against the wall just a few feet away.

No. Not now. Jess froze.

Kim stepped close. "You okay?" she asked, her voice soft and warm.

One look into Kim's loving blue eyes stripped Jess bare.

She was sure Kim could see into her soul, straight down to her deepest shame. Panic struck as swift and painful as an arrow's point. Jess spun on her heel and fled. She heard Kim call out, but her shame gave wings to her feet.

Jess paced around her office. *You knew this would happen. It was just a matter of time.* The demons of her past were slowly, but surely destroying her future. *Myra had it right all along. You're damaged goods.*

Despite the current situation, the past month had been the happiest Jess could remember. Each day, she fell deeper in love with Kim. They had not spent a night apart since Christmas.

But one thing had marred that happiness. Jess slammed her fist into her palm. No matter how hard she tried, she was not able to stifle her reaction whenever Kim tried to take control of their lovemaking.

The lie that there was nothing wrong had become a draught almost too bitter to swallow. Every time Jess uttered the lie, the light in Kim's eyes dimmed a little more.

Jess was trying. Just last week, she had allowed Kim to go down on her for the first time. Granted, she had had to be in the upper position, but still, it was an intimacy she had never allowed anyone before.

And still you lie.

Many times in recent weeks, she had longed for the courage to tell Kim what even Sam didn't know. But just the thought of seeing disdain and pity replace the love in Kim's vivid blue eyes made her sick to her stomach.

You're a coward. Why else have you been hiding out from Kim all afternoon?

Jess had avoided Kim since seeing her outside the sexual assault victim's room. She had not come back to her office until she was sure it was well past the time when Kim left for the day.

And now you're hiding in your office to avoid going home.

Jess dropped into her chair with an sigh. She buried her face in her hands. *God. What am I going to do?*

Jess parked in front of the house. An icy ball filled her stomach. The house was dark, and Kim's Jeep was not in the driveway.

It had never dawned on her that Kim wouldn't come home.

She looked into the backseat at Thor. "I really fucked up, boy."

Pain weighted her shoulders as she unloaded Thor and then made her way into the dark house.

The silence was oppressive.

"Come on, big guy. Let's get you fed."

Jess went about feeding Thor on autopilot. With Thor taken care of, she returned to the living room and flopped down on the couch.

She stared at the cold, dead ashes in the fireplace. They were the perfect representation of what her life had been like before Kim. Kim was the spark that breathed life and fire back into her world.

If you don't do something, your fear is going to cost you the best thing that has ever happened to you.

Steely resolved filled Jess. *No. It's not going to end like this.*

She grabbed her keys and headed for the door. *Please let her be where I think she is.*

The meager light from the fireplace did little to pierce the darkness of the room. A musty, unused smell permeated the air.

Kim sat huddled in the corner of the couch, her knees drawn up to her chest. She stared into the flickering flames.

Her mind was filled with memories of Jess. In front of this very fireplace, Jess had held her and comforted her over a patient's death.

Tears flow down her face. *This is what happens when you open your heart and let yourself love someone.*

She had been happy with Jess. Her relationship with Jess was unlike any of her previous ones. She had opened herself to Jess in a way she had never done with anyone else.

That was what made Jess's repeated lies all the more painful.

Memories of the past tortured Kim every time Jess looked her in the eyes and lied. She shut down a little more each time it happened.

You love someone, and in the end they will leave you. They lie and then leave you—one way or the other.

Something had snapped inside her today when Jess ran from her. All those old fears she had tried so hard to overcome came roaring back.

A knock on the door startled Kim. *I can't deal with anyone right now.*

The knock came again, louder than before. "Kim? Are you there?"

It was the last voice Kim expected to hear. *She came for me?*

Kim wiped her face on her sleeve. She flipped on the lamp next to the couch and then moved to the door.

Her hand hovered over the knob.

Jess knocked again. "Please let me in."

Kim opened the door and found a very disheveled Jess. She looked as if she had raked her hands through her hair countless times.

"You weren't at home," Jess said.

Kim was tempted to correct her but bit her tongue. "I had some things I needed to get done around here." *Now who is lying?*

Jess shoved her hands into her pockets. "Can I come in?" Her voice held a pleading note.

Every instinct told Kim to say no. She gazed into Jess's vulnerable blue eyes and lost the battle. She didn't have the heart to refuse her.

"Okay."

Kim walked away, leaving Jess standing in the doorway.

Jess stared after Kim for a moment, then stepped inside and shut the door behind her.

Kim sat on the couch and stared into the fire.

Jess followed and eased down on the opposite end of the couch. She had never seen Kim like this—so closed off. Even her position reflected her withdrawal. Kim's knees were drawn up to her chest and her arms wrapped tightly around herself. She reminded Jess of a flower bud, its petals folded over each other in a tight cocoon, protecting the vulnerable inner center.

Fear shafted through Jess. *You're losing her.* She scrubbed her hands on her pants. "I'm sorry about what happened at work."

Kim turned her head. Her gaze pierced Jess. "The case upset you?"

Jess's jaw clenched. *Don't lie.* "Yes ... It reminded me of the past ... of what happened ... to me." Her hands gripped her thighs with viselike force. "I've wanted to tell you. I swear. I ... I ..." *Tell her.*

Her heart was roaring so loudly in her ears she missed Kim's words.

"What?"

"I've never told you about my dad."

Jess blinked at the non sequitur. She stared at Kim. In all the time she had known her, Kim had mentioned her father only once. She never talked about him. *Why now?*

"I was such a daddy's girl," Kim said. "Even at sixteen, I still loved going places and doing things with my dad." Her eyes took on a faraway look as if she was seeing another time and place.

"Right around the time I turned seventeen, things began to change. Small things at first. I'd find my dad sleeping in his recliner on a Saturday afternoon. He was never one to sit around, much less sleep during the day." Kim's arms tightened around her legs. "Then it got too obvious to ignore. He didn't have any energy and was losing weight."

Kim turned and looked at Jess. "I kept asking him, 'What's wrong, Dad?' He always said the same thing, 'Just a little under the weather.'" Kim's hand slashed sideways. "'It's nothing.'" Her hand slashed again, punctuating each word, "'No. Big. Deal.'"

Jess flinched hearing her own words.

Kim's eyes locked on Jess's with laserlike intensity. "And I believed him."

Realization slammed home. *Oh, God. No.*

A single tear slid down Kim's face. She rested her chin on her knee.

"Four months later, he was dead."

"I'm sorry," Jess whispered. Her heart broke for Kim. She longed to reach out and comfort her but feared her touch wouldn't be welcome. She sat on her hands to keep from giving in to the impulse. "I'm sorry," she said again, at a loss for exactly what to say.

Pain and sorrow filled Kim's eyes. "For a long time I thought he had been trying to shield me from what was happening." She rocked back and forth. "But no matter how he rationalized it to himself, what he was really doing was protecting himself."

Just like you. Jess's stomach lurched and bile burned the back of her throat. She struggled not to give in to the nausea.

"He didn't want to face telling me he was dying. He set all his affairs in order. I found out later, even my older brothers knew." Kim let her legs drop to the floor and turned to faced Jess fully. "I loved him so much. But right up to the end, he looked me in the eyes and lied." She captured Jess's gaze and held it. Her eyes glistened with tears, but her voice remained firm. "I can't do that again. I won't do that again."

Jess's restraint broke. She slid across the couch and wrapped her arms around Kim. "I'm so sorry. So sorry." Her words held a multitude of meaning.

The twisted knot in her stomach let go when Kim's arms wrapped around her waist.

Jess buried her face in Kim's neck, only then becoming aware of her own tears. "So sorry," she whispered again.

A soul-deep sigh escaped Kim's lips. She soothed her fingers through Jess's sweat-damp hair. Although she didn't quite remember how, they had ended up face to face, entwined on the couch. Their shared tears had mingled in a cathartic release.

Seeing Jess struggle earlier had made Kim realize just how difficult what she was asking of Jess was.

Jess had her face buried in Kim's neck.

"Jess?" Kim pulled back a little.

A whimper escaped Jess, and she tightened her arms around Kim's back.

"Come on," Kim said. "You must be smothering."

Muttering something unintelligible, Jess pressed closer.

Kim brushed Jess's hair back and placed a soft kiss on her jaw line.

Jess lifted her head. Her eyes were red-rimmed, and her face was splotched with color.

Kim was sure her own appearance was a similar sight. She pressed her forehead to Jess's. "I've said it before and I'll say it again. We're quite the pair—aren't we?"

A wobbly smile trembled on Jess's lips. "Yeah."

After disentangling herself from Kim, Jess sat up. She reached down with a trembling hand and gently stroked Kim's face.

Kim leaned into the touch. After having shared her deepest pain and secret fear, there was no keeping an emotional distance from Jess. She sat up next to Jess. Her brow furrowed when Jess moved away to sit on the far side of the couch.

Jess wedged herself into the corner and drew her legs up under her. She wrapped her arms across her belly.

She's trying to comfort herself.

"Jess?"

"I should have told you. You deserve to know."

Now that Jess had admitted what Kim had suspected all along, she wasn't sure she wanted to hear the details. *You owe it to Jess to hear them, no matter how painful.*

She faced Jess and waited.

Jess rocked back and forth. "I ... It was ... He ..."

It killed Kim to watch Jess struggle, stopping and starting but never quite getting the words out.

This is hurting her too much. You can't force this.

"Jess. It's okay. I know."

Jess shook her head roughly. "I have to tell you." Her gaze met Kim's.

Worry gripped Kim at the look in Jess's eyes.

Jess's demeanor reminded her of an abused dog she had once seen—eyes filled with fear, yet desperate to please.

Kim moved closer, then slid off the couch and knelt in front of Jess.

"And you will tell me, but it doesn't have to be today. Whenever you're ready." Kim leaned up and softly brushed their lips together. "You're worth waiting for."

A sob escaped Jess's lips. "Thank you." She brushed at both their tears. "Will you come home? Please."

A kiss filled with all the love in Kim's heart was her answer.

CHAPTER 35

Still half-asleep, Jess reached for Kim's warm body and encountered empty space. She jolted into full alertness, and her eyes popped open. That was when she became aware of Kim spooned up against her back. She went limp with relief.

How did she end up behind me? She always held Kim, not the other way around. Then she remembered the dream. A cold shiver chased down her spine.

Kim stirred, and her arm tightened across Jess's belly.

She comforts me even in sleep. Jess's heart filled to overflowing with love.

Kim lifted up and placed a sleepy kiss on Jess's temple.

Shifting onto her back so she could see Kim's face, Jess smiled at her. "Morning."

"How are you doing?" Kim propped her head on her hand and used her free hand to stroke Jess's belly. "You were pretty restless last night."

"I'm fine. It was noth—"

Kim stiffened. Her hand froze on Jess's abdomen.

Don't lie. Jess bit her lip. She forced herself to meet Kim's eyes. The warmth there just a moment ago had dimmed.

"I had a bad dream." She swallowed heavily. "About the ... past." Jess looked down, unable to hold Kim's gaze.

The tension drained from Kim's body. She resumed

her gentle stroking of Jess's belly.

Jess braced herself for all the questions. She was determined to answer them, no matter what it cost her.

The questions never came. She started when Kim finally spoke.

"The alarm is about to go off," Kim said.

As if on cue, a strident beeping filled the room.

Jess slid across the bed and shut off the alarm and then scooted back over next to Kim. "I'm sorry. I have to get ready for work." She met Kim's gaze. "I'm not trying to avoid—"

Kim pressed her finger to Jess's lips, her gaze full of love. "We're fine. I promise." She kissed Jess gently on the lips.

Jess sank into the loving touch. She drew Kim into her arms and held her. "I love you," she said, soft and low.

Kim's arms tightened around her back. "I love you too."

Loath to move, Jess sighed. "Duty calls." She reluctantly released Kim and climbed out of bed. Despite Kim's reassurances Jess still felt vulnerable and unsure. Kim running from her yesterday had spooked her. She gazed down at Kim. Although nauseated at the very thought, Jess knew she couldn't put this off. "We'll talk tonight. After work."

Kim sat up. "You don't have to do that, Jess."

Resolve stiffened Jess's spine. She locked gazes with Kim. "Yes. I do."

Kim stopped outside the staff lounge door to try and tame her smile. *This couldn't have come on a better day—for either of us.* It had filled Kim with guilt to see Jess so tentative and scared this morning. The depth of

Jess's reaction to her running had shocked her.

This will cheer her up. Kim poked her head in the door.

Jess was getting herself a cup of coffee.

A quick glance around showed the lounge was empty. *Perfect.*

"Hey, Jess. Have you got a minute? There's someone I'd like you to see."

"Sure." Jess set her coffee down. "What have you got?" she asked as she followed Kim down the hall.

Kim tried hard to hide her smile. "I need to show you." She stopped outside an exam room door.

Jess arched an eyebrow.

Biting the inside of her cheek to keep from grinning, Kim pulled open the door and stepped inside before Jess could question her.

What the heck is she up to? Jess followed Kim into the exam room.

Kim headed straight for the woman standing next to the gurney.

Jess quickly surveyed the scene.

A thirty-something, stocky man, dressed in faded blue jeans and a flannel shirt, stood on one side of the gurney.

The woman, about the same age, also dressed in jeans, stood opposite him. She was what was commonly referred to as pleasingly plump.

A dark-haired little girl, maybe four years old, sat on the gurney, playing with a stuffed animal. There was something vaguely familiar about the little girl, but Jess saw so many patients she couldn't place her.

Kim motioned Jess forward. "Mr. and Mrs. Bailey, this is Dr. McKenna," she said.

Mr. Bailey strode over and grabbed Jess's hand. He pumped it enthusiastically. "We can't thank you enough for what you did for our little girl."

Am I supposed to know them? Jess shot Kim a puzzled look.

Kim grinned. She gestured to the little girl on the gurney. "You remember Tara?"

The little girl looked up at the sound of her name. Bright blue eyes met Jess's.

Jess's jaw dropped and she stared. *That's Tara?* She could not reconcile the filthy, skinny little girl they had taken care of with the pink-cheeked, cherubic angel on the gurney. She took a step toward Tara, then stopped. She gazed over at Kim.

Happiness shone on Kim's face. She moved over next to Jess. "Mr. and Mrs. Bailey are fostering Tara until they can adopt her."

Jess smiled. *Oh, little one. I'm so happy for you.*

"I helped Daddy," Tara said. She stood up and leaped off the gurney into Mr. Bailey's arms.

Fear widened his eyes even as his arms wrapped tightly around Tara.

"Land sakes!" Mrs. Bailey said. She came around the gurney. "None of your antics, young lady." She tugged on Tara's pant leg. "We've had enough excitement for one day." Standing on her tiptoes, she pressed a kiss to Tara's forehead.

"Daddy makes me fly," Tara said. She laid her head down and snuggled against Mr. Bailey's chest.

Mrs. Bailey wagged her finger at her husband. "No more flying today." Her husband glanced away, a sheepish look on his face. She looked back at Kim. "Those two are going to make me gray before my time."

They all shared a laugh.

That's when Jess remembered just where they were—the ER. Tension stiffened her muscles. She had not seen any sign of injury, but that didn't mean anything. Her gaze darted to Kim. "Is she okay?"

"She's perfect," Kim said. She unobtrusively touched Jess's back.

She's got your number. Jess threw Kim a grateful look.

"She was helping her daddy in the garage and stuck a metal screw up her nose," Mrs. Bailey said. "I was going to take her over to our family doctor's office, but someone," she shot a mock-scowl at her husband, "panicked and insisted we rush her to the ER."

Mr. Bailey flushed and shuffled his feet.

"But I'm glad we did." Mrs. Bailey met Jess's gaze, and her eyes misted with tears. "We can't thank you enough for what you did for Tara."

Jess shook her head. "It was really the police. I just checked her out when they brought her in."

"You did more than that." Mrs. Bailey moved forward and gave Jess a quick hug.

Jess felt her cheeks heat.

"We're friends of Val Williams," Mrs. Bailey said.

Was she supposed to know who that was? Jess's brow furrowed. She glanced at Kim.

Mrs. Bailey answered before Kim could. "She's the police officer who brought Tara in that day. She told us how gentle and caring you were with Tara."

A moment's confusion cleared at the memory of Officer Williams coming into the room after she had finished her exam. Jess had been sitting on the gurney with Tara, gently rocking her in her arms, singing softly to her.

Mrs. Bailey smiled brightly at Kim and reached out to squeeze her arm. "You and Dr. Donovan both."

Jess didn't know what to say.

Kim came to the rescue. "You're very welcome. It's wonderful to see Tara so healthy and happy."

Mr. Bailey moved up next to his wife. His big arms were wrapped securely around Tara. "She's the light of our life," he said.

Jess's pager shrilled. She glanced down at the screen. "I'm sorry. I have to go."

"We appreciate your time. We just wanted a chance to thank you," Mrs. Bailey said.

After taking one last long look at Tara, Jess waved and headed for the door. She turned back at the last moment and sent a bright, loving smile Kim's way.

CHAPTER 36

Kim watched as Jess pushed her food around her plate. She had been quiet since they got home from work. The shadows in Jess's eyes had lifted after her encounter with Tara earlier in the day, but they were back now, deeper than ever.

Jess looked up. Stress lines framed her eyes.

"Done?"

Nodding, Jess rose to her feet and began to gather up the plates.

"I can do that," Kim said.

"No. I've got it. Go relax. I'll be right there." Jess walked away before Kim could protest.

Should I go check on her? Kim glanced toward the kitchen doorway. Jess had been gone far longer than it took to clean up. Before she could get up, Jess appeared, carrying two glasses of wine.

Jess set both glasses on the coffee table and offered her hand to Kim.

Kim allowed Jess to pull her off the couch. She could feel the tension pouring from Jess. "I meant what I said earlier. You don't have to do this today."

"Yes. I do." Jess stared intently into Kim's eyes as if she was trying to look into her soul. She leaned in and brushed a soft, sweet kiss across her lips. "Come what may, I love you. Please remember that."

What the hell? Tears prickled at the corner of Kim's

eyes. It sounded as if Jess was saying goodbye. She reached up and cupped Jess's face. "I love you too, Jess. Nothing is going to change that." Disturbed by the melancholy smile and almost defeated look in Jess's eyes, Kim tried to wrap her arms around Jess.

Jess pulled away. She sat down on the couch and turned so that her back was against the arm of the couch. She patted the open space between her legs. "Sit with me?"

Kim was struck by the dichotomy of the position Jess had chosen. She obviously didn't want to look at Kim while she told her, but at the same time wanted Kim sitting between her spread legs and against her chest like a protective shield.

Realizing she was falling into her clinical mode, Kim stopped herself. *Jess is not a patient. You don't need to analyze to distance yourself emotionally.* She was aware enough to admit that she was trying to protect herself. This was going to be very difficult to hear. *Stop stalling.* She looked down at Jess to see that her expression had closed off. Kim carefully took her place between Jess's legs.

Some of the strain eased for both of them when Jess wrapped her arms around Kim's abdomen and settled her close against her chest.

As the silence grew, Kim began to wonder if Jess was going be able to do this. She started when Jess placed a kiss on her temple.

"You know by now how much I need to be in control." Jess snorted self-deprecatingly. "Obviously, there's a reason for that."

Kim could feel the coiled tension of Jess's body against hers. She stroked Jess's arms.

"It happened in my senior year in high school. Not only was I a loner, but I wasn't the most feminine of girls either. I'd already gained most of my height. And at that time, I was big into lifting weights. Not too many guys were interested in dating a muscular, almost six-foot-tall girl." Jess shrugged. "And I really wasn't interested in guys that way."

Jess pulled one arm from around Kim and reached for the wine. She offered Kim a glass.

"No, thanks," Kim said. Stress was making her stomach queasy.

Keeping the wine for herself, Jess settled back in place. She took a healthy drink before returning to her story. "I realize now that I must have subconsciously known I was attracted to girls and that was why I avoided having any female friends. If there were any other gays at my small town high school, I never knew it."

Kim's heart ached for that younger Jess. It must have been so hard growing up and knowing you were different, but not realizing why. That was one advantage of attending a big city high school. Kim had been exposed to other gays in school.

"By my senior year, my mother was becoming increasingly concerned that I wasn't dating. My dad didn't seem to think it was a big deal. Anyway, it was around that time that I was approached by one of the guys on the football team. He was a big guy, six-six and well over two hundred pounds. He looked and acted like the all-American boy next door." Jess's hand stiffened on her wine glass.

But he wasn't. Bastard. Kim bit her lip to keep the comment to herself.

"My mother was thrilled when I told her David had asked me out. We started dating pretty regularly, mostly going out as a group with his football buddies and their dates. When we did go out alone, he kissed and touched me, but never anything beyond light petting. He always stopped when I asked him to. I never felt anything, but

I guess I was trying to fit in and it made my mother happy," Jess said, a bitter edge to her voice.

Kim entwined her fingers with Jess's and gave her hand an understanding squeeze. Kim had been there before. Trying to make her mother happy had resulted in some of her most miserable moments. Now that Jess was talking, she didn't want to interrupt her.

Jess finished off her wine in one gulp. "You sure you don't want that?" She pointed to the other glass of wine.

"No. Go ahead," Kim said.

After exchanging the glasses, Jess was silent for several minutes.

Kim wasn't sure she was going to continue. *You're doing great. Keep going.*

Finally, Jess took up the story again. "We had been dating for a month when he asked me to the homecoming dance. It was a huge deal in our town. My mother was ecstatic. She took me on a special trip to San Francisco to find the perfect dress."

Hoping to comfort her, Kim stroked her hand up and down Jess's thigh. The muscles felt rock hard under her fingers.

"My parents extended my curfew to two a.m. for the night. David and his buddies had rented a hotel room so we could all hang out together after the dance. Or at least that's what I thought." Jess blew out a shaky breath. "Pretty fucking naïve, huh?"

"Jess—" Kim tried to turn in her arms, but Jess stopped her.

"Let me finish."

Kim resumed her stroking of Jess's leg.

"David had been trying to convince me to sleep with him for the two weeks leading up to the dance. He kept telling me how much he cared for me and how on homecoming night he wanted to make me truly his. I thought about it, but just wasn't sure I could go through with it." Jess pulled her free hand off Kim's belly and raked it through her hair. "We got to the hotel room, and several of David's buddies and their girlfriends were already there. The guys had gotten hold of some liquor, and we started drinking. After a couple drinks, everyone started making out with their date. When David pulled me off the couch and urged me toward another door, I really didn't think about it and followed him. I trusted him."

Jess fell silent.

Kim could feel the tension radiating off Jess in waves.

Jess's chest hitched, but she remained silent. She took several sips of her wine as if hoping it would provide her with courage.

"Jess, you don't have to tell me the details. I have a pretty good idea what happened." Kim turned in Jess's arms until she could cradle Jess's face in her palm. "It wasn't your fault. He forced you."

"No. That's just it, Kim. He didn't." Jess looked everywhere but at Kim. "I need to tell you this. I just hope ..." Jess's voice deserted her for a moment. "I pray you'll still want to be with me after I tell you," she said, her voice filled with pain. Tears glistened in her eyes.

Oh, Jess. Kim could feel the frantic beat of Jess's heart against her breast. "I love you, Jess. Nothing you tell me will ever change that." She brushed her lips gently over Jess's. "Go ahead."

Jess nodded. She set her wine glass on the table, then urged Kim back around so that her back was once again against Jess's chest. She wrapped her arms around Kim's middle as if Kim were her lifeline.

"When we got into the room next door, he immediately started groping me. He had always been so gentle before, it really shocked me. He pushed me back onto the bed and lay down on top of me. I kept telling him to wait, slow down, but he wouldn't listen." Jess's breath hitched. "Before I knew it, he had pushed my dress up and was pulling my panties down."

Kim could feel tremors rippling through Jess's body. She tried to turn in Jess's arms, but Jess held her fast against her chest. She was totally caught up in the agonizing memories.

"It happened so fast," Jess said in a choked voice. "I never even realized he had his pants open until I felt him push my legs open and start probing between my thighs." Jess's arms clenched painfully tight around Kim.

Oh, God. Kim's eyes stung with repressed tears.

"He was hurting me, and I panicked. I shoved against his shoulders, trying to get him off of me. I kept saying, 'Stop, David. Please. Stop.' He pulled my hands off his shoulders and pinned them above my head. I started to protest again, but it was too late ... a searing pain streaked between my legs and he was ... he was ..." Jess's body shook as she struggled for control.

Anger burned deep in Kim. *You bastard.* She tried to turn again, but Jess stopped her.

"I need to tell you ... I need to tell you the rest," Jess choked out.

Kim stroked Jess's arms where they were clutched around her until she calmed enough to continue.

"I just laid there while he thrust into me, grunting in my ear. I never fought him. I just let him do what he wanted." Jess's fists clenched against Kim's stomach. "When he was finished, he got up and grinned down at me as he pulled his pants up. He stuffed my panties in his pocket. Then he patted my cheek and thanked me, smirking the whole time. We went back to the other room and he took me home as if nothing had happened. I trust ..."

Jess's emotional control broke. She released her hold on Kim and broke down in great heaving sobs.

Her own tears flowing, Kim quickly moved from between Jess's legs. She edged onto the couch next to Jess's thigh so she could face her. She wrapped her arms around Jess and drew her tightly against her chest. "That's it, sweetheart. Let it all out." She petted Jess's hair and murmured softly to her as Jess purged some of the pain of the long held secret.

Finally, Jess pulled back and swiped at her tears. She tentatively peered into Kim's eyes as if afraid of what she might see.

Kim met her gaze and held it. She gently brushed at both their tears. "I love you," she said, her voice soft and tender.

Jess clutched her painfully tight to her chest. "I love you." She heaved a sigh and pulled back. "That's not the worst of it."

Not the worst? Acid poured into Kim's stomach, and she was sure she was going to be sick. *What else did that fucking bastard do to Jess?* Kim forced herself to be calm. She stroked her fingers through Jess's hair letting it soothe both of them. "Tell me, sweetheart."

Jess picked up the glass of wine. She downed it in a single gulp, then put the empty glass back. "When I got to school on Monday, I noticed right away all the snickers and looks I was getting from everyone. David had wasted no time. He bragged to anyone who would listen how he bagged me. He made the rest of my senior year a living hell. Every time I saw him in the hall, he smirked at me."

"I'm so sorry," Kim said, her voice shaking. She didn't know what else to say.

Jess didn't seem to hear her. She was still caught up reliving the past. "I didn't learn the rest of it until almost a month later."

Dear God. There's more? Kim tried to brace herself for what was coming.

"David was waiting for me outside the library one night. I guess he decided that humiliating me at school wasn't enough. He wanted to show off his new leather jacket and thank me. Turns out that he and one of his buddies had made a bet. They each picked an outsider, an 'untouchable' for their little game. Whoever in his words 'popped their chosen girl's cherry first' won. That's what he was thanking me for that night. Winning the bet for him."

Unable to distance herself emotionally, the depth of Jess's pain staggered Kim. *Betrayed, raped, and publicly humiliated. My God, Jess. It's a wonder you've ever let anyone close.*

Jess's eyes went cold and flat. "I swore right then and there I would never trust anyone like that again. It was all my fault. I allowed him to control me and then use me. I vowed I would never put myself in a position to be controlled or used again."

How can you blame yourself? Kim cradled Jess's chin gently in her hand and gazed into her eyes until some of the light came back into them. "Jess, I want you to listen to me. You're not to blame for what happened. You told him to stop, and he didn't. That's rape."

Jess pulled away. "No. I let him—"

Kim cut her off. "As a wise woman once told me, that's bull. You're not responsible for other people's actions. The only one at fault was the bastard who raped you."

"That's not true." Jess vehemently shook her head. "I didn't fight back. I let him take my power and violate me. I was weak and pathetic. I didn't claim my own power."

It sounded as if Jess was quoting someone. The phrasing struck a chord in Kim. She had heard this same crap from some of the radical women's groups when she was in college. A woman could only be raped if she chose to let it happen. It was total bullshit then, and it was total bullshit now.

White-hot anger flashed through Kim. *All these years! All these years she has suffered because of something she was probably told in college.* "Who told you that?"

Jess jumped. "I … um … I was having some trouble adjusting my first year in college. I saw a doctor that volunteered at the student union medical clinic for a little while. She talked a lot about taking responsibility for your actions. People could only do what you allowed them to do. And about letting people take your power."

Unable to contain herself any longer, Kim sprang off the couch and began to pace. "Was she a psychiatrist or psychologist? Or at least a trained therapist?" She gesticulated sharply with each question.

"I don't know," Jess stammered. "She called herself doctor. She was a professor at the college."

Kim threw up her hands. "Oh, and let me guess. She taught women's studies or intro to psych."

Jess swung her feet off the couch and sat up. "What? How do you know that?"

Fucking amateurs! They had no idea the damage done to young women like Jess with their horseshit! Kim's hands clenched. She struggled to get control of her temper. Blowing out a breath, she scrubbed her hands over her face. She looked down at Jess, who was staring at her with wide, shocked eyes.

Kim sat down next to Jess and took both of Jess's hands in hers. "I need you to really hear me. You've told me over and over what a good psychiatrist I am, and that you trust my judgment." She locked gazes with Jess. "Trust me on this. I would not lie to you." Her hands tightened on Jess's. "What that woman told you was total bullshit. It was never your fault. Period."

She stroked the backs of Jess's hands. She could see the wheels turning in Jess's head as she tried to re-evaluate all that she had believed for so long. Kim knew things wouldn't change overnight, and Jess would need lots of repeated reassurance. But now that she knew what they were dealing with, they had a real chance at a life together.

Jess met Kim's gaze. For the first time, in far too long, her beautiful blue eyes were filled with hope. "So where do we go from here?"

Kim released Jess's hands and moved to straddle her lap. She brushed away the last traces of Jess's tears. "We go on with our lives—together." She smoothed her fingers through Jess's hair and smiled—already sure of Jess's answer. "If that's what you want?"

A heartwarming smile spread across Jess's face. Her eyes danced with light. She slipped her hand into the hair at the nape of Kim's neck and gently drew her close. Her lips inches from Kim's, she whispered, "I do," before closing the distance and sealing the deal.

EPILOGUE

SEVEN MONTHS LATER

L aughing, Jess raced across the deck. *Oh, she's going to make you pay for that.* She pulled open the patio door.

"You better run," Kim called from behind her.

Jess dashed into the living room. The slap of her bare feet against the wood floor echoed in the empty room. She tugged her towel tighter around her chest as she made a break for the hall.

Rapid footsteps sounded behind her.

She glanced back and saw Kim hot on her heels.

Kim had a towel on as well, only hers was wrapped around her hair. The rest of her was gloriously bare.

Oh, man. No fair. Jess's steps faltered. Her momentary inattention cost her. *Ah. Shit.* Her feet slid on the freshly buffed wood floor, and she grabbed at the wall to keep from falling.

Kim was on her in a flash. "Got you now." She grabbed for Jess's towel.

Not yet you don't, but hopefully soon. Jess grinned. She was having too good a time to end the game now. She stuck out her tongue and let go of her towel. Jess sprinted naked toward the bedroom.

"You're going to get it, McKenna."

Jess threw her head back and laughed. *Promises,*

promises.

As Jess reached the bedroom doorway, Kim caught up with her again. Jess groaned when a warm hand brushed over her butt. With one last burst of speed, Jess launched herself at the large air mattress in the middle of the room. She landed face-first and bounced.

Seconds later, Kim landed right next to her.

A brief wrestling match ensued.

"Wait, no. No tickling," Jess said, breathless with laughter. She rolled onto her back, taking Kim with her. Arousal flared at the feel of their bare bodies pressed together.

Kim sat up, straddling Jess's hips. "You give?"

Jess spread her arms wide. "I'm all yours."

A dazzling smile flashed across Kim's face. "That you are," she said. She planted her hands on Jess's shoulders and stared lovingly into her eyes.

God, kiss me already.

As if Kim had heard her thoughts, she leaned down and took Jess's lips in a searing kiss.

When Kim's tongue pressed into her mouth, a moan was torn from Jess's chest. Her hands came up and clasped Kim's hips. She whimpered in protest when Kim broke the kiss.

Kim sat back up and looked around the empty room. "Are you going to miss this place?"

Jess blinked, trying to get her brain working. She was much more interested in the feel of Kim's sex pressed against her belly. She shook off the sexual fog and gave Kim's question due consideration.

"No. As many good memories as we've made here, it was a place of hiding for me. Our new house will be a place for living. For us to spend our life—together."

That declaration earned Jess another soul-searing kiss.

"I love you," Jess said when Kim pulled back.

Kim caressed Jess's bare chest and belly. "I love you too, sweetheart."

Jess gazed up at Kim, her heart filled to overflowing with love for this incredible woman. Her hands stroked the tops of Kim's smooth thighs. It was hard to believe sometimes that they had met only a year ago. From their first meeting, Kim had slowly but surely turned her world upside down. And Jess couldn't be happier about that.

There had been some tough times over the past months. Jess had finally given in and seen a psychologist Kim recommended. It had been hard, but in the end, Sandy had been a godsend.

"What're you thinking about?" Kim asked, startling Jess out of her thoughts.

"About how amazing this last year has been," she gently squeezed Kim's thighs, "and hard too. For both of us."

"It has been a whirlwind," Kim said.

Kim's love and support had allowed Jess to contemplate things she had never dared dream of before. *Just talk to her. You don't have to be afraid anymore.* That was true. Jess didn't feel the need to hide her feelings or fears from Kim any longer.

"You know, I've been thinking," Jess said. She blew out a breath. "With the new house and everything ..." *Come on, you can do it.* This was something they had never talked about. "Well, this place was small ... even with just you, me, and Thor. But the new place is much bigger, so if we wanted to expand our family ..."

Kim's brow furrowed. She stared down at Jess.

Great, Jess, she has no clue what you're trying to say.

"You want to get another Great Dane?" Kim asked.

Of course, she would think that. It's not like you haven't referred to Thor plenty of times as your furry son.

Jess shook her head and smiled. "Ah … no. Puppies are cute, but I was thinking about something …" She reached up and tenderly stroked Kim's flat belly. "Or rather, someone else."

Kim's eyes went wide and her jaw dropped when she finally got it.

Disappointment shafted through Jess. She struggled not to show it. "It's okay. I just—" Jess's breath whooshed out when Kim landed on her chest.

Kim wrapped her in a bone-crushing hug.

Jess held her close, her heart tripping double time. *That's a yes? Right?* She wanted this so much, she couldn't help but be nervous.

It was several long moments before Kim released her and sat up. Tears glistened in her eyes. "You want us to have a baby?" she asked, her voice trembling.

"Yeah." Jess swallowed heavily. She didn't want Kim to feel pressured in any way. "I mean if you would even con—"

Kim pressed her fingers to Jess's lips. "Yes."

Jess's heart soared. "Yes?"

Kim nodded. The happiness shining in her eyes left no doubt.

Jess grinned. She waggled her eyebrows at Kim as she slipped her hand between Kim's legs. "Wanna practice getting pregnant?"

Kim groaned and her hips thrust forward. "Oh yeah. Practice. We'll need lots of practice."

THE END

ABOUT RJ NOLAN

RJ Nolan lives in the United States with her spouse and their Great Dane. She makes frequent visits to the California coast near her home. The sight and sound of the surf always stir her muse. When not writing, she enjoys reading, camping, and the occasional trip to Disneyland.

E-Mail: rjnolan@gmail.com

Website: http://www.rjnolan.com

OTHER BOOKS FROM YLVA PUBLISHING

http://www.ylva-publishing.com

MANHATTAN MOON

Jae

ISBN: 978-3-95533-012-5 (epub), 978-3-95533-013-2 (mobi), 978-3-95533-014-9 (pdf)

Length: 28,500 words (novella)

Nothing in Shelby Carson's life is ordinary. Not only is she an attending psychiatrist in a hectic ER, but she's also a Wrasa, a shape-shifter who leads a secret existence.

To make things even more complicated, she has feelings for Nyla Rozakis, a human nurse.

Even though the Wrasa forbid relationships with humans, Shelby is determined to pursue Nyla. Things seem pretty hopeless for them, but on Halloween, during a full moon, anything can happen...

SOMETHING IN THE WINE

Jae

SOMETHING
IN THE WINE

ISBN: 978-3-95533-006-4 (epub), 978-3-95533-007-1 (mobi), 978-3-95533-008-8 (pdf)

Length: 99,100 words (novel)

All her life, Annie Prideaux has suffered through her brother's constant practical jokes only he thinks are funny. But Jake's last joke is one too many, she decides when he sets her up on a blind date with his friend Drew Corbin—neglecting to tell his straight sister one tiny detail: her date is not a man, but a lesbian.

Annie and Drew decide it's time to turn the tables on Jake by pretending to fall in love with each other.

At first glance, they have nothing in common. Disillusioned with love, Annie focuses on books, her cat, and her work as an accountant while Drew, more confident and outgoing, owns a dog and spends most of her time working in her beloved vineyard.

Only their common goal to take revenge on Jake unites them. But what starts as a table-turning game soon turns Annie's and Drew's lives upside down as the lines between pretending and reality begin to blur.

Something in the Wine is a story about love, friendship, and coming to terms with what it means to be yourself.

HOT LINE

Alison Grey

ISBN: 978-3-95533-016-3 (mobi), 978-3-95533-015-6 (epub), 978-3-95533-017-0 (pdf)

Length: 27,188 words (novella)

Two women from different worlds.

Linda, a successful psychologist, uses her work to distance herself from her own loneliness.

Christina works for a sex hotline to make ends meet.

Their worlds collide when Linda calls Christina's sex line. Christina quickly realizes Linda is not her usual customer. Instead of wanting phone sex, Linda makes an unexpected proposition. Does Christina dare accept the offer that will change both their lives?

COMING FROM YLVA PUBLISHING IN SPRING AND SUMMER 2013

http://www.ylva-publishing.com

BACKWARDS TO OREGON
(revised and expanded edition)
Jae

"Luke" Hamilton has always been sure that she'd never marry. She accepted that she would spend her life alone when she chose to live her life disguised as a man.

After working in a brothel for three years, Nora Macauley has lost all illusions about love. She no longer hopes for a man who will sweep her off her feet and take her away to begin a new, respectable life.

But now they find themselves married and on the way to Oregon in a covered wagon, with two thousand miles ahead of them.

CROSSING BRIDGES
Emma Weimann

As a Guardian, Tallulah has devoted her life to protecting her hometown, Edinburgh, and its inhabitants, both living and dead, against ill-natured and dangerous supernatural beings.

When Erin, a human tourist, visits Edinburgh, she makes Tallulah more nervous than the poltergeist on Greyfriars Kirkyard—and not only because Erin seems to be the sidekick of a dark witch who has her own agenda.

While Tallulah works to thwart the dark witch's sinister plan for Edinburgh, she can't help wondering about the mysterious Erin. Is she friend or foe?

SECOND NATURE
(revised and expanded edition)
Jae

Novelist Jorie Price doesn't believe in the existence of shape-shifting creatures or true love. She leads a solitary life, and the paranormal romances she writes are pure fiction for her.

Griffin Westmore knows better—at least about one of these two things. She doesn't believe in love either, but she's one of the not-so-fictional shape-shifters. She's also a Saru, an elite soldier with the mission to protect the shape-shifters' secret existence at any cost.

When Jorie gets too close to the truth in her latest shape-shifter romance, Griffin is sent to investigate—and if necessary to destroy the manuscript before it's published and to kill the writer.

WALKING THE LABYRINTH
Lois Cloarec Hart

Is there life after loss? Lee Glenn, co-owner of a private security company, didn't think so. Crushed by grief after the death of her wife, she uncharacteristically retreats from life.

But love doesn't give up easily. After her friends and family stage a dramatic intervention, Lee rejoins the world of the living, resolved to regain some sense of normalcy but only half-believing that it's possible. Her old friend and business partner convinces her to take on what appears on the surface to be a minor personal protection detail.

The assignment takes her far from home, from the darkness of her loss to the dawning of a life reborn. Along the way, Lee encounters people unlike any she's ever met before: Wrong-Way Wally, a small-town oracle shunned by the locals for his off-putting speech and mannerisms; and Wally's best friend, Gaëlle, a woman who not only translates the oracle's uncanny predictions, but who also appears to have a deep personal connection to life beyond life. Lee is shocked to find herself fascinated by Gaëlle, despite dismissing the woman's exotic beliefs as "hooey."

But opening yourself to love also means opening yourself to the possibility of pain. Will Lee have the courage to follow that path, a path that once led to the greatest agony she'd ever experienced? Or will she run back to the cold comfort of a safer solitary life?